Bone Song

Bone Song

John Meaney

GOLLANCZ

LONDON

The right of John Meaney to be identified as the author
of this work has been asserted by him in accordance with
the Copyright, Designs and Patents Act 1988.

First published in Great Britain in 2007 by
Gollancz
An imprint of the Orion Publishing Group
Orion House, 5 Upper St Martin's Lane,
London WC2H 9EA

A CIP catalogue record for this book is available
from the British Library

ISBN-13 978 0 57507 955 7 (cased)
ISBN-10 0 57507 955 X (cased)
ISBN-13 978 0 57507 954 0 (trade paperback)
ISBN-10 0 57507 954 1 (trade paperback)

1 3 5 7 9 10 8 6 4 2

Typeset by Deltatype Ltd, Birkenhead, Merseyside

Printed in Great Britain by
Mackays of Chatham plc, Chatham, Kent

www.orionbooks.co.uk

The Orion Publishing Group's policy is to use papers that are natural,
renewable and recyclable products and made from wood grown in sustainable
forests. The logging and manufacturing processes are expected to conform to
the environmental regulations of the country of origin.

One

Amber eyes watched from thick darkness beyond the stone steps. Donal sketched a fingertip salute. Stuffing his hands in his overcoat pockets, he looked up at the two hundred storeys of Police HQ, rearing upwards, dark and uncompromising. It was late and cold and the sky appeared deep-purple, heavily opaque.

Somewhere near the top, Commissioner Vilnar's office waited. And reading between the lines of this morning's phone call, the Commissioner had a new job lined up for Donal – something he was not going to enjoy.

'Son of a bitch,' he muttered.

From the shadows came a low growl.

'No offence,' he added.

Donal unbuttoned his coat and moved easily up the steps, two treads at a time, and passed between tall stone pillars surmounted by orange glows. He stopped at the big bronze-and-steel doors.

'Lieutenant Donal Riordan.' He spoke clearly. 'Badge number two-three-omicron-nine.'

A tingling swept down his skin, then huge locks rotated and *clunk*ed, and the doors swung inwards. He passed inside, into the vault-like reception chamber.

To the right, the duty sergeant, Eduardo, was a shadowy figure above the imposing granite block of his desk; otherwise, the place was deserted. Donal's footsteps echoed back as he headed for the bank of cylindrical lifts at the rear, his coat swirling cape-like in the mixed cool and hot breezes that swept through this place.

He stepped into an empty lift.

'Hey, Gertie. Floor 187, please.'

For a moment, nothing. Then:

Anything for you, hon.

1

The words felt like a caress.

Donal's stomach tipped as he shot upwards.

Ten seconds later, he stepped out into a half-lit corridor.

Later, darlin'.

'See ya.'

In the reception offices, Commissioner Vilnar's secretary, known to every cop as Eyes, was sitting with her back to Donal. Slender silver cables hung around her switchboard-like console. Without turning, she waved her pale hand, which Donal took as a signal to go straight in.

'Thank you.'

'You're welcome, Lieutenant.'

He strode past a row of ordinary-looking filing-cabinets. Each was marked with a tiny fist-shaped sigil, indicating that they were in fact secure, and he wondered what they contained. Probably the Commissioner's expense sheets.

The black doors in front of Donal pulled apart, and he stepped through into Commissioner Vilnar's office. There was a lone visitor's chair made of black iron, set before the imposing desk. Behind him, the doors closed with a faint screech.

On the other side of the desk, the big chair rotated, revealing the Commissioner's bald head, the wide shoulders of his black suit.

'Sit down.'

'Thanks.'

'Have you ever been to the opera, Riordan?'

'Sir?'

'That' – the Commissioner's flat features moved: a sketched rehearsal for a smile – 'is what I thought you'd say. Read this.'

A desk drawer slid open, and Commission Vilnar pulled out a broadsheet newspaper. It looked like a luxury edition, on warm yellow vellum bearing a curlicued violet script: a copy of the *Fortinium Times*. Its layout was similar to the *Tristopolitan Gazette*, though not the flimsy edition that Donal read: the plebeian version shredded apart within hours.

'Um ...'

There was a gangland killing featured on the bottom of the first page. A blue-and-white photograph showed an innocent victim, a passing nurse who'd stepped between a slowing car and the real target, Bugs Lander.

'Try the Culture section,' said the Commissioner. 'Under Theatre.'

'You're kidding.' Donal turned the heavy pages. 'This? About the opera singer?'

Purple ink shimmered as his gaze moved across the description of Maria daLivnova's performance in *The White Masque*.

'I don't see.. Oh. She's coming to Tristopolis. The Théâtre du Loup Mort.'

The venue was an ornate building off Hoardway that Donal had passed many times.

'That's right. And while the Diva is here' – Commissioner Vilnar reached over and took back the paper – 'absolutely nothing bad is going to happen to her. Am I right?'

Donal closed his eyes, opened them again.

'Are you suggesting protection duty, sir?'

'I don't have to *suggest* anything.'

'Um ... No, sir.'

From another drawer, the Commissioner removed separate vellum sheets. Indigo typeface delineated a series of crime report summaries, each headed with a location and date, the first crime scene being in Fortinium. Two other sheets were reprinted newspaper articles.

'Six months ago,' said Donal.

'Read the details.'

The report described a famous actor falling dead on stage, accompanied by surprised applause from some of the audience who failed to realize how premature the death scene was.

'A fake ambulance crew,' added Commissioner Vilnar before Donal could finish the paragraph, 'came to take the body away. Five minutes before the real medics arrived.'

'Thanatos,' muttered Donal.

Commissioner Vilnar frowned: he disapproved of bad language. Donal continued to read, scanning reports from three other countries in Transifica, plus one from Zurinam.

'The bodies. That's the common factor.' Donal looked up. 'Someone's after the performers' bodies.'

'That's right.' Commissioner Vilnar pointed at the third report, of family bodyguards at a heavily fortified mausoleum, who shot first and asked no questions. They had killed two of the intruders and driven off the others. 'That was Trelway Boskin the Third, and his body is still in its sarcophagus.'

One of the dead actors, Sir Alyn Conroly, had made it as far as the city morgue. That was in Lorgonne, on the dank south coast. There, forensic seers found microscopic holes left by dissolving toxic slivers.

But the morning after their examination, when a seer's assistant pulled open the lead-lined drawer that should have contained Conroly, the drawer was empty.

'And it *is* murder,' said Donal. 'Not just body-snatching.'

'In a courtroom, in the other cases, that would be idle speculation.'

'Yes. I see.'

The reports covered twelve murders in total.

In Zurinam, where a popular foreign singer called Shalaria was visiting – just Shalaria, no last name – the same kind of thing had occurred. But after Shalaria's collapse, according to local custom, city officials had fed her corpse to the glistening albino snakes which lived in the city's largest cathedral.

In the blue-and-white photograph, the snakes were coiled impassively around the stone columns, while a congregation prayed, with no sign of the digested remains.

The reprinted article, written by a Tristopolitan journalist, commended the city fathers for their speed in committing Shalaria to the snakes 'without those bothersome delays incurred by forensic examinations'. Luckily, the authorities were trustworthy, the article continued, otherwise 'one might even doubt that it was Shalaria's body at all.'

Donal pushed the papers aside.

'It could be coincidence.'

'So. What else could it be?'

'A conspiracy across two continents. With resources and rigorous planning.'

'And a burning desire,' said Commissioner Vilnar, 'to go for lucky thirteen?'

'It could be.' Donal tapped the papers. 'Even if not, this Diva will need a protection detail. It's a question of how thorough the protection is.'

What Donal meant was, how much money the department was prepared to spend. For a moment, a flash of something that might have been humour passed through the Commissioner's eyes.

'She'll be safe in our city.'

Donal understood that statement for what it was.

'When do I start, sir?'

'You just did.'

In the antechamber, a folder was waiting for Donal on the desktop. He opened it, and drew out a letter.

'You're supposed to read it.'

'Yes,' Donal said to Eyes. 'Thank you.'

Being polite to the Commissioner's secretary was a basic survival skill in the Department.

Donal checked the letterhead, which bore the embossed Tree Frog insignia of the City Borough Federation, as well as the federal Salamander-and-Eagle.

> Xoram Borough Council
> 99 Phosphorus Way
> Xoram Precinct
> Tristopolis TS 66A-298-omega-2

Tristopolis Police Headquarters
1 Avenue of the Basilisks
Tristopolis TS 777-000

42nd Quatrember 6607

Re: Meeting with Malfax Cortindo, Director, City Energy Authority

Dear Commissioner Vilnar

It has been absolutely my pleasure to arrange a meeting between one of your officers and Director Cortindo of the City Energy Authority. The latter body are of course a credit to our city, and the Director evinced no hesitation in ensuring me that any technical assistance which is germane, he will be overjoyed to provide.

I have communicated with Director Cortindo that Lieutenant Donal Riordan will be meeting with him, as per your indicated request of 40th ult., on the evening of 37th of Quintember at nineteen o'clock, at the Downtown Core Station. All facilities will be placed at the Lieutenant's disposal.

Kindest regards

K Finross

Alderman Kinley Finross

P.S. All best to your honoured wife. Sally and I hope to return the favour at the Styxian Ball.

Donal checked his watch, worn military-style inside his wrist. The appointment was for tonight in less than an hour.

'Sweet bleeding Death. How am I supposed to get there on time?'

The receptionist, Eyes, shrugged without turning away from her console.

'Sorry. I didn't make the arrangements.'

'No, of course not.' Donal replaced the letter in the folder. 'You want me to leave this here?'

'Yes, please.'

'Then I'll get going.'

Gertie took Donal down fast to the twenty-seventh floor, without a word: Donal's mood was obvious. He swept through the squad room, ignoring Levison who was waving a piece of paper. There was no time.

Inside his office, Donal pushed back with his heel to slam the door shut.

'Death damn it.'

Putting his phone's handset to his ear, he span the first four combination wheels to dial an internal number, then waited.

'*Garage.*'

'Hey, Sam. It's Donal. You got any squad cars down there ready to go?'

'*Sorry, Lieutenant. O'Doyle and Zachinov took the last one. The others are still hooked up to the—*'

'Shit.'

Donal hung up. How—?

A dark cable hung outside his office window, and he remembered that the cleaners were working on the exterior this week.

I must be insane.

But he was in a real hurry now, so he reached inside his desk drawer and hooked out a pair of black liquid-metal gloves, and pulled them on. Flipping up the window catches, he took hold and heaved.

It was a long drop down.

Ah, shit.

He flexed the black metal gloves, thought about it for a moment, then climbed up on to the window sill and threw himself out.

The gloves took hold of the rope by themselves, and a smell like burning oil rose up and the air was cold as Donal's feet touched the wall every fifty feet or so, an insane abseil ... while behind a window, a woman jumped back, her mouth wide in an unheard scream.

6

Gripping harder now, the gloves slowed Donal's descent – *for Thanatos' sake* – leaving it to the last moment but his feet touched lightly and he was down.

A purple taxi slowed, the driver catching sight of Donal, but then began to speed up again.

'Hey!' shouted Donal.

Just then a dark shape shot into the road from beyond the HQ steps. Amber eyes blazed and the taxi screeched to a halt, rocking on its suspension. Donal stared at the sight for a moment, then pocketed his gloves and strode to the taxi, his heart still beating fast from the effort and adrenaline.

He pulled open the passenger door and stopped.

'Thanks, FenSeven!'

The huge deathwolf grinned, sitting on its haunches in front of the vehicle. Then it nodded, and trotted back to its place in the shadows, as Donal climbed inside the taxi and pulled the door shut.

'Police emergency,' he said.

'Uh … Yeah?'

'Thousand and seventh street. Let's not hang around.'

The driver turned around, an unlit black cigar hanging from his lips.

'Police?'

'What, you want to see my handcuffs? Or my gun?'

'Uh … No, chief.' The driver gunned the engine and pulled away from the curb. 'No need.'

'Good.' Donal's voice was soft. 'That's a good thing.'

From the corner of Avenue of the Basilisks and Hellvue Boulevard, a white-skinned woman in a pale-grey skirt suit watched the taxi depart. She liked the way that he had exited the building directly without caring too much what people thought.

'That's a quality that could be useful.'

A streetcleaner, in his black uniform, paused on the other side of the street. He wondered what such a pale pretty lady was doing talking to herself … But then, just for a millisecond, he glimpsed a shift of movement in the air. He jerked back. Some things are not meant to be stared at directly.

Grabbing a broom from his cart, the cleaner got to work in the gutter, no longer looking up or sideways. Not even from the edge of his vision.

You think he's honest? the air whispered.

The woman in the pale-grey skirt suit pulled a compact out of her handbag, and flipped it open. The mirror was one-third silver, the remaining two-thirds black but still reflective: plenty of time remaining.

She snapped the compact shut, replaced it beside her platinum-coated pistol, and slung the bag back over her shoulder.

Well?

'I don't know,' she said. 'Do you think we could use him if he isn't?'

No.

'Neither do I.' The woman looked down the long perspective of the dark avenue, watching as the purple taxi hooked into a fast left turn and was gone. 'If he doesn't survive, it doesn't matter either way.'

I thought I was the negative one.

The woman turned and strode towards the nearest black hydrant. Her dark, finned car – a Vixen – was waiting at the curb. As she walked, a half-glimpsed ripple passed through the air alongside her, keeping pace.

Or maybe you're afraid to let yourself fancy him. Is that it?

The woman stopped, fingers touching the car's doorhandle. She looked up at the air.

'Am I that transparent?'

There was another ripple, altering the outline of the art gallery beyond.

Is that meant to be funny?

'Well, I laughed.' The woman got inside the car and slammed the door.

After a moment, she opened the passenger door from the inside, waited for approximately thirty seconds, then reached across and pulled it shut.

'Let's go keep watch. If Lieutenant Riordan doesn't reappear, we'll have someone to charge with his murder. There's always a bright side, Xalia. Didn't you know?'

I prefer the darkness, Laura.

'You would.'

And you don't?

The car slid away from the curb.

Two great pillars of stone reached up. If you craned your head back, you would see, against a background of purple sky, that each pillar was surmounted by a skull wearing an Ouroboros headband, a flattened Möbius serpent twisting around and swallowing its own tail.

Lowering your gaze just a little, you would take in the immense size and weight of the solid black iron gates, and the great walls formed of granite stretching off to either side, encircling the Downtown Core Complex.

The taxi stopped, small in the foreshortened black drive that stopped at the gates. Behind the taxi, beyond the street, rose the attenuated blocks of old denuded buildings, empty niches showing where gargoyles had perched before leaving en masse.

'Man,' murmured the taxi driver. 'This place ...'

Donal said: 'Sound your horn.'

'Oh, I don't—'

'Sound it.'

A long howl rose from under the taxi's purple bonnet. 'There. Are you—?'

There was a grinding sound, and the taxi shuddered as the gates began to move, sliding to either side. Donal remained impassive while the driver swallowed twice, three times in succession, then rolled the taxi forward.

As they entered a gargantuan courtyard, the driver almost had his eyes shut; but Donal was scanning the environment, checking the gun slits on the walls, noting the internal stairs that led to watchtowers.

Then the taxi slowed and halted on a brass circular area at the courtyard's centre. The brass disc's diameter was perhaps twice the length of a delivery truck.

'PLEASE CUT THE ENGINE.' The voice reverberated around the courtyard.

'Oh, man ...'

'Do it.'

As soon as the driver switched off the engine, the taxi shuddered once more. The courtyard wall begin to slide sideways ...

'Sweet Hades.'

... except that it wasn't the wall that was moving, it was the taxi and the great brass disc it was parked on, slowly rotating.

'Is the handbrake on properly?' said Donal.

'Yeah.' But the driver yanked up hard on the lever. 'Yeah, we're OK.'

The wall moved faster now, and Donal could feel the sinking motion as the brass disc screwed itself downwards. The driver clutched his face and tried not to look at the hollow threaded wall rising past the windows.

The disc screwed into the earth, carrying the taxi down.

It took seven minutes by Donal's watch to descend through the shaft. Then the walls were gone, replaced by a vast underground space ... as the giant screw continued to lower the taxi, down to the floor of the cavernous complex.

The place was vast, with great shadowed aisles separating the huge, square-edged stone piles. Even the darkness seemed to flicker; and that might not have been Donal's imagination.

For these were the necrofusion piles, the reactors that kept the city powered and its inhabitants alive.

When the brass disc finally slowed and stopped, the driver was muttering a prayer over and over: 'St-Magnus-slayer-of-evil-behead-my-enemies-and-keep-me-safe. St-Magnus-slayer-of ...'

Donal pulled out his wallet, and counted out thirty florins, in accordance with the needle on the dashboard's dial. 'I'll need a receipt.'

'... enemies-and-what? Say what?'

'Receipt. Please.'

'Oh. Sure.' The driver pulled a receipt book from under the dashboard, and looked for a pen.

'Behind your ear,' said Donal.

'Huh? Oh.' The driver found the pen, pulled the cap. He tried to write while casting glances out of the windshield and side windows; but his hands were shaking. 'Look ...'

'What?'

'Take the receipt, man. Write in your own amount, OK?'

Donal handed over the florin notes and took the blank receipt. 'All right. If you wait for me on the street up above – out on the street, mind you – you'll get another fifty for the journey back.'

The driver stared at Donal in the mirror, then nodded his head, fast. Outside, figures in overalls were walking this way.

'You won't be there,' said Donal.

'Man, I ...'

'Better not lie.' But Donal had work to do. He opened the door and stepped out on to the brass. 'Don't break any speed limits.'

He slammed the purple door shut, and walked off the brass disc and on to solid stone. Behind him the brass cylinder began to screw its way upwards once more.

But it was the three men in grey overalls that dominated Donal's attention. He noted the skull-and-Ouroboros symbol on their chests, the calm look in their eyes ... and the protective platinum earplugs, the liquid amber vests inside their coveralls.

'I'm here to see Malfax Cortindo.'

The brass column had reached the cavern ceiling, and was now a solid rotating column, bearing the taxi upwards through solid ground.

'Of course, sir. Director Cortindo's office is this way.'

'How do you know he'll see me?'

'You're on his schedule,' said the largest of the three men. 'Lieutenant Riordan.'

Donal had presented no ID.

'That's nice,' he said.

The large man gestured. 'Sir?'

'Lead on.'

In fact the men walked beside and behind Donal, escorting him along a vast black-floored alley that separated two rows of necrofusion piles. Even with the lead-and-carbon cladding, Donal felt a twisting in the air, and his chest laboured as he walked.

'You ever had a leak in here?' Donal's voice sounded softer than he had intended.

But none of his escort answered; they walked on in silence. There was only the hum of the reactors (overlaid with gut-liquefying sub-sonics) plus an ozone tang that hooked at Donal's nostrils and something else ... a feeling that was dry and damp, like poisoned silk drawn softly across his skin.

This was where the dead paid back for the comforts of their life.

And kept repaying.

'Up the staircase, sir. The Director's assistant will be waiting at the top.'

Repaying for ever.

'Thank you.'

It was an ordinary iron spiral, and Donal began to climb.

Two

At the top of the spiral staircase was a landing, also of black iron. Set in the stone wall was a circular door of polished steel, on which the skull-and-Ouroboros was inlaid in shining brass.

The door swung inwards with a faint sucking sound.

'Good morning, Lieutenant.' The grey-haired secretary drew her shoulders forward, hollowing her chest, as though afraid to take up too much space. 'Director Cortindo will see you straight away.'

'That's good of him.' Donal scanned the outer office. There was a low ceiling, and black-flame candles in niches on the walls, with true illumination being indirect, from channels at the floor's edge.

He pulled off his overcoat, and hung it on the black iron coat-stand.

'Can I bring you a cup of tea, Lieutenant? Zurinam Black, or we have Axil Red.'

'Not for me.'

Donal wanted to tell the woman to straighten up and breathe deeply. He wondered if she had always stooped like this, or whether the dark oppressive weight of this place had pressed her down over the years.

He smiled, but the woman looked uncertain as she flicked three glass toggles and waited. The big steel door to the inner office swung open.

The man who rose from behind the blue glass desk was perhaps sixty years old, with a grey goatee.

'Lieutenant Riordan. How wonderful to meet you.'

This had to be Malfax Cortindo. He wore a silver cravat instead of a tie, and a suit cut from some soft, dark fabric. A walking stick leaned against his chair: ebony, with a plain silver handle, instead of the skull-and-worm that Donal had half expected.

'Thank you. Likewise.'

12

They shook hands. Cortindo's hand was smooth – there was a hint of lilac scent – but strong. Donal decided that there was more to this man than an air of elegance.

'Won't you take a seat.'

'Thanks.'

Donal sat down. On the other side of the desk, Malfax Cortindo sat in his more ornate chair, with curved back and arms. Then Cortindo crossed his legs and steepled his fingers together.

'I'm really happy to help you. Your visit is something out of the ordinary routine, Lieutenant. Thank you for that, at least.'

'And the department is grateful for your agreeing to help.'

Donal and Cortindo looked at each other. In this insulated office, richly appointed with carvings and other ornaments, the reactors' sound was a background hum. A golden clock formed of interlocking metal bones wielding a miniature scythe sliced away the half-seconds from a vertical thread of flowing amber liquid, cutting the thread into discrete drops.

They fell into a cup: *snick-snack, snick-snack.*

Malfax Cortindo broke the impasse. 'I'm not entirely clear on how I'm supposed to help, mind you.'

Donal let out a breath. 'You want the truth? Neither do I.'

'In that case' – with an elegant chuckle – 'can I tempt you with some brandy, while we try to work this out? I have Sintro Mundo, shipped in from Alfrikstan.'

'No, thank you.' Not in this place. 'Now, I have to be careful about giving away specifics about this case.'

'Of course. I understand.'

'In addition to which, it's more a case of preventing a crime than solving one.' Donal never used the word 'solve' when talking with fellow detectives; he had never thought of his job as a puzzle or a game. 'But in other cities, some notable people have been murdered—'

Something shifted in Cortindo's eyes.

'Murdered? This is serious.'

'Yes.' Donal held back what he wanted to say: that otherwise, he wouldn't be in this place. 'And in several cases, the death has been in a public venue, before an audience. The link is that someone took the bodies, sometimes in audacious ways.'

Malfax Cortindo uncrossed his legs and leaned on the dark-blue desk. 'This sounds like some kind of widespread conspiracy.'

'Oh, no,' said Donal, lying. 'I just mean, there's a particular type of crime that sometimes occurs. A type we've identified, and would like to prevent.'

'Interesting.' Malfax Cortindo's gaze remained fixed on Donal. 'Interesting ... Do I take it you're going to be in charge of Maria daLivnova's security?'

'What?' Donal straightened up in his chair. 'Who said anything about her?'

'Ah. You did, Lieutenant. You provided a strong hint, anyway, which you've just confirmed.'

'This isn't a game.'

'I've always thought a playful spirit allows one to work so much better. But we don't have to agree on that ... You want me to explain my thought process?'

'Why not.'

'The guesswork was this: when you mentioned deaths in public places, and audiences, and the stealing of bodies, I assumed you meant the ... victims ... were performers or artists of some kind. Once I'd got that far, the subsequent deduction was obvious.'

'You mean about the Diva.'

'I mean Maria daLivnova, of course. Her forthcoming performances will be the highlight of the current season, as I'm sure you're aware.'

'Naturally.'

'Ah ... Not an opera fan, Lieutenant?'

'I sometimes sing in the shower.'

Malfax Cortindo gestured at his office. 'Take a look. You see that statuette? It's Zurinese, maybe four hundred years old. And that painting, the dark one, is by Turinette in the last month before his death. And that embroidery of a poem? If you look closely, you'll see the verses are from Zar Cuchon's epic *Gladius Mortis*, the part where he's in the forest and—'

'Fascinating.'

Donal was less interested in statuettes and embroidery than he was in Malfax Cortindo himself. A blizzard of fine-sounding words could not disguise the intuitive leap that made Cortindo identify public performers as the victims of murder and body-stealing.

But the man was too self-possessed to crack easily ... and he was supposed to be a resource, not a suspect, for Death's sake.

'The point is, Lieutenant, the people who created these works were very special. Even if they didn't know it themselves, their dreams

14

were priceless, beyond any kind of material worth I know.'

'If you say so.'

'Perhaps we should take a look at the facility. It'll be a start in explaining what I mean.'

This was the part that Donal had not been looking forward to.

'Good idea,' he said.

'First, let me show you the overview.' Still sitting, Malfax Cortindo made a gesture over the blue glass desk. Something rippled inside the glass. 'Here we are.'

There was a soft groan, and then the wall to Donal's right began to move. It slid slowly, a vast yard-thick slab of granite, into a recess, revealing the caverns beyond. This room was high up, close to the ceiling. Down below, seven rows of reactor piles were visible; others were out of sight, hidden by supporting columns and walls: this was a whole system of caverns, not a single space.

'See, below the ground' – Malfax Cortindo pointed – 'where the air appears to shift and waver?'

'Um ... Got it.'

'Those are the power conduction channels. The necroflux itself must remain confined within the reactor piles, or there would be a hetero-dyning build up that would become catastrophic.'

'You mean an explosion?'

'Exactly.' Malfax Cortindo took hold of his elegant cane and stood. 'Shall we go down and take a look?

Down at the floor level, the air seemed thicker, and a buzz appeared to float inside Donal's head. Each reactor was taller and more solid than it had appeared from Malfax Cortindo's office. Workers in grey overalls moved constantly among the piles, and Donal could see the stress-lines clamped on their faces: the price of non-stop vigilance.

They walked, Donal and Malfax Cortindo, for ten minutes along one wide aisle, with minimal conversation. The scale of it was greater than Donal had thought it would or could be. Finally, they came to a reactor whose casing was open.

'Don't worry,' said Malfax Cortindo. 'It's been scrubbed and decon-taminated, ready for recommissioning.'

Seven men in heavy protective suits and helmets were working on the casing.

'Could I poke my head inside the cavity?' said Donal. 'Just to take a look.'

Malfax Cortindo shook his head. 'I wouldn't do that if I were you, Lieutenant.'

'Didn't you say it's been scrubbed?'

'Cleanliness' – with a quarter-second smile – 'is relative, sir. Everything here has a memory, which is part of the problem.'

One of the workers stopped and stiffened. Then one of his colleagues snapped open a lead-lined case. 'OK, Karl. I'm ready.'

Donal started to step forward, but Malfax Cortindo touched his sleeve. 'We need to keep our distance, I believe.'

'All right.'

The bent-over worker, Karl, was wearing heavy stub-fingered gauntlets as part of his protective gear. It must have made fine work harder, but after a few seconds he straightened up and backed out of the hollow reactor casing, bearing something in one palm. It was a sliver of grey, a bone splinter, no more.

But immediately Donal felt sickness clutch his stomach, and the floor seemed to sway.

'Come along.' Malfax Cortindo's grip was strong on his upper arm. 'Let's leave these gentlemen to their work.'

Screaming, the inchoate mix of faces and touch, softness and the feel of intestines bursting, tears and the stink of . . .

Then they were further along the aisle, and the air seemed clear, though still heavy.

'What the Hades was that?'

'Sorry, Lieutenant. The splinter was bigger than I thought, or I'd have got us out of there straight away.'

'A bone splinter? Just a splinter?'

'Yes . . . A fragment that's spent considerable time as part of the reactor fuel. You understand what goes on inside these things?'

'We touched on it in school' – Donal wiped his face with the back of his hand – 'which was a bloody long time ago.'

'Best days of your life. Isn't that what we tell our grandchildren?'

Donal doubted whether he and Cortindo had attended the same kinds of school. There are places where you need fists as well as brains in order to graduate.

Malfax Cortindo gestured up at the nearest reactor with his cane.

'It takes the bones of two thousand corpses,' he said, 'to form the critical mass for a single pile. What we're talking about is a resonant cavity, where standing waves of necroflux vibrate and strengthen, giving off a plethora of harmonics.'

16

Two thousand people's remains, just in that one reactor.

'OK.' Donal blinked, forcing down his natural dread and sadness. 'Two thousand. Large number.'

'There's no shortage of raw components, Lieutenant.'

After a moment, Donal said: 'I don't suppose there is.'

As they walked back to the staircase together, Malfax Cortindo spoke more of the underlying process. Donal tried to follow, not knowing whether any of this had bearing on his job.

Cortindo explained how the microstructures of living bones are altered by the perceptions and actions of the body they're encased in. But after death, when those same bones are part of a reactor pile, the necroflux moans and howls, diffracted by the bones' internal structure, replaying the memories of the dead.

'But not in a coherent whole,' said Malfax Cortindo. 'They're just mixed-up memory fragments from two thousand individuals. The conglomeration does not truly think or feel anything.'

Donal stopped, and looked back at the long straight rows of reactors.

'Not even pain?'

'No.' Malfax Cortindo looked at him for a long moment, then tapped the stone floor with his cane. 'At least, that's what I'll tell anyone who asks me officially. You understand me, Lieutenant?'

Biting his lip, Donal thought of how the city would react if there were suddenly no power, no transport, and therefore no food in the shops.

'I understand.'

On the wall beside the staircase was a row of brass-encircled, glass-covered dials. The leftmost dial was labelled $MN f^{-2}$, and Malfax Cortindo stopped to check it. Beside it, a dial labelled GW showed the total power output, Donal assumed, in gigawatts.

'What's the first dial?' he asked.

'It's the mean flux rating across all piles,' said Malfax Cortindo, 'in meganecrons per square foot.'

'Oh. Of course.'

'Hmm. Shall we go back up' – with an elegant smile – 'and have a cup of tea?'

In Malfax Cortindo's office once more, Donal accepted the offer of tea. The grey-haired secretary brought it on a tray, served with best bone china.

Hoping to Hades that there were no real bones involved in the cup's manufacture, Donal took hold of the fragile handle and sipped the dark strong tea. It was the best he had ever tasted.

'That's good.' Carefully, he replaced the cup on the saucer. 'That's very good.'

'I'm glad you approve, Lieutenant. Now ... Once you've finished your tea, I've one more thing to show you. Don't worry, there's no more walking involved.'

I wasn't worried, Donal was tempted to say. Instead he took another sip of tea.

Wonderful.

'Let's do it now,' he said. 'Whatever it is.'

'Since you insist ... bear with me a moment.' Cortindo went to the bookcase which covered the rear wall. He stared at the books' spines for a moment, then tapped the shelves with his cane, in a pattern of strikes that Donal could not follow.

Malfax Cortindo turned around, just as a circular section of the carpeted floor rotated, and a yard-wide cylinder of metal rose up to chest height and stopped.

'Here we are.' Cortindo laid his cane against the desk, and inserted his fingertips into brass-coloured depressions in the metal cylinder. After a moment, a steel door popped open on the cylinder's side. 'OK, this is what you need to see.'

It was a platinum case sealed with a golden catch. Perhaps the size of a gun case for an antique pistol, it looked heavy, and Donal wondered what it could contain.

There was a kind of reverence in the way Malfax Cortindo held the case, snapped back the catch, and pulled open the lid. Then he turned the case around so that Donal could see inside.

On scarlet velvet lay a desiccated bone.

'You can touch it,' said Malfax Cortindo, 'but—'

Too late.

Something had already drawn Donal's fingertips forward, as though he had relinquished control of his own neuromuscular system, and then he touched the bone and he was lost.

It was a form of drowning.

There was a silver sea, its gentle breakers spreading on a pink beach, while transparent birds flew overhead, singing arias of such magnificence that Donal began to weep. There were flowers inland, on fantastical green-glass structures that might have been plants or might have been art, and the minutest detail of their texture was fascinating. Here a drop of water glistening like a—

Something snatched at him.

No!

—crystalline world in its own right, and all around the fabric of existence was threaded deep with colour, strange nude figures moving in the distance, and landscape filled with—

Another tug, which he tried to fight.

—bands of heavy yellow and red and indigo, the trees which—

Were gone.

Everything was gone.

'NO!' Donal hurled himself at Malfax Cortindo who backed away in a deceptive circular motion, bypassing Donal's momentum. 'Give it—'

'Sorry.' Cortindo's footwork became a spiral, then a twisting reversal, avoiding Donal's charge once more.

'Give ...'

Donal bent over from the waist, wheezing, more out of breath than after a ten-mile run. He squinted, salt-sweat half-blinding him, and he wiped his face with his hand.

What the Death was going on?

'You were lost,' said Malfax Cortindo, 'in an artist's dreams.'

'But you—'

Heavy gauntlets on Cortindo's hands must be shielding him from the bone's influence. Moving with apparent slowness – he was deceptive in his fluid motion – Cortindo replaced the bone inside the platinum case and pushed the lid down shut. Immediately, the air inside the office seemed to clear.

Donal staggered back to the visitor's chair and sat.

'Ah, Hades.' He picked up the cup, and took a slug of tea. 'Ugh!'

It was cold.

'Sorry, Lieutenant. But you had to see.' Malfax Cortindo was inserting the case back inside the cylinder's opening. 'If you didn't experience it for yourself, everything I told you would have been fragile words, immediately forgotten.'

'I've got a good memory.' Donal made a sour face as put the teacup down. 'How did that grow so—?'

'Do you remember how much time passed in your dream?'

'Excuse me?' Donal twisted his wrist and checked his watch. 'No. That's ...'

The time was 22:63.

'. . . impossible.'

As soon as Malfax Cortindo pushed the metal door shut, the cylinder began to sink back down into the floor.

'Is it, Lieutenant? Surely not.'

Malfax Cortindo was right, because there was no reason for Donal to think that his watch had been ensorcelled, or that some eldritch process had been used to suck the heat from his teacup. Instead, there was only one conclusion to be drawn.

Donal had been lost in the bone's dreams for nearly three hours.

Sitting down behind his dark-blue glass desk once more, Malfax Cortindo stripped off the heavy protective gauntlets.

'I could have snatched the bone back,' said Donal. 'What would have happened to me then?'

'My dear Lieutenant, I have trained since childhood in *pa-kua*, a soft art which enabled me to avoid your somewhat, ah, unsteady lunges.'

'I'd just been ripped out of . . .' Donal let his voice trail off.

Out of paradise.

'I know, and that was in my favour. If there'd been more risk, I'd have had Security in here with me, you understand.'

It sounded as if Cortindo expected Donal to thank him. Instead, Donal opened his suit jacket and let it fall open as he sat back, allowing the shoulder holstered Magnus to show.

'You want to explain what just happened?'

'Ah. Perhaps I should apologize for the graphic demonstration—'

'Perhaps you should.'

'—but it was in the common good, I assure you. That bone you just touched was part of a common intake, ordinary bones destined for the reactor piles.'

Donal shook his head. He knew he shouldn't have come here.

'But our staff are dedicated,' Malfax Cortindo continued, 'and highly trained. All bone shipments pass through necroscopic examination procedures. If a gifted artist has died a pauper's death, this is the final chance of our discovering their existence.'

The cylinder had sunk into the floor, become integral with it, and was hardly noticeable now.

'Who was that?' said Donal. 'Whose bone did I touch?'

'It was an ulna' – Malfax Cortindo gave a precise smile – 'from Jamix Holandson, whose works now command exceptional prices. Several of his pieces are on show in the Federal Centre for Modern Art, in Fortinium.'

'Oh. Him.'

'Our procedures are rigorous and our staff are highly trained.'

'Too bad this Sorenson—'

'Holandson.'

'—Holandson, didn't get famous before he died.'

'As I said' – Malfax Cortindo rubbed his grey goatee with one finger – 'it is the artist's *final* chance.'

'More like the postultimate chance,' said Donal, 'if there is such a word.'

'I don't believe there is, old chap.'

Donal looked at him. There was more to be discovered here, but how much of it related to his job, Donal could not tell. He had a strong desire to get the Hades out of here, but he forced himself to slow down.

'What has this got to do with murders?' he asked.

'Isn't that obvious?'

'I don't know. Explain it to me, Mr Cortindo.'

The plaques on the wall indicated that he was Director Cortindo or Doctor Cortindo … or in the case of Donnerheim University, Herr Doktor Direktor Cortindo.

'If you were a certain kind of collector – a rich and influential collector, you understand – would you not pay a considerable amount of money to take possession of such bones?'

Donal stared at him. 'Perhaps.'

'Well … *Perhaps* if you were a certain kind of dedicated collector, you might not be able to wait for the natural course of events, let's say, before your favourite artist's bones became … available.'

'Oh, shit.'

'After all, there's no guarantee that you'll outlive the object of your desire, is there, Lieutenant? Does any of us know when he's going to die?'

Donal stood up.

'Thank you for the tea. And the … enlightenment.'

'Why, Lieutenant.' Malfax Cortindo also stood. 'It's been my absolute pleasure.'

They shook hands.

'I hope to see you down here again soon,' added Malfax Cortindo. 'Oh … I mean socially, of course. Not—'

21

'I understand.'

Donal picked up his overcoat from the secretary's outer office. The black liquid-metal gloves were still in the coat's pockets. For a moment Donal considered putting them on, going back into Cortindo's office, and stuffing the dead artist's ulna down Cortindo's throat.

But Donal had a job to do, and beating the crap out of a civilian adviser was not the way to go about it.

'Thank you very much, Lieutenant. I hope you had a wonderful visit.'

'The tea was great. Thank you, ma'am.'

Donal left through the door to the spiral stairs, and descended the black iron steps to the cavern floor. The same three men in grey overalls were there to escort him back to the surface.

'Nice seeing you guys again.'

'This way, officer. You got no car?'

'I don't need one.'

'The elevator for people, like, is this way.'

The trio led Donal to a curved black door set in a stone pillar. The door rattled and slid open. Donal stepped in, finding himself on a scratched steel floor. Lanterns were set on short stubby metal stands, forming a circle around him. Craning his head back, he could see only thickening shadows, and total darkness overhead.

'Is this—?'

But the door was already sliding shut.

'Oh, well.'

The floor scraped a little as it rose, then moved faster, and in seconds it was accelerating hard, pressing his feet against the steel. The stone shaft wall went past in a blur; reaching out to touch it would be a bad idea.

Then the rising floor decelerated, and Donal's bodyweight felt normal as the floor clanged to a halt, jolting him. He was in a black hollow hemisphere.

'How do I—?'

At that moment the metallic hemisphere split into flanges that folded themselves back, leaving him standing on open concrete, inside a small courtyard.

He stepped quickly off the disc in case it was set to return below. Uniformed guards nodded to him – Donal recognized one as a former patrol officer who'd been kicked off the force for getting freebies in the

Scarlet Quarter – and he gave them a fingertip salute as he headed for a small exit door.

The door's height and width were for a single person, but when the door swung inwards, he saw that it was foot-thick metal, and could not imagine the weight of it. A small wisp of steam escaped from the powered hinges.

He gave a half-wave to no one behind him, then stepped through the doorway and on to the sidewalk. Behind him, valves hissed and pistons swung the heavy door shut.

'Wonderful.'

He was stuck in a dilapidated area, outside the fortress which was the above-ground manifestation of the Downtown Core Complex. Few people ventured here except for work, travelling on the Energy Authority's own buses.

What he should have done was called a taxi or a squad car from the secretary's office; but he had wanted to get out of the Complex straight away.

Several furlongs down the street, a dark, finned car, a Vixen, was parked. Donal considered asking the driver for a lift, but as he turned his attention to it the car started up. It pulled away from the curb.

'Damn it.'

But the driver had been a woman: Donal had glimpsed permed pale-blonde hair. There would have been no reason for her to offer a lift to a lone man walking these particular streets.

Beside him lay a derelict site, a scree formed of rubble from which skeletal ribs of rusted girders poked. Three pale lizards, scuttling across the ruins, froze when they realized Donal was staring at them.

He shook his head, and looked up at the solid purple-black sky.

Then he pulled his coat around himself and began to walk. As he did so, a light quicksilver rain began to fall. Tiny mercury droplets spattered from the long coat.

I hate this place.

On the sidewalk, liquid metal puddles were already forming, shining and glutinous. If it hadn't been for the regular injections Donal received as an active police officer, he would have been less blasé about walking down the street without a hat.

There was a scratching sound as the lizards scrabbled for cover.

Donal wondered where the Diva, Maria daLivnova, was right now. Rehearsing in some swanky theatre or dining in a fantastically appointed hotel restaurant. Not walking alone down streets where lizards hid from the weather.

But as he walked, he remembered something more, against his will: the deep richness of the world seen through Jamix Holandson's eyes.

Through one of his dead bones.

Three

Back in his own office, Donal beckoned Levison to come and join him. Levison was tall and gangly, bald save for patches of carrot-red hair over his protruding ears. As usual, his shirt's top button was open and his tie was loosened.

Picking up a folder from his desk, Levison entered Donal's office and pushed the door shut with his elbow. He adjusted the gun slanted forward on his left hip, as he sat down in front of Donal's desk. Levison's weapon had seen little action on the street, despite the well-worn look of the leather holster. Levison had never confused marksmanship with being a good cop.

'You know,' said Levison, 'there are only twenty-five hours in the day. Perhaps you should have a word with the Commissioner and let him know.'

'On account of how,' said Donal, 'me and him are such great pals, right?'

'Yeah ...' Levison placed his folder flat on the desktop. 'This came down from above while you were out swanning around with the high and mighty. How was the Energy Authority, anyway?'

'Filled with piles of bone, like you'd expect.'

'Pleasant place.' Levison shook his head. 'Sooner you than me, boss. Did you learn anything?'

'Only that certain sickos' – Donal remembered the wonderful dreams: there was nothing sick in them – 'would have a great reason for offing the Diva and stealing her bones.'

'Wonderful.'

'Or professionals, working on behalf of rich sickos ... That scenario works.'

'It sounds like a lot more effort, Donal, than guarding against one nutcase. This Diva's landing in a week's time at Tempelgard. It's all in there.' Levison pointed at the folder.

'Justice never sleeps.'

'Naw, it just gets schizophrenic hallucinations caused by dream deprivation, and then blows out its brains with a silver-loaded Magnus.' The humour seemed to sink inside Levison's long face, leaving a serious mask. 'You heard about Peters, out at the hundred-and-first?'

'Peters?'

'He did himself in last night.'

'Shit, I was at his wedding.' Donal stared out of the window at the rearing blackstone corporate building across the street, seeing nothing. 'His widow . . .'

'The guys are making a collection.'

'Put me in for fifty florins, will you? I'll pay you tomorrow.'

Levison nodded, knowing that Donal was good for the money. 'You're going back out?'

'Yeah . . .' Donal pulled the folder to him and flipped it open. 'Need to check out the environment, the route from the airport. Like that.'

'She's staying at the Exemplar.' Levison reached over and turned back two pages. 'There, see. Got her own suite. No expense spared.'

'Shit.'

'Right. You want reasonable coverage, you'll need guys in the room across the hall. You need full cover, that'll be the rooms on either side, on the floor below – that's three separate rooms, actually – and the one above. That's another suite.'

'Thanatos.'

'When I talked to the lovely Eyes on the phone' – Levison grimaced – 'she passed on Commissioner Vilnar's favourite phrase.'

'Tell them not to go mad on the overtime?'

'The very one.'

'Accounts are going to go ballistic. I'd better go see the hotel first, see if I can charm them into giving us a better discount than usual.'

'How about them paying us, considering we'd be saving them embarrassment?' said Levison. 'Not to mention lost business.'

'If you say so.' Donal put his feet up on the desk. 'Or maybe the public would come flocking in to stay at the place where the Diva was murdered.'

'Hades, Donal. Don't let anyone hear you say that.'

'Yeah . . . I might give someone a bright idea. Or dark idea. Whatever.'

*

Donal avoided Gertie's elevator shaft, and walked along the dark corridor to a colder shaft, where rime formed on the steel casing and the shaft's enslaved wraith carried out its duties in perpetual silence.

There was little time, but Donal had not practised today, and if you let it slip once, then it would be easier to avoid practice the next time. Before you knew it, you'd end up a soft bureaucrat like Commissioner Vilnar, whose knowledge of street policing was based on ancient memories, plus the reading of endless memos and precinct reports.

Inside the shadowed shaft, Donal plunged fast, feet first. The icy slipstream whipped his coat upwards, but he paid no attention. After thirty floors his descent slowed. By the time he reached the minus-thirteenth floor, his downward motion was infinitesimal.

Donal stepped into a cold half-lit chamber.

He pulled his Magnus from his shoulder holster, slipped out the magazine to check it was full – chitin-piercing load with silver-crossed bullets – then slapped it back in and reholstered. Donal took in a deep chest-full of cold air, then expelled a long calming breath.

In front of him was an iron-bound door. Donal pushed it open. An empty counter stood to one side.

'It's Riordan. You there, Brian?'

'Sure, Lieutenant.' A bald man with bluish skin and a pot belly levered himself up from behind the counter. 'What can I do you for today?'

'I need' – Donal glanced at his watch: he would have to make this fast – 'a box of fifty rounds, that's all. The usual.'

'OK.' Brian reached underneath the counter, and came up with a three-inch cardboard box filled with shells. 'You wanna sign?'

'Sure.' There was a clipboard and Donal pulled it towards him. He wrote LIEUT. D. RIORDAN in capitals and added his signature. 'Six targets, please.'

A howl echoed from the corridor outside.

'What's going on?'

'Little combat shooting competition.' Brian slid out flat drawers from the wall behind the counter. 'The boys from seventy-third are up against our guys. You weren't thinking of making an illegal bet now, were you, Lieutenant?'

'Wouldn't dream of it. If, hypothetically speaking, someone *were* taking bets, what odds would they be offering on our boys winning?'

'Evens, is all. Woulda been three-to-one against, but them seventy-thirds had a lotta gang trouble last year. Sharpened 'em up.'

Donal shook his head.

'Some other time.'

'Your loss, boss.' Brian pulled out several sheets from the drawers. 'Awright, we got yer basic roundel – one of those? – and some outlines. One ghoul-with-human-hostage. One human-with-ghoul-hostage. One—'

'I'll take two of those.'

'OK. And for the last ...' Brian slid the two-foot by four-foot sheets of paper across the counter. 'I heard someone's been sketching well-known figures on big bits of paper, y'know? Like various Aldermen, including Finross and O'Connell. Maybe even the Comm—'

Donal reached across the counter and clapped a hand on Brian's shoulder. He smiled, keeping it friendly, as his grip tightened and his fingers dug in.

'Now, Brian? You know why we don't just shoot round targets any more?'

'Um ... No, boss. Listen—'

'It's because it makes it easier for us to shoot real people. Or real ... whatever. They call it operant conditioning, and it helps keep cops alive. Because we don't freeze on the street when it goes down hard.'

'Ugh, sure. But you're hurting—'

'So we don't ever make a joke of it, or use individual people on the pictures. Do we?' Donal released his grip. 'Do we, Brian?'

'No, Lieutenant. I mean *no*, for Hades' sake. Wouldn't dream of—'

'Good. Because when the inspection comes tomorrow, this place will be ship-shape. And if I hear rumours of anything else ... But I won't, will I?'

'No, sir.'

'Good man.' Donal gathered together the four sheets of paper. 'I'll need two more targets, please.'

In silence, Brian took two more standard targets from a drawer and laid them down.

'Thank you very much, Brian.'

It took fifteen minutes to unload sixty rounds into the targets: the magazine clip plus the fifty rounds he'd got from Brian. That was a long time, but the ceiling cables used to carry the targets out to varying distances in the subterranean range were slow.

Silver sea, gentle breakers on a pink beach, while transparent birds sing overhead ...

Donal was right-handed but with a dominant left eye, which meant he had to tilt his head down to his right shoulder when he aimed. It looked odd – when he was a rookie, fellow officers called him Cockeye Riordan – but it stabilized the head and made him a better marksman.

That, and the daily training.

On the last magazine-load today, Donal sent the target right back, turned away, then squeezed his eyes shut before swivelling round and firing ten rounds in even succession.

When he opened his eyes, the target was in tatters.

'Good enough.'

Because you don't always get good lighting on the street. Sometimes the bastards come at you from darkness.

A series of loud percussive bangs echoed down the range. Donal had thought he was the only person here. Whatever the load the other guy was using, it was heavy duty. Donal felt curious, but ... he checked his watch. He still wanted to visit the Exemplar Hotel tonight, and check out the floor where the Diva would be staying.

Another sequence of bangs sounded.

'Just a peek,' Donal told himself.

Walking slowly, not wanting to startle the officer with sudden movement at the edge of his vision, Donal passed seven empty lanes on the gun-range until he could see the shooter.

The man was huge, nearly seven feet tall, with massive shoulders stretching his dark-burgundy leather jacket. Round blue glasses perched on his long nose.

He fired a heavy silver gun single-handed. The weapon was heavy, designed for a two-handed grip: an abbreviated machine gun.

'Ha.' The big man put the emptied weapon down, and pulled out his earplugs. Donal did likewise.

'What kind of—? Hades. Look at that.' Donal peered down the range, then placed his hand on the green Retrieve button beside him. 'Can I?'

'Go ahead, Lieutenant.'

So the man knew who Donal was. Well, that happened. A drawback of rank: they knew you and you didn't know them. Donal pressed the button and held it in as the target holder whined its way back along the ceiling.

But there was little target left. By the time it reached Donal's position, he had verified that only a few flapping ribbons of paper remained.

'Not bad. What kind of beast is that?'

29

'Oh, her?' The big man ran a finger along the weapon, which lay flat on the shelf. 'I call her Betsie. She's a Howler 50.'

'I thought it – she – might be. I've read about them. Not bad.'

'You want to give her a try, Lieutenant?'

'Er ... Damn it, I'd love to. But not tonight. I've still got stuff to do.'

'But you made time to come down to the range? Understood, sir.'

The man was unshaven, and his face was tanned and ugly. Donal had already decided to like him.

'What's your name, Detective?'

'Viktor Harman, sir. I work out of the, ah, seventy-seventh. They call me Big Viktor.'

'I'm not surprised. You'll be round here again?'

'Oh, yes, sir. You can count on it.'

'See you then.'

'Lieutenant.'

Out on the street, Donal had no trouble in flagging down a purple cab. Earlier, after leaving the Energy Authority complex, he'd walked over a mile before finding a phone booth that worked, so that he could call a taxi. It had come surprisingly quickly.

Now, the driver pulled into the heavy flow of traffic and halted. It was too close to rush hour and Donal regretted not having chosen the hypoway. On the other side of the street, further down, he could see two prospective customers – a couple of tourists from Kaltrin Province, judging by their blue coats – talking to a cab driver.

The driver was shaking his head: they weren't going far enough to make it worth his while.

Welcome to Tristopolis.

The driver of Donal's cab stared impassively ahead. He hadn't asked where Donal was going until Donal was inside the vehicle. That was one advantage of picking up a ride directly in front of Police HQ.

Donal crossed his arms and leaned back, settling for a moment's calm. He thought about the big officer – Viktor, what was it, Harman – and the way he'd handled the .50 calibre weapon with ease.

'I work out of the, ah, seventy-seventh.'

That's what Big Viktor had said ... but Donal wondered now at the precinct number. Had he meant to say seventy-*three*, implying he was with the team competing against the local cops? It would have furnished an excuse for an uptown precinct officer to be here in the mid-Tristopolitan district.

Brian, on the desk, was competent enough on security. And Eagle Dawkins, the range safety officer, was always around, observing. An imposter could never make it into the practice range.

Donal came back into the moment. The taxi had moved less than a block before traffic congealed once more.

Digging into his wallet, he said: 'I'll walk. But here's the fare.' He handed over two florins.

'Aw, man ... How am I—?'

Donal leaned over, eyes hardening. 'You hook a U at the end of the block, and go back. There was a couple in blue coats standing there.'

'Um, I saw them.'

'Take them wherever they want to go, Mister' – Donal's eyes flickered towards the municipal licence tag on the dash – 'Boudreaux, driver number fourteen-oh-three. You got that, right?'

'Yes, sir. My pleasure.'

'I thought so.' Donal reached inside his pocket, and found a seven-sided half-florin coin. He reached through the partition and dropped the coin on the seat. 'You're a good man, Boudreaux.'

The driver swallowed.

'Thank you, sir.'

Donal slid out of the cab.

His first stop was the Exemplar Hotel on Ninety-ninth and Two-hundred-and-first. It was a grand old dark-grey building that rose up fifty storeys before reaching over and staring down in the form of a massive granite eagle's head. The east and west walls represented furled wings.

At street level, the originally plain talons were now decorated with upturned brass bowls in which eternal orange flames flickered and danced. Moving patterns swirled across marble steps leading up to the foyer.

Donal had never been inside.

Entering the polished reception hall, he passed gothic bronze dragons, gleaming with reflected dancing flames. Slender women in fur stoles, brandishing long cigarette holders, were waiting for their portly, rich husbands.

A bell wraith, almost corporeal, said: 'Can I help you, sir?'

Donal stared into the darkness where its eyes would have been. 'You got a house detective here?'

'Um ... Why would you—?'

Donal flashed his badge, replaced it. 'I'd like to chat with him, if that's all right with you.'

'Right away, sir.' The wraith began to float away, its cap maintaining a constant height above the brass floor. 'This way.'

Behind the reception desk, one of the people in dark-green suits had exceptionally white skin. He looked up at the wraith's approach.

The wraith bent close, leaning inwards until its face partly melded with the pale man's head. It was the most private way to whisper.

As the white-faced man nodded, the wraith drifted back. The man approached Donal.

'I'm Shaunovan. Sounds like you want to talk to me.'

'Can we do it on the move?' said Donal. 'While you show me around?'

'No problem.' Shaunovan led the way to the rear. 'The restaurant and kitchens first?'

'Sure.'

'So I'm guessing it's the Diva. She's the highest-profile guest checking in soon.'

'You keep an eye on bookings?'

'Part of my job, officer. Um, Fred didn't say what your name was.'

'Riordan. Donal Riordan.'

'Oh, Lieutenant. Of course.'

They walked through the bar area. Two glasses floated past, twisting and shivering: airborne cocktails, heading for one of the secluded booths at the rear.

'Who else works as detective here?' asked Donal. 'Got a replacement for other shifts?'

'Just me.' An odd look passed through Shaunovan's eyes. 'I'm here twenty-five nine.'

'Never sleep, huh?'

'No.' Shaunovan's voice went cold. 'I never do.'

Donal was impressed with the building's layout, which combined safety – easy access to fire exits and emergency evacuation-wraiths – with security. But the management had drawn the line at the use of in-house seers: the Exemplar's guests expected privacy.

'Come back tomorrow afternoon,' said Shaunovan, 'and Whitrose will sort out the bookings for your people. He's the senior manager, and he's got more ... discretion ... on rates than he'll admit to.'

'Claims to have no leeway when he's negotiating?'

'Right. But Whitrose can reduce the rates all the way ... if you can persuade him.'

'You're a good man, Shaunovan.'

'Are you sure of that?'

'Well ... You're good, anyway.' Donal held out his hand. 'Nice meeting you.'

'Likewise, Lieutenant.' Shaunovan's grip was like frozen steel. 'Likewise.'

It wasn't a long walk to Ninety-second Street. Close to the Hoardway intersection loomed the massive construction which was the Théâtre du Loup Mort. From across the street, Donal watched a party of school-girls gathered outside the main entrance: a school outing.

The play was one that Donal had studied in school, a study of war-riors who were facing their last battle, and he remembered the spears flying across the stage in the final scene, and the howling as the heroes died.

It had been shocking then, and still seemed dreadful all these years later, despite the real terrors he'd experienced on the street.

Up top, through a window, Donal caught a glimpse of a woman's outline and her perfect, bouncing breast, strawberry nipple against pale skin, and then it was gone. *Hades ...*

One of the high windows opened on to the actresses' changing rooms, and the evening's performance was less than an hour away. Donal blew out a breath, watched the window for a moment longer, then forced himself to turn away.

Side alley. A lane at the back, and a loading bay for trucks large enough to transport scenery. Fire escapes. This was going to be hard. There were so many opportunities for a trained hitman to—

Another actress walked past the window high up, pulling her blouse over her head as she walked. If Donal didn't move on, a beat officer would arrest him for peeping.

He walked to the corner with Thousand-and-first, stopped in a small café-bar and ordered an espresso. It came thick and dark in the tiny cup, and he shuddered as he drank it.

Then he walked to the big amber P-shaped sign, lit from within, that surmounted the iron steps leading below. Donal descended into the Pneumetro station, along with hundreds of other commuters forcing their way down to the platforms.

He looked for the red signs indicating the Z line – he didn't usually travel from Thousand-and-first – and made his way there just as seven big slugs arrived, one after the other.

Donal wondered how often the guests at the Exemplar travelled by hypoway.

The tube was convex and sort-of transparent against the platform, though the hexiglass was scratched and stained and maybe five years overdue for replacement. Each red slug held two hundred people, and Donal made his way to the third opening – Z3 was his branch line.

He was one of the last people to squeeze inside before the door wheezed shut. Everyone waited, crushed together and sweating. Then there was an explosive cough, and all seven slugs shot out of the station together.

It was a twenty minute ride back towards Donal's neighbourhood, but at least he didn't have to change trains. The slug flicked on to the third branch of the Z line without incident, and it only took seven more stops, and seven more explosive bursts of acceleration, to reach Halls.

No one greeted him as he walked down the street amid bluestones and converted temples, until he reached the apartment block. He opened the outer doors just as old Mrs MacZoran was leaving, laundry bag in hand.

'I'll pop round to the washeteria in a while,' Donal told her. 'Check everything's all right.'

'Don't worry about me.'

'Then I won't. I'll just—'

But Mrs MacZoran was already gone, head bent and hearing only the voices in her head, memories of days long lost.

'—go out for a run.'

Donal climbed upstairs, let himself into his fifth-floor apartment, and locked the door behind him. Moving quickly – because to sit down would be to make the discipline more difficult – he used the tiny bathroom, then stripped off and pulled on a long one-piece black running suit, and his old black shoes.

He performed stretches and lunges on the bare floorboards, and used the exposed ceiling pipes to haul himself up through a series of chinups, interspersed with press-ups performed with his feet up on the bed. Sit-ups and leg raises on the hard floor followed.

He rose to his feet, picking two splinters from his clothes.

The gun had always been problematical, and tonight he decided to run without it. Leaving the shoulder holster slung over the bedpost, he went out and locked the front door: all three locks. Keys and badge clutched in his left fist, he went downstairs.

Out on the sidewalk he jogged slowly to the corner.

The purple sky looked dark. The washeteria, known as Fozzy's Rags, shone its lights hard and white. Mrs MacZoran was in there, sitting side by side with another of the neighbourhood's old biddies. Wicker baskets, for transferring cleaned washing into the big dryers, waited at their feet.

None of the neighbourhood tearaways appeared to be lurking around the place. Not this evening.

Good.

Donal jogged on to the next corner, where a dank stone pedestal stood, slightly wider than a man and about eight feet high. A stone door's outline was scarcely visible on its side, but the hand-sized opening beside it was clear of obstruction.

Donal inserted his police badge, waited a long moment, then pulled the badge back out. This was what you might call a perk of the job.

The heavy door ground its way open.

Inside, the pedestal was hollow, revealing the beginning of a stone staircase that spiralled deep underground. Donal went down the first five steps and waited. The door groaned shut behind him.

Nodding slightly, he continued downward. Phosphorescent runes cast enough ghostly light for him to make out the steps. In any case, he had been down this way thousands of times before.

It took maybe ten minutes to descend to the tunnel, and step on to squelching grey ground: fine particles of stone, wet, on top of worn flagstones. Donal's foot splashed in a black puddle.

No cars moved down here, polluting the air or taking over the streets. Generally speaking, no people moved in this place. There might be guards, but the newer mausoleums were further downtown. Everything here was ancient: relics of once-powerful families, now forgotten.

These were the catacombs, cold and quiet.

End of another day.

Donal began to run.

Pounding now, ten minutes into the run and warmed up, Donal raced along a winding tunnel that dipped and widened out into a low cavern where half a dozen stone sarcophagi were interred. Each sarcophagus had melded with the stone floor and wall, like some kind of cocoon.

Donal ran past, feeling the faintest of whispers like a spider's web slide across his skin.

Then he was out of the chamber, into an unmarked tunnel, and the sensation was gone. He followed one of his three usual routes, looping back until he was eventually at the stone steps once more: chest heaving, body slick with sweat, ready to ascend.

Climbing the steps forced him to slow the pace, and the tension in thighs and calves was a kind of joyful pain as he reached the top. He stepped out on to the sidewalk.

Donal half-jogged past Fozzy's Rags, reached his apartment block, and took his time climbing the final stairs.

Home once more, he used the shower in its tin stall, rinsed off, and used one of his old, scratchy towels to dry with. Then he pulled on fresh underwear and a shirt, the same suit he'd worn earlier but with a different tie, dark-green. He went back out.

There was a secondhand (and third- and fourth-hand) bookstore two blocks away, and that was Donal's first stop. He went inside, and picked up a battered copy of *Human: the Revenge*, one of a fantasy series set on a parallel Earth where the only sentient beings were human, and necroflux was either undiscovered or non-existent: he hadn't worked out which.

'Thirty centals, to you.'

'Hey, Peat. How's it going?'

Peat was well named, from the spongy aspect of his skin to the dark woody scent that wafted from him. Not that Donal knew much about the countryside.

Each of Peat's hands ended in three stubby fingers, currently holding a massive stack of old books. He weighed about four hundred pounds, was three times stronger than a human, and knew every epic poem and sonnet of the last three centuries by heart.

'Well, Donal, as always.'

'Good.' For a man – a being – with such literary knowledge, actual conversations with Peat had a tendency towards abruptness. 'Listen, I need to get some dinner. But ...'

'Later, my friend.'

'Yeah.' Donal put the coins down on the counter. 'Later.'

He left with the book in hand, and crossed the street to Freda's Diner. There, Marie, a short waitress with missing teeth and a gentle manner, took Donal's order.

Sipping weak coffee, Donal read from the book until his food came.

Then he continued to read while shovelling eggs and tubers into his mouth. It was greasy and filling and he ate too much.

Then he went back home, stripped off his clothes and hung them up, and lay on his bed, reading. It was the end of a normal day.

But when he finally put the book down and slid into sleep, the dreams that visited him were of a rich, coloured texture such as he had never experienced before: meadows of impossible emerald brightness beneath a sky that was pale instead of dark, where winsome fantastical semi-transparent creatures out of legend grazed on blue lawns. Finally, a black crack appeared across the sky and Donal began to run, ever faster without making distance, while words – or were they fingernails? – scraped across his skin, and whispered words he could not hear, not quite.

We are the bones, the grass beneath his feet seemed to say.

Donal ran faster in his sleep.

We are the bones. We know you now.

Four

Nine days later, Donal was sitting in his office with Levison, checking his watch and wondering whether the Diva's flight could possibly land on time. All of yesterday, thick fog had cloaked Tristopolis, until virtually nothing was moving. Today it looked like being more of the same.

'Accounts will have my hide,' Donal said, 'if our guys have got an extra night in the hotel and the Diva isn't going to make it here today.'

'She'll make it.' Levison looked up from the puzzle in his folded newspaper. 'I'm telling you.'

'Uh ... OK.' Donal leaned sideways in his chair, trying to see outside. From here, he could not see the sky, but he could judge the light in the artificial canyon of buildings, and note the silver-lilac reflections in the windows. 'I'm tempted to bet on it.'

'Listen,' said Levison. 'You haven't been up to anything you shouldn't, have you, boss?'

'All my life.' Donal focused on Levison's serious expression. 'Nothing illegal, though. What's on your mind?'

'Nothing.'

'Right ...'

'It's just, er, I was chatting with Helven in Records—'

'And how is she? Have you asked her out for coffee yet? Has she asked you? Does your missus know?'

'—anyway, so I happened to notice this woman among the personnel files.'

'While you should have been paying attention to Helven. Come on, Lev.'

'Your dossier, Donal. That's what this nice-looking blonde had in her hands.'

38

'Uh.' Donal's chair creaked as he swung his weight back. 'So?'

'So she had a weapon and she weren't no bureaucrat.' Levison's accent reverted to the streets, and to his childhood. And Donal's. 'Got it? Looked like IntSec to me.'

'Ain't no reason for Infernal Security to worry about me, pal.'

'Well.' Levison nodded. 'Good.'

'Apart from those millions I got stashed away ...'

'Hades, Donal. Don't joke about this stuff.'

'All right. Have you got a car arranged?'

'For the airport? Yeah.' Levison checked the small clock on top of Donal's book cupboard. Inside the bi-chambered clock, dark-green fluid dripped upwards from the lower chamber to the upper, causing the second-hand to move. 'Fifty-five minutes, down below.'

'Great. You carry on drinking coffee.' Donal climbed out of his chair. 'I've got stuff to do.'

'OK, boss.'

Donal picked up his suit jacket and pulled it on as he left the office. That was mostly in case he ended up talking to a civilian before returning: hiding the gun usually made conversations proceed more quickly. Except during interrogation.

The elevator shaft opened while he was ten feet away.

Hey, lover. Missed you. And, as he stepped inside: *How long's it been?*

'All of an hour.'

Feels like longer.

'Range, please, Gertie.'

Invisible fingers seemed to cross his torso. *Where would you like me to range?*

But Donal was already falling down the shaft.

'Behave.'

All right. The hands began to slow Donal's descent. *Behave well, or behave badly?*

'Hades.'

Mind your language. Gertie exerted horizontal pressure on Donal's back. *Bad boy.*

The force expelled Donal into the corridor. He turned to say something but the shaft had already sealed up. His snappy retort would have to wait.

Flat bangs sounded from the practice range. Someone was hard at work.

When Donal reached the entrance, Brian was sitting behind his desk, wearing a smart shirt and tie, his fresh skin bluer than normal. Behind him, two blank-faced men were flipping through folders, and the boxed records of who'd signed equipment in and out.

'Hey, Brian. How's life?'

'Got my IntSec pals visiting. Right, boys? Other than that, biz as usual, Lieutenant.'

Brian dropped Donal a wink, as if thanking him for the warning that Internal Security were going to be here. But it was Donal who had called IntSec and told them to check out the range, and if Brian had failed to get rid of his stupid targets – sketches of Tristopolitan politicians and the like – then Brian would have been out.

Donal leaned over the counter. The IntSec men looked up.

'Don't take any crap from Brian,' Donal told them. 'OK?'

'We won't, Lieutenant.' There was no humour in the reply, just leaden fact.

Neither of the IntSec guys matched the description that Levison had given: a nice-looking blonde who'd been holding Donal's personnel file in her hand.

'Gimme two hundred rounds,' Donal said to Brian. 'And a pile of targets, ghouls and humans mixed.'

'You got it.'

'Er, Lieutenant ...' One of the IntSec men, the quieter one, held up a folder. 'You signed for ammunition yesterday. Can you remember how many rounds that was?'

Brian's blue skin began to shine paler. Donal shook his head. Was Brian really that stupid, to change numbers of rounds handed over, overstate the expenditure, and pocket the surplus?

'Sorry,' Donal said. 'Can't remember.'

Donal fired off the two hundred rounds and went back to the counter. The IntSec guys were still there, peeking in the target drawers and archive cupboards. Donal got Brian to give him another hundred, and went back into the range and shot his targets into shreds.

When he returned the second time, Brian was alone.

'Your IntSec pals,' said Donal. 'They gone for the day?'

'Er ... Sure. Why wouldn't they be?'

'I know for definite the inventory's fine. It is fine, isn't it, Brian?'

'S-Sure.'

'You worked the streets a long time. I appreciate that ...'

'Thanks, Lieutenant.'

'...but if I think ammo or weapons are going astray, I'll put a bullet between your eyes myself. You got that?'

Brian's mouth dropped open. It was all the answer Donal was going to get.

'Shit.' Donal turned his wrist over. 'And now you've made me late.'

'S-Sorry.'

Donal strode out of the range office and headed for the elevator. Gertie's door whisked open, and she bore him up to the garage level with only the faintest saucy humming in his ear, snatches of an old song he barely recognized and could not have named.

Coming out into the echoing concrete garage at a run, Donal spotted a squad car idling with its rear door open. Two uniformed officers sat up front, and Levison was in the back, on the far side.

'Airport,' Donal muttered to the driver as he got in. 'Quick as you can.'

He pulled the door shut with an unnecessary slam.

The uniforms got the message. They pulled the car out into the traffic flow, using the black-light strobe and switching the siren from *wail* to *maximum thunder*.

For several blocks, the traffic was too heavy for it to make a difference, but then they were out on streets where cars were moving – this was late morning, not rush hour – and frightening other drivers became a valid timesaving tactic.

Flashes of blackness reflected back from the buildings as the car accelerated, weaving in and out of half-filled lanes. They ran three stop lights in succession before reaching the Orb-Sinister Expressway.

All nine lanes flowed directly towards the centre of the two-thousand-feet-high skull that marked the eastern boundary of midtown. There, the lanes peeled upwards into the left eye socket of that vast construct – or maybe relic, no one really knew. They entered a mile-long round tunnel lit only by disembodied flamewraiths, dancing overhead.

The wraiths were indentured for short periods these days, because the stress of passing traffic was great, and everyone remembered the tunnel crash of '93 in the Orb-Dexter Freeway. Then, a kind of group hysteria seized the flamewraiths, many of them into their second century of servitude. Wraiths discorporated explosively into showering sparks; drivers swerved in sudden shock. The hundred-car pile-up killed dozens.

41

Soon the squad car was out into the open. The sky was heavy with purple-grey clouds; and Donal still felt closed-in. They passed through the mercantile district of Prismatic Trance with its rainbow adverts and myriad illusions.

Finally they reached the turn-off for the airport, and the driver pulled the car out on to the fast lane and floored the acceleration.

Fog was thickening overhead by the time they turned through the glowering twin-panthers gateway of Brody Airport (named after Fisticuffs Brody, still remembered as the best mayor the city had ever had). They slowed as they came to a police-only entrance, then turned and went down a ramp, into the depths of Terminal Aleph.

'Good work guys,' said Levison. He looked at Donal.

'Uh, yeah. Good job.'

'Sir.' The driver wheeled them neatly into a parking slot.

'You reckon the flights are on time?' said the other uniformed officer.

'Not with this fog,' muttered Levison. 'Gives us more time to check around. Right, boss?'

'Right.' Donal sat unmoving for a moment longer. His unease might have been kicked off by some subliminal perception ...

'You OK?'

'Yeah.' Donal retraced the drive in his mind, the route into the airport, and felt no specific reaction to any part of the route.

Shit.

It was the entire operation that worried him. A killer could strike from anywhere.

'Let's get going.'

They slid out of the squad car.

Whatever Commissioner Vilnar had said about keeping overtime payments down, there was only one way to stop the hit, and that was to ensure a visible presence. It would make two things clear: the killer would have to give up his (or her, or its) own life; and no one would be stealing the body afterwards.

There was an escalator formed of rising glass slats, their lev-runes solidly encased and glowing darkly. Levison stood on the step above Donal as they rose through a seven-storey atrium.

Donal scanned the crowds. There were men with Fedoras tipped down over their eyes, hands in their overcoat pockets, standing at corners and pillars and other vantage points.

42

'They're all ours,' said Levison.

'Good.'

'But you want I should take a walk later. Right, boss? And check them out personally?'

Donal glanced up at Levison. 'I hate being predictable.'

'I knew you'd say that.'

'Piss off, Lev.'

'And I also knew you'd—'

'I mean it.'

But Levison was grinning as they got off the escalator. They both knew he'd won that round.

The flight arrived late. Fog was thick and pale-grey everywhere when the four-propeller Dagger Airlines plane came to a stand near the terminal building.

Ground crew wheeled the steps into place and rolled out the long strip of crimson carpet. Reporters and photographers crowded as close as they could, held back by officers of the 1005th Precinct. Several local dignitaries including Alderman Alexei Brown were there to greet the Diva.

The props were rotating slowly, and finally they stopped, one by one.

Magnesium bulbs popped white as the Diva appeared at the open door and paused on the top step. From the small crowd's edge, Donal looked up, and saw the triangular, fine features he recognized from the magazine articles he'd read during the week.

He hadn't realized how beautiful Maria daLivnova was; but as she descended, a kind of iron elegance ruled every motion, and when she paused once more at the bottom of the steps, the sense of her presence was overwhelming. Her smile, as she looked around, was wide and white and shining with the message: *I'm full of joy, being here.*

Her gaze passed over Donal without pausing.

Expecting her to cavil at the arrangements had been one thing, but this was worse: her failure to recognize Donal's existence.

But why should he care? This was work, the Diva was a commodity to be protected, and if he had to step between her and an assassin's bullet, well, that was what he'd become a cop for, what they paid him to do.

'What's it like to be in Tristopolis?' called out a reporter. He wore a dark hat, and held his notepad and pen ready for the Diva's reply.

'Nice fog you people have here.'

There was a round of laughter among the reporters.

After the handshakes, three black limousines with black windshields pulled up on the tarmac. The Alderman's aides escorted the Diva to the centre limo. She got in and perched, half sitting but with one stiletto-shoed foot on the crimson carpet outside, for a final round of bulb-popping photographs.

Then she pulled her foot inside and an aide closed the door; and Donal let out a tiny breath. This was the first possible fixed ambush point, and they'd got through it. If everyone could just maintain highest-level vigilance, nerves strung taut for the next eighteen days, they would make it.

Two weeks.

At least the time would pass quickly, because there'd be no time to stop and rest. That was Donal's theory. He got into one of the squad cars that pulled up, while the remainder moved into formation before and after the limos.

He looked back at the plane. The journalists were dispersing, the dignitaries were in the limos, and now the ordinary passengers were beginning to descend the steps, allowed to disembark.

No one was waiting to take their photographs or ask them what it felt like to be here.

There were outriders on low-slung motorbikes, officers with helmets and leather jackets, over-and-under spitguns clipped to the sides of their fuel tanks. They swung in on either side of the cavalcade.

All the cars slid into motion. Donal watched in every direction.

He had wanted a helicopter overhead, but the fog was even better, providing visual cover from rooftop snipers: not so much here, as when they reached the high midtown skyscrapers.

Except that in those architectural canyons the fog would be thinner.

Damn it.

Opportunities to make the hit were everywhere.

The Diva's limo pulled up before the Exemplar. Here, not just journalists but fans had gathered on the sidewalks. Donal's nerves tightened as he exited his car fast, and held his badge out for the uniforms to let him through.

'Nice to see you, Lieutenant,' said one of them, a grey-haired veteran that Donal recognized. 'Looks like everyone's here to get your autograph.'

'It's your picture they're taking.' Donal gave a half-salute while scanning the windows high up across the street. 'OK, here goes.'

The Diva was exiting her car, and the officers linked arms against the increased chaotic pressure of the crowd, as those farther back jostled. The dancing flames above the steps cast golden highlights on the Diva as she stopped to wave at the crowd – *don't stay in the open, damnit* – and then ascended the steps so that she was under the decorative canopy in front of the door.

Even here a Seeker round would pick her out through the obstacles. Donal waved at the doormen to usher the Diva indoors. One of them bowed and murmured a greeting as he gestured inside, and the Diva seemed to flow into the foyer.

Inside, Donal's own men were already posted at vantage points. He began to feel happier.

While the Diva took the elevator – operated by a human attendant, suitably humble-looking – Donal went up the stairs three treads at a time. By the time he reached the third floor, his breath was coming in big loud inhalations, as his body sprang a layer of sweat: reacting to the promise of a hard run.

But the Diva's suite was on the forty-seventh floor, too high to sprint, so Donal walked along the corridor to the laundry lift where Levison was already waiting, holding the brass door open. Levison had come here ahead of the cavalcade, and he was looking almost sleepy as he said: 'Which floor, sir?'

But he had already pressed 47 and was hauling the door shut before Donal had finished stepping inside. The elevator car lurched, ascended a few feet and rattled, then rose more smoothly as it gathered speed.

'Nice to see you looking calm,' said Donal.

'If Commissioner Vilnar's got every confidence in you' – Levison spoke with a straight face – 'then who am I to argue?'

'You're absolutely right.' Donal pulled his Magnus a quarter way out of his shoulder holster, then pushed it back in. No problems there. 'In your place, I'd be calm, too.'

'And what about you?'

'I'm scared shitless. I'm looking forward to the whole thing being over, the Diva off somewhere else on a plane, heading to Rio Exotico or someplace.'

'Ah.' Levison nodded as the dial-needle swung through 40 and the elevator's ascent slowed. 'That's why the rest of us are relaxed. When you're strung out, everything's under control.'

'That's nice to know.'

The elevator clanked to a halt, and Levison hauled the brass door open. 'Looks like we're ready.'

Twelve uniforms were posted along the corridor. Detectives on the floors above and below were already in place. Two of Donal's squad opened the door of the suite across from the Diva's and grinned.

'Hey, boss. Lev. You want anything on room service?'

'For Hades' sake ...'

'Just kidding, Donal.'

'Where's the D—?'

'She's coming now.' Levison touched Donal's arm. 'Here.'

They walked down to the main elevator bank just as the Diva's elevator arrived and the golden doors slid open. She stepped out, Maria daLivnova, Diva extraordinaire.

The hotel's general manager, Whitrose, was beside her, fawning.

'Um, Miss daLivnova, you'll have met Lieutenant, um, Riordan? In charge of the ... arrangements for your visit.'

'No, I've not had the pleasure.' Her gaze on Donal was amused, nothing more.

But she stopped his lungs and maybe his heart.

So beautiful ...

And a target, unless he did his job properly.

'Honoured, ma'am.' Donal made himself speak. 'If we could talk some more about the security prec—'

'A glamorous detective. For me. My, how I'm touched.'

Then she swept past him, followed by her two female assistants. Both women were employees of the Théâtre du Loup Mort, assigned by the management (they'd been in the limousine to meet the Diva). Donal had interviewed both of them; afterwards, Levison, who was much better at forming a rapport with strangers, had talked to them individually. Neither seemed to be a security risk; both of them were already looking as stressed on the surface as Donal felt inside.

Glamorous detective.

Donal watched the door to the Diva's suite swing shut. He blew out a breath.

That'll be me, all right.

The first performance changed everything.

Donal was standing in the shadowed interior of a box on the top level. Commissioner Vilnar was one of six dignitaries seated officially inside it.

Down below, armed officers were obvious outside the actual performance hall; in here, two Department snipers in plain clothes were in another box, their rifles at their feet. Levison was seated in one of the stalls. Other members of Donal's team were scattered among the audience.

The visible presence outside presented the first layer of deterrence; but Donal assumed that a trained killer might spot the two snipers: their grim gazes continually swept the audience below. Neither one looked like an opera lover despite the tuxedos.

They were the second, also visible, layer. The third layer was Donal's squad. If Levison hadn't told him, Donal would not have guessed that the overweight grey-haired lady with the diamonds and fur stole was Sergeant Miriam Delwether, one of the Department's finest shots.

This was the opening night, and if there were to be an attempt on the Diva's life, this would be the most dramatic time to stage it.

The lights went down, shadows growing unevenly inside the auditorium, and Donal was alert for any shifts of movement, any gleam of reflected light – *there* – forcing himself to relax – *just opera glasses* – and to keep scanning, looking for any sign of a weapon being brought to bear.

On stage, the production swirled into life. Colourful costumes were bright, almost blazing at the edge of Donal's peripheral vision: the *Mort d'Alanquin*'s opening scene took place in a royal court amid pageantry.

None of it helped Donal's vision to remain dark-adapted. He continued to scan the audience.

Donal was half aware of the dancing on stage. As the scene progressed, the cast tended to stand still more, and the singing became more important. When the Diva stepped out on to stage left, at the entrance to the royal court, Donal's gaze snapped back and forth across the auditorium: stalls, circle, boxes, flicking to the stage itself, then back to the seats below.

And then she opened her mouth to sing.

Oh, my Death ...

The Diva sang, pure and crystalline, captivating everyone with her innocent enquiry of the court: is this where the great king holds judgement?

When the solo was finished, the Diva lowered her head as waves of applause washed through the auditorium. Donal rubbed his hand across his face, and realized he had been aware only of her, for the past several minutes as the aria proceeded.

Minutes that could have been a lifetime.

Just keep bloody focused.

It wasn't only the danger to the Diva. If bullets started flying through the audience, if his own people opened fire, he would be held accountable. And if someone important died, and their relatives claimed blood-price, it was Donal, not Commissioner Vilnar, who would be served up as payment.

But during the next solo from the Diva, Donal – though he kept pushing himself to look elsewhere – kept returning his gaze to her, like an exhausted man whose chin keeps falling to his chest no matter how often he jerks back upright, trying to maintain wakefulness.

So much for security.

During the intermission, Donal faded out of the box. He went downstairs, and made his way backstage past two hulking uniforms that he knew well: the Brodowski Brothers. In the weightlifting room, their fellow officers called them the Barbarians.

'All clear, guys?'

'Sure, but I think Al cried during the last song.'

'Like you didn't.'

Hades, they were as bad as him. Donal climbed up a flight of wooden steps, and stepped through the heavy overlapping curtains.

Men in brown coveralls were pushing heavy façades – castle battlements – on industrial-sized castors. Cast members who had not spent much time on stage were murmuring to each other; the others would be sitting down and rehydrating in the changing rooms.

A lithe young woman walked past half naked, pulling on a peasant's blouse. Donal swallowed before forcing out a long exhalation.

'Can I help you?' asked a stagehand.

'No ... Yeah. You see anyone here that doesn't belong?'

'Er, don't think so.' The stagehand glanced at the young actress straightening her blouse, then back at Donal. 'Apart from you, Officer. The rest of us are used to this.'

'Must be a hard life.'

'Don't talk so much about *hard*.' The stagehand winked. 'Some of the boys might get excited.'

Hades ...

Donal took a last look around the stage. Up top, beyond the overhead spotlights, a gantry allowed objects to be lowered on near-invisible cables. There was a heavy man up there, script in hand, ready to call down: he was to be the ghost's voice in the next act.

There were also two plain-clothes officers, one of whom waved Donal a half-salute, which Donal returned.

All clear.

Donal went back out to the Brodowski Brothers. 'Guys, it's a good job you're holding the fort out here. It's hell backstage.'

'Why's that, Lieutenant?'

'All those naked actresses getting changed. Bosoms bouncing everywhere. My blood pressure's gone through the roof.'

'Aw, man ...'

Third act.

The plot was beyond Donal's comprehension, but he wasn't being paid to follow the story. Still, he kept glancing down at the stage.

Commissioner Vilnar was equally captivated. The Diva, whether singing solo or as now, part of an intricate duet as she called out the prince on his impetuous treatment of the populace, captivated Donal along with everyone else in the theatre.

Fourth and final act.

The entire company was on stage, enacting the battle scene and then the coming together of both sides to mourn. When the Diva sang that heartrending farewell to the slain prince, Donal felt his nerves hooked out of his body, his soul dragged out by talons.

Tears ran in silent floods down his cheekbones.

No shots rang out. No one sprinted on to the stage and ran a dagger into the Diva's heart. It was just as well, because neither Donal nor any of the officers, not even the spellbound snipers in the opposite box, could have processed the danger or made a move while that pure sublime sound continued to emanate from the Diva's perfect mouth.

And then the aria was ended.

Donal bowed his head in silence. Backing out of the box, he wiped tears from his face with the back of his hand, and by the time he reached ground level he was practically normal. The two detectives stationed at the side entrance to the auditorium were still damp-eyed.

'Be professional,' said Donal as he went through.

'Sir.'

From the side, Donal watched as multiple bouts of applause rose, ebbed, then washed higher once more. The company took bows, but the greatest cheering was reserved for the Diva (and secondmost for the Prince, or rather the man who sang that part, whose name a quarter of the audience and none of the police knew).

Flowers arced through the air, hurled by enthusiastic opera-goers, and Donal winced each time one of the snipers moved up in their box. But neither of them raised his weapon over the balcony's edge.

A young girl brought a huge bouquet, taller than herself, up on to the stage. The Diva accepted it and kissed the girl's cheek, which brought renewed clapping and cheers.

Finally, the curtain went down and stayed down. The lights came up, causing Donal to squint against their brightness. Happy people, murmuring and chattering, threaded their way up the aisles to the exits, while Donal's tension was strung tight.

He had been relieved in the emotional aftermath of the final aria. But now everyone's guard was down, and this was a danger moment. No one had said the Diva had to be on stage for the killing to occur.

'Stay alert, damn it,' he said to the two Brodowskis as he climbed backstage.

'Huh? Right.'

'Got it, Lieutenant.'

There was a press of well-wishers in the Diva's dressing-room, champagne in a silver rune-chased bucket and woven heptagrams of blue orchids and indigo roses, and a chattering cacophony of congratulations. Levison, in his unassuming way, stood in the background assisting with the bouquets.

'Thank you so much,' Levison murmured to the florid son of a well-known businessman, owner of the Black Viper supermarket chain.

The businessman's gaze didn't even flicker in Levison's direction.

From the doorway, Donal watched, and raised his eyebrows as Levison took charge of another bouquet. The slightest of quiet smiles passed across Levison's face: it meant everyone was ignoring him, unaware that his presence ensured the Diva's safety in this room.

Donal checked the sycophantic rich visitors, breathless in the presence of fame ... but also of genuine talent, and perhaps that excused them. Platinum skull-shaped cufflinks, white-gold torcs with diamond insertions ... no overt weapons. And no body language that betrayed anything more urgent than the need to bask in the Diva's presence.

For a second, the Diva noticed Donal, and gave the tiniest of nods. He felt a sensation like a multitude of sprite fingers playing down his spine. Then the Diva's attention was on a large woman in an ivory white gown who was offering congratulations, and the moment was past.

Donal forced his way back into the narrow corridor. Then he went back to the stage, checking angles and examining shadows. All clear. The Brodowski Brothers were now at the side exit, and Al – the slightly taller one – opened the metal door for Donal.

Outside, the limo was ready. Two of Donal's squad, Petrov and Duquesne, dressed in their best suits, were standing by the vehicle. Their gazes roved the rooftops as well as ground level.

'So far, so good,' said Duquesne. 'We got Avram up on the roof. No problems there.'

'No relaxing yet.'

'Right.' Petrov spared a second to look at Donal. 'And how many nights do we keep it up for?'

Donal didn't answer. The question was rhetorical and Petrov's tone was mild: not a complaint but an observation.

Damn, damn, damn.

Because no one could keep alert for ever.

At the official reception afterwards, there were canapés and hors d'oeuvres and who-knew-what savouries on the buffet. Commissioner Vilnar looked resplendent in his cummerbund, and even congratulated Donal on the arrangements so far.

'Thank you, sir,' was all Donal said, ignoring the final words: *so far*.

If all went well, the Commissioner would be happy to receive a shower of happy messages from the city's politicians; but if anything happened to the Diva, a different kind of pungent shower would ensue. It would be directed on Donal's head.

Donal circulated around the party's edges, stopping to talk to Levison, who was nibbling from a plate of finger-sized *things* that each appeared to end in a single black eye.

'What are you eating, Lev?'

'Haven't a clue, but they're lovely. Try one?'

'Not a chance.'

As he moved on, the Diva noticed him and beckoned. There was a tight half-circle of important-looking people focused on her.

'And this,' the Diva said, 'is my glamorous personal detective. See how the city treats me?'

'That's our pleasure,' said a Tristopolitan councillor who wore his platinum chain of office atop his frilled dress shirt. 'And you'd be Captain—?'

'Lieutenant Riordan. Glad to be of service, Councillor.'

'Talent and beauty like this' – with a soft-fingered gesture – 'must be preserved, no matter what.'

'Oh, Edward. You flatter me.'

Donal gave a tiny bow and stepped away. As he did so, the Diva glanced at him, and perhaps he saw irony move inside those dark and perfect eyes. Then she returned her attention to the councillor, resuming their decorative and meaningless conversation.

Glamorous detective.

Staying on the periphery until the party ended at two a.m., Donal followed as the Diva finally went down to the limo. The streets were eerie valleys almost devoid of people or cars as they drove to the Exemplar Hotel.

At this hour, the flames dancing above the entrance moved slowly as though tired, but the doormen were alert enough as they opened up for the Diva. She and her two assistants climbed the steps, with Petrov and Duquesne on either side and Donal following.

The night shift was in place and Donal's duty was over. Still, he could not help taking a last walk around the hotel's deserted corridors, the darkened restaurant and the quiet (though not entirely empty) residents' bar. Everything was clear.

He took the hypoway back to his apartment, ignoring the drunk who stared at him for most of the trip. No one disturbed him as he walked to the apartment building and let himself in.

Once in his own place, despite the lateness of the hour and the groan of the ancient plumbing, he showered in the old tin stall with soap. The water cut out before he had fully rinsed off.

Donal towelled himself dry, then sat at the single unadorned wooden table with a bottle of Jacques Dauphin liquor. Twisting the cap off, he saluted the shadows of his room, and drank a slug.

It tasted like fire as it went down.

Two more slugs, and he screwed the top back on. Then, feeling scratchy and unclean, he forced himself to lie down on the plain bed and look up at the ceiling, waiting for sleepiness to manifest itself.

Some kind of glamour.

At five a.m, in a deserted street two blocks from the Exemplar Hotel,

a supine body moved along the sidewalk. Head supported by nothingness, heels dragged along the ground, he moved.

Waves of dark refraction shimmered. *Something* was dragging the
unconscious man.

It pulled him around the corner, then released him. The man's head
fell to the sidewalk with a sickening thud. His nose was smashed, and
there were torn gashes in his cheek.

Beside his head, two expensive, elegant shoes glistened black. Their
owner wore a grey skirt suit, and her hair and skin were pale.

'What's this?' she said.

Lurking near the Exemplar. I found him.

'And that's all?'

Hardly. Take a look in his pockets.

The woman glanced into the shadows. Then she went down on one
knee, and inserted her gloved hand into the beaten man's pockets,
retrieving a dart-gun, its loaded bolt coated with a dark fluid whose
scent she recognized immediately.

'Moonshade. Fatal dose.'

The injured man also carried a stranglewire noose, treated so that
it would tighten of its own accord when tossed around a victim's soft
throat. It would contract to a fist's diameter ... but *slowly*. Not a pleasant way to die.

Straightening up, the woman held the weapons in her hand. The
man moved a little, eyelids fluttering, then lapsed into stillness.

'You got any suggestions, Xalia, as to what we do with him?'

The darkness rippled, then:

Nothing at all.

'What do you mean?'

Just that.

The woman looked up and down the street and then she saw it: two
pairs of amber eyes glowing briefly in black shadows.

'Just leave him? For them?'

Come on, Laura. He was going to kill the Diva.

'I know. But he's not Black Circle. Just a lone sicko.'

My point – the words seemed to float on wind – *precisely.*

The woman, Laura, looked down at the injured man once more.
'Shoulda stuck to beating off with your fist, sick visions in your
mind.'

Then she walked away and, after a moment, the disturbance in the
darkness floated after her.

Five

Donal woke at 5:23, seven minutes before his alarm was due to go off. In the tag-end of his nightmare, swirling out of memory like fluid down a plughole, he imagined a fading scream. Then it was gone.

He used the facilities, drank brackish water from the tap – at least it was working – and pulled on his old black running-suit, and left the apartment. No one moved on the street, not this early.

A hundred feet overhead, a Department scanbat moved in a straight line, and Donal gave it a wave. Perhaps later one of the surveillance mages, absorbing the bat's memories, would recognize him.

At the stone pillar on the corner, he did the usual thing with his police badge and the door scraped open. He descended the spiralling stone steps.

Do you feel it?

Donal stopped, shuddering, and then told himself to stop being stupid. This place was empty. He continued going down, until he reached the catacombs.

There, he began to jog along the ancient stone floor.

Do you feel the song?

Coldness scraped along his skin as he ran, forcing the pace before his muscles were warmed up. Then he was into the chamber where sarcophagi stood melded into the earth.

Do you hear?

He pushed himself to run faster, while talons that were pure imagination raked at his nerves, dragged like hooks through his body.

Do you hear the bones?

Donal's arms were shaking by the time he returned to the stone steps, and the big muscles of his thighs felt soft as he ascended, fearing he might fall at any time. When the door scraped open, it jammed momentarily partway before freeing itself, and a huge sensation of dread swept downwards through his body.

Then he staggered on to the sidewalk, heading for home.

Donal made time in the afternoon for a nap in the back of a squad car. There was no opportunity to practise in the range at HQ, so after he woke, before opening his eyes, Donal sent himself into trance.

He visualized a training session where he fired straight into the target's vital points. Then, with a long, deep, shuddering breath, he returned to reality.

'Hey, Lieutenant. Need coffee?'

'Only if there's doughnuts.'

'We can manage that.'

The two uniforms, Belden and O'Grady, had left him alone in the car while he slept, staying within earshot of the radio in case it squawked for them. Now, they got back in and drove out of the alleyway. They pulled up on the ultraviolet no-parking lines in front of a Fat'n'Sugar. Belden went inside.

'He prefers Tarantula Creams,' muttered O'Grady. 'Make your teeth black.'

'Wonderful.'

But Belden brought back plain and redberry, just what Donal would have ordered, and big snakeskin cups filled with coffee that was so-so. Volume over taste.

'You getting cultured, Lieutenant?' Belden, in the front passenger seat, pulled back the little snakemouth opening on his coffeecup lid. 'All that opera and all?'

'Absolutely, my good man. One is getting cultured up the wazoo.'

'Hear that Diva's a cracker.' O'Grady, sitting behind the wheel, took a mouthful of doughnut and a large slug of coffee, and commenced chewing. 'She as gorgeous as they say?'

'Oh, yeah.' Donal's voice went soft, and he put his coffee down. 'She is that.'

The second performance bettered the first. The audience, affluent but not the city's most influential folk, were less restrained in their applause. That triumphant mood fed back to the opera company, raising them to a new level.

Not just the Diva, but everyone sang their hearts out. Several of the soloists reduced the audience to tears, capturing that ability to entrance

55

the listener and weave patterns with their soul.

This time, the Brodowski Brothers were stationed backstage – it turned out they'd had a word with Levison – and, after the performance, Al Brodowski pulled Donal aside.

'Hades, Lieutenant. You wuz right. Twenty bare bods, big titties everywhere. Bud's had to lie down.'

'Er ... Glad you were paying attention.'

Then Brodowski left, leaving Donal to wonder whether they really had seen twenty naked women, or whether they were winding him up in revenge.

'Hey,' said Levison. 'What's up? You were staring into space.'

'Thinking strategic thoughts. Have Petrov and Duquesne got her car ready?'

Her meant the Diva.

'All set. She still going to the Five Seasons?'

'Yeah. Seven-course meal.' Donal and the others would get to stand around and watch. 'All the trimmings.'

Levison said, 'You managed to eat already?'

'Sure. You?'

'Brought a bean sprout sandwich in with me. Tilly made it last night. What about you?'

'Two redberry doughnuts and a Fat'n'Sugar max-size coffee. With Belden and O'Grady.'

'Fat'n'Sugar?' Levison sighed. 'Lucky bastard.'

The Diva left shortly afterwards, trailing a cloud of hangers-on and admirers. Donal wondered if she ever grew sick of it.

Sitting in the back of Belden and O'Grady's car, Donal watched the streets, his stomach sour, not from the bad coffee but the knowledge that a killer could be anywhere.

Once more the team deployed to vantage points, three men having spent the day at Five Seasons, getting in the head chef's way and trying not to get noticed by diners. Donal roved around the positions and the streets outside, watching for anything out of the ordinary, anything to break the pattern, finding nothing.

Three hours later it was back to the Exemplar.

Donal was technically off duty now, but could not resist wandering through the corridors and facilities. He chatted briefly with Shaunovan, the Exemplar's house detective who never slept or – it seemed – left the building.

It was late when Donal finally went home.

Next morning, he rose at seven, itching to go for a run. Although traffic was beginning to take over the streets at this hour, he chose to run along the sidewalks, not the catacombs. Nothing whispered to him at ground level.

Donal showered, in hot water that lasted as long as he wanted, had scrambled eggs for breakfast, and pulled on a clean shirt and his other suit. He'd had the suit steam-cleaned at Fozzy's Rags.

Today felt like a good day.

There was a matinée performance, which drew a different crowd, with children accompanying their parents. They sobbed and laughed at the right places, though the plot must surely be beyond them.

Donal was finally getting the hang of the intricacies of the story that mixed innocence with ambition, social justice with revenge. He had learned to be in the deepest shadow when the Diva sang that final aria over the body of the dead Prince Turol. That was when Donal's professional instincts failed and unearthly grief poured through him.

Afterwards, the Diva returned to the hotel to rest, and while she remained there, Donal walked the streets around the Exemplar. Once he saw a dark Vixen among the purple cabs, and remembered the car that had been parked near the Energy Authority complex that time, more than a week ago.

It was an unusual car but not unique, and by the time he drew near the lights had changed. Donal saw nothing of the driver as the Vixen moved off.

In the evening, it was time for the Diva to return to the Théâtre du Loup Mort. Once again the limo, bracketed by two unmarked cars and two squad cars, made its way across midtown.

At this hour the traffic was heavy, and Donal had insisted that Levison and Duquesne – the department's finest shot in close conditions – ride in the limo with the Diva. She had been furious, only calming when Levison asked her about what breathing techniques she used to hold such a range of tones.

To Donal, the change of subject seemed forced and obvious, but something in the way Levison did it – as always – let the conversation flow the way he wanted. Perhaps it was just that Lev was so focused. You knew he *absolutely* wanted to learn the answers to his questions.

The Brodowski Brothers were out front tonight – 'We had to change position, Lieutenant. All that flesh, we couldn't concentrate' – and

Donal went through the drill, checking the windows in the opposite buildings, scanning the crowds for unusual body language.

This was the third night in a row. It was beginning to feel like routine.

Dangerously like routine.

To the family who had seats in the top-right box, plush and comfortable, Donal pretended he was part of the theatre management, here to see that everything was just right for valued guests. The husband preened, his chest swelling as he told his boys that influence was what life was all about.

His wife nodded quietly, absorbing everything, but there might have been an amused sparkle in her eyes as the family took their seats. The children looked more like her, which Donal could only think of as a good thing.

The lights dimmed.

Drums rolled, and the orchestra began the overture.

The first two acts proceeded with the same magic as before. During the intermission, Donal walked around the auditorium and went backstage. Everything looked clear.

No. Check again.

Because he felt as if he were going through the motions. This was *serious*. So he backtracked, checking every stagehand and performer he walked past. He checked the overhead scaffolding, and the spaces behind curtains. He went back out into the auditorium, using the internal staircase, taking a tour of all the boxes.

Still clear.

Intermission over, the audience filed back into their seats. Donal remained at ground level, standing by the door with one of the ushers. When the third act commenced, he remained in the shadows, captivated as before by the Diva's performance.

He applauded along with everybody else; and when the fourth act proceeded to Prince Turol's inevitable death, he was even more stricken than before. With the Prince's body draped across the stone bench where he had declared his love to Lady Arla, the Diva stood and faced the audience.

Hands spread wide, she commenced the aria and that was when it happened.

Something black moved through the air and every member of the audience sat rigid.

Donal did not react.

The small group of singers on stage, the Prince's erstwhile allies who had betrayed him, were frozen like statues ... but the Diva continued to deliver the heartrending aria, not realizing anything was wrong.

But a second later, the first three rows of spectators stood up *in exact unison* as if they were a single body. Donal could do nothing but watch, frozen as all the rest. The front row took a pace forward, and the next two row began to file out into the aisles, their footsteps in time.

A note faltered in the aria.

Trance. Have to—

When all the standing people were free of the seats, the entire aggregate, some hundred men and women, took a single step forward. And another.

Like the start of some macabre dance.

—break it.

Ensorcelled, the hundred people advanced, blankness in their eyes. The music died and the Diva's voice trailed away. She stood paralysed: not by a spell but by fear.

This was what had happened in the other theatres. Some part of Donal's captured mind realized that every report and article he had read in preparation had been a lie. Any power great enough to ensorcel a hundred people in public had enough capability to alter the memories of everyone here.

Something clicked inside Donal.

NO.

If felt like a sound, a wooden click inside his head as the trance-training broke in and sheets of ice seemed to slide away from his body, and then he was free.

Move.

Donal crouched, scanning the auditorium, but everyone – even his officers, even Petrov, in theory trance-shielded – was frozen in place.

Move now.

The orchestra remained unmoving. But a hundred people were advancing as Donal sprinted across the intervening space, and leaped into the orchestra pit, heading for the stage.

It was like some sort of signal: every musician swivelled their head towards Donal, their eyes dead. Hands reached for him, but he elbowed a cellist in the temple, thrust-kicked a woman violinist out of his way, and grabbed the edge of the stage.

He pulled himself up, kicked out at grasping hands, and rolled up into a crouch.

'Come on! Maria!'

The use of her first name seemed to break the Diva's stasis. She whipped her gaze from side to side, breathing fast in panic, and backed away with shuffling steps. Behind her, the Prince sat up, and the other performers took a synchronized step forward.

Shit.

Donal ran to the Diva, grabbed her round the waist and said: 'We have to run. Do you understand?'

'Yes ...'

He wanted to tell her to stop taking shallow breaths, but something, perhaps her singer's training, made the Diva take a single deep, calming breath as she kicked off her shoes.

'Which way?'

'Left.'

Donal kept his arm around the Diva's waist as they ran to the side of the stage, through the wing where a stagehand reached out and Donal whipped an uppercut elbow under the man's chin. Then they were sprinting past, clattering down the steps and reaching a fire exit. Donal kicked the bar mechanism open.

There was a dark alleyway outside, but three men reached out from behind them – spearholders from the previous scene – and grabbed the Diva's gown.

Donal span, throwing a hard overhead left into the side of the nearest man's neck – *got it* – and that man was down, but more were advancing in the shadows. Donal kicked the second man in the knee, collapsing the leg, then grabbed hold of the man's head and twisted him aside.

The Diva was struggling with the last man but Donal whipped his Magnus from his shoulder holster and hammered the butt into the back of the man's neck, dropping him.

'Come on.'

A hand reached from the floor – one of the fallen men – but Donal stamped down, heard a liquid crunch, and then he was pulling the Diva towards the exit.

Out in the alley, he crouched. A man at the corner, who had been walking by, now shivered and took a stiff step into the alleyway.

Ensorcelled.

Thanatos. How far can one spell spread?

'This way.'

Around the back of the theatre, Donal ran with the Diva keeping pace. The ground was cold and hard, and she was in bare feet. They skirted shards of broken glass, remnants of a dropped beer bottle that sparkled with reflected light.

In front of them was another alleyway: too narrow for them to walk side by side, and one hell of a potential trap but there was no choice. Donal ran first, dragging the Diva along.

Then they were out on to the sidewalk of Ninety-second Street.

Bright lights, moving cars, and a crowd of passers-by: for maybe twenty seconds it seemed as though they were safe. Donal was starting to flag down a purple cab when he saw a group of Zurinese tourists, cameras in hand, shudder and grow blank-eyed.

The ensorcelled tourists turned their attention on the Diva.

She's the locus.

Wherever they went, the trancing spell would coalesce and fall upon anyone within seeing distance. It was like some kind of infection. Donal batted aside a tourist's grasping hands and tugged the Diva – 'Ow!' – into motion.

Her ivory gown had slipped and Donal caught a peek of her breast – Hades, there was *no* time for this – and then he spotted a stone pillar, wider than a man, across the street on Hoardway.

Donal reholstered his gun, took hold of the Diva's left wrist, and ducked under. He straightened up with her weight across his shoulders into a fireman's carry.

'Hold on.'

Then he ran.

Horns blared and someone shouted, then two cars crunched together in a shower of broken glass as ensorcelled drivers turned their attention to the fleeing pair. But Donal had run every day for twenty years, and a kind of joy flared through him as he dodged the vehicles, leaped up on to the opposite sidewalk and kicked out, hard, despite the Diva's weight on his shoulders, and a heavy man fell.

Twenty more yards, then Donal crouched down, almost throwing the Diva off him as he felt for his wallet, got it, and pulled out his badge. He slammed it against the stone slot.

The metal door moved, revealing steps leading down.

'You first.' Donal pushed the Diva inside. 'Hurry.'

'Yes …'

Blood shimmered on the Diva's bare foot. She might slip, but there was no choice. Donal pushed her again, but gently, then followed her inside and worked the door mechanism. Dozens of people were advancing and the door was slow—

Shit shit shit.

—but it closed in time. For now, they were clear.

'They're going to, to—'

'No. Keep moving. Distance and stone will shield us.'

It was the only thing that would stop the ensorcelment: getting clear of people.

'Where to?'

'Just keep going.'

It took maybe two minutes to reach the rough-carved tunnel at the foot of the stairs.

'Is this ...? Where are we, Detective? The catacombs?'

'Call me Donal. And yeah, this is the catacombs.'

They moved along at something between a fast walk and a jog. Donal would have preferred to move faster, but the Diva could never maintain the pace.

Sound ...

Donal stopped dead.

'What's wrong, De— Donal?'

A distant rumble emanated from somewhere up ahead.

'We need to go back the other way. Now.'

'Oh ...'

The Diva broke into a stumbling half-jog as he pulled her back along the tunnel, and took a turn to the right. After a moment she pulled away from him but continued staggering forward.

'Don't you even know your way around?'

'Not these particular catacombs.'

'Shit.'

That sounded un-Diva-like.

The city's catacombs weren't all joined up, but any given network was likely to stretch for miles. Occasionally they linked through to the hypoway or sewage system.

In the distance, a thump sounded.

'Can you go faster?'

'Oh, Hades ...'

'Can you?'

'Yes.'

Here, some sarcophagi were so ancient they seemed mere geological bumps in stone. Others looked freshly carved, just decades old. Donal and the Diva ran past them.

Do you feel the bones?

Donal shuddered. 'Ugh.'

'What is it?'

'Nothing. Run.'

They moved faster.

Do you kiss her bones?

Terrible feelings tugged at Donal as they passed into a wider cavern. Odd, fragmented images assaulted him. There was *hunger*, as if every cell in his body needed to absorb ... something.

Or do you taste the song?

But then they were through the worst of it, leaving the sarcophagi behind. A closed ceramic door in front of them bore a red mu-sigma-tau logo, on an alpha-shaped shield. The Municipal Subterranean Transport Authority.

Once again the emergency lock responded as Donal rammed his police badge into the slot. He leaned back, tugging at the door until it groaned and began to shift.

'You first.'

'It's dark.'

'I know. Go.'

The Diva stepped inside and Donal followed, hauling the door shut. There was a soft pressure wave against his face as the door clicked. They were into the subway system, and it was total blackness.

'Grab my hand. OK ... Stretch out with the other hand, with your fingertips.'

'All right.'

'Feel anything?'

'No ...'

'With me, then.'

Donal led the way. There were no obstacles until his reaching hand felt for the tunnel wall and got it.

For a long time – or maybe just ten minutes – they travelled like this, until his fingertips touched a sheet of heavy, flexible material that might have been rubber. It formed a curtain to hold out dust.

He found a vertical slit in the sheet and pulled it open. His eyes blinked, stinging at the sensation of distant light.

'Safe ...' murmured the Diva.

'Perhaps.' Donal helped her through. 'Let's try to stay out of sight.

There are MSTA workers over there.'

'The ensorcelment …'

'Can reach down here.' Donal's tone was rough.

'What can we do, then? Will it wear off?'

'Not while you're alive.' Donal took hold of her shoulders. 'Trust me, all right? I'm going to find somewhere isolated with a telephone. One call, and they'll be flying in federal spellbinders from Fortinium. The feds can break any enchantment there is.'

'OK …'

'They can have a chopper airborne in minutes. What I need is—'

'A phone. That way?'

'That way.'

There was a flat cart on a dark section of the subway track. Donal thought the cart might be called a bogey, although in the orphanage a bogey was something you picked from your nose.

At any rate the cart looked as though it drew power from the rail. It was obviously for maintenance; but there were workers farther along, in the lighted area, and Donal did not want to steal the thing unless it was necessary.

Flying headlong through darkness, possibly straight into an oncoming train, was not the kind of safety he'd promised the Diva.

Her hand grasped his upper arm and squeezed: a primate response, a youngster clinging to an adult for protection.

Just then a hammering series of thumps echoed down the corridor, and a thunderous compressor started up. Several pneumatic drills, powered by the compressor, added their own noisy contribution to the din.

Donal and the Diva continued to advance along the dusty tunnel, keeping away from the live rail. Finally they reached a length of platform on the right: a disused station. Beyond, stood portable floodlights and a big compressor, with the workmen further inside the tunnel.

Do you hear the bones?

In the cacophony some strange combinations of tones must have …
No. Donal pushed that from his mind. He had work to do.

He climbed on to the deserted, grey platform and pulled the Diva up after him. They moved into a short corridor, looking for a maintenance engineers' office, and that was when Donal bumped straight into a barrel-chested mustachioed man.

Hades …

Donal slammed the palms of both hands against the man's body,

64

knocking him against the hard ceramic-tiled wall, and slammed a rising elbow just below the man's sternum. The big man fell, mouth working like a landed fish.

He lay there, groaning.

Donal considered tying the man up, but there was nothing obvious in sight for the task, and they had to move fast. He stepped over the man and pulled open a plain door. An office. An empty phone socket was on the wall, round and black like a mocking eye.

'Why ...'

This was the Diva.

'What is it?'

'... don't you kill him?' Hand shaking, she pointed at the fallen man.

If the bastard wakes up, we're done for.

Donal had no proof, but he had an idea that if the ensorcelment took hold of this man, it increased the chances that the maintenance team further down the tunnel would change, slip into trance, and that would be the end.

'Is he the enemy?'

'I ... I don't know.'

A blue-and-white schematic was pinned to the wall, and a true-scale map lay flat on a worktable.

She didn't even remember my name.

Irrelevant. He had to work out where they were, and where they could go.

Not till I told her again.

This seemed to be a disused branch off the Twenty-third Line.

She's probably forgotten already.

Donal traced the intersections. Police HQ was less than two miles away, but there was *no* tunnel in the right direction. It would take three changes, no, four changes to reach the place.

Every crowded train, every packed platform en route would contain a multitude capable of transforming into murderous parazombies.

'Shit shit shit.'

'What's wrong, D-Donald?'

He hated being called Donald.

'Nothing.' He could see it now. 'We've got a route out of here.'

But the man on the floor was looking up at them.

Thanatos.

Donal kicked the man in the temple.

'Y-You said he wasn't the enemy.'

'Yeah. But' – Donal stared down at the unconscious man: overweight, his breathing unsteady – 'they might be able to see through his eyes.'

Donal thought back. He had said nothing about where they might run. The small logo on the map, skull-and-Ouroboros, did not particularly stand out. If the enemy had linked in to the man's perceptions, they would not know ... unless they could read the man's own knowledge of where he was.

'We're moving now.'

Ten minutes later they were on the bogey, using its headlamps now they'd rounded a bend in the tunnel. They sped south, Donal keeping the throttle handle pushed all the way.

At some point they hurtled through another abandoned station where men were working. Several heads looked up but then they were through.

The Diva placed her cheek against his shoulder.

Ha.

Earlier, she'd paid no attention to the man who'd risk everything to protect her, but now ...

Do you taste the song?

He had to pay attention, that was all, and he counted disused stations as they passed through them. These were truly abandoned, save for a twenty-foot white snake curled up on one of the platforms.

Then Donal cut back the power, letting the bogey decelerate by friction. A faint patch of pale-grey up ahead was growing brighter.

They coasted to a halt.

Here stood a clean platform, its indirect lighting growing stronger as Donal and the Diva climbed from the bogey. Was this in use? There were no exits up to ground level – not according to the map he'd seen – but perhaps freight slugs used these places.

'Where are we?'

Donal pointed. Where the station name should have been, an Ouroboros worm encircled a skull, headband-like, swallowing its own tale.

'Energy Authority,' he said. 'Downtown Complex.'

'Is it safe?'

'I hope so.' At the platform's end, Donal saw a man-sized door bearing a smaller version of the logo. 'I bloody hope so.'

Six

They passed along a horizontal shaft, and came out at the edge of the vast cavernous Complex. Rows of huge reactors stretched back, filling the immense dark space.

A million fingers seemed to slide across Donal's skin, and the Diva moaned.

'There's shielding here,' Donal whispered. 'Look. See up there?'

He pointed to a small shape set high up on the left-hand wall: the Director's office. His fingertip traced the path of the rising black iron staircase that led upwards.

'All right.' The Diva clasped his upper arm, released it.

They stepped into an aisle, and commenced walking. It was more like a roadway, and they kept to the left, walking close to each reactor base, as they moved from one pile to another. No one was—

Damn.

A man in a bulky protective suit was working on a reactor casing, maybe twenty yards down the cross-aisle to the right. But he didn't look up, and then Donal and the Diva were past.

'He didn't notice us,' the Diva whispered.

Donal lowered his voice to a murmur, which was less likely to carry. 'His protective gear. It might have blocked the spell.'

It had been part of what he'd counted on, taking her to this place.

They walked on, passing seven more reactor piles, and the staircase up to the Director's office was within sprinting distance when everything went to Hades. Four men in grey overalls stepped directly into their path.

'Um ... Hi. I'm Lieutenant Riordan, here to see ...'

But their eyes were blank. Donal glanced at the Diva. Her pale, beautiful face was bone-white now.

Had she noticed that the men had not shuddered as they saw her?

Almost as if they were *already* en—

'Move it.' Donal whipped a circular kick into the first man's thigh, paralysing the leg and dropping the man. He punched the second man twice, then grabbed hold of the Diva and ran, pulling her *through* the foursome, raking another man's eyes and then they were clear.

'Fast ...'

They began to accelerate but then a larger group – seven, eight men – was blocking their way. Donal stopped, looked back – reinforcements there as well – and dragged the Diva sideways, quickly, jerking her arm in its socket, pulling her into a cross-aisle ...

No.

... and stopped, because the way down here was blocked as well.

'I'm sorry.'

Every route was a no-go.

Donal's shirt was soaked with sweat. He'd run hard, but the Diva ... Her feet were bloody, her dress ripped; and yet her face and body were the most sublime creation of the universe. She was so beautiful.

'Save me, D-D ... Please. Save me.'

Donal swallowed, and pulled out his Magnus. He raised it up, lowered it, and squeezed off a shot. The Diva yelped at the loud bang.

One of the men fell.

He was innocent ...

But the other ensorcelled men did not hesitate. They continued to walk towards Donal, closing in from both ends of the aisle. Donal glanced upwards. It might be possible for him to scale the side of the reactor ... but with the Diva? No chance.

Thanatos.

Donal fired into the advancing group, swivelled fast, and shot down two more men from the other contingent.

Then both groups swelled with reinforcements, more men wearing Energy Authority overalls, bearing heavy shotguns. Now they had no chance.

Donal lowered his Magnus.

'Save ...'

Do you taste the song?

'... me.'

There were six rounds left in the magazine before he needed to reload. There were more than twenty men advancing on him; half were armed with shotguns that could blast him into redberry spray. It was over.

The men advanced closer.

'Please ...'

Donal was tempted to ask the Diva if she remembered his name. Such a petty thought to have before dying, before his personal universe blanked out like wiping down a writing slate back in the orphanage school.

He remembered Sister Mary-Anne Styx drilling him in maths, and bandaging him after he took down the three bigger boys who—

The men shuffled to a halt.

What's happening?

One group parted slightly, allowing another figure to advance. He was narrow-bodied, with a grey goatee, and Donal had a bad feeling he should have expected this all along. It was Malfax Cortindo, Director of this place.

There was nothing blank about Cortindo's dark and sparkling eyes. Nothing blank at all.

'Ah, Lieutenant. How nice to— Careful.'

As Donal's Magnus came up, all the ensorcelled men who bore shotguns brought them to bear on the Diva. With the two groups facing each other, the men were likely to blow away each other's legs at best; but ensorcelled men care nothing for their own safety.

They were kamikaze pawns.

Donal lowered his gun, then let go. It clattered on the flagstones.

'Did I come here of my own free will?' He hadn't intended to say this out loud.

'Aren't our own motivations' – Malfax Cortindo's voice was courtly, devoid of tension – 'an eternal mystery to us all?'

'Screw you.'

'Oh, please.' The derringer that Malfax Cortindo pulled from his waistcoat pocket was a gleaming antique. The ends of its twin abbreviated barrels were dark, malevolent. 'A sense of style, if you would.'

Cortindo swung the derringer round to face the Diva.

'Time to die, my loveliness.'

Do you feel the song?

'No.'

That was the moment.

Do you touch the bones?

The ensorcelled men held their shotguns steady, but that was not the reason. In the name of Death, fear could never be the reason.

But that was the moment.

'S ... Save ...'

'He can't.'

The moment when Donal could have moved.

Do you taste the ...

The derringer banged, flashed strontium-red.

Crimson was the spray of drops from that pure ivory neck as the Diva span, toppling to the stone floor as arterial blood arced forth.

And died.

... bones?

Too late.

The moment when—

A second shot, red flame, flat bang, a third eye appearing in the Diva's forehead ...

— when Donal could have saved her, but it was too late, would always be too late, a lifetime and a universe beyond the second when he could have acted and made a difference.

'No!'

... and dark blood pooled, spreading from her shattered skull.

Then Donal *did* move.

He flowed into motion, and Malfax Cortindo circled, fast with the *pa-kua* moves, but he wasn't the only one to have studied the internal arts. Donal followed with a *pa-kua* palm-change of his own, flipping the derringer aside, then stabbed fingertips into Cortindo's eyes, whipped an elbow into the bastard's throat, and a knee below the ribs, targeting the spleen and finding it.

Wrapping one arm round Cortindo's neck, Donal span round, keeping their bodies close like lovers because that's how fulcrums work, whipping him towards the flagstones, and Cortindo was down.

The ensorcelled men were frozen.

Do you feel the ...

Down but not dead. Cortindo was a threat. Donal raised his knee.

...song?

And stamped down.

Hard.

All around, ensorcelled men dropped and lay sprawled on the hard floor in thaumaturgical coma. Not dead.

Only Malfax Cortindo and the Diva were corpses now.

Expected me to save her.

Donal wiped hot fluid from his face with the back of his gunhand. It might have been sweat; it might have been blood.

To save her. Couldn't even remember ...

It was blood. Some injury he hadn't noticed getting.

Bitch couldn't remember my name.

But she was so beautiful, even now, splayed with eyes open on eternity, pale skin splashed with red, that fine dress soaking with the hot slick fluid of life. While all around, the reactors seemed to glow black, to howl silence.

Do you hear the bones?

Slowly, slowly, Donal retrieved his Magnus and reholstered, all without removing his gaze from the Diva, the beautiful Diva.

He squatted down beside her perfect form.

So lovely.

Donal slid his hands beneath her body.

Perfection.

Steadied himself.

Do you taste the ...

And then he pushed himself up to standing, the limp weight of her across his arms. He took one step and then another, and then they were leaving, Donal and the greatest perfection in the universe, leaving this place for good.

  ... song?

He used the personal elevator that he remembered from before, standing proud with the Diva in his arms, one of her arms dangling, as the steel disc rose through the shaft.

Then it shuddered to a halt inside the dome formed of black flanges. The metal folded back on itself. Donal was in the small enclosed courtyard.

In the internal wall, an iron door stood half open, two collapsed men on the ground. Like their comrades below, they were the ex-ensorcelled, so deep into coma that only thaumaturgical intervention could save them.

But that was not Donal's concern.

Perfection.

He stepped over the fallen men, carrying the Diva into the larger courtyard where three finned black cars were parked, each with a raised black skull-and-Ouroboros on the doors. No one was moving.

Half-squatting, Donal tried the door handle of the nearest car. It clicked open.

Good.

So he carried her around to the rear, his perfect Diva, half-squatted again to twist the handle – *careful, don't drop her* – and stood back as the boot lid rose up. Then, with perfect care and a tender smile, he rolled the Diva's wonderful body into the boot.

And slammed the lid down.

Donal went to the gatehouse, where he found two more slumped men. Three sets of car keys hung from hooks, and he took them all. Then he wrenched down the series of brass levers that would cause the outer gates to open.

Crossing back to the car, he tried the keys, and the second set fitted. The huge steel gates were groaning back as Donal walked over to a drain in the ground and dropped the two remaining sets of keys through the grille. There were two viscous splashes in darkness.

He climbed into the car, pushed the skull-embossed lever into first, and drove forwards, through the huge gates while they were still opening, and turned on to the empty road where derelict buildings stared at him.

Overhead, the sky pulsed dark-purple as he drove.

It took two hours to clear the central Tristopolitan districts, using backstreets and odd lanes where possible, staying off the main grid. Donal kept under the speed limit, drove courteously . . .

So beautiful.

. . . and tried to keep his attention on his driving, despite the flawless wonder in the boot of his car. It was difficult, and he wanted to stop and allow the stupefied trance to swallow him. He needed to stop the car and go back to touch his beauty . . . but not yet. Not yet.

Beautiful.

And not just beautiful, but *his*, wasn't that the point?

Once past the city limits, Donal turned the car towards Black Iron Forest, where few people ventured and fewer lived. Perhaps that was why the orphanage never sold the cottage for their own gain; or perhaps it was Sister Mary-Anne Styx who had arranged things to Donal's advantage.

While Donal's parents had died when he was a week old, his grandfather, dour and solitary, had survived for thirteen more years. Unwilling to raise a grandchild, he nevertheless acknowledged Donal. When Jack Riordan died a year before Donal's 'graduation' from the orphanage – before they kicked him out on his fourteenth birthday – Donal received title to the cottage, plus the small amount of savings that had allowed him to continue in school and work towards the military entrance exams.

As far as he knew, none of his Department colleagues were aware of the place. He had never mentioned it, rarely visited, and for sure had never brought anyone here.

Not until now.

The long car growled along ever-darkening roads, the trees becoming odd-patterned shadows against night, twisting perspective. There was a long period when Donal drove without any conscious thought, lost in beautiful dreams – *oh, my Diva* – and when he came back into the moment, he was entering the Dispersed Vale.

They – he and the dead Diva – were deep inside Black Iron Forest now. Someone would have discovered the mess back at the Downtown Complex. Scene-of-crime diviners might already be at work.

The time when he could have given it up and returned to Police HQ was hours past.

It's all right, my love.

It was better when the path was clear, all choice removed.

With its immense fuel tank, Donal had felt the car could gone on for ever. But eventually the time on the skull clock – the hands fashioned in the form of slender bones: one femur, one radius – passed twenty-five o'clock. It was the early hours of the morning.

He continued to drive.

Eldritch howls and half-perceived shadows with amber eyes moved in the darkness. Donal branched off the already-narrow forest road, on to the Tartrous Trail, dropping his speed. Grit seemed to have gathered in his eyes.

By four a.m., he was in familiar surroundings. Donal drove the car quietly down to a clearing, and stopped.

And waited.

He switched the engine off.

Lost in trance for a time, Donal eventually came to. He inhaled, then forced himself to move, pushing the car door open, and stepping out on to dark mud. The sky was featureless purple. Looking downslope, he could see the lake.

It was a massive shadow that would never grow lighter. The lake had no name, and its waters were permanently black, perpetually still. Donal had never seen it any other way.

73

He walked to a wide silvery tree that stood on a hillock, dragging a key out of his pocket. He inserted the key into a knothole in the bark. There was a hesitation, then a cracking sound.

The slope's mulch slid back to reveal the cottage's steel windows, and the carved blackwood door.

Grandfather Jack's legacy.

Donal opened up the front door, then went back to the car, and hauled the dear Diva from the boot. Gently he carried her to the cottage, *their* cottage, and laid her down on the long dining-table.

He snapped the flint switches on two oil-lamps. Their yellowish light danced and flickered before growing strong and steady.

Perfect ...

No. There was work to be done.

Forcing himself not to look at the perfection spread out upon the table, Donal looked around the low-ceilinged room, avoiding the overhead beams, looking for something heavy.

He stopped when he came across an old Zurinese stone skull, some beloved totem of his miserable old Grandfather Jack who had never come to visit his grandson, never mind take him away from the prison that was ...

Irrelevant now.

So beautiful.

Stone skull in hand, Donal made his way downslope to the car. He pushed down the boot lid, climbed into the driver's seat, the skull in his lap as he drove in first gear, bypassing a large tree root. Then he stopped, but left the engine running.

Directly below, the nameless lake was thick and dark as ever.

Donal slid out from the driver's seat, jammed the stone skull down on the accelerator, let go of the clutch pedal and leaped back. The car bumped its way down toward the waiting lake.

It's going to stall.

For a second Donal thought he had failed, but then the car was over the edge into the lake with a heavy plop, no more. Black viscous waters surrounded the car's roof, pulling it under, and then it was gone.

One long curved wave moved across the viscous surface like a satisfied smile, then attenuated into nothingness. Lake and forest had returned to dark normalcy.

After a moment, Donal turned and made his way back to the cottage. To the object of his dreams.

Seven

For the next three days and nights there was no sleep – no true sleep – for Donal. He slid in and out of strange half-waking dreams where the Diva sang arias that were purely his, amid impossible white sands by a quicksilver sea born of the memory of that other artist, Jamix Holandson, whose dead bone Donal had touched.

But it was the Diva who remained with him, laid out on the long table beneath the low ceiling, her flesh pure and radiant ivory.

So beautiful.

Donal washed the wounds, scraped dried blood from perfect skin – a spatula from the kitchen served for that – and cut away the bloodied portions of her dress – *oh Thanatos, such perfection* – and wrapped a white bedsheet around her body.

Afterwards, he pulled the only armchair close, turned it away from the table, and used it to kneel upon, his forearms across the chair's back. He contemplated the drying perfection of his desire.

Soon, she would be ready for the flensing.

Do you hear the bones?

Not every moment was spent in contemplation. For the beautiful dark act to take place, it was necessary that the Diva – and Donal – remain undisturbed. So he was able to drag himself into the kitchen, drinking cold canned soup as he dug through the old toolbox and equipment chest.

In a forest such as this, Grandfather Jack had needed to prepare for dangerous times. There were thirteen old iron life-wards: narrow, heavy objects the length of his forearm, ending in a rough spike so they could be jammed into the ground.

Designed primarily to ward against packs of deathwolves, the devices would repel all living organisms above the level of plants.

The life-wards were heavy as Donal lugged them outside. When he

pushed them into the hard soil and leaned on them, the life-wards'
spikes slid easily into place. It took an hour – as much as he could tell:
time seemed to be moving strangely – to set them all in place, in a
rough ring around the cottage.

As the last ward entered the soil, a great shimmering hemisphere
descended, shielding the entire cottage from invasion.

Safe.

Donal went back in to contemplate the Diva.

After a long, rapt period, Donal shook himself into awareness. He was
kneeling on the reversed armchair. When he pushed himself to standing, his sinews ached with unaccustomed use.

He wiped his hand across his face, feeling rough stubble. Then he
moved towards the bathroom, and each step was hot agony.

Finishing, he drank brackish water from the tap. Then he walked,
still in pain but with more mobility, to the kitchen. He opened another
can of soup, took three cold sips from it, and put it down.

There was something important he had to do.

What is it?

The toolbox.

From it, Donal drew the rusted scythe that Grandfather Jack once
used to cut back the long dark grasses. He found the stone sharpen-
ing-block, poured seven drops of moth-oil upon it, and began the long,
careful process of sharpening the scythe.

Soon, the flesh would begin to soften with a hint of liquefaction.

Beautiful. So …

Then, only then, could Donal begin the slicing and cleansing process,
which would culminate when he polished those dear bones, one by
one, with every ounce of skill he possessed.

Donal worked, until he could stand it no more: the presence of
perfection in the next room while he scraped blade against stone in
here.

He went back into the lounge and resumed his kneeling position
upon the armchair, contemplating the dead, perfect Diva laid out upon
his table.

So perfect …

And that was the position he was in, kneeling and frozen in rapt
awe, when the front door blew apart in splinters and the windows
exploded inwards.

*

76

No ...

Dark-clad troopers in hexlar armour stormed inside, dropping to crouch, some rolling and coming up with weapons trained on Donal.

You cannot ...

Donal's hand moved toward his shoulder holster.

... have her!

He clasped the butt of his Magnus, drawing it out.

And in that moment a woman clad in a pale-grey skirt suit stepped through the splintered remnants of the doorway. She raised a heavy dart-gun, aimed at Donal's heart.

The world was moving so slowly.

'Too late.'

She fired.

The ceiling span past and he was flat on the floor, limbs rigid, ribs paralysed, scarcely breathing. Darkness circled and shifted around the edges of his vision.

'How ...?' It was so hard to speak. 'Wards ...'

'That was your mistake. They're *life*-wards.'

The woman leaned over him, and brushed back her white-blonde hair with one gloved hand. Donal's lips moved to ask the next question, but only a gasp came out.

'The ward shield keeps out' – she smiled – 'only living beings.'

Donal's eyes shifted towards the troopers.

'Oh, *they're* alive all right.' The woman tapped Donal's forehead with one finger. 'It's me you didn't count on.'

Darkness was closing in.

'—take the Diva and—' was all he could hear of the troopers' voices.

A hush surrounded Donal, blanketing him.

No. She's mine.

Even the air was thicker, viscous. It was difficult to drag the stuff into his lungs.

Do you hear the ...

Silence.

A shadow-fist closed around the world and snuffed it out.

Eight

Delirium followed chaotic dream followed a thrashing in his bed, limbs screaming with pain as Donal – or the near-mindless thing that had been Donal – fought against the restraints, and howled. Then he would lapse into comatose darkness.

Afterwards, liquid fire would spread along each fine nerve, igniting it with agony, as the cycle of torture began again.

For nine long days and nights, nurses with vertically slitted eyes watched over him, their skins shifting through hues of violet as his writhing body threw back refracted energy from the thaumaturgical field. They were immune to the field's effects: Night Sisters with delicate fangs and elegant limbs, revealing hints of their feline aspect.

They watched, and cared for him.

On the tenth night, something burst inside Donal, something in his mind ... and he gave a great agonized gasp and fell back, slipping into peaceful sleep. Above him, the ten-foot-long shield casting the healing field glowed strongly and then began to fade. The thaumaturgical field shifted hue, and became a pale-blue volume that smelled of ozone and lilacs.

Two of the Night Sisters looked at each other, the vertical slits of their eyes growing more circular as the light faded once more.

'He'll be fine, don't you think?'

'Yes. You did a good job, Sister Felice.'

'Thank you. Shall I ring the Commander, or do you—?'

'I'll let you make the call.'

The younger Night Sister, the one known as Sister Felice, walked along the central aisle of the shadowed ward. It was night, and the room was in darkness, save for one of the beds which glimmered with a sapphire glow: radiant energy from an ensorcelled victim trapped deep within the paralysing influence of a deathmoth's bite.

Other sleeping forms were just lumps beneath the bedclothes, unmoving, while tiny monitor-sprites hovered over each pillow, ready to flare with brightness should any vital signs drop below the parameters that the Night Sisters had set.

In the nursing station, Sister Felice picked up the phone. With one long retractable fingernail, she rotated all ten combination wheels to a memorized sequence. She listened for the ring. Though it was the middle of the night, someone picked up the phone immediately at the other end.

'Hello?'

'Is this Commander Laura Steele?'

'Yes.'

'You wanted to know when a patient called Lieutenant Riordan underwent a phase shift in his condition?'

'What's happened?'

'It's an improvement, not a decline. Although, not having died in the first three days, he had a good chance of—'

'He's going to live?'

'Yes, that's—'

A burr sounded.

Sister Felice held out the receiver.

'You're welcome.' Her voice was a predator's whisper.

She put the receiver down.

On the seventeenth day – after Donal had woken for an hour at a time, three times in twenty-five hours – Sister Felice hauled Donal from the bed, on to a wheelchair whose frame was formed of interlocking silver heptagrams.

'For luck,' she murmured, as Donal ran his fingertips along the soft metal. 'And for healing.'

'Where ...?' His voice was a croak. 'Going ... where?'

'Rehabituation.' Sister Felice pushed the chair into motion. 'Don't believe what they say about mystical therapists.'

She let go of the chair's handles and walked in front, heading through open double doors and into a square-cross-sectioned corridor. The wheelchair trundled after her, bearing Donal's pain-wracked form.

'What do they ... say?'

'Oh' – Sister Felice looked back over her shoulder at him – 'that they're evil and sadistic and delight in torturing you until you scream.'

They continued on, until they came to a floating hand-shaped sign, hanging in mid-air in a five-way intersection of corridors.

'Rehab,' said Sister Felice loudly.

The hand swung left.

'Everything moves around in this place.' She shook her head, then headed into the indicated corridor. 'Come along.'

The wheelchair followed.

'The ... therapists.' Donal's voice was tight, but he had to ask. 'Don't ... torture patients?'

'Oh, they torture you, all right.' Sister Felice slowed before a set of black opaque doors labelled RD. 'It's just they don't enjoy doing it.'

Then she grinned, showing needle-fine white fangs.

'Only kidding.'

The doors swung open of their own accord, and Sister Felice stepped aside as Donal's wheelchair rolled forward and took him into Rehab.

A soft feminine chuckle sounded as the doors closed behind him.

'Ah, so you're our latest vic— patient.' The androgyne in white tunic and trousers had wide shoulders and ten-inch-long fingers. A smile stretched its long features. 'That's our little joke. Don't you worry.'

'Thanatos.' Donal was not up to this.

'All right, my name's Jan, and the first thing we have to do is restore some basic thought and movement patterns. You with me?'

'Uh, if you say s—'

A strangled gargling sound came from one corner of the Rehabituation Department. Donal was confused by the strange geometric shapes of apparatus designed for Hades-knew-what functions, but then he saw the patient trapped inside.

Gross distortions rippled across the man's body. Then his right hand flared to maybe four feet in length, and he moaned in pain.

Then, just for a second, his whole form pancaked outwards to ten or twelve feet in diameter, amoeba-like, before retracting into a normal human shape. The man bent forward on his couch, retching. Another androgynous therapist held a cardboard bowl beneath the man's mouth.

'That's Andy' – Jan used one frightening, long finger to indicate the patient – 'and the therapist is Alyx.'

'Very good,' Alyx was murmuring to the wretched man, Andy.

'Are you trying to tear him apart?' Donal felt an urge to get off his wheelchair and run, but when he commanded his muscles to move, only hot pain resulted. 'You're killing him.'

'No. Relax.' Jan ran its long fingers, ending in soft padded tips, down

80

Donal's face. 'Andy's been infected with an attenuation field. We're teaching him to hold himself together.'

'Oh.' Donal's eyelids fluttered.

Again, Andy's hands ballooned, the right more than the left, and his face grew larger and larger.

'See the natural precursor to complete expansion?' Jan gestured, and Donal's wheelchair rolled closer to Andy's couch. 'That's how your nervous system views the world, in terms of touch. The hand and face are more sensitive than—'

All of Andy's body started to rip outwards, to flow across the room, but Alyx shouted at him: 'NO! Pull yourself together!'

'Can't ...'

'Now.'

With a whimper, Andy sucked his body back into normal configuration. Then he looked over at Donal, and gave a tiny smile, ignoring the tears flowing either side of his mouth. 'Some people would pay good money for this.'

'I'd pay a shitload to be somewhere else.'

'Don't' – a painful ripple spread across Andy's chest and face – 'make me laugh.'

Then Donal's chair swivelled away. It was time for his treatment to begin.

Back in the ward, body aching in what might have been a good way – Donal hovered in that strange place between hurt and joy – he was sitting up beside the bed, in a hard wooden chair, when he heard strange voices coming from the nurses' station.

'—Commander? I'm not sure he's up to it yet.'

'But it's just me, and I'll keep it low key.'

'You mean' – this was Sister Felice's voice, and she gave a soft hiss before continuing – 'the both of you?'

After a moment: 'Very perceptive, Sister. I can see that Lieutenant Riordan is in good hands.'

'Ha. Come this way.'

Sister Felice came walking down the wide aisle between the beds, her feline eyes slitted, her ears flattened against the sides of her head, and her hair flowing straight back, not hanging down. Behind her walked the pale woman who had shot Donal with the dart gun, wearing a pale-blue skirt suit today, with dark-blue gloves. And behind her ...

Something?

'Yes.' Sister Felice bared her delicate fangs. 'That's right, Donal. Call me if you need anything.' She placed a green stone in his hand. 'Squeeze it, and I'll be here in a second.'

Behind the woman, the air rippled. But if Donal turned his head and closed his eyes nearly all the way, the wavering became almost human-shaped.

'Thank you,' he told Sister Felice. 'You're the best.'

'I know.' She gave a soft laugh. 'Remember, you just need to squeeze the callstone.'

Then she walked away, silent and elegant . Both Donal and the pale woman watched her go. After a moment, the pale woman said: 'Do you remember who I am?'

'Yeah ...' A knot of pain was forming over Donal's right eye. 'Not your name, but I remember in the cottage, when I ...'

Do you hear the bones?

But the words were distant, no longer clinging: just an abstract memory. It was the image of the Diva stretched out upon the table – the *dead* Diva – that made Donal's gorge rise. He turned to one side, grabbed a wastebin, and vomited into it.

'Perhaps this is too soon.'

'No, it's all right.' Donal wiped his mouth with the back of his hand. 'So who are you?'

'Laura Steele.' She held out her gloved hand. 'Nice to meet you properly.'

'Er ...' Donal sniffed. 'We should shake when I've cleaned up. And does that mean you're *Commander* Laura Steele?'

'That's right. And this' – Laura nodded towards the wavering in the air – 'is Xalia. She's a member of the federal task force that I'm heading up.'

'Ah.' Donal leaned back against the hard chair. 'Are you here to cheer me up or to interrogate me?'

'Neither one. We're here to recruit you.'

'You're joking.' Donal closed his eyes, and remembered the long drive into the forest, and the blur – how many days? – that was his stay in the cottage, while he kept the Diva's corpse laid out and made his preparations for scraping clean the bones. 'How many laws did I break?'

'You were effectively ensorcelled.'

'Yeah, but not actually ... Doesn't that make me *effectively* guilty?'

'No, it makes you a damned victim, especially if you keep acting like one.'

'Thanatos.' Donal looked at her, then at Xalia's near-invisible shifting form. 'Nice bedside manner you got. You say you're heading up a task force. So what are you working on?'

'Well, it's a task ...'

'That is so fuckin' funny.'

'We're investigating the exclusive little club that Malfax Cortindo belonged to. We call them the Black Circle—'

'That's original.'

'—because their real name is a secret only they know.'

Then a soft whisper that might have just been a breeze sounded:

I wanted to call them the Pink Collective.

A smile twisted Donal's face, despite himself. 'How about the Lilac Conspiracy?'

Xalia's form rippled.

'So how big is it?' added Donal. 'This conspiracy?'

'Let's just say' – Laura's glance flickered towards the end of the ward, where Sister Felice sat at the nurses' station, drinking helebore tea – 'the BC have gone for quantity over quality, when it comes to recruitment.'

'But not just in Tristopolis.'

'Why do you say that?'

'Because you're federal, even if you're based here. And because of the background to my screw-up. We were supposed to be on alert, because of what happened in other cities. Including overseas.'

'Hmm.' Laura walked over to the bedside cabinet. On top stood a cheap stained vase containing two black dandelions. 'I think Sister Felice likes you.'

'It's her job. She's good at it.'

'Whereas you let your principal die seconds before killing the chief suspect.'

Donal consciously relaxed his shoulders. 'You said you were here to recruit me, and now you're telling me how badly I performed. Interesting tactic, Commander.'

'The thing is, we' – Laura nodded towards the near-invisible wavering of the air that was Xalia – 'understand more about ensorcelment and the ways of manipulation than your superiors do. Or more than they'll pretend to, for the sake of political expediency.'

'You mean I'll be a scapegoat? But it *was* my operation, didn't you know?'

In lucid moments, Donal had wondered what might have happened

83

to his career. Or whether he was going to jail, or worse.

'You were the only person in the whole theatre, cops included,' said Laura, 'to break the trance. If you hadn't been there, the Diva would have died anyway, with police protection all around. The story that everyone remembered would not have been what happened.'

'So I resisted the influence.' Donal looked down at the floor, remembering. 'One kind of influence, anyway.'

'Cortindo sowed the seeds of what happened to you,' said Laura, 'when he showed you the artist's bone. He did show you the bone, didn't he?'

'Thanatos, yeah ... How did you know?'

Another ripple moved through Xalia's discorporate form. This time, Donal sensed no amusement in her.

'We investigated his office.' Laura nodded towards Xalia. 'Every nook and cranny. It was no big extrapolation to work out what happened. We already knew you'd been ordered to go there.'

Donal stared at Laura's pale face, trying to read between her words. Without using Commissioner Vilnar's name, was she accusing him of being a member of the conspiracy? Or of abetting it without realizing?

Sister Felice was a long way down the ward, but Donal already knew how sensitive she was, how acute her hearing. It was best not to discuss specifics.

'So the only reason I've got for joining your team,' he said, 'is because my current bosses are going to leave me twisting in the wind.'

No. Xalia's insubstantial form drifted closer. *That's not the only reason.*

'And the other is ...?'

Laura answered for Xalia. 'She's talking about revenge.'

'Ah. That.'

After discussing a few specifics about the job offer, Laura said she wanted to check with Sister Felice regarding Donal's progress. Laura walked with Xalia beside her, down to the nurses' station.

There was a brief discussion, which Donal observed, watching without making judgements. Then Laura returned while Xalia remained hovering by Sister Felice.

'Nine days or nineteen,' Laura told Donal. 'Or ninety, if that's what it takes to get you rehabituated. What's rehab like, anyway? Rewiring-body-and-mind thing, right?'

'Exercise and illusion, to restore the old patterns of thought and movement,' said Donal. 'With plenty of pain, so you know it's doing you good.'

'Sounds ... interesting.'

'Uh-huh.' Donal wondered what she was thinking. 'You understand, I still haven't agreed to join you.'

'There's no rush.'

'All right.'

'So I wondered ... You understand Xalia's nature, right?'

'What? That she's a freewraith?'

'Exactly. She's not bound to a crane or an elevator, or a ... wheelchair. She's a member of the team, not some kind of *device*.'

'Obviously. Though I think you don't know Gertie very well.'

'Who's Gertie?'

'Elevator 7, at HQ. Next time you ride up, tell her you know me.'

Laura's pale eyes narrowed. 'A lot of cops wouldn't feel that way.'

'So they're assholes. It's cos they don't know any better.'

She opened her mouth to speak, closed it, then spoke up. 'I hope you decide to join us, Lieutenant Riordan.'

'Thank you.' Donal wondered what it was she hadn't said. 'Thanks for coming out here.'

He watched her leave, accompanied by the wavering of the air that was Xalia. The heels of Laura's shoes were high stilettos, and the fit of her skirt was snug; her motion caused him a certain feeling in his gut that was unexpected.

'Oh ...' Sister Felice was standing beside Donal's bed, her slit-eyes widening into roundness. 'I guess the lady Commander made an impression on you, huh?'

'Not really.'

'Ha.' Sister Felice gave a tiny cat-smile, allowing her claws to flick in and out a centimetre. 'You are such a liar, Lieutenant.'

'Shit.'

'Oh, do we need to use the bedpan?'

'No, *we* don't.' Donal swung his legs over the edge of the bed. 'But *I* am going to walk to the bathroom by myself.'

'Really?' Her eyes were slits once more.

'Yes.' Donal's voice was tight with pain.

'Good for you. If you fall over, just shout.'

On the following day, the liquefying patient called Andy, the man who had difficulty in maintaining his normal form, began to softly scream.

The sprites floating around his bed went wild, emitting banshee yells of their own, flaring from bright-orange to blazing white and back again.

Sister Felice came running, stared at the silver bands wrapped around Andy's bed, and checked the intricate device that appeared welded into the bedframe. She hurried to the wall-phone.

'Get Thaum Support here, stat. We've morph-support equipment failure.'

Donal sat up in his bed, watching but unable to do anything. Even Sister Felice appeared helpless now, as she reached towards Andy's bubbling form then drew back, unwilling to disturb his equilibrium further.

Donal wondered what would happen if Andy's skin burst.

Soon a young man with ivory Oriental features was walking quickly into the department, with two older, grey-haired men following. All three wore rust-and-brown jerkins embossed with brass-coloured runes.

Sister Felice said: 'Thank Thanatos you're here, Kyushen. Can you fix it?'

The younger man, Kyushen, carried a steel tool-chest. One of the older men nodded as Kyushen took a silver forked rod out of the chest and ran it above Andy's bed.

'The hex-flux integrity failed.' Kyushen looked up. 'We can handle that.'

The three men worked with tools, muttering about resonant frequencies and shifted octaves, replacing a blackened valve with a shining amber new one.

Suddenly a clear sheet of light passed across the bed and Andy's suffering form shivered into stillness. His body was still distorted, but static.

'Good work,' said Sister Felice. 'I'll call Dr Drax, and we'll take it from here.'

'But it's fixed,' said Kyushen.

'I know. But' – Sister Felice pointed at Andy's twisted, elongated body frozen in the bed – 'he isn't.'

'Oh. The patient.'

'Just a little detail,' said Sister Felice, but she was smiling. 'Like I said, leave it to us ordinary mortals. You thaumies go back to your labs.'

'All right.'

*

By the end of the week, Donal was hobbling around the silver lawn in thin mist (while mistwraiths floated around in odd patterns, murmuring encouragement) beneath a dark-purple sky. You couldn't call his motion running, not yet.

His firearm was in a secure locker, somewhere – according to Sister Felice – so Donal did the next best thing. He stood at the lawn's edge, using an imaginary gun, visualizing in his mind's eye the attacking figures, feeling the imaginary pressure of the trigger, and the recoil as he fired again and again into the shadows advancing on him.

Rehabituation continued, using pressure and psychic stress to re-establish the neural patterns of the pre-ensorcelled Donal. Jan told him that the old patterns would re-emerge stronger than before: a virtual guarantee that he would remain free of senility in old age.

On the third morning, he hobbled to the nurses' station, and asked Sister Lynkse if he could use the phone.

'Sure.'

She left him while he made the call. Silvery fingers seemed to play around the handset: he'd used a secure number.

* What can I do for you, Lieutenant?*

'Put me through to Commander Steele, please.'

One moment.

A strange sighing drifted down the line. Perhaps the countermeasures ached for the chance to defend against spikewraiths infiltrating the network.

Putting you through.

'Hello?'

'Commander Steele, this is Donal Riordan.'

'Lieutenant. Have you considered the job offer?'

'Yeah, and I'm accepting it.'

Again, the line sighed.

Then: 'Good,' said Laura. 'Report for duty as soon as you're discharged.'

'All right.'

'I won't send you into anything strenuous until you're fully fit.'

'That's all right, I didn't expect to—'

The line went dead.

'Nice talking to you, too,' said Donal to the silent receiver. 'Rats.'

Sister Lynkse, returning, gave him a strange look.

'Just renewing my membership,' Donal said, 'in the Rat Fancy club.'

Half-revealing her slender fangs, Sister Lynkse gave a silent laugh.

'Kill some of those rats for me, OK?'

A black low-slung ambulance came to take him back to the city. The vehicle was wide, with flared housings along the running-boards.

Sister Felice pushed Donal in the wheelchair he no longer needed, while Sister Lynkse walked alongside. They stopped at the edge of the dark-blue gravel drive.

The ambulance rear door rose up, and Donal stood. He kissed Sister Felice on the cheek, and patted Sister Lynkse's hand.

'You're wonderful,' he said. 'Both of you.'

'Well, we *knew* that.'

'Yeah.' He smiled at Sister Felice. 'Look after yourself.'

'You too, Lieutenant.'

Two black-suited paramedics with bone-grey skins descended from the ambulance.

'I can climb in,' said Donal, 'by myself.'

The paramedics watched in silence, unblinking, as Donal hauled himself into the rear compartment. He sat down on one of the stretchers that were fastened in place. The two paramedics looked at each other, exchanged some form of silent communication, then bowed to each other.

One of them climbed into the back and sat down on the opposite stretcher from Donal; the other returned to the front and slid into the driver's seat.

Sister Felice waved.

Donal blew her a kiss, and then the rear door lowered itself into place and clicked shut.

And that's that.

The ambulance rolled into motion, scrunching its way along blue gravel until it reached the road. The driver hauled the vehicle through a tight turn – the paramedic sitting opposite Donal gave a tiny grin – and then they were accelerating smoothly, back towards Thanatopolis.

And then, when they were a mile from the hospital grounds and the road was wide enough, the housings alongside the chassis split open. Bat wings unfurled, stretching to either side.

The engine note dropped as the front of the ambulance tipped up, gathering speed.

And the ambulance rose into the air.

Nine

The bat-winged ambulance howled low over dank marshes until it reached the city limits, where the density of thaumaturgically charged airborne particles forced the vehicle down to the ground, for fear of a flame-out in the engines. Pollution can be fatal.

Slowing to a normal crawl, the paramedic driver took the black ambulance through desolate west side streets before reaching mid-town.

'You live in Lower Halls, yes?' asked the paramedic riding in the back with Donal.

'Yeah, but ... Take me to HQ, why don't you?'

'HQ?'

'Police Headquarters. It's Number One, Avenue of the Basilisks.'

'Yes ...' The paramedic's voice grew oddly sibilant. 'We know where it is.'

He blinked: a slow wet motion of nictitating membrane preceding the flicker of his eyelids. In the driver's seat up front, the other paramedic gave a slow nod.

Neither spoke a word for the remainder of the journey.

Donal exchanged greetings with FenSeven and another deathwolf that he didn't know well, FenNineBeth. FenSeven sniffed, tasting the air for evidence of Donal's health. Then his tongue lolled in a lupine grin.

Once inside, the first thing Donal did was to descend to the gun range level. Gertie made no smart remarks during the descent, and she was gentle pushing him out of her elevator shaft and into the corridor. It disconcerted Donal more than anything else might have done.

Brian, behind the counter, his skin a healthy medium-blue, waved to Donal. 'Hey, Lieutenant. How's life?'

'I've still got one,' said Donal. 'And yourself?'

'I'm in the pink.' Brian patted his bald pate. 'Or in the blue, at least.'

'And in the clear?'

'Lieutenant. Everything's clean. Really.'

'Good. Gimme two hundred rounds and a bunch of targets, mixed.'

'None of the, ah, *specials?*'

'Brian ...'

'Just kidding. We're all legit here.'

Donal took the targets through to the range, sent the first of them back to maximum distance, then whipped out his Magnus and blew the target into shreds. He changed targets, reloaded, and got to work again.

Over and over he fired, blowing tightly clustered shots into the targets, until the air stank and his ammunition was gone.

Good enough.

Donal walked back to the elevator bank.

'Something new for me, Gertie. Down to minus 27.'

Have you been a bad boy, Donal?

'New job. I'm going to be working out of there from now on.'

So you have been a bad boy.

Donal said nothing more during the descent. Finally, Gertie brought him down slowly, slowly, towards minus 27, as if giving him time to reconsider.

At the doorway, Donal floated for a long moment while Gertie hesitated. Then:

Your funeral, lover.

She pushed him through.

A hulking figure was waiting for him. Donal recognized the guy from that time at the gun range, from before the debacle with the Diva. Viktor Harman, the guy had said he was, and had claimed to be from the 77th Precinct.

'My name really is Viktor Harman,' the guy said now. 'But I've never been inside the seventy-seventh.'

'OK ... I'm guessing we have the same boss.'

'You're guessing right. Laura's looking forward to seeing you.'

When Donal walked into Laura Steele's glass-walled office, she looked up, and just for a second her eyes looked as grey and metallic as her name suggested. Then a change shifted inside her gaze.

'I thought you were only being discharged this morning.'

90

'I am. Was. I came straight here.'

'So what do you expect to be doing on your first day in the team?'

Donal looked out at the communal office, dark polished desks and ancient phones, and Viktor Harman's hulking figure chatting to himself ... no, to the wavering in the air that was Xalia.

'Don't tell me,' he said. 'You've a bunch of really interesting files for me to read.'

'You got it.'

'And stuff you don't have written down?'

'Some of that, too. But this' – Laura pointed at her own head – 'isn't guaranteed indestructible. Most of it's down in writing somewhere.'

'Well, that's something.' Donal looked at her. 'Who are we investigating?'

'We call them the Black Circle.'

'Yeah, I remember that much.'

'You looked woozy. I wasn't sure how much you'd recall.'

'Uh-huh. You mentioned Malfax Cortindo.'

Like some attenuated echo, he half-remembered a whispered *Do you feel the bones?* Then the disconcerting memory was gone, and he was back in the moment.

'Don't worry about the flashbacks,' said Laura. 'They'll— Never mind. Not my business.'

She was right: this was none of her business.

'Malfax Cortindo,' said Donal. 'You said he was part of the club. Part of the Black Circle.'

'Yeah, well. The BC – the name *is* embarrassing, right? – seems to include your favourite Alderman. Some of the paper trail is in the files, as you'll see.'

'You mean Finross? I haven't had any dealings with him. Er ... Not directly.'

Donal's visit to the Energy Authority had happened because Alderman Finross had made the arrangement. That was one thing Donal would not forget.

'I'd guess they were trying to work out how much you knew, or how hard you were going to work to prevent the kill.'

Donal shook his head. He *hadn't* prevented the kill, had he? But his own remembered actions seemed like a stranger's.

'It was Commissioner Vilnar who contacted Finross initially, I think. You can't suspect the Commissioner.'

Laura cocked her head to one side, saying nothing.

'Thanatos,' muttered Donal. 'But he was the one who briefed me in the first place.'

'Well, he had to, didn't he? Once he'd been tasked with protecting the Diva. The orders didn't originate with him, but the City Council.'

'Oh.'

'And that thought is most certainly *not* in writing. How well do you get on with the Commissioner, Donal?'

'We're like' – Donal pretended to have difficulty crossing his fingers, as if they were repelling magnets – 'that. Damn. Just like that.'

'Good answer. I should've asked you earlier.'

'Perhaps, Laura ... If I can call you that.'

'What I think is, if you have to ask—'

'—it's probably too soon. So can I get you a cup of coffee, Commander?'

'Yeah. Black and strong.'

'You got it.'

Donal fetched coffee in ectofoam mugs, and left one on Laura's desk. She was in deep in phone conversation with someone now, but she'd left the door open so it wasn't confidential.

Going back out into the main office, sipping his too-hot coffee, Donal nodded to Viktor. Then he made his way to the only clean desk.

That's mine.

Suddenly the air was wavering in front of him.

Yours is the messy one over there.

A faint outline of a raised hand pointed.

'Thank you so much.'

Donal sat down, kicked a grey metal wastebin into position, and slid the papers from the desktop, plus the old-fashioned blotter, straight into the bin. Then he pulled open the tall lower drawer, designed for hanging files, and stuffed the bin inside.

'There we are. All tidy.'

Donal pushed the drawer shut with his foot.

Aren't you going to ask why I need a desk?

Donal looked at her.

'Xalia, come on. I can see right through you. You're fishing for compliments.'

Like I haven't heard that one before. But what do you mean?

'You're solidly beautiful. You're gorgeous. Why wouldn't you have somewhere to sit?'

Ha. You're a piece of work yourself, Donal Riordan—

'Back at ya.'

—but you're not fooling me. I know who you've really got your eye on.

'I don't—'

But his gaze had already shifted towards the door of Laura's office before he could stop himself.

'Shit.'

Ha.

Then Viktor was returning to his desk with a flimsy report clutched in one big hand, and Xalia faded into near-invisibility. Donal pretended to find something interesting in the upper drawer of his new desk.

A detective, not part of the team, passed through the office. He was big, almost as big as Viktor, and his eyes were the colour of slate – in fact, they appeared to be *made* of slate. Donal had seen stone lenses before, during his Army days: they were sniper implants, and they were for life.

Kresham's grip, like Viktor's, felt capable of crushing Donal's hand. 'Good to meet ya.'

'Likewise.'

Kresham nodded, as though a one-word reply was a point in Donal's favour. Given the reticence of most snipers, that was probably the case.

Viktor said, 'Who's on Blanz, then?'

'Harald's got him.'

'Long-range?'

'Yeah. I'm going back to my own desk, for some peace and quiet. Don't call me.'

Donal looked from one to the other.

'You guys wouldn't be talking about Sherman Blanz, would you?'

Viktor shrugged. 'Why not?'

'Senator Sherman Blanz.'

'Right.'

'You have a visiting federal senator under surveillance.'

'Uh-huh.'

'Shit.' A slow spread smile across Donal's face. 'I think I'm going to enjoy it here, if we all stay out of jail for long enough.'

Ain't the jailhouse we have to worry about. It's the graveyard.

Donal stared at Xalia, whose form seemed to grow as opaque as mist just for a second. He remembered that smartwraiths like Xalia would be classified as non-human under Blanz's proposed Vital Renewal Bill, with no more legal rights than a piece of furniture.

'But we wouldn't do anything illegal or bad to Blanz, would we?'

We're professional police officers.

'Even though Blanz is a cretinous bigoted motherfucker who deserves to die in long-lasting agony.'

Even though.

Donal let out a long breath.

'You guys got any other interesting surprises for me?'

'Dozens,' said Viktor. 'But if we told you, they wouldn't be surprises.'

'Shit.'

That evening brought a different kind of surprise into Donal's life: the sudden experience of being homeless.

When he arrived at his neighbourhood, no one paid him any attention, but that was business as usual. Walking past the washeteria, Fozzy's Rags, he saw old Mrs MacZoran give a start at his appearance; then she turned and said something to the large woman sitting beside her. Behind them, the washing machines churned on.

Donal would have gone in to chat with her, but he'd drunk too much coffee and his guts were still shaky: he needed the bathroom. When he reached the apartment block and climbed to the fifth floor, he knew straight away that something had changed, even before he saw and smelled the fresh coat of black paint on his front door.

Except that a tiny handwritten label said 'Davinia Strihen,' which meant it was no longer *his* front door, exactly.

For a moment, hand inside his jacket and resting on the butt of his Magnus, Donal was tempted to kick the lock out of the jamb. But this Strihen woman probably knew nothing of Donal Riordan, and she might be an old dear liable to drop dead of a heart attack if he burst in.

'For fuck's sake.'

He went downstairs, pushed his way between cardboard boxes in the ground-level hallway, and made his way back to the super's office at the rear. That was a door he could kick in, and did.

It crashed open with a satisfying sound of splinters ripping from wood.

'Hey—'

'Right, fuckin' hey. What's up, Ferd?'

'Oh, Hades, Loot ... Er, Lieutenant. It wuz the landlord. Bastard made me.'

'Made you do what, Ferd?'

Ferdinand was old and fat and hadn't shaved for ten or twelve days. If Donal needed a decent opponent to fight, Ferd wasn't it, and this wasn't the place.

The landlord lived a long way uptown from here.

'They said you wuz in the hospital, like. Didn't think you'd come out again.'

'Nice of everyone to care.'

'Yeah, well ... We did. Old Mrs MacZoran wanted to send flowers, but I didn't know where the hospital was.'

'Where's my stuff?'

'Oh, Thanat— Sorry. It's ...' Ferd's voice trailed off, and he swallowed.

'You trashed it?'

'Hades, no. It's outside.'

'In the backyard.'

'No ... I mean yeah, but it wasn't my idea. Honest.'

Donal started to raise his fist, then he turned away and slammed the rear door open with the heel of his hand. It bounced back from the wall, and he kicked it. Then he went out into the narrow alleyway of broken concrete.

Small black ferns were growing in the cracks. Four dented cardboard boxes lay there, stained in the aftermath of quicksilver rain. One of the boxes was torn. Donal's old brown jacket looked shredded.

He went back in to Ferd's room. Ferd had pulled on his coat, trying but failing to button it across his globular stomach. He stopped, swallowing, as soon as he saw Donal.

'I was just, er, just—'

'About to phone for a taxi for me. Right?'

'Er, right, Lieutenant. Right.'

The rent hadn't been paid for a month, that was true. But beyond that ... damn it, Donal would sort it out tomorrow. But he needed a place to stay for the night.

He stared around Ferd's tiny room, with torn wallpaper hanging in triangular patches from the walls. It was filled with an old dank rotten smell, and the couch was torn, its springs exposed. He could have forced Ferd to let him stay here, but he'd rather sleep in the open.

'Taxi. Outside. As soon as possible. Got it?'

'Got it. Thanks, Lieutenant.'

Thanks for what? For not punching his head in?

Donal back out and picked up two of his four boxes – half of everything he owned, how wonderful – and headed inside. Ferd was already dialling, and Donal pushed his way through to the front hallway.

He set the two boxes down just inside the closed front door. Going back to fetch the other two, he heard Ferd say: 'Please, Joe, for Hades' sake. He'll kill me, otherwise.'

Donal felt the anger rise inside him and for a blinding split-second he could feel himself ripping out the Magnus and whipping it backhand across Ferd's flabby face, cutting open the skin … then he throttled down and pushed the anger back inside him, where it belonged. Coiled up, ready for use when he needed it.

Ready for when he met the true killers responsible for the Diva's demise.

Out on the sidewalk, he waited for the purple cab to appear. While he did so, he wondered where the Thanatos he was going to stay for tonight, and the nights to follow. A month's unpaid rent was the equivalent of what, two days in a hotel?

Just as a cab appeared at the left-hand end of the street, a Vixen slid around the corner of the opposite end, its curved, finned shape out of place in this neighbourhood. It slowed, cruising. Then Donal recognized the blonde-haired silhouette behind the windshield.

He held up his hand in a static wave.

'Hey, bud.' The taxi driver leaned out of his window. 'You Riordan?'

'Never heard of him,' said Donal. 'That's my lift over there.'

'Hades, I hate this rat-damned place. Lower Halls.' The driver stared at the apartment block's scratched and scabby door, obviously debating the merits of going inside to raise hell while leaving his vehicle exposed on the kerb.

On the far side of the street, two shifty youngsters with yellow eyes (nephews of the Fozzy who owned the washeteria) slouched against ruined brickwork, watching Donal and the taxi. That was enough for the driver, who gunned the accelerator and said: 'You want my advice, you get far away from this dump.'

Donal said nothing as the taxi pulled away from the kerb and twisted into a U-turn, engine growling as it headed back the way it had come. Then Laura's Vixen pulled up, and the taxi was forgotten.

'You throwing out the garbage, Lieutenant?'

'I *am* the garbage, Commander. Me and my worldly belongings here are headed for a hotel.'

'For fuck's sake.' Laura glared at the apartment block. 'You're not saying they chucked you out?'

'While I was gone, yeah.'

She stared at him for a moment. Then: 'The boot lid's unlocked. What are you waiting for?'

'Thank you.'

Donal went round to the back of the car. Low and solid, it appeared to purr as it sat there idling. Donal had to use both hands to twist the twin handles; then the lid raised itself up on the sprung hinges, revealing the near-empty compartment.

He hesitated, then transferred the first of his boxes from sidewalk to boot, squashed it into one corner, then followed it with the remaining boxes. He slammed the lid down, walked around to the side of the vehicle, and slid in on the passenger's side.

'You've booked a place?'

'I thought I might try the A.' The Agnostic Men's Association ran hostels, as well as the jailhouse gyms that Donal often trained in. 'There's one on Thousand-and-third.'

'That'll be a no, then.'

'I— Right.'

'I've got a spare room. More than one.' Laura slipped the car into gear. 'But you'll have to fend for yourself when it comes to food. I've nothing in stock.'

'No problem.' Donal watched the apartment block slide away. It felt as though a chunk of his life had come loose and fallen into a wild, cold ocean. 'I'm not used to ... Well. Thanks.'

Laura nodded, her mouth tightening, as though she were engaged in some kind of internal argument with herself. Donal decided he should keep quiet.

So why was she driving this way in the first place?

The old, damaged neighbourhood fell away behind them, as the Vixen arced upwards on to a curving overpass, slipping among fast-moving cylindrical lorries, ignoring a blast of horns as she pulled in front of a triple-decker transporter stacked with five-wheeled quin bikes. The Vixen accelerated harder.

They pulled on to the Midtown Expressway, and Donal's heart rate increased. Laura must be so much richer than him. He could not make a play for her now, not when she was acting on a charitable impulse to a coworker, one who reported to her.

Do you hear the ...?

Shut up.

They soared into the heart of the city, among the hard-edged gothic-deco towers, then pulled into a helical off-ramp.

Oh, shit.

Donal hated these things.

'You're all right with thaumatunnels, right?' Laura was already taking them off the main overpass and into the mouth of the spiral. 'Right?'

'Yeah ... Sure.'

The car flipped upside down as it span through the helical descent.

Shit shit shit.

Then it was righting itself as it slid into a basement garage, screeching echoes bouncing back from stone walls carved with malevolent hard-angled protective runes.

Most of the parked cars were bigger and grander than the dark-but-sporty Vixen, but there was one thing every vehicle had in common: Donal could never afford to rent one for a weekend, never mind buy one.

'Home bitter home,' said Laura, with no trace of emotion, and slammed the car into a decelerating turn that pushed Donal to the side, pressing him against the door. 'Here we are.'

And screeching and yowling ...

What's she trying to do?

...the Vixen pulled to a halt, its nose just inches away from a wall of grey-black polished granite. In it, flakes of quartz sparked with malevolent light.

Give me a heart attack?

Then Laura gave him a sideways look.

'Sorry,' she muttered. 'I forgot, you're just an ordinary— Never mind.'

Perhaps that dismissal – of Donal as ordinary – was the most devastating thing that had happened in a confused and disturbing night.

A black trolley pulled up beside the car, and Laura popped the boot before stepping out. By the time Donal had walked back to the rear, all four of his battered boxes were already in place on the trolley's flat bed, held in place by four fat pulsing arms.

At the trolley's front end, two large yellow eyes turned to look at Donal, and gave a long slow blink. Then the trolley rolled into motion.

Donal began to follow, but Laura said: 'The people elevator is this way.'

'Uh ... OK.'

He watched the trolley make its way past a gigantic Nebula limousine to what looked like a blank concrete wall. An opening drew apart and the trolley rolled forward into a darkened, empty shaft. It hung in mid-air as the wall clamped shut behind it.

Where the Thanatos am I?

Laura was heading for a buttress of the same shining granite-and-quartz rock, in which a silver elevator door was set. Over it was a dial, its needle currently indicating the 227th floor.

A flare of blue light travelled down the door at Laura's approach. The needle began to swing, indicating the elevator's descent.

Soon the doors were sliding open to reveal a steel-floored elevator with walls that curved inwards to a point overhead. As Donal stepped forward, metallic thorns slid like cat's claws from the walls; but then Laura touched Donal's arm. The thorns retracted.

Security system.

At least Laura had identified him as a friend. Donal wondered just what the building would have done otherwise.

Sealing itself up, the elevator rose fast, its floor pressing against Donal's feet. It hurtled upwards with relentless speed, then began to brake. The ascent slowed, then they bumped to a halt and the doors slid open.

They were in a twenty-foot high lobby with only one doorway: massive black steel double doors, which swung inwards as Laura walked towards them. Donal hung back.

Beyond was a huge reception area decorated in steel-grey and matt black, all of metal. On twisted helical stands, metal cups bore dancing blue flames whose motion matched the near-subliminal music of Illurian harps seeping through the obsidian floor.

A pale ethereal hand at the end of an insubstantial arm headed towards Donal, its fingers lengthening as it drew close, reaching towards Donal's Magnus in its concealed shoulder holster. At a tutting sound from Laura, the hand froze, then withdrew back towards the wall, sank inside and was gone.

'This is just like my old neighbourhood.' Donal looked around the chamber. 'They try to steal your weapons there, too.'

Laura half-smiled. 'Don't worry. I'll look after you.'

'Yeah ... And you're not doing a bad job so far.'

'You're welcome. The apartment's through there.' She inclined her head towards the solid-seeming wall, its surface decorated by a twelve-foot high steel mask: a man's face, hook-nosed, eye shut.

'The apartment? So what's this place?'

'Kind of a hallway, I suppose. A, what, antechamber?'

'Antechamber,' murmured Donal.

The mask's eyes opened, stared at Donal for a moment, then opened its mouth, wider and wider like gaping jaws, splitting apart to form an entranceway into a large room with a dark-blue floor that looked like solid glass. Laura led the way; Donal caught up with her, glancing back as the steel mask folded and slid back into place.

Here, the air was chill.

'Sorry,' said Laura. 'I wasn't expecting— Well. You know.'

'What are you sorry for?'

'I meant, it's cold, isn't it? That's all.'

At her words, shafts of orange flame slid up the walls from controlled vents at floor level. Waves of warmth washed over Donal, as he wheeled around, checking over the huge room: bigger than his old apartment, almost as big as the entire apartment block.

'You're rich,' he said. 'I mean really rich.'

Laura shrugged.

'Are you asking why I'm a police officer?'

'No, but ... Why *are* you in the force? I take it you don't need to earn a living.'

'A living ...' Laura shook her head, an odd look in her eyes. 'That's one way to put it, I guess.'

She led him across the forbidding high lounge, to the twenty-foot dark windows that reared upwards, looking out on to the nightbound city towers. In the distance, a lone smartbat sailed against the background of a moon-illuminated cloud.

'Tristopolis,' she said. 'Is it worth it, do you think? Should we even try to save it from itself?'

Donal shook his head.

'I don't even know what you're talking about.'

'Excuse me?'

'A city might be a thing in its own right, like a living being ... but it ain't the city we're here to protect, y'know? It's your average man or woman struggling through life, who doesn't deserve to become a victim as well – that's who we're here to help.'

Donal could not stop himself scanning the high room, the black iron-and-quartz chandeliers, the tall twisted sculpture of what looked like a melting warrior, standing in one corner.

'You've got a problem,' said Laura, 'because of my wealth. Because I'm so well off, is that it?'

'No.' Donal blew out a breath. 'I don't figure you for a career politician. Not if you're running a task force that's investigating federal senators ... unless you're *really* figuring to make a name for yourself as a moral crusader.'

'Thanatos ... Me, a crusader. I've enough trouble just— Well.' Laura crossed her arms. 'If I let you stay here until you sort yourself out, we're not going to have a problem with each other, are we?'

'You run the task force. You're the boss. Although if I'm stuck here until my life's sorted out' – Donal couldn't help grinning – 'we're going to be putting up with each other for a long time.'

'Ha.' Laura uncrossed her arms. 'Come on. I'll show you around.'

Ten

The place was huge, and 'apartment' seemed such a tiny word for the wide, gothic dwelling which Laura kept. She owned the whole 227th floor of the building, Darksan Tower, which was the uppermost residential level: the higher, narrower levels housed maintenance rooms, and the huge motors and drums of the seven elevators that serviced the building.

The rooms were cold, simultaneously grim yet palatial, and Donal's breath steamed as he stood in a huge bedroom with a clean, polished obsidian floor, and a four-poster bed whose coverings were of silver fabric, interwoven with dark-purple runes of a kind he had never seen before.

Black vase-like constructs, dotted around here and there on low tables, sprouted dancing pale-blue flames when Laura snapped her fingers near each one in turn.

'Not flamewraiths.' Donal frowned. 'I'm not sensing ... There *are* no boundwraiths here, are there? Of any kind.'

'You think there should be? That I should have spirits enslaved inside my household appliances?'

Donal thought about the moans echoing through the subterranean avenues of reactor piles, spill-off from necroflux waves passing inside the bones of the dead

Do you feel the—?

No, not any more.

'Maybe it's no worse,' Donal murmured, 'than whatever's waiting for the rest of us.'

The expression in Laura's eyes was unreadable.

'I should show you the kitchen,' she said after a moment. 'You'll be able to fix yourself some supper. This here is your room, and there's a bathroom through there.'

102

She pointed at a solid-looking wall decorated in vertical ten-foot-wide panels of alternating grey and black. 'Third panel's the bathroom door.'

Donal's four cardboard boxes of belongings were already stacked in one corner. The trolley – which *was* a wraith container – must have used an alternate route, perhaps through some kind of maintenance shaft, to reach the room. There was no sign of the trolley now.

Perhaps it belonged to the building management, rather than Laura.

He followed Laura into the ice-cold kitchen. Cupboards opened at Laura's command, revealing a stasis-pantry full of food cartons, and chinaware stacked away as though it had not been used for ages.

'Help yourself,' Laura said. 'I'll see you in the morning.'

'Um ... OK. Thank you.'

Donal felt let down, knowing it was an unreasonable reaction.

Do you—

Never.

After all Laura had done for him, sharing supper was too much to expect. She would be going out to dine with her rich friends, moving in strata that would be alien to any normal working cop.

'I appreciate this,' he added, as she left the kitchen.

'You're welcome.'

The door – simply ensorcelled, not requiring a wraith – swung shut of its own accord as Laura's heels clicked along the hallway floor, fading from Donal's awareness.

'Well,' he murmured to himself. 'Let's see what's for supper.'

In fact, Donal no longer felt hungry, but he had a brief memory of Sister Felice back at the hospital, telling him to eat or his recovery would take longer. He supposed that still applied.

Donal found a greasepaper-wrapped brick of Alcadian pink cheese, and a cardboard carton of blacksprout broth. Some black crackers from the stasis pantry. And that was it. He searched for a saucepan.

There were none that he could find.

'Bleeding Thanatos.'

In the end, he settled for drinking the soup cold, straight from the container, standing at the counter. The cheese and black crackers tasted ... interesting.

The wrapper on the cracker box bore a date: 22nd Sextember, 6604. At least they were all right to eat: the stasis pantry looked top-of-the-line, guaranteed against decay.

But what kind of luxury apartment was this, where the rooms were kept icy cold and there was no fresh food, only three-year-old crackers and frozen cheese?

Donal ate slowly, cleaned up the crumbs he had spilled, and stacked the dishes in the sink – which coughed up rust-coloured water, as though unused to working, before the water flowed through long enough to clear. Then the sink swilled the dishes, small extruded arms washing and polishing the plates, before setting them to one side to dry.

Donal walked back through the echoing hallway to the tall, dark bedroom. He stared at the four poster bed for a long time, before stripping down to his skivvies, finding the right cardboard box and retrieving a battered book with the covers torn off. It was the copy of *Human: the Revenge* that he'd started before the job with the Diva.

Do—?

No.

He took the book into bed with him.

Donal sat propped up against silk-covered pillows with a mercury sheen, reading by the light of flickering pale-blue flames, finding some comfort in the words of an imaginary story. Real life and the actual world had slipped far away from logic and ordinary purpose.

And at some point he closed his eyes to rest, laying the book on his lap. He drifted into a warm, blank orange dream.

Donal woke thirsty. Still in his skivvies, he went back out to the kitchen ...

And stopped.

Do you feel—?

Oh, my Death, yes.

Laura was in the hallway, totally nude. Behind her, tall windows stood open to the icy night. Quicksilver rain fell almost horizontally through the powerful wind.

And Laura's perfect, pale skin was silvery. If Donal didn't know better, he'd think she'd been outside.

'You're so warm,' she whispered. Her eyelids fluttered. 'I didn't mean to—'

Part of Donal's mind cried out a warning, but most of him thrummed with a resounding affirmation as he took a step towards her.

'So close to the living. All day, at work ...'

'You're perfect.' Donal's voice was rough.

Feel the song?

Something, some powerful force, washed through Donal's being.

I don't know.

Perhaps he struggled against that tidal attraction for a moment; or perhaps he imagined that, and gave himself up immediately to what was happening.

His hand cupped against one cold breast. Her nipple was erect and frozen, like steel.

'Thanatos.'

And they were embracing, desperate to cling to each other, and the time for thought was past as they stumbled towards the bedroom.

Laura straddled him, pale and strong, laughing as he came inside her, a nova burst of white joy as he cupped her small breasts. He rolled sideways, bringing her down to lie on the bed, and kissed her icy nipples as he hooked his fingertip inside her and in a moment she screamed aloud, shuddered, then laughed once more.

Do you—

Not now.

Donal kissed her pale soft skin, so cold against his lips, his body. In minutes Laura was aroused again, arcing back as Donal used his tongue, and then he was inside her once more, climbing to that pinnacle of explosion which this time occurred simultaneously for both of them.

'Oh, Death ...'

'You're wonderful,' he told her, suddenly able to speak.

'And you, lover-man.'

They snuggled close, holding each other.

'Shit.' A cramp seized his ribs. 'Sorry.'

He rolled back away from her.

'You all right, lover?'

'Yeah.' Donal stretched, even though it hurt. 'You wait till I get my full strength back.'

He rolled back over and kissed her cool lips.

'Yes ... You should sleep, dear Donal. Or you'll be no good to me in the morning.'

Did she mean at work, or in bed? Smiling, he meant to ask her, but he was lying in a bed more comfortable than he had ever known, exhausted from ongoing trauma and recent lovemaking.

Do ...?

Dunno. Can't remember. Who cares?

Donal slipped into a state that might have been sleep or might have been trance, but was in any case disconnected from the ordinary world. It was bliss, and nobody experiences that often in their life.

Donal drifted.

When he woke, the room had grown chilled once more. It remained dark, lit only by one pale-blue flickering flame. Laura was not in the bed.

What have we done?

Desire had overwhelmed them. But how had that happened?

'Laura?' Donal blinked and pulled himself half-upright on the bed. 'Are you—?'

She was there.

Oh, black Thanatos.

Still nude, Laura sat cross-legged on the floor. A narrow black cable, hanging in a catenary curve, connected her to a power valve in the wall. The cable pulsed with necrotonic power. But on her left breast—

No. I didn't realize.

—a large flap of pale skin hung back, a triangle of that perfect skin he had kissed and run his tongue and fingers over—

Or did I? Did I know?

—revealing the hollow in her chest, and the slick black wetness that pumped and beat in a regular, never-changing rhythm, recharged for another night and day.

A repressed memory rose up.

'The ward shield keeps out only living beings.' That was Laura, back in the cottage with the troopers who had burst in.

Now, Laura's eyes were shielded by shadow as she watched him watching her.

Then, 'What's the matter?' she asked, her voice harsh. 'Haven't you ever fucked a zombie before?'

Donal tried to speak. Something clutched his throat, and it was exactly like being strangled. He tried to tell Laura that it didn't matter, but it was impossible as she stood up, pulled the power cord from her beating slick black heart, flicked the cord aside and sealed up her thoracic cavity and her pulled her breast-skin back into place.

The edges joined up and faded so that her skin was whole once more.

'I—'

'Don't worry yourself, Donal.'

Laura's discarded clothes remained behind as she walked nude from the room, her perfect convex buttocks clenching and relaxing in rhythm, and then she was gone and Donal was cursing himself.

'Ah, Death ...'

He swung his legs off the bed and came to his feet in one fast motion.

She regrets it. It just came over her too, that desire—

Donal was used to moving athletically, but not in his current state. Blood pooled from his head and Donal swayed, tottered, and then the bedsheet seemed to rise to meet his face – *Hades, I'm bloody fainting* – and he was falling forward but could not stop himself as everything went.

Black.

In the main lounge, Laura stood nude, shivering but not with the chilled air, because she was no longer human and how could a dead thing feel the cold? She stared back at the hallway and the bedroom door – her own bedroom, where Donal lay.

The room she had not used since ... since it happened.

There were six guest bedrooms but the seventh bedroom was her own: though she had not consciously planned to make love to Donal, some part of her must have known all along that it was going to happen.

Thanatos. Balls.

Giving Donal a moment longer to follow her and apologize – *Death, he was so warm* – she gave up – *but I'm his Commander* – turned to the massive open windows, and climbed out on to the sill.

So I found myself a real man at last.

Laura was two hundred and twenty-seven storeys above street level. The purple sky was edged with silver: the moon shrouded behind impenetrable cloud.

Too bad I'm not a real woman.

She grabbed hold of a skeletal head carved in the wall, and pulled herself upwards. Using other carvings – here of a Zurinese komodo, there a Balkran carnivulcan next to a ghouleagle – she climbed steadily, naked in the night.

Great stone demonic heads, part of Darksan Tower's massive superstructure, stared at her with dark-green eyes bigger than cars. They followed Laura's ascent to the next, narrower level.

Finally she reached the roof which ringed the final, tall spire rearing into the night.

Laura sat down, her nude buttocks pressed against the root of one of the four great demons' necks. She stared into the night, seeing nothing beyond the depths of her own stupidity.

A dark-grey cat padded up towards her.

'Hey,' Laura murmured.

The cat's eyes glowed scarlet.

'Will you sit with me for a while?' she added.

Silence, then:

+Yes, I will.+

The cat sat next to her, blinking its shining scarlet eyes.

Across the human- and wraith-built canyon that was the street, Laura's dark-adapted sight focused on the opposing towers, and the narrow spars of stone that linked them: channels for necrotonic cabling as well as phone lines.

No person could traverse within the spars – the internal spaces were too narrow – but wraiths could, and did, flow along the wires from building to building as required. And, externally, if they chose to risk the turbulent winds that battered the heights, other creatures might walk (or occasionally slither) atop the stone spars, crossing the spaces and the vast drop below.

Now, on other rooftops, pairs of scarlet eyes blinked, feline and knowing, at Laura's appearance, sitting nude at the base of Darksan Tower's spire, staring into the night.

The night to which she belonged.

Donal slipped back into wakefulness. He padded into the bathroom, drank musty water from the tap, then left it running. A second glass, after a few minutes, tasted fresher.

No sign of Laura.

He went back to the small stack of cardboard boxes, searched inside, and pulled out his old jump-rope. The cord was black and slick and shiny with age: a narrow length of manticora gut, well-worn.

Dressed only in his shorts, Donal slowly skipped, beginning with the simple two-footed jump, then alternating feet. He interspersed the steady aerobic rhythm with bursts of high-speed footwork. Mal O'Brian, his old boxing coach, would have been proud.

It was half an hour later, with Donal just about to finish up, when Laura walked into the bedroom, fully clothed. She was wearing one of her severe skirt-suits, this one navy-blue, along with high-heeled shoes of the same colour. Her iridescent lipstick matched the shade.

'I see you're fit enough,' she said.

'Fit for anything' – Donal whipped the rope around himself fast, spectacularly, then tossed it on to the bed – 'you'd care to attempt with me.'

'Excuse me?'

'I feel much better now.'

'No.'

Donal let out a long breath.

'I'm ...'

No. He would not apologize.

Do you feel the—?

All the bloody time.

Donal wanted to tell her that he loved her, even as the rational part of his mind yelled that it was a hangover from ensorcelment, a rewiring of his basic animal drives.

'We don't need to talk about it.'

'No,' he said.

They stared at each other.

Do—?

And swallowed.

Laura unbuttoned her jacket and blouse, took hold of his right hand, and cupped it against the black lace of her bra, cupping her left breast, covering her heart. 'Do you feel the black pump ... slithering ... inside me?'

'Yeah.' Donal closed his eyes and shivered. 'Yeah, I feel it.'

'Oh, Thanatos.'

They pulled each other to a unifying embrace, as though every cell in their bodies was sucked towards the joint organism they formed together, as though they could be one single being, filled with the joy of lust and love, sweaty and salty mingling fluids, and then he was pulling off her clothes and his shorts were off and yet there was a gentleness here, not the rapid urgency of last night.

And it was deeper and far more satisfying as they cried aloud and laughed as they came together: once, twice, and a third time. They lay back naked atop the tossed silver sheets and laughed again, soft and satisfied.

'Well,' said Laura. 'I guess we've done it now.'

'I guess we have. You're seducing a minion, and I'm—'

'—involved with a non-person, at least by Senator Blanz's criteria.'

'Fat lot that bastard knows.'

They stared at each other.

109

'Is it always going to be like this?' Laura said.

Donal shook his head. 'I don't know anything.'

'Me either.'

He could guess at the origin of the desire sweeping through him. But why would Laura feel that attraction to him?

I don't know.

But he knew that she *did* feel it, that was the thing.

Donal propped himself up on one elbow and looked down at her, tracking his fingertips along her cool and flawless skin. Her icy darkish nipples peaked and crinkled at his touch.

'Ah ... You like? So why are you on the senator's case, Laura? Why is Blanz your enemy?'

'Besides the obvious? I didn't say he was my enemy.' Laura's lips curved, and she raised her head up to kiss him, then lay back. 'Of course he *is* ... I just didn't say so. He's the enemy of all my kind, mine and Xalia's.'

'Xalia's a smartwraith. That's hardly in the same category as you—'

'You think she's less than human, then?'

'No I bloody don't. How can you ask that?'

Laura shook her head, her blonde hair swirling across the silvery satin pillows. 'Sorry, I'm still not used to ... The world's not supposed to change in an instant.'

'Yeah, but it can.'

And had she known this would happen? Had she planned it?

I don't care.

'Right.' Laura rolled herself up to a sitting position, and checked the angular needle-hands twisting into position on the bedside cabinet, indicating the time: 11:07. 'Death, do you have any idea how late we are?'

'Yeah ... We'd better travel to HQ separately.'

'No.'

'Or you can drop me off maybe five blocks away, somewhere discreet. I can pick up some take-out coffees which have to be better than the muck that Viktor makes.'

'I don't think so.'

'You can't like Viktor's coffee. Tell me you don't.'

'I've never tasted it,' said Laura. 'Never felt the need. And I don't feel the need to disown you either, my hot lover.'

She touched her fingertips against his chest, and for a moment a hint of steam played around her fingertips and evaporated.

110

'Er ... I don't hurt you, do I?' Donal realized consciously for the first time how different his body temperature was from hers. 'I mean, my skin doesn't burn you, does it?'

'Oh, yeah, my fine lover. But not in a bad way.'

'You said' – Donal responded to her kisses, blood leaping back into his tumescence – 'we're late for work, remember?'

'Mmm. Lucky I'm the boss.'

They slid together, forming one being once more.

'Lucky, lucky ...'

And they headed for the nova-burst that awaited them.

Laura drove the Vixen, which seemed ideally suited to her. Even the crescent-shaped steering-wheel was fitted to her exactly, as if she could wheel the car through massive turns with the tiniest fingertip pressure.

They slid through the half-busy streets, enjoying the respite from peak-hour traffic. Only near Police HQ did the cars grow packed together, and then Laura used her Vixen's black-strobe light – bands of shadow flitting across the street as the siren moaned – and pedestrians retreated as Laura edged one tyre up on to the sidewalk and drove along the edge of the street.

At the cross-junction the lights were red, but the drivers had seen the strobe and everyone pulled to a halt as Laura's car streamed through.

'I want you to take the Diva Trail,' she said, hauling the car into a right turn across three lanes of traffic, ignoring the horns. 'All right?'

Steel doors, carved with dragons' heads, slid apart to either side at the Vixen's approach – moving improbably fast for such massive constructs.

'That's like, what, some kind of cross-country hiking route?' Donal forced his hands to relax – he'd been about to tense them into fists – as they swung past carved stone pillars that bore brooding stylized eagles' heads. 'Or what?'

'If the trail takes you across country, then that's what it does.' The tyres screeched and howled as Laura pulled the Vixen through another tight fast turn, startling a uniformed chauffeur who was starting up his big armoured limo. 'But I was thinking of paper trails, the boring unglamorous kind.'

'What about the Diva?' Donal was amazed there was no pain left when he said her name, or rather her title. Donal was only now realizing: he hadn't known Maria daLivnova at all.

And how little that mattered now.

'Malfax Cortindo,' Laura said, slowing the car at last, wheeling past bronze pillars and descending a long, red metal ramp that led into a bowl-shaped parking area.

The parking slots were arranged radially as tear-shaped depressions in the floor, like a potter's marks in clay; and three of them were occupied with rich-looking empty cars.

'You'll need the paper trail there. See why Alderman Finross was so keen to send you to him in the first place.'

'You don't want me to talk to Finross.'

'Not yet, Donal. Let's not reveal our thinking at this stage. The bastard probably thinks he's got away with everything ... and I'm not even sure what he *is* guilty of. I think he might have brokered a deal ... I don't know.'

'Cortindo was a middleman.' The Vixen rolled to a halt, and Donal closed his eyes and let out a gentle breath, then opened his eyes again. 'But that doesn't rule out your theory on Finross ... One man brokering a deal with another broker. Two layers of indirection between the crime and whoever paid for it to happen.'

'Hmm. Like I said, that's your job, lover.' Laura leaned over to kiss him, then winked and pushed open the door and stepped out with one foot. 'Come on Lieutenant, we're not hanging around here.'

Donal gave a crooked half-smile and exited. As he stood on the hard parking garage floor, the door pulled itself from his grasp and swung itself shut. It locked with a loud click.

'Er ...' He hadn't realized the Vixen was wraith-enabled.

'Don't worry about it. She's quite tame.' Laura patted the already-shut driver's door. 'Aren't you, dear sis?'

'What?'

Laura shrugged. 'A story for another time ... But we're only half-sisters, so it's not as strange as you might imagine.'

Thanatos.

Life really had taken a sudden swerving turn for Donal. But there were richly suited men – dressed in dark business suits – accompanied by overdressed wives heading for a trio of silver limousines. Donal kept his thoughts to himself as he and Laura walked past.

'We're not in HQ yet,' he said instead, staring up at the curved red-brown ceiling with bas-relief designs of what looked like smiling parrots. 'Which building is this? The Redburn Centre?'

'Yeah, you got it. The Five Circles is two hundred floors up, if you

112

want to eat dinner with senators and aldermen and similar fauna from the fishtank of local politics.'

'Nice description. I don't think they'd let me in.' Donal walked alongside Laura, shoulder close to her but not holding hands. 'Not with my suits and ties.'

'You're probably more welcome in there than I am. And I'd be happy to take you there once for the experience, you know?'

In his mind's eye, Dona imagined some portly maître d' attempting to stop Laura from entering his restaurant, and her iron reply: 'What's the matter, haven't you ever served a zombie before?'

But that was in Donal's imagination, as they walked past the entrance to the upper levels, and continued along the silver-and-white tunnel whose name signs proclaimed it to be Deepway Fast 17. Secondary notices bore a list of buildings it linked to, including Police HQ.

There were shops and small eateries, but the prices behind the counter were enough to make Donal wince.

'I guess I'm moving in new circles now.'

'Huh.' Laura shook her head. 'Not much of a social circle, hooking up with me.'

'Is that what we've done? Hooked up?'

They walked on in silence, with Donal wanting to hold hands but knowing he should not – Laura was a senior officer and he was on her team and that was it.

At the subterranean silver-grey metallic entranceway to HQ they stopped. An open-mouthed wolf formed the design, some thirty feet high, the upper fangs raised above their heads and the long tongue forming a ramp.

Donal nodded to the real deathwolves stationed on either side.

'Hey.' He moved slowly, pulling out his wallet and flipping it open to reveal his badge. 'Riordan.'

'Don't know ... you.' The deathwolf on Donal's left raised its head and focused its amber eyes on his face. 'Lieuten-ant.'

'FenSeven is my friend.' Donal held up his hand, and allowed any microscopic residual scent to waft into the warm air. 'Can you tell?'

'Ah. Yes-s-s.'

The other deathwolf was already staring at Laura. She looked back at it, as if in silent exchange. Then the deathwolf growled, ducked its head, and padded away inside the building. When it came back, two more deathwolves accompanied it.

'This is Donal.' Laura nodded towards Donal, then to each deathwolf in turn. 'He's my—'

'Mate.' The biggest wolf, old and silver grey, pulled back its – her – upper lip in a lupine laugh. 'We know.'

Then the pack parted, two to each side, and watched as Donal and Laura entered the building. It was oddly ceremonial.

He dared not look at Laura.

Seconds later, they were ascending in a lift shaft – not Gertie's – headed for another day at the office.

There was an odd thrill – except that it seemed not so strange, given the sudden shifts in his life – but Donal felt that familiar start-of-term sensation, that feeling of entering another year, another adventure. They walked through the team room together, heading for Laura's office.

Viktor was seated at a desk, his fingers encased in wire claw-gloves as he wrestled with a compositor framework, like a three-D abacus, harder to use than a typewriter. A pale woman Donal did not know appeared, her eyes serious.

'Alexa,' said Laura. 'I want to introduce you to—'

'It's Sushana,' the woman, Alexa, said. 'No one's seen her for thirteen days. Last night, she was supposed to be with her cousin, and never turned up.'

'Shit.' Laura looked away. 'Shit.'

'We're backtracking, as quietly as possible, but you know how hard it is.'

Donal looked from one to the other. 'What was she doing?'

'Undercover sorcerer,' said Alexa. Then, when Laura did not intervene to prevent further explanation: 'It was a mixed coven, thirty-seven acolytes, meeting over a used tyre garage uptown. Rumours were that Sally C, aka Sally the Claw, funded the place.'

'The coven or the garage?'

'Both. You know of Sally?'

'I met his brother Al once. Al Clausewitz.'

Alexa blinked slowly. 'I didn't know Sally had a brother.'

Donal waited a beat.

'He doesn't,' he said. 'Not anymore.'

Laura's cold lips tightened in a smile. 'You're the right man for the job, I think.'

'Tracking down this Sushana?'

'What about Harald?' said Alexa. 'If he gets his network looking for Sushana, she'll turn up. One way or the ... other.'

'Look, she's undercover,' said Laura. 'Once Harald's tame pimps and fortune tellers start spreading the word, they'll know we're taking a special interest in Sushana. If they think she's a made woman from Selvikin City, like her cover story says, then no harm done. But if they think she's a snitch ...'

'Or that she's a cop.' Donal shrugged. 'She's dead, either way.'

'The missed meeting is one day old,' said Alexa, 'but it's thirteen days since anyone's seen her.'

Laura said nothing for a moment. Donal knew what he would do, and he'd suggest it if Laura asked.

'Do it,' Laura said then. 'Get everything going that you can. Any hint of someone who knows Sushana, if we don't already know the person, we snatch 'em and sweat 'em.'

Alexa whirled away, back to her desk, and ripped up the phone.

'That's a go,' she said, and slammed the handset down. Then she looked up at Laura and gave a bright girlish smile. 'I had it all arranged, because I *thought* you'd say that.'

'I hate,' murmured Laura, 'being predictable.'

Donal said to Alexa: 'Remind me to introduce you to my pal Levison some time.'

But the humour was a coping mechanism, no more. A missing undercover cop, on the first full day that Donal was on the team ... Luckily he didn't believe in omens.

Do you hear the—?

Oh for Death's sake, not now.

Eleven

The task force sent their contacts, their snitches and sympathizers, their paid informants and the weaklings they threatened, searching the unofficial labyrinths which defined the city. They looked for Sergeant Sushana O'Connor, or rather Sorceress Shara Conrahl who had expressed such an interest in exploring the darker sides of her professed art.

That night, Laura remained in the office, coordinating. Donal's eyes were drooping, and she finally said he ought to go home. There were camp beds he could have used, but that seemed more conspicuous in terms of staying here all night with Laura.

Finally, he gave up and did what she suggested. He descended to ground level, where he chatted with FenSeven for ten minutes until the purple cab arrived.

The streets were empty and it took little time to reach home. His new home.

Darksan Tower's guardians were eight-foot behemoths with single slit eyes, who stood aside to allow Donal entry. An elevator whisked him up to the apartment, where he wandered around its metallic gothic-deco spaces before collapsing into bed.

Dark dreams enveloped him.

Donal woke late, a sign that he was not yet fully recovered. He changed into his old running-suit and took the elevator down to the basement levels. A maintenance worker with grease-stained skin, and two wraiths hovering behind him, showed Donal how to access the deep stairwells that led into the catacombs.

He ran, along routes that were unfamiliar to him, the length of twisting long-abandoned ways. Then he was in a cavernous area where newer family mausoleums, some of polished brass and silver, were ringed with pale amber lanterns. Running on, he finally entered a region that he knew, and grew certain that he was not imagining it.

Something had changed.

Catacombs persisted for centuries or even millennia. If there was a change, it could not be in them. Yet odd whispers began now, falling silent whenever Donal neared a sarcophagus or a mausoleum. It was almost as if—

Don't be insane.

As if the dead had grown afraid of him.

Back at the apartment, Donal's breakfast consisted of cold blacksprout soup and coffee. If this arrangement was going to last longer, he was going to have to see about shopping and cooking. He checked his Magnus load, then dialled down to the concierge and asked him to call a taxi.

'I could get used to this,' Donal muttered after putting down the phone. 'Maybe.'

The elevator which he rode down in was like a giant's bullet, very fast. It stopped at the fifty-ninth floor to take on two passengers, a man in a dark suit with a sine-wave weave, and a woman with ballooning features and too much jewellery, all of it real.

The man wore a monocle. Both he and his wife stared at Donal with superior mild curiosity, as though wondering what sort of new servant had been hired by the management.

When the elevator reached the ground floor, Donal pressed his palm against the elevator's steel wall and murmured: 'Thanks.'

The couple sniffed and frowned, passing through the doors before Donal. But the elevator wall delivered a cold shiver, and Donal knew he had been right: it was a wraith-capsule. He wondered how long the wraith had been in service.

When Donal told the taxi driver where he was going, disappointment descended down the driver's features. Probably he'd figured on a big tip from one of the rich bastards who lived in Darksan Tower; but a hard-faced man headed for Police HQ didn't fit the type.

At the corner of Fifth and Avenue of the Basilisks, the traffic was thick with the post-late-lunch hour crowd, and the taxi slowed to a halt. The driver frowned, thought a moment, then turned and said through the partition: 'Know what, mac? It'll be quicker an' you walk.'

Donal looked at the sidewalks. The driver was unlikely to pick up another paying fare for a while. It was a fair assessment.

'Right,' he said, and counted ten bills from his wallet and handed them through the gap in the partition. 'Keep the change.'

'Really?'

'Yeah.' Donal slid out and slammed the door shut behind him. 'Cos I'm a soft touch, really.'

The sky overhead was a medium purple, with no scanbats in sight. The faintest hint of quicksilver was upon the air, but it wasn't raining yet. Donal pulled up the collar on his overcoat, and walked fast for five blocks, until he reached the familiar tower that was HQ.

'Hey, FenSeven. Met one of your cousins yesterday.'

'Yes-s-s.' Amber eyes glowed. FenSeven pulled back his upper lip, slobbering. 'You are ... mat-ed.'

'Thanatos, does everybody tell everyone everything in this place?'

'Not the ... hu-mans.'

'Well. Good.'

Another two deathwolves rounded the nearest pillar and sat down next to FenSeven.

'Loo-ten-ant Riordan.' FenSeven performed the introductions. 'FenSevenThree. GrimwalTwo.'

Both deathwolves looked young – too young for this assignment.

'Good to meet you both.' Donal tipped his forefinger against his forehead in salute. 'And any daughter of FenSeven has a lot to live up to.'

The smaller wolf, FenSevenThree, ducked her head and gave a low growl of acknowledgement.

'See ... you.' FenSeven nodded to Donal.

'Later, pal.'

Donal climbed the dark steps, passed through to the hall with the purple and white chequered floor, and skirted a bickering group of young-looking scarred whores from the dockside. On the granite desk, Eduardo – his lower body long melded into the granite – waved a hand towards Donal.

'You're wanted upstairs,' Eduardo called out.

'The Commissioner?'

'That's the upstairs I was thinking of.'

One of the whores raised a finger and said: 'Climb upstairs this.' A thin man who might have been her pimp backhanded her across the face. 'Dumb pig, shaddup.'

A uniformed cop kicked the pimp in the side of the knee.

'Hey—'

As Donal turned away, Eduardo called: 'Good to see you back.'

This was from a man turning into granite. Perhaps Donal's experiences with the dead Diva and the hospital could have been worse.

'Thanks, Eduardo. Good to be here.'

From the floor, the pimp called: 'Ooh, Edu-*ar*-do. What a lovely name. Are you man or a statue up in your—Mmmph.'

There was a dull crack, and the whores fell silent, while the pimp uttered a tiny moan.

Donal continued to the elevators without looking back.

Commissioner Vilnar's secretary, the lovely Eyes, turned towards Donal, but continued working. Silvery fibres clamped against her eyes joined her to the switchboard-like console, filled with tiny levers, linking her to the city-wide network of rooftop surveillance mirrors.

Donal had never seen Eyes any other way. It occurred to him that if he passed by her in the street, he would never recognize her.

'The Commissioner will see you straight away, Lieutenant.'

'Is he in a good mood?'

Eyes' fingers paused, hooking the air, as though using imaginary controls to parse meaning from Donal's words. Then, saying nothing, she turned back to her console.

The doors to the Commissioner's office parted.

Do you feel the—?

No. Never.

It seemed to take an age for Donal to pass through the doorway, as if something were dragging at his skin. This was new.

Or I've changed.

Secure sites sometimes used time-distorting hex-fields as one layer of protection. Such fields could slow down intruders long enough for deadlier countermeasures to swing into action, or for the intended targets to make an escape.

But here, inside Police HQ? Were such defences really necessary?

Commissioner Vilnar, fat unlit cigar in hand, pointed towards the black iron visitor's chair.

'Sit.'

'Sir.'

'You're on this task force, Riordan, which I am not bloody happy with, understand?'

'Um ... OK.'

'What's that supposed to mean?'

'I mean I understand now, but I didn't before … Sir, I volunteered.'

'That zombie, what's her name—'

Donal felt his voice drop an octave. 'Commander Steele.'

'—right, she led the squad that broke you out of the cottage, so I couldn't refuse the request. But …' Commissioner Vilnar let the sentence hang there. 'I could have shit-canned you. That possibility is still there.'

'Sir? Am I under internal investigation?'

'No.' Vilnar placed his big pale hands flat on the desktop. 'You called in IS to check out the gun range, which doesn't mean you're clean yourself, but it helps. You still allowed yourself to be ensorcelled in a high-profile assignment that I gave to you right here.'

'Yes. I remember.'

'There are people who weren't happy how that turned out.' Commissioner Vilnar meant important people, high enough in Tristopolitan society to matter. 'Some of them tried to give me a hard time.'

'Oh.'

'Which is why I'm giving you a chance, because I don't like being threatened. By anyone.'

A desire to smile tugged at the muscles around Donal's mouth. Underneath it all, the old man had this kind of iron strength. That was what Donal admired about him.

'If anything strange crops up in your investigation,' Vilnar continued, 'anything that might affect the security of our city' – he meant the safety of his own career – 'you'll let me know here, in private, as soon as you can.'

'Right, sir. I'll use my judgement on that.'

'OK, you can go, Riordan.' Vilnar raised his scarcely-existent eyebrows. 'I gather there's some kind of commotion going on at present. Hammersen's network is causing waves.'

'There's an officer missing.'

'Right. Sushana something? But the street networks are shaking' – Vilnar gestured with a fat hand at his office – 'from what I can gather up here.'

'I don't know anything about Hammersen's snitches,' said Donal. 'Only that he has them.'

Harald Hammersen sounded like the most impressive of the team members that Donal had yet to meet. An ex-Marine with the most widespread network of underworld contacts that any working police officer had come across: that was Harald's reputation.

'It would be interesting,' said Vilnar, 'to learn more about that.'

'Yes,' muttered Donal, getting up from the chair. 'I suppose it would.'

And if Vilnar thought that Donal was going to hand over any details he might learn about another cop's private network, then Vilnar was insane. After a moment, a tiny glimmer appeared in Vilnar's eyes: it might have been anger or amusement.

'Go,' said Vilnar. 'And keep in touch.'

'Yes, sir.'

He went out, passing Eyes who was bent over her console, fingers flickering across the tiny levers. Just as well: if Donal had said anything, it might be a bad decision.

You want me to spy on Laura?

Donal really didn't think so.

In Gertie's elevator, Donal muttered: 'Take me to the gun range, will you.'

What's the matter, lover? Need to pull your trigger desperately?

'Just do it, Gertie.'

Well.

She dropped him fast down the shaft. At the subterranean level of the range, she dragged him to a bouncing halt.

Go play with your bangs.

The invisible hands that expelled him into the lobby were rougher than usual.

While Donal was blowing targets apart on the range, an army of informants was working the labyrinthine byways of the less-than-legitimate world. The people involved ranged from fruit stall owners in Mixnatine Market close to the docks, who turned a blind eye to the odd carton that slipped away from the delivery lorries belonging to the large chain stores, to a bent enforcer working for Sally the Claw.

This enforcer had been caught to rights by Harald Hammersen three years before, with photographs taken by city technicians. Harald sent him back to work in Sally C's organization with the understanding that spying on his own boss was preferable to the official Tristopolitan execution pit, where wraiths with ravening, insane minds manifested hard talons and claws and beaks to satiate their hunger on the living.

'Dropping the hammer' was what Harald threatened as the last resort. He looked pale and thin, with dead white hair and strange eyes, and there was a rumour that he had once eaten an informant's eyes, when said snitch failed to notify Harald of an arms shipment arriving at Buldown Docks inside crates of herring.

Whether the stories were true or not, Harald made tactical use of their implied threat. That was one of the reasons that Brijak Nelsan, a hard-faced stevedore with hooks for hands, was willing to share a bottle of vodka with Harald, in the untidy 'office' space at the rear of his warehouse. Nets strung across old boxes formed a kind of swing in which Harald sat, watching Brijak's face grow redder as he drank.

'You?' Brijak offered the vodka bottle.

'No. You finish it.'

'Ha.'

'So what have you heard?'

'Nothin'.'

'Brijak ...'

'Nothin' about why there's a bonded warehouse in North Dock that's going to be empty tomorrow night. I mean, no guards at all.'

'A robbery?' Harald was disappointed. Sushana was missing and he was learning about a stolen shipment of cigarettes or booze.

'Dunno. Maybe a transport.'

Harald ran his fingers through his white hair. He had the skin of an eighteen year old and the hair of a grandfather, but he was neither. His hands were slender but iron-hard.

'Tell me about it,' he said.

'The transport? You wanna get on a ship to, I dunno, Zurinam, how would you go about it?'

'You mean, other than buy a ticket like a normal person would?'

'Normal?' Brijak smirked. 'Don't know much about what that means.'

'Tell me.'

'Stuff's en route to another dock, just passing through here. Steal something, and eventually someone notices. But add a little extra shipment, who's gonna find out? Specially when you can just fill in some blank paperwork to make it right.'

Harald thought about this. 'You mean, someone's breaking in to put a crate *inside* the warehouse? Not to steal one?'

'What I said, ain't it?'

'Huh.' Harald pulled out his billfold, counted out three blue twenty-

122

sevens, a single three and an eleven, and passed the notes over. 'Interesting story.'

'Was it what you wuz after?'

'No ... But you've done good, all the same.'

'Told ya. Sure you don't want a swig of this rotgut?'

'Some other time.'

Harald went out quietly. Outside, on its stand, his bone-coloured motorcycle stood waiting. Its ceramic duckbill snout was close to the ground, the headlights like angled eyes, the handlebars swept back like twisted horns.

When Harald drew closer, he saw a smear of bright red across the bill.

'What's happened?'

Something faint glimmered inside the headlights. Harald crouched down, breathing in the dockland scent, and then he saw it: the faint trace of blood, dark upon dark. Two hundred yards away, two figures, bulky in shapeless clothes, were helping each other to limp away as fast as their broken limbs could manage.

'I don't like thieves much myself—'

The headlights flared amber, then dimmed.

'—but I'm glad you didn't kill them.'

Harald swung his leg over the saddle.

'You ready?' He took hold of the raised handlebars, which reconfigured themselves as he gripped, bringing his hands lower. 'Cos I am.'

The bike growled into life.

'I need to talk to you,' said Donal, waving at Laura. 'If ... that's all right.'

Viktor and Alexa looked up from their desks. Whether they sensed something was happening between him and Laura, Donal had no idea.

'Can it wait?' Laura was standing over a purpleprint of some building.

'I've just been chatting with Commissioner Vilnar.'

'So did you shoot the old bastard?' Alexa's tiny nostrils flared. 'I smell smoke and cordite.' She licked her lips. 'Yummy.'

Donal looked at her for a moment, then turned and followed Laura into her office. The door swung shut behind them, deadening the sound from outside.

'Thanatos,' Donal said. 'Am I the only normal one around here?'

For a moment, Laura's face was a pale mask. Then she relaxed and half-smiled. 'If you're the most normal person we've got,' she said, 'then Death help all of us.'

Donal looked at the visitor's chair, decided he would remain standing.

'How would you rate me as an undercover operative?' he asked.

'If you're asking could I send you in as Sushana's replacement' – Laura's face was a mask again – 'the answer's no, even *if* I could find a role for you. You're not a sorcerer and she was specifically—'

'That's not what I meant. Vilnar wants me in here so I can spy for him. On you.'

'Oh.' Laura blew out a cold breath, steaming faintly in the warm room. 'That makes life interesting.'

'Yeah. I don't suppose Eyes is a spy *you've* planted on *him*?'

'I wish. That cold bitch is a mystery to me.' Laura's breath steamed again, and she saw Donal looking at the dissipating vapour. She half-grinned, half-looked about to cry. 'Shit. I'm just so funny. What do you see in me?'

'The most amazing person,' said Donal, 'that I've ever met. Or just about, anyway.'

'Hey.' Laura blinked. 'What do you mean, just about?'

'I had quite a crush on Sister Mary-Anne Styx, back in the orphanage. Everyone else thought she was a hard bitch.'

'Oh.' Laura looked at her desk, as if its blank surface had become interesting. 'Guess I can't compete there, then.'

But there was more to it than that. If Donal had known the words, he would have asked Laura about the traumatic transition into paralife ... but not here, and not now. Not in the office.

Instead, he told her: 'I'm going to do what you said, and follow the trail. If Vilnar's dirty, there'll be a link between him and Alderman Kinley Finross somewhere in the Archives. All I've got to do is wade through several lifetimes of boring shit to look for the shining nugget, right?'

'Right.'

'And—'

Donal threw his fear aside. Life, and paralife, were too short for nervousness or complexity.

'—I love you, Laura, in case you didn't know.'

Laura's mouth opened in surprise.

Death. I didn't mean to say that.

He blinked, not knowing what had come over him.

Do you hear the—?

Not now.

Donal turned and banged into the door, moving fast enough to take it by surprise. It recovered with a jolt and swung open, letting Donal into the office, where Viktor and Alexa were staring at him.

The door shut behind Donal, and he passed through the office, heading for the elevators. He was almost there when a handclap sounded back inside, along with laughter, and Alexa called: 'Way to go, Riordan!'

The muscles of Donal's face tightened in what might have been a grin as he stepped into the shaft and began to freefall. For perhaps twelve seconds he dropped, heart thumping as he screwed down his fear and refused to yell, and then invisible hands surrounded him and slowed his descent.

Where you going, darlin'?

'All the way, Gertie. The Archives.'

Then I'll forgive you. Maybe.

She continued to lower him, under control, inside the two-thousand-foot shaft.

You got a real hankering for dead things, don't you, lover?

Strong feelings roiled in Donal, preventing his reply.

Twelve

Vaults filled with obsidian sheets of runic transcriptions floating among the racks, vibrating against their tethers; strange half-physical, half-discorporated bird-forms who cried out and wept as they recited the recorded conversations of long-dead men in the exact tone of voice – so the Archivists claimed – of the original speakers.

There were pits of magma fire where the researcher could chain himself (or herself) and relive the Farseers' visions of distant events, for as long as they could stand the pain. There were sealed-off shafts from which subtle rustling and the occasional inhuman groan emanated, with no explanation provided to the ordinary visitor.

Worst of all were the Vacua, those zones of nothingness that could drive even a federal spellbinder into madness. They promised the wisdom not of fact but of intuition, to any who could withstand the nine-day torture it took to traverse a Zone.

Such was the outer ring of the Archives.

Donal's coat flapped in breezes of alternating cold and hot vapours as he passed along the half-lit colonnade that ran alongside the Junior Archivists' pit. The wizened, grey-skinned forms mostly sat, bent and unmoving, poring over ancient records written on faded skin, some of which was not human.

They all appeared to be working on the same project, but Donal knew better than to stop and ask them what they were about. One of them looked up, his eyeballs crawling with tiny red mites, each giving and receiving the blood of the Archivist's fellows, sharing the stuff among the thirty-seven strong team. Lines of the tiny mites stretched across the desktops, in their endless march among the ancient-looking Junior Archivists.

Just why the Archivists shared their blood, and in such a way, was another mystery closed off to outsiders.

'What the Thanatos are you doing here?'

The voice was harsh and loud, causing Donal to stop and scan to every side, before looking down at the ten-inch stone figure standing near his foot, gesticulating.

'My job,' said Donal, drawing out his Magnus. 'What about you?'

'I'll accept that answer,' said the little homunculus, and then it began to shiver ...

'Hold on.'

...and melt, as it slipped down and soaked into solid rock, and was gone. Donal reholstered his Magnus.

'Nice place you've got here,' he muttered to no one and nothing.

In the distance, there might have been stones falling into dank pools; or perhaps the sound was of laughter, mocking Donal's presumption in entering the Archives.

He continued until he was in a chamber of razor-edged glass sheets, arranged in a haphazard fashion at every possible angle in three dimensions ... and possibly beyond, as occasional twistings occurred at the edge of Donal's vision field, where he glimpsed geometrically impossible arrangements of glass that blurred or became invisible when he tried to stare at them directly.

'Lieutenant Donal Riordan,' he said, 'badge number two-three-omicron-nine, requesting Bone Listener assistance for Archive exploration.'

Around him, huge glass sheets seemed to rearrange themselves, although he could not actually track any motion: it was as if the glass moved without moving.

There was the potential for the new arrangement to slam into existence where Donal stood, carving him into geometric blocks of meat. The Archivists' criteria for acceptance often seemed arbitrary to the outsider, and cops told rumours of investigating officers chopped apart for no reason, except perhaps that the Lattice required fresh bones.

The air shifted – somehow, in some direction not easily perceived – and then vibrated in Donal's ears, with deep harmonics he felt only in his gut.

~~WE REQUIRE THIS KNOWLEDGE: WHY ARE YOU HERE?~~

Donal clenched inside and fought his reaction to the subharmonics, because to show fear was to lose: the orphanage had taught him so.

'To track down a network of corrupt sorcerers and politicians,' Donal said, 'and take the bastards down.'

There was a silence like the false calm of water flowing massively fast but without surface turbulence to reveal its power. Beneath, there was the sense of dark beings carrying out portentous unheard conversations. Donal's safety meant nothing here.

Laura had expected him to follow the paper trail, not the bone trail, but the real information was held in the Lattice. It always had been. There was every reason to suppose it always would be.

~~THE DIVA'S KILLERS?~~

'Yes. Among other things.'

~~DO THEY NOT SING, THE BONES?~~

Were the subharmonics mocking or sympathetic? Donal could not tell. Those words disturbed him, yet he had half-expected them, in this place.

'If you say so.'

~~WE TASTE THEM ON YOU STILL.~~

'Piss off.'

The sound that echoed among the glass sheets now *was* laughter, but not from any human throat. Donal felt the blood draining from his face, from the skin of his torso.

'Are you going to fuckin' help, or what?'

Now the sound that washed around him was a torrent of strange whisperings, layer upon layer of them, building up a thunder that drowned even the blood rush in Donal's ears.

Then:

~~YES.~~

A pale white light floated in the air at head height. It shifted shape: first a tiny winged human, then a kind of wriggling featureless white caterpillar, then a convoluted tangle of finger-thick cords, like some form of living knot. Whether it was alive, Donal could not tell.

As he focused on the knot and took a step forward, the glowing shape morphed once more, turned itself inside out, then glided through the dank air to Donal and stopped.

It hovered.

'You want me to follow?'

Donal stepped one pace in its direction, and the glowing shape drifted a yard farther. Donal followed again, and the shape began to move steadily, into an arched, darkened tunnel formed of cubic stone blocks that were worn and distorted with the centuries.

Somewhere, something screamed. Donal forced himself to ignore the sound.

There were steps leading downwards, which Donal descended carefully because it would be easy to slip and end up lying there with a broken leg. In this place, there was no certainty of help.

Then there was a series of twisting tunnels, some that were intended to be straight but had warped into irregular configurations, others that deliberately wound back on themselves, and in one place, where a fluid that smelled like blood trickled between the stone blocks, the tunnel was a slanting spiral that corkscrewed downwards.

This was deeper into the Archives than Donal had ever wanted to go. And all the time, the glowing shape led the way, occasionally morphing into bizarre shapes, always to return to the knot-form that perhaps approximated its true shape.

In an area floored with sandy dirt, ringed by openings to seven dark tunnels, the knot stopped its onward motion and twisted in place, hanging there.

'This is as far as you go, right?' said Donal.

The shape gave one final twist, then creased over in the middle as if bowing, and shot off into one of the tunnels and was gone.

'Thank you,' Donal called out after it.

'You're welcome,' said a dry voice behind him.

Thanatos ...

There had been no footstep, no sensed presence, but when Donal span around the woman looked solid enough: tall, pale skin, a bald forehead and lank milk-coloured hair that began halfway back along her scalp and hung to the small of her back.

The woman was lean but her wrists looked thick and strong, her jaw square, her gaze calm but redolent with something more, as if she had looked upon things that Donal could only half-imagine. Those eyes had dark-brown irises that were double the normal diameter, so that only tiny hints of white appeared at the corner of her eyes.

She was a Bone Listener.

'I'm Feoragh Carryn,' she said. 'You can call me Feoragh, Lieutenant.'

'In which case I'm Donal to you.'

Feoragh acknowledged this, inclining her head. Then: 'Do you have a worthwhile search goal? Something worth bothering the Lattice for?'

'I don't know,' said Donal. 'I know nothing of the Lattice, but it's worth a lot to me. The case is ... political ...'

Feoragh frowned.

'... which I don't give a rat's ass about,' Donal continued, 'but it makes it hard to track down the killers. And if I do find the triggermen, the principals are going to be protected by massive layers of indirection.'

'Killers,' murmured Feoragh.

'Including Maria daLivnova, the Diva. They tried to take her bones.'

'Ah.'

When Feoragh blinked, her eyes went momentarily black. Donal shivered.

'Tell me more, Donal. Tell me everything you know.'

Donal related what he remembered. The period before his hospital stay was a little blurry, and the final days in the cottage, before Laura broke in and pulled Donal away from the bones' spell, formed was a traumatic pain buried in his subconscious; but he could remember enough.

There was the meeting with Commissioner Vilnar which had started it all, the newspaper clippings from foreign cities about theatrical celebrities unexpectedly dying. Donal surprised himself by recalling all the names and locations ... or at least, he *thought* he remembered them all.

Then there was the meeting with Malfax Cortindo—

'Oh, yes,' said Donal. 'I nearly forgot. There was a letter from Alderman Kinley Finross, who arranged for me to visit the Energy Authority. He obviously knew Cortindo ...'

Beneath Feoragh's dark and steady gaze, Donal found he was able to recall the letter word for word.

Then he told her of the visit itself. When he talked about picking up the bone and slipping into dreams, Feoragh sucked in a breath. And he told her of Cortindo's snatching the bone from his grasp, dumping him back into the real world after three hours had passed, though it had seemed only a minute.

And finally, voice unsteady, he related the Diva's final performance, the ensorcelled audience, and his flight with the Diva down through the tunnels that led to the Energy Authority.

'That was a mistake.' Donal's chest was heaving now, his skin covered with a slick layer of sweat as though he had been running. 'Because of course Cortindo was behind it.'

He told of the confrontation among the reactor piles, surrounded by ensorcelled workers, and Cortindo giving the order to fire.

'I could ...' Donal's throat felt as if the Diva's ghost were strangling him. 'I hesitated. I could have saved her but I froze for half a second ...'

'Ah.'

'... as if I *wanted* her to die. As if I wanted to touch her bones, caress them. Shit. You know ...'

Do you feel the bones?

Yes.

Always.

Donal stared at the Bone Listener.

'Yes,' murmured Feoragh. 'I do know.'

And Donal realized that she did, that Feoragh Carryn knew exactly what he was talking about.

'Malfax Cortindo,' he said after a moment. 'Thanatos. I didn't check the autopsy report ...'

'I can find out,' said Feoragh. 'Come with me.'

They walked along a sand-floored stone tunnel, and stopped before a plain dark-green door. Feoragh opened it and went inside. There was a simple wooden desk, sealed document boxes on a shelf, and a solitary telephone. Feoragh picked up the phone.

'Padraigh Fasheene,' she said. 'If you would.'

Donal shook his head, smiling at his own preconceptions. He'd been expecting some kind of esoteric device, not a telephone.

Feoragh covered the mouthpiece with one hand. 'Padraigh's my cousin. Works for Mina at the OCML.'

'You mean Wilhelmina d'Alkarny?'

'Who else?'

'That's— Good.' He'd been about to say it was an interesting coincidence, her cousin working at the Office of the Chief Medical Listener, but then he realized that perhaps it was no kind of coincidence at all. What did he know about Bone Listeners?

'Could you ask your cousin,' he said, 'what the—'

Feoragh held up her hand.

'Padraigh ... The autopsy on Malfax Cortindo. Yes, the one from the Energy Authority.'

Donal watched, trying to read something into Feoragh's tense pale features.

'You're sure,' said Feoragh: not quite a question.

Again there was a delay while Donal failed to guess what Feoragh's cousin was saying on the other end of the line.

'Yes? All right ... Could you get her to notify Lieutenant Donal Riordan when it happens? *If* it happens. Fine.' She glanced at Donal with those too-dark eyes. 'Thanks, Padraigh.'

131

She put the handset down.

'Don't tell me,' said Donal. 'They've lost the report.'

'Hardly.' Feoragh shook her head. 'They haven't done the autopsy yet. Cortindo's body is suspended in a stasis hex.'

'But ... That's impossible. I was in the hospital for over a week.' Donal knew there couldn't be that many bodies in the morgue. Not even the lowest priority case could be held back this long. 'What's going on?'

'Nothing.'

'I don't believe—'

'By order of Commissioner Vilnar's office,' said Feoragh in a hard tone, 'absolutely nothing is happening.'

'Oh,' murmured Donal. 'Like that.'

'Exactly like that.'

Donal stared at the blank stone wall, seeing nothing. Vilnar had put him on the Diva assignment originally, but Laura believed that had been because Vilnar was under political pressure.

Could Vilnar really be holding back his own department's investigation?

Except that the task force had federal authorization. It wasn't truly under departmental jurisdiction.

'All right.' Donal was trying to work out whether he could ask Feoragh to circumvent the restriction, to somehow get the OCML to carry out the autopsy anyway. It seemed unlikely. 'What about the information trail? In the Lattice?'

An odd-looking smile pulled at the muscles of Feoragh's face.

'Well that's why you're here, isn't it?'

'Yes ...'

'Then let's go.'

It was impossible to tell how big the Lattice was. Donal followed Feoragh along a convoluted route that led in the end to a long low chamber filled by struts and nodes – the struts of titanium-wrapped bones, the nodes formed of carved bone inlaid with strips of some green-and-black mineral.

The chamber reminded Donal of a wine cellar. It was arranged so that Feoragh, provided she was willing to crawl on hands and knees or to stretch up on tiptoe, was capable of touching every bone node with her bare hands.

But that was only one chamber, one tiny cell among thousands – maybe tens of thousands or more.

They had used a stone bridge to reach this place, and Donal had stopped at the midpoint to look over the edge, down into the shadowed abyss. It plunged down as far as he could see, and the Police Department's medics had always rated Donal's long vision as excellent. There were narrow bridges everywhere, entering the vast subterranean edifice that contained a three-dimensional array of bones many times bigger than the greatest buildings Donal had ever heard of.

Far below, on separate bridges, Donal had made out the figures of three Bone Listeners: two entering the Lattice, one shuffling and bent over, stopping to catch his or her breath partway across the bridge's span. Did they pay a price for working in the way they did?

'I'm ready.'

Feoragh's voice brought Donal back to the moment, to the cold chamber in which they stood. This close to the Lattice, Donal felt as if the air were fractured and his body was brittle. If he turned too quickly he thought his eyes might fall out.

'For the information quest,' Feoragh added. 'You might want to listen to anything I say. Because if I speak it means I'm not retaining what I hear.'

The atmosphere was different from the Energy Authority with its rows of reactor piles. There, a form of chaos had lapped at the edges of Donal's awareness, threatening always to explode; but here in the Lattice cell, it was more as if glass razors filled the air. There was a sharpness, a *density* that scared him.

'We need links,' he forced himself to say, 'between the Diva and Alderman Finross, and between—'

'That much I remember.'

Whether Feoragh was offended, Donal could not tell. She was slipping into some form of trance state, though not a relaxing kind: her limbs twitched, a short-lived rictus jerked several times across her face, and her eyelids fluttered for longer than seemed probable.

Then Feoragh's dark eyes snapped wide open, and she was expressionless as she walked into the midst of the Lattice and reached out towards a node. Her sleeve dropped back and, as she reached, a sharp-edged node cut a thin red arc on her pale skin. Tiny beads of blood glistened as Feoragh's fingertips touched the node.

The blood-drops grew smaller and sank inside the bone, like water into a sponge.

Feoragh's mouth stretched open as she screamed ... except there was no sound. To Donal it seemed that she was howling in agony, but that the sound failed to reach him: something in the air cut the vibration apart and fed on it, absorbing it.

Then Feoragh bowed her head, and Donal thought he saw some dark vibration ripple along the struts, play across nodes, and flow outwards into the greater Lattice.

I'm sorry.

But this was what Feoragh did for a living.

It hurt her, in fact it seemed to be torturing her, but Donal knew that he would ask her again to engage on an information quest if it was important. In fact, it seemed to him that a touch of ruthlessness was required in order to be a successful candidate in the first place: the Bone Listeners did not respond to everyone.

And there were rumours of candidate clients who had entered the depths of the Lattice buildings – if not here, into the core – and simply never returned.

Feoragh shuddered once more.

'Going—'

Her voice reached Donal as if through ocean waves, attenuated and broken.

'—to Ill—'

Strange ripples broke up the air.

'Illurium. That's where—'

Feoragh clamped her mouth shut, and now stood catatonic, un-moving save for the blood which started at her lip and trickled down towards her chin.

'Wake up,' said Donal, changing his mind. 'Whatever it is, I don't need to know this badly.'

But it seemed his decision was too late. Feoragh began to shiver, and her hands sprang off the bone nodes as though she'd been burned. Then, stiff as a two-by-four, Feoragh toppled to the floor.

For a split second Donal thought that he wouldn't be able to react fast enough, but his body had already shifted and the next thing he consciously knew, he was kneeling with Feoragh in his arms. Her head was two inches from the hard flagstone.

He laid her down on the too-cold floor.

'Shit.'

Now what was he supposed to do? Did this happen to Bone Listeners all the time? Or was Feoragh ill? Could something she had discovered inside the Lattice have *made* her ill?

Donal shifted Feoragh into the recovery position, checked that she had not swallowed her own tongue, then got to his feet. There was nothing in the chamber – or cell – that would let him communicate with the outside world: no phone, no alarm button. Nothing.

He went out to the colonnade which led to other cells. No one was there.

'Hello? Can anybody help?'

From the balustrade he leaned over, to stare down into the shadowed abyss crossed by thin stone bridges. Again, no one. He looked up at the undersides of further bridges, but there were no sounds of movement.

'I've a Bone Listener in trouble!' Donal's voice echoed back at him. 'Feoragh Carryn needs your help!'

The shadows were still.

'Thanatos,' he muttered, and went back inside.

But Feoragh was already sitting up on the floor. When she saw Donal she stretched out one hand so that he could help her to her feet.

'It happens sometimes,' Feoragh said before he could ask. 'When the depth of information is too great, when there are thaumaturgical safeguards to navigate, we pay the price.'

'I'm sorry.'

'It has nothing to do with you.'

'Oh.' Donal stared at the bone nodes, the titanium-and-bone struts that supported and linked those nodes.

Do you feel—?

Yes, and I wish I didn't.

'This isn't,' said Donal, 'what I sensed near the reactors. They were dangerous and I knew it. Fragments of agony ...'

'Yes.'

'This is different.'

'We have clear information, incised deeply.' Feoragh paused, then: 'The bones are a medium with vestigial trace of their memories from life. New bones are formatted first, utilized later.'

Donal nodded, only half understanding what she meant.

'Surely it's fuzzy,' he said. 'The information. Unfocused.'

Feoragh shook her head.

'Information etching is a precise process,' she said. 'There's nothing fuzzy about the results. Nothing at all.'

She rubbed her fingers across her forehead in what Donal thought was an unconscious gesture.

'What is the process?' he asked her. 'The etching ... How does it work, or are you not allowed to say?'

Feoragh stared at him for an extended moment. Then: 'Suffering,' she said. 'That's where the focus comes from.'

Donal had no idea how to respond to that.

Thirteen

The information quest did more than disturb Donal. Bloodied, Feoragh seemed matter-of-fact about what it took to be a Bone Listener; and she had uncovered some positive results.

She told Donal as much as she'd been able to discover about the people-behind-the-people-behind-the-people involved in the Diva's and the other performers' deaths. There were 'unfulfilled links' – as she described them – to Zurinam and other countries.

Feoragh recited a short list which Donal memorized.

'But the clearest trail,' Feoragh said, 'leads to Silvex City. Councillor Gelbthorne is the name you need. I rate him at ninety-three per cent likelihood of belonging to the same group as Cortindo.'

'Silvex City? That's in—'

'Illurium, yes. And one of your colleagues is Illurian. Though she has no meaningful contacts that I can discover, she should be able to brief you on what life is like in Silvex City, when you decide to go there.'

Donal scarcely noticed the 'when' rather than 'if'. The colleague that Feoragh referred to was Xalia, and quite what a wraith could tell Donal about surviving in the city, he was not sure.

'Senator Blanz has been dealing with someone in Silvex City,' Feoragh added. 'I can't track down the name. I'm sure that Malfax Cortindo knows it.'

This made a kind of sense.

'Cortindo's dead,' he said. 'But why is his body still in stasis?'

'I didn't pursue that question,' Feoragh answered. 'There's no point in looking inside the Lattice for information that fresh.'

'Shit.'

Donal needed to get an autopsy scheduled. Perhaps Laura's influence ... but even she couldn't move openly against Commissioner Vilnar. And if Vilnar really was dirty, and suspected that Laura's task force was investigating him, he would have the power to shut them down, provided he resorted to dirty tricks.

And Donal thought that Vilnar, if he were fighting for his own survival, would have little hesitation in pulling out every nasty tactic he knew, from discrediting Laura or her officers to having them arrested or worse.

There were many bad things that could happen to a police officer whose own superiors had turned against him ... or her.

'Talk to Padraigh,' Feoragh said. 'Tell him I sent you.'

'All right.'

'That's not a promise that he'll be able to help you.'

'I understand. Thanks. And thank you for—' Donal gestured towards the cell. 'You know.'

Feoragh bowed her head. 'What else could I do?'

'I don't know. But thank you anyway.'

Harald was crouched low over his Phantasm Mk IV, travelling at a hundred mph along the overpass. This late at night there was little traffic, though it was still dangerous as he hurtled from the orbit-opening in the thousand-foot skull that overlooked the city's midtown.

He accelerated, weaving between three freight trucks and their loads of scared-looking lizards in their crates, destined for the foodmarkets. The Phantasm's handlebars had already morphed to their lowest configuration, and the engine growled, certain in the knowledge that there was more power to give should Harald need it.

Then there was a spiralling down-ramp and Harald took it at speed, feeling the bike's joy as he banked through the continuous turn, through some thousand degrees of spiralling curve, until he was on the level and shooting forward between two vast supporting pillars, screaming through blood-red stop lights as horns honked – even at this hour there were people to be scared by his tactics – then slowed

He followed a zig-zag route through nine city blocks, then turned into the gentle off-ramp that led on to Avenue of the Basilisks. It was the same street but several miles away from Police HQ: the Avenue stretched for over a hundred blocks.

There. He could see the green headlights now.

Brijak, his snitch, had been telling the truth. There had been a bonded warehouse exactly where Brijak had said.

A lone low-slung car had pulled up at the gate. Its driver had got out and talked to the security guards for a couple of minutes, before getting inside the car and driving off. The driver had been wearing a dark suit, and he had scanned the streets – security conscious – before walking over to the guards' booth.

But there was no way he had spotted Harald, on his silent bike parked in deepest shadow.

When the car moved off, Harald had waited nearly two minutes before setting the Stealth switch and turning the engine into mumbling life, and moving slowly in the correct direction. There was only one sensible direction for someone leaving the warehouse district.

Harald didn't open the engine up to normal power until he was on the Expressway. Red strontium-vapour streetlights turned the highway into a glistening blood-river as Harald gunned the Phantasm, bringing the car into sight.

He remembered the way that the driver had checked the surroundings. Damn it. Because as Harald followed along the high expressway, the bastard had to have spotted the Phantasm trailing him.

When the car took the off-road that ended five miles later at the Avenue of the Basilisks, Harald had taken the penultimate exit, the spiralling ramp that rush-hour drivers crawled down carefully in their complaining cars. For a minute, he would be out of sight of the car's rearview mirrors.

Now, Harald manipulated switches and spoke the keywords that he preferred not to use: they made the Phantasm uncomfortable. It stretched out, wheels rotating as it elongated its chassis in preparation, then it hunched back and raised its handlebars into a vertical attitude.

A shivering change washed over its bone-pale skin. The fairings broadened and darkened towards green. It no longer looked like a Phantasm.

To a bike enthusiast its outline was closest to a Maleville Seven, a low-performance classic. It was the best the bike could do, for disguise.

Up ahead, a car swung into view. Green headlights, a cautious driving style: yes, that was the bastard.

'Let's go.' Harald laid his hand flat on the fuel tank. 'And thank you.'

The first stop was at the rear of a garment store which should have been deserted at this hour. In the alleyway round back, the car stopped.

The driver got out and crossed to a metal door, and spoke a password that Harald failed to lip-read. Silver sparks flickered across the metal as a hex-field dissipated. The man opened the door and went inside.

Harald left the bike: it was gently thrumming in Stealth mode and fully armed should anyone touch it in Harald's absence.

On foot, Harald went down the alleyway, keeping to the edges as it opened out to a yard paved in black oily gravel. Despite the footing, Harald moved with scarcely a sound. At the lighted, barred window, he peeked inside.

Two short men with square jaws and massive shoulders and arms were shifting a coffin-sized container into position on a table. The man in the suit was standing in an internal doorway, only partly in Harald's line of sight.

They said something more, then the dark suit disappeared from the doorway and Harald realized the meeting was already over. He moved fast, disappearing into the narrower alley just as the metal door banged open.

'—course it's light when it's empty,' a rough voice was saying. 'Obvious, innit?'

'Then you won't have any problem being there.' This man's voice had a trace of an accent. 'Will you?'

'Er ... No, boss.'

Harald waited in case they might say something obvious, like a place or time. If they did, he would have to evaluate whether it was the truth or a fabrication – the latter would mean they'd spotted him.

But there were no further words as footsteps scrunched across gravel, the car door opened and slammed shut almost in time with the building's metal door, and Harald was already moving. Beneath the car engine's sound, he could hear the deeper rumble as the bike switched itself out of Stealth mode in readiness for the chase.

'Well done.'

By the time the car pulled out on to the Avenue of the Basilisks, Harald was already riding the still-altered bike in its Maleville form, following from in front. The car overtook him but not at high speed, because this was close enough to Police HQ, and the driver would not want to be stopped. Not tonight.

Then the car pulled off to the right, into Kilbury Circle, and Harald had to think fast, taking the bike into Melville Square and cutting down a small alley, knowing that he could no longer afford to be spotted. He'd thought the car would have overtaken him, but this was the way life turned out: there was no use worrying about it.

There.

Harald caught a glimpse of the target car, saw the wash of its lime-tinged headlight beams play across a dustbin – they were into a residential area, five-storey town houses from the turn of the millennium replacing the huge towers – and he turned the bike to follow.

'I think you can relax,' he shouted above the slipstream, and squeezed inwards with his knees.

There was a warmth against his inner legs: a signal of gratitude as the bike began to morph itself back into default shape.

It lengthened and lowered its configuration, paling back to the colour of dried bone.

Harald lay forward, close against the armoured fuel tank, and the Phantasm growled its delight as its natural form returned. It banked over as Harald directed the hard-accelerating turn, and they arced into Pallas Heptagon.

Slowing now, the car had already passed along two sides of the heptagonal central park. On the other side of the road, although it was late, lights were burning in many of the grand old buildings. Outside two of them, soldiers in unfamiliar uniforms stood on guard duty.

This was the diplomatic district, where embassies and consulates had stood for centuries.

The bike switched its lights off and slowed simultaneously with Harald's decision to do just that: it was no longer clear which of them was the rider and which the vehicle. Sometimes they acted together like a single being.

Coasting to a silent stop, the bike-and-Harald reflexively chose the darkest spot. A large parked limousine with obsidian windows and flared fins helped obscure them. They quietly observed the target car slowing and then halting before armoured gates that let into a yard beside one of the older and more luxurious embassies.

A white-helmeted guard came out of a sentry box, looked in at the car's driver and nodded. At the same time the armoured gate slid to one side on impressively quiet rollers – Harald assumed that diplomats liked to sleep soundly – to reveal a darkened yard.

The car slid forward, entered the yard, and disappeared from sight as the gate rolled across and clicked into place. Pallas Heptagon was still once more.

Harald squeezed his knees and the bike slipped into Stealth without his having to use the controls. Then it rolled backwards until they had reached the next corner of the heptagon, before spinning around and taking them out of there, heading for the nearest police phone.

It was the early hours of the morning, but there was at least one person that Harald knew would not be asleep. Every member of the team had Laura's home phone number, and the Police HQ switchboard had it set up as if it were an internal extension.

Harald wondered what he was going to say.

Sushana was missing, that was the thing. Was any of this going to help? A bonded warehouse, a covert shipment ... It might be nothing to do with Sushana's disappearance.

There was an all-night convenience store on the corner. Here the houses were dark and crumbling. Harald stopped and parked the Phantasm.

'I'll just be a moment.'

The engine purred.

Inside the store, Harald nodded to the owner, who was a tall man with pale-brown skin and three purple scars along his left cheek.

'Have you got any maps?' Harald asked. 'Local maps?'

'Yes, I think we have—' The man started to point, then his gaze flickered towards the street outside. 'Is that your bike?'

'Uh-huh.'

'Please, shall I call the police? I think a man is trying to steal it.'

Harald felt himself relax, listening.

'Everything's fine,' he told the store-owner.

'But he is going to take your motorcycle!'

Flicking through the maps, Harald found the one he wanted. He pulled it open, checked the index, and turned to the Tristopolitan Midtown section and found the page that showed Pallas Heptagon. As he'd hoped, the embassy names were marked.

The man he'd followed had entered the Illurian embassy.

'Please sir, I'm thinking I should really call the—'

A scream echoed from the street.

'No need to panic,' said Harald.

There was no need for the switchboard to patch Harald through to Laura's home. She was in the office, as was Donal. He'd found a small cot to sleep on, from among the four set up in the supply room at the end of the corridor.

Viktor and Alexa were in the squad room, bruised arcs beneath their eyes, showing the strain. Waiting was worse than being on the streets.

After a while, Viktor pulled on his leather coat and said he had to get out. Alexa, staring into space, scarcely acknowledged the words.

When the phone rang, Donal was standing in Laura's office while she sat, flicking through the same reports she'd already read twenty times. Donal felt sweaty and unclean, his shirt rumpled and his suit in need of a steam-clean, his tie half-undone.

Laura picked up the handset.

'Harald? You've found something?'

There was a pause.

'Sounds thin,' she said then. 'Sounds like you were following a different kind of lead – no, I don't blame you: a bonded warehouse job is big news. Coincidence?'

Laura listened some more, then glanced up at Donal.

'We might be in luck,' she said into the phone. 'Let me talk to Donal a moment. Just so you know, Donal's uncovered another trail, and it also pointed to Illurium. To Silvex City.'

Laura covered the mouthpiece with one hand.

'Harald's found a driver from the Illurian Embassy,' she told Donal, 'who's connected with a bonded warehouse job. They're going to insert some container into the warehouse.' She continued with the details that Harald had given her. 'What do you think?'

Donal was used to running his own team. It was good of Laura to recognize that.

'Go with it,' said Donal. 'But don't commit all our resources.'

For a few moments, Laura considered. Into the phone she said: 'Sorry, Harald. Just planning. D'you have any input?'

She listened, eyes hardening.

'Intelligence,' she said then. 'Damn it.'

Donal guessed what they were talking about. 'You want to call in the spooks?' Even to someone used to freewraiths, some of the DIO's operatives were hard to take. 'They'll crawl all over the place and shut us out.'

Laura tapped her desk with her diamond-hard fingernails.

'That's not good enough ... Look, Harald.' She switched her attention from Donal to the phone. 'You know Alf Zentril? From Robbery-Haunting? Good. I'm going to call in a favour. Expect to see his team at your location shortly. If not, we'll send our own people. Got it?'

She listened a bit, then nodded. 'Sounds good. Make sure you're not spotted.' And, after a moment: 'Good luck.'

Laura put the phone down.

'I didn't figure you for a territorial animal,' she said to Donal. 'We've an officer's life at stake, and the Distributed Intelligence Organization has resources we could never—'

'It's not Sushana I'm thinking of,' said Donal. 'Ah ... I don't mean that the way it sounds.'

'You don't?'

'The driver that Harald followed,' Donal said. 'He's not an Illurian agent.'

'Why not?'

'Because if you needed to ship something – or a dead someone – out of the country, and you're a foreign intelligence officer, you'd use the diplomatic bag.'

'Diplomatic bag ...'

'That's just what they call it. The "bag" could be a shipping crate.' He was sure of himself now. 'If it's from an embassy, Customs don't open it.'

'Damn it,' said Laura.

'It's as if the embassy mail room were a bonded warehouse all by itself.'

'All right. I've worked it out. But someone official in the embassy might want to run an operation off the books. I've heard people do that sometimes.'

A tiny smile tugged Donal's mouth. 'That's terrible.'

'Right. Like we'd never do that.'

'Thanatos forbid.' Donal sat himself down in the visitor's chair. 'So what are we going to do, boss?'

'We're going to track down whoever's got Sushana,' said Laura, 'and deal with the fuckers.'

'On or off the books?'

'Either way.'

Harald's network of snitches was huge, but he wasn't the only one with resources. Big Viktor had contacts of his own, and right now he was busy bouncing one of them, hard and repeatedly, against a brick wall.

Still, Franz was refusing to talk. His eyes had widened at the blue-and-white photograph that Viktor had shown him: the photo of Sushana. But Franz had shaken his head, clamping his mouth shut.

This was unusual for Franz. Unfortunately, his reticence guaranteed that Viktor would keep hammering until he got answers.

'How's business?' asked Viktor, using a paper towel to wipe blood off his fist. None of the blood was his own. 'Well enough to miss it when it's gone?'

They were behind Franz's largest gambling joint. In a parlour at the front were stone couches where wraithing addicts slid into trance, their disembodied viewpoints hooking on to wraiths, and following them in their races through channels beneath the city.

Viktor hooked his fingers into Franz's collarbone and pulled downward, tugging at the friable bones and bringing a wince to Franz's face. Then he hammerlocked Franz's arm, and propelled him indoors, through the dingy hallway to the parlour.

No clients lay on the deserted stone couches. Each couch was a single hollowed stone, shipped from upstate Orebury, quarried from the Resonant Caves. In a low-class joint, these were expensive items.

Viktor bared his teeth in something that was nearly a smile. He pushed Franz away from him, then reached inside his leather jacket crossing his arms, and drew out two square-edged Grauser automatics.

He took aim at the nearest couch.

'No.' Franz swallowed. 'Don't you know how much they—?'

Viktor pulled both triggers.

Shards of stone blew in all directions. One sliver cut Viktor's cheek but he ignored it.

'*No,*' Franz whispered.

Viktor swivelled and took aim at couches either side of him, arms spread dramatically: a calculated stance. Intimidation is a skill best learned on the streets.

'All right.' Shoulders slumped, gaze weakening, Franz said: 'The woman ... There was one like her.'

He meant Sushana, from the photograph.

'Tell me.'

'I heard ...' Franz swallowed again. 'She was in the docks, with Tax Silberman's crew. You know them.'

Viktor nodded.

'It was a snifferwraith.' Franz spoke quickly now, as though some internal dam had broken. 'What I heard, anyhow. They scanned her, found she was a plant, and ...'

'What?'

'Either they dumped her straight into the Plax with chains on, or they took her to Sally the Claw and he did it. I ain't sure which version is true, and I didn't try to find out.'

145

There was a rage building up inside Viktor, but now was not the time to release it.

Sushana, my love.

Franz looked up, regaining a little of his composure. 'Was she one of yours?'

'Was ...?'

Then it burst out, a black flood inside that Viktor made no attempt to rein back as his hands raised of their own accord and the twin Grausers thundered loudly, shot after shot crashing through the air as stone couches blew apart into sharp-edged fragments.

Franz was on his hands and knees, crawling back towards his office for safety beneath the maelstrom, then giving up. He crouched on the floor like a face-down foetus, shivering while the world disappeared in the cacophony overhead ...

'*Sushana,*' Viktor whispered.

... and the guns clicked empty, half a second apart, and Viktor's rage dissipated more quickly than it had come, blowing away like smoke in a sudden wind. What remained in Viktor's core was something harder and darker, and as patient as it needed to be.

It would take time to reach Sally the Claw, past all the cut-outs, the lieutenants and footsoldiers; but Viktor would do it. What happened next would be up to Sal, but Sal was not the kind of man to submit to arrest.

Viktor was counting on that.

Donal looked ready to fall over. Alexa had already gone, finally giving in to Laura's order to get some rest. Nothing more was likely to happen tonight, or this morning.

It was already two a.m, and the only thing Laura had achieved since Harald's phone call was to despatch a team from Robbery-Haunting to act as Harald's surveillance team.

Now she told Donal: 'You need to go home.'

'What about you?' He was too tired to argue much, but had no wish to leave her here.

Laura looked around the office, then decided quickly, rolled up two charts from her desk and tucked them under one arm. 'I'll come with you. All I need is a phone, and the switchboard can patch through to the apartment.'

'All right.'

Picking up the phone, Laura waited for the internal operator to come on, then gave her instructions, thanked the wraith, and put the phone down.

'Let's go via the street,' she said. 'I need some air.'

'Me too.' He thought perhaps it was for his benefit, because Laura looked exactly as she always did.

Donal and Laura left together, and descended in the elevator shaft side by side, borne by Gertie who remained silent all the way, giving them only a normal impersonal push to assist their exit from the tube.

At ground level, they passed along the stone halls that became the outer reception, where Eduardo was on perpetual duty, melded into the stone block of the reception desk.

'She'll be all right,' Eduardo said, meaning Sushara. 'I'm sure of it.'

Donal nodded, but Laura shook her head, rejecting the assurance. She was sure – or almost sure – that Sushana was already dead.

Out on the street, the sidewalks were slick with puddles through which fine silver threads swam, glinting orange or crimson where they caught the streetlights' reflections. Donal and Laura walked in silence, until a purple cab appeared and Laura flung her arm out.

'It'll be quicker than retrieving the car,' she said.

'Um ... All right.'

Perhaps she was too tired to drive. Or perhaps it was just that she wanted to be out of contact for minimal time. Donal followed her into the cab, and told the driver to take them to Darksan Tower, fast.

It took only minutes to reach the tower, and draw to a halt outside.

'Good man.'

Laura paid before Donal could move. They got out and passed the entranceway's guardians. Laura's heels clicked on the black-glass floor as they crossed the lobby to the express elevator and ascended straight to the apartment.

At first Donal thought he was too wired to rest, but once inside the bedroom he pulled off his jacket, and sat down on the edge of the bed to pull off his shoes. He felt the lure of the bed and lay back and slipped into relaxation and then he was asleep.

'Very good,' murmured Laura.

She kicked off her shoes, took off her jacket, undid her skirt and let it slip to the floor. Then the blouse went. In her dark lingerie, she stood there for a long moment staring at Donal as he slept.

It was hard for Laura to remember sleep, and dreaming.

Then she walked out into the hallway, and stopped before the dark-grey wall with the fifteen foot mirrors shaped like elongated upside-down shields. Her own reflection was of no interest to Laura.

Clapping her hands softly, she spoke the keywords that activated encrypted spells inside the hidden mechanisms. She stopped, listened – no sound came from the bedroom save the softest of snores – then clapped once more.

This was the quickest way up, faster than ascending the outside of the building – that was something she did only when she needed to feel alive ... or to try recapturing that feeling.

The mirror shifted, then swung back, revealing a narrow portal. It led to a darkened shaft. Inside, a slender ladder formed of struts that might have been bone glimmered with a grey-green luminescence.

Laura stepped through the portal and directly on to the ladder. She grabbed hold with both hands, swung her other foot on to the same rung, and waited. The door swung shut behind her, the concealing mirror once more in place.

After a quick glance down – the ladder disappeared into the black depths – Laura craned her head back, focusing on the faint heptagonal outline high above. She returned her attention to the ladder.

Slowly at first, Laura climbed.

Ten minutes later, she was at the hex-guarded hatch, muttering the keywords that would let her through. In moments, the hatch flared silver and swung itself up and back. A sudden vicious draught caught hold of Laura, but her grip was tight. After a moment she moved, pulled herself up on to the roof, and stepped into the turbulent night.

The hatch swung shut behind her.

Laura was high above the streets now, on the complex gothic-deco spire that rose high above Darksan Tower proper, hundreds of feet above her apartment on the two hundred and twenty-seventh floor. As always, necrotonic cables hung in dark catenary curves, linking her building to the other towers that stood like giant sentinels high above the city streets.

Hunkering down to present a lower profile to the wind – not against the cold, simply against a capricious force that could tug her straight off the roof at any time – Laura watched the night and waited.

Soon, pairs of glowing scarlet eyes were visible amid the darkness, where Laura's enhanced vision could scarcely make out the cables and skywalks. The tiny scarlet beacons moved through darkness, drawing closer.

Laura's cats were coming.

Fourteen

One by one the small shapes slipped across the narrow stone bridges, the hanging cables and the tiny translucent filaments that normally bore only sprites engendered by the splitting-off of insubstantial fragments from large wraith-forms.

Now the cats moved steadily across these narrow byways, their forms undulating as necessary to counteract the chaotic wind-turbulence that swept these high places. Their eyes glowed, powerfully scarlet when a distant reflection caught them.

Once, as a scanbat glided past overhead, two of the cats hunkered down on the skywalk they were traversing, alert to the opportunity to catch new prey; but the bat was past soon enough, and after a moment the cats continued on towards Darksan Tower.

If Sushana was alive, Laura needed to know. She had lost officers before, but not in this team, not during this job. What Laura did for a living – or whatever she should call it now – had always defined her. And now that she had allowed Donal into her life – unlife – the job mattered more than ever.

Not the politics, not the ticking-off of boxes when cases cleared or budgets were secured. The real people.

The first of the cats licked her hand, and settled down beside her to wait.

While Laura thought about the ways she could direct her friends of the night, which buildings they might investigate, which people they might observe unsuspected from the darkness, the cats themselves gathered in a widening circle around her on the rooftop. Behind her rose the skeletal needle that was the final upthrust of Darksan Tower, making its mark in the night sky.

Then the cats were gathered, and Laura began to speak.

While Donal dreamed – bizarre, broken images that might have been nightmare, might have been a way of dealing with the dark reality *without* frightening himself – and while Laura laid out her plans for the cats' approval, the rest of their team were busy.

Alexa, after calling in at a cops' bar and sinking back three flame-tequilas in rapid succession, was now in her own apartment, inhaling lilac clarity-smoke from broken twigs burning in a copper bowl. She was attempting to reverse the drunkenness and cough her way back to sobriety.

But the other members of the team were more active. Harald, though he had not slept in three days, looked entirely alert as he sat astride his stationary motorcycle and told his new colleagues, the team from Robbery-Haunting, everything he knew about the embassy's layout, and the driver who was their target.

'When he moves, we follow, hanging back but not enough to risk losing him.' Harald's gentle eyes did not change as he added: 'If he spots us, we'll need to shut him down.'

'Shut down? How permanently?'

'An officer's life is at stake.'

The R-H guys looked at each other. 'That explains it,' one of them said.

'What?'

'Why our boss is doing your boss a favour.'

'And,' said one of the others, 'why none of us is on duty right now, unless we have to be. No reports.'

'Off the books?' asked Harald.

'Completely. Unless something exposes us.'

'Good,' said Harald. 'Let's try and keep things quiet. I like quiet.'

Around him, the R-H team nodded. They had lives and families to return to, when this thing was over.

While this was happening, Harald's friend Viktor was on the West Side, near the dockyard district, only a few miles away from the bonded warehouse where Harald's trail had begun. But Viktor's target was something else.

There were several acres of concrete beyond the chain-link fence. Stacks of pallets and crates stood haphazardly between a half-dozen block-shaped office buildings and warehouses. They provided reasonable cover from the swinging silver beams cast by slow-gliding jelly-lights overhead. Each floating jelly-light trailed venomous thread-like tendrils.

In the office, a surprising number of windows were lit. Men in ties and shirtsleeves were going about their business (most of which, Viktor knew, would be legitimate, for this was a real trading company).

Strange ripples of darkness moved across the chain-fence. Atop it stretched razor-wire that slowly twisted and turned, animated by tortured wraiths whose forms had been dragged thread-thin along the wires' lengths. They screamed for ever in a realm where no human could ever hear, hanging on only so that they might catch a living person, and deliver agony of their own.

At the gateways, guards stood smoking and watching the street outside and the unlit buildings beyond, occasionally fingering their weapons. As Viktor watched, an older, grey-haired man approached them. The men dropped their cigarettes and ground them out with their heels.

Alertness was everything.

But still, thought Viktor, as the older man retreated to one of the buildings, the setup was less secure than it looked. That was partly because Sally the Claw was running a mostly legitimate business here. But it might have been a miscalculation, or an over-reliance on Sal's reputation as a stone killer with an organization of psychopaths at his back.

To Viktor, the outer defences looked strong; but once inside the perimeter, the site was poorly guarded.

Even as he thought this, Viktor noticed the grey-haired man re-entering a building without having to use any kind of password or submitting to personal inspection. The building's doors were not even locked.

From his hiding-place inside a blackened alley mouth, Viktor smiled: cold and predatory, as hard and unforgiving as the punishment Sal so easily handed out.

In the apartment, Donal sat bolt upright on the sweat-soaked bed, sheet falling away from his bare torso. His eyes snapped open, seeing nothing but the fading tag-ends of his own nightmares. The bedroom was empty save for him, with no sign of Laura's presence.

'Oh, Thanatos,' he said.

Then his eyelids fluttered and he lowered himself back on to the mattress, shivered once, and slipped straight back into his dreams. He

151

smiled briefly, but even with his eyes closed it looked like a humour-less smile, predatory and remarkably akin to the expression on Viktor's face, at almost the same moment.

Donal slid deeper into sleep.

Viktor remained standing in the alleyway, knowing he should take action, not knowing why he wanted to stay as he was. But he had worked the streets for long enough to trust himself, to trust his own subconscious that saw more of the world than the surface mind.

After a few minutes he got it.

On the very edge of his peripheral vision, five storeys overhead in what had seemed a deserted building, a shadow shifted within dark-ness: just the tiniest of movements.

Snipers.

Well, one sniper at least, in this building. Even if the man was solo – which was probable – he would not be the only man stationed around the perimeter. Other buildings would have their watchers armed with rifles, observing the surrounding streets, and watching the compound fence from the outside.

There was a chance that this was some enemy of Sally the Claw, whether police or criminal, watching the premises with much the same intent as Viktor himself ... but that seemed improbable.

The man would be solo because being alone in darkness creates fear and therefore alertness. It gave Viktor a chance he might not otherwise have. Thinking that, he began to move down the alley's length, careful to move his feet slowly, just above the broken concrete surface.

Once, he touched a half-brick with the toe of his shoe, and stopped himself from scraping the brick across concrete. Instead, he circled the small obstacle with his foot and took another silent step. With such slow motion, he took an endless time to reach the back of the build-ing.

The rear entrance was of metal, rust-patched but solid enough.

Digging deep into his pocket, Viktor's hand came out with the set of hex keys that he always carried. A pale-blue phosphorescence washed across the keys.

The door was protected.

A chain of tiny glowing heptagons appeared around the threshold. They spread along the rust-covered lintel and down both sides. That was where Viktor got to work first, scratching tiny anti-patterns to dissolve the geometric setup that stood against him. It was painstaking work. It could collapse in an instant if he made a mistake.

In that case, would he sense the final flare of light that accompanied his death? Or would his world already have blanked out for ever?

Viktor let experience guide his hand, working around the edges of the doorway. Then he scratched a knot-shape on the concrete threshold. His key flared blue-and-white, burning him, freezing him …

Bastard. Bloody hurts.

… as chain and anti-chain writhed together, grew brilliant …

Bloody bastard.

… and collapsed, fading from existence.

The first barrier was down.

There were three more barriers that Viktor could detect. There might be further shields inside. But Viktor was the best, and this was what he enjoyed.

Sushana. I'm coming.

He moved on to the second layer of defence, and got to work.

Wilhelmina d'Alkarny, known as Mina to her few friends, walked the long stone passage that led to the underground labs. Deep below street level, they were arranged in two concentric heptagons around the central morgues.

Earlier, one of her most promising young employees, a junior Bone Listener called Padraigh, had mentioned that Feoragh Carryn had been enquiring about one of the many bodies stacked up in morgue-storage. They were held in non-decay stasis, awaiting the decision: postmortem or disposal.

Usually, any pressure came from none-too-subtle hints from the Energy Authority that their stockpile of bones was growing depleted, and could they have some more as soon as possible? It was a request that Mina normally ignored.

Her distaste regarding the necrofusion piles was born of a deeper understanding than a normal person's. Mina knew for sure how much suffering remained, intensified beyond anything a living person could withstand, inside reactor piles filled with standing waves of necroflux … providing heat and power for every living citizen of Tristopolis.

It was a form of balance, of paying back for the luxuries of life once that life was over. It was not a form of fairness that appealed to Mina.

In this case, the strange enquiry had come on behalf of a Lieutenant Riordan, whom Feoragh had referred to as Donal (a familiarity unusual enough in its own right). When Padraigh had investigated, he found that the hands-off stasis order had originated in Commissioner Vilnar's office.

While that request was not totally unusual, it wasn't an everyday occurrence. What interested Mina was that one of Vilnar's own senior officers was questioning the ruling.

None of that would have necessarily caused Mina to undertake a personal investigation. She was Chief here, with the whole OCML to worry about ... not just the postmortems, but salaries and staff morale, whether they had enough cleaners and whether the plumbing worked, and the myriad other bureaucratic administrative tasks that came with being the boss.

But there was something else unusual here: the identity of the body in question.

The dead man's name was Malfax Cortindo. Until dying at the hands of one Lieutenant Donal Riordan, this Cortindo had been the unpleasant, manipulative City Director of the Energy Authority. He had supervised the Downtown Complex, where he kept his office amid the necrofusion piles that groaned with replayed agonies.

Why wasn't he reactor fuel himself?

Two uniformed officers stood to attention, shoulders pulled back and gaze straight ahead. Mina could taste the subliminal pheromones of their fear – to her, noradrenaline was bittersweet with a hint of almonds: a synaesthetic illusion – but she did not smile. After all these years, Mina no longer cared what ordinary humans thought of her.

She was a forensic Bone Listener, the best of her generation. That was enough.

'I need to go inside,' she said.

'Yes, ma'am.'

Behind them, the big circular steel door looked impenetrable and probably was. Wisely, no one had ever attempted to break the security in this place. Pale waves passed through Mina's tall, bony form. The scanwraiths finished their check and approved her entry.

On the door, complex heptagonal wheels and cogs rotated in different directions – one of them appearing to circle through an impossible arc that existed outside of normal geometry – and a sudden draught tugged Mina's lank hair forward as the metal door swung inwards, sucking air from the surrounding corridors into its cold low-pressure interior.

Mina hesitated a moment, reflecting for perhaps the ten thousandth time that she was lucky to be here, in what others found a forbidding place. It was the ultimate calling for a Bone Listener.

She went inside and the big door swung shut, generating a pulse of air pressure that propelled her steps. Mina walked through a thin sheet of shimmering coldfire – a second-layer defence that could turn nova-incandescent – and entered the outer chambers.

Two junior Bone Listeners, neither of them Padraigh, were at workbenches in the admin area, filing cards in the metal cases that would go into the vaults before scanning for Archive entry. Both Bone Listeners wore purple robes streaked here and there with black, where some corpse had spilled its decay fluids as they cut it into it.

It was the bonework which was important, not the cold flesh. In any case Bone Listeners were almost impervious to normal infections: wearing stained robes in this place was business as usual.

'How goes it?' Mina asked the two young men.

'Well, ma'am,' said one, pale-faced with a dead expression. 'We're just filing the results of yesterday's intake. Nineteen incomers.'

'Excellent,' said the other, a frog-like grin distorting his bony face. 'Picked up a resonant trace from a young girl who was flamewraithed. Thought they'd destroy her bones, but we' – he glanced at his companion – 'managed to drag out the perceptions we needed.'

'Good enough to make a match?' asked Mina, meaning a visual ID of the killer.

'Done it already, ma'am,' said the serious one.

But something in his voice told Mina that it was the enthusiastic guy who'd done the real work, not the plodder who was sharing the credit. These were two people she needed to keep an eye on.

'All right,' Mina said. 'I'm going to make an inspection of storage. No need for you to help,' she added, seeing the enthusiastic Bone Listener starting to rise. 'I like to wander round the place alone.'

His answering grin was immediate, and Mina realized that he did exactly the same thing: allowing the low vibrations of the bones' trapped memories to play at the edges of his awareness, as he walked around the morgue labs and repositories. It was a way of getting a feel for the atmosphere of the place, of noting anything unusual in advance, of being prepared when the postmortem began.

'You're Lexar, right?' said Mina.

'Uh— Yes, ma'am.'

'Keep up the good work.' Part of Mina laughed at herself for using the trite phrase. 'I mean it.'

'Thank you.'

When Mina stepped through into the interior tunnel, she remembered that the other young man was called Brixhan, and realized that he had scowled as she left. Did he think that Mina wouldn't notice?

Thanatos save her from such subordinates ... But it was unwise to make enemies, even junior ones. Especially when you were planning to break the laws you were supposed to help enforce.

Mina entered the metallic space they called The Honeycomb. Heptagonal steel cells contained the bodies of the dead awaiting analysis. The ends of those cells were sealed with a mist-like wavering of the air: a side effect of the stasis-hex that filled each cell.

Stasis prevented degradation of the interference patterns laid down in bones, the same interference patterns that the most experienced of forensic Bone Listeners might deconstruct and reconstruct, as they relived the final moments of the dead person's life.

Most often the interference patterns merely confirmed a medical diagnosis, at least within the normal parameters of a physician's ability. Down here, the Bone Listeners knew better than most how much guesswork filled medical science.

By definition, Mina and her colleagues only ever met the patients who had died.

The metal floors were gently sloping, and suffered sudden reversing turns, so that they zig-zagged deep down into the subterranean volume of The Honeycomb. Five levels down, Mina came to the section she wanted. She slowed down, checking the numbers on the labels that bore the deceased's details.

Here were some of the long-term stasis cells, where bodies were preserved for years or even decades, usually waiting for some judicial process to complete, so that a body's ownership could be established. There was one corpse, known affectionately as Fat Fredo, who had been in stasis for over a hundred and twenty years, while generations of lawyers argued with their counterparts in distant Zurinam.

Fredo had been some kind of junior diplomat killed in a bar brawl, but there had been complications due to the Tristopolitan mayor's daughter who had been the cause of the affray, and allegations that Fredo had used his position to illegally influence certain business deals. The battery of entwined legal cases dragged on with a life of their own, with the original participants long gone.

Then Mina found the cell she was looking for. The name was written in an ornate script that most Tristopolitans could no longer decipher.

It read *Malfax Cortindo*.

Mina stared at the shimmering stasis field, thinking about what she was going to do. Most forensic Bone Listeners needed the fully resonant chambers that were the autopsy rooms in order to work.

But Mina was aware of her own capabilities, straightforwardly and without a sense of ego. With the right tools, a scalpel and a bone cutter, perhaps a platinum divining-scope, she could analyse Cortindo's skull right here.

The question was whether the powers that be were going to insist on holding the corpse in stasis indefinitely – in which case Mina would be safe, because no one ever looked in on the bodies once the stasis field was plugged. Not until it was time for the autopsy.

But if the postmortem decision was made soon, then the interference would be obvious. So would the trail of blame.

'Shit.'

Mina's colleagues would have been surprised to hear her now. She was renowned for her equanimity in difficult circumstances, and her insistence on clean language even when there were only corpses to hear.

Mina placed a hand against the steel rim of the heptagonal cell, as though gaining strength from the metal. Then she pulled away and headed back up the long sloping floor, climbing towards the autopsy rooms where she kept her own personal set of tools and devices.

Cats moved across the rooftops, searching, comfortable in the darkness, lithe and agile, enjoying their own abilities as they slipped through the night. They hunted tiny silvermoths that flickered in the air. As they spread out across the city, they were alert for any sign of the people that Laura Steele was tracking.

Sometimes the cats met others of their kind, and spread the word in a manner undetectable to humans (though Laura might have sensed a little of the phenomenon, had she been present).

That was why one of their number, a scrawny little silver tabby called Spike by the humans who sometimes fed him, was perched on a damp brick wall near the docks, watching a big man in a leather jacket working on the ensorcelled rear door of a mostly deserted building.

Mostly deserted, but not entirely. Spike's feline senses could taste the air that revealed the rifle and the hidden sniper deep inside, as sour tastes or bitter scents, and a sense of compressed violence barely kept in check by the need for discipline, along with the fear of punishment from someone more evil than himself.

Lights flared across the door, dissipated, and were gone, leaving no defences behind. The leather-clad man, Viktor, drew the Grauser from beneath his left armpit, leaving his left hand free to push open the door.

The little cat, Spike, had been inside Laura Steele's mind often enough to know that she would approve of Viktor's actions.

In the fictional representations Laura held in her mind – Spike experienced fiction secondhand as a form of dreaming which was dangerous to bring into the real, waking world – cops went through doors with one gun held in outstretched hands. The result of that would be a hostile hand snaking out, grabbing the cop's hands and twisting, so that the firearm became a leverage tool for snapping the cop's fingers. Then the unseen assailant would rip the firearm out of the cop's grasp, and use it.

Viktor went through the doorway with his stance low, left side first, left hand outstretched, gun held tight against his chest with his right hand. No one could take the weapon from him.

Most cops who die from bullet wounds are shot with their own weapon.

As Viktor went inside the building's interior and was lost from sight, Spike hunched on the wall, a tiny ball of fur, and commenced a tiny buzzing purr.

Donal rolled awake off the bed, stumbled, then hauled himself vertical and stretched hard, vertebrae and tendons popping. Barefoot, he walked around the bedroom, looking for signs that Laura was there, knowing she was gone.

He padded out to the kitchen which he still hadn't stocked, detecting no sounds in the apartment anywhere, save the soft ongoing sibilant hiss of the internal systems that kept Darksan Tower operational. He called out Laura's name, got nothing back except a micro-echo of his own voice.

Definitely gone.

Perhaps she had scarcely been here, for Donal remembered only that Laura had stood outside the bedroom as he fell on to the bed and into sleep. Perhaps she had left straight away and gone back to HQ, having made Donal get the rest he needed.

'Shitfuckbugger,' Donal muttered. 'Laura, for Thanatos' sake.'

Then he blew out a breath, and allowed himself to grin. At least Laura cared about him.

Picking up his discarded suit jacket from the floor, Donal searched through the pockets until he found a scrap of notepaper he'd stuffed there earlier. It was a list of phone numbers, some of them home numbers, which he could use to contact members of the team at odd hours.

Donal squinted at the steel-handed clock on the wall: it was eleven minutes past nine in the morning. But everyone had been working during the night, so the normal standards failed to apply: they might be asleep.

He took a guess, set the rotary wheels on the bedside phone to Alexa's number, and waited for the ring.

The tone sounded twice, and then there was a click and Alexa's voice said: 'Hello?'

'Hey, it's Donal. I'm glad you're up.'

'*Right.*' Alexa sounded hoarse. '*You going in to HQ now?*'

'I would've but' – Donal looked at the tangled bedsheets where he'd slept alone – 'I've a feeling no one's going to be there, not even Laura.'

'*Why? Aren't you and her—?*' Alexa coughed. '*Sorry. Forget that. None of my business.*'

'Maybe.' Donal's laugh came out easily, surprising him. 'I am in her place. It's just that she isn't. I think she just wanted me to crash.'

'*And then what? She went out on the streets?*'

'Yeah, I reckon. Where would she go?'

'*Hang on a minute.*'

Donal listened to coughing on the other end of the line, then some muted sounds followed by the sound of a tap running, filling a glass. After a few moments Alexa came back on the line, her voice clearer.

'*Two possibilities,*' she told Donal. '*One, she went to Harald's location to join the surveillance team. Second ...*'

'What?'

'*Something else. She followed up some lead of her own. She's ... Well. She's like that.*'

'Thanatos.'

'*Yeah, precisely. You OK?*'

'Not really. See you near the Illurian Embassy?'

'*Yeah. See you there.*'

Donal put the phone down, found his Magnus and checked it over, ejecting the magazine and snapping it back in before reholstering.

Time to go to work.

Fifteen

Viktor moved further into darkness.

There was a stairwell, and he tested the narrow treads carefully. They were old and prone to creaking, but the edges seemed solid enough. Viktor began his ascent, feet pointed side-on to the treads, using cross-steps to climb. He moved carefully, slowing when he reached the first landing. Were there trip wires?

None. Not that he could detect.

With his left hand Viktor drew out his lockpicks and continued to climb, knowing that the keys would fluoresce at any hint of a hex field. But there were other, equally dangerous traps. As the gloom intensified, he slowed the pace once more.

The sniper was four more storeys up. At this proximity, if Viktor tripped something then if the trap itself wasn't fatal, the sniper's response would be. He would come out of hiding and fire down into the stairwell, and that would be it.

Slowly ...

But there were tricks to do with time passing. While part of Viktor's mind remained in the moment and alert to the smallest stimuli, other layers altered their time perception, slowing down to a leisurely pace, to a kind of moving meditation.

Viktor moved upwards, further and further into the danger zone. Finally he was on the fourth landing, and everything clicked into place inside his skull. The night burned with a dark and silver life.

Where the stray moonlight was coming from was impossible to tell. It was enough to cause the hairs to rise on the back of Viktor's neck as he saw the sliver – *Thanatos and Hades* – like a single thread spun by a nocturnal spider. It stretched across the floor and touched, just touched, the material of his trouser leg.

Trip wire.

Another millimetre and he would have tripped the thing.

Viktor retreated three paces.

Beyond the wire was a shut door which would open inwards. As always there were two choices: to creep in slow or charge in fast, hoping that momentum would take him beyond whatever trap waited inside. The third choice was to kick in the door and then retreat, ready for what followed ... but the man inside was a sniper, and the last thing Viktor wanted was the sound of a firefight.

On the other side of the street lay several acres of yard and buildings owned by Sally the Claw. While many of the people there were office workers, there would be a couple of dozen footsoldiers at least, all of them ready to shoot.

Viktor's keys remained dull, so there were no hex-shields to contend with. Perhaps the elaborate hex-alarm down below had seemed enough for the sniper.

With no time left for deliberation, Viktor moved. His foot crashed into the door just below the handle, smashing the lock apart. The door flew inwards. Viktor leaped, clearing over ten feet as the prone sniper jerked himself upwards.

Down below, on the street outside, the gates to the complex had swung open and a glimmer of bright yellow indicated an unlikely sight, which Viktor would later think had distracted the sniper for those few extra milliseconds.

But Viktor's own momentum saved him the necessity of processing the sight, and he swung his leg powerfully forward and kicked the sniper in the ass: a move that might have looked comical but crushed the coccyx and caused the man to arch back, voice frozen, and in that moment Viktor descended.

Knee-drop on to spine, Grauser-butt hammered into the back of the neck, then Viktor slipped his left forearm under the sniper's chin, pressed down with his right elbow, and applied a sleeper hold, hard.

The man was probably unconscious before the strangle went on, but this would make sure (though it added the risk that he might never wake up). After thirty seconds, Viktor released the hold. He stood up.

The sniper remained prone, unmoving.

As part of checking the environment, Viktor allowed himself to sink quickly, deeply into trance, checking for ensorcelment. If the various parts of his mind were no longer in synch with each other, then it might indicate that some form of hex was distorting the neural patterns in his brain, causing hallucination.

161

Nothing.

That meant several things: not just the lack of hidden, subtle booby-traps in this place, but also that the vision Viktor had glimpsed earlier had been real.

Just why the gates outside had swung open to let out two dwarves riding a canary-yellow tandem bicycle was unclear ... but that was exactly what Viktor remembered seeing. Either that, or twin children wearing false beards.

The sniper began to groan and shake.

Good.

Meanwhile Spike the alley kitten was already on his way, moving among shadows. He darted across a wall surmounted with fragments of broken bottles. They were fastened in place to discourage human intruders; Spike circumnavigated the sharp-edged shards with ease.

Then he was scrambling up a long-dead tree that looked like splayed bones against the night, and slipping along one dry branch that led to a rooftop. High above, a noxeagle glided below moon-tinged clouds; but Spike was aware of the danger. In seconds he was hidden beneath a rusted water tank, waiting for the flying hunter to pass.

Yellowish eyes regarded him from across the roof. It was a parafox, not a deathwolf, but the look in its eyes was nothing like friendly. Even as Spike began to realize the danger he was in, two pairs of eyes suddenly glowed scarlet, followed by a third pair, and a fourth.

The parafox blinked at the appearance of more cats, these ones rangy and muscular. In a second, the parafox had turned with one flash of his bushy tail and slipped away. After a moment, one of the cats, old and grey and torn-eared, made his way across to the water tank where Spike crouched.

The other cats maintained their watch. They were far from familiar territory.

Ducking low, the tomcat peered in at Spike. The tomcat was a tough customer, but in a few seconds Spike had decided that he was also fair and trustworthy. Spike stared back, and the two cats – the old warrior male and the determined youngster – were locked in a mutual staring match as information passed along the entangled channel of feline communication that slips through the deepest geometry of spacetime.

Spike began to purr.

Then the older tomcat turned and moved away, slipping across the rooftop and accelerating. It took a few seconds for the other cats to realize what had happened; then they too were on the move, into the night, heading for their rendezvous with Laura Steele.

There was a spare medical robe in her locker. Mina drew out the robe and pulled it on over her ordinary clothes. The robe was clean and smelled good. She ran her finger across her instrument case, then rejected it: the damned thing was too heavy to cart several storeys down.

Mina had a smaller, zipped travelling case of instruments, which had been given to her by Aldinov, her old boyfriend back in graduate school. Aldinov had lost interest in direct proportion to Mina's success and prospects outshining his. Aldinov had been rich, or rather his parents had been, and a useful-but-expensive present like the portable instruments had been a clever idea.

After their affair's bitter ending, Mina had almost thrown away the shining instruments rather than continue with a reminder of her stupidity. In the end, though, she had kept the case and settled on using it only when it was necessary, when carrying a full kit was impractical.

Mina slipped the small instrument case into the pocket of her robe. She stared at herself in the small mirror fixed inside her locker door, then swung the door shut. She exited and found herself in Autopsy Room 3, where concave steel benches with inbuilt drains and antiseptic nozzles were empty and shining.

No stains marked the tiled floor, no scents hung in the air that could penetrate the eternal mist of disinfectant that pervaded this cold place. Perhaps a hint of steam marked the exhalation of Mina's breath as she saw once more the room that meant so much, where she became alive.

Knowing enough to smirk at this thought, Mina shook her head and crossed the autopsy room and pushed her way through the triple sets of doors. She did not look back as the steel floor began its downward slope towards The Honeycomb, where Malfax Cortindo's corpse waited.

Something rumbled deep beneath her feet. Mina stopped.

'What the Thanatos—?'

Mina held herself still, expecting something more. There was nothing. It had felt like a distant train; but no tunnels ran beneath this place. If it was a freak trick of geology and happenstance, then that was all right; but Mina decided she would report this.

All the more reason for doing what she had to do quickly, quietly and privately.

Her pulse began to beat visibly beneath her thin, white Bone Listener's skin. She took out the instrument case and unzipped it as she walked, drawing out a long slender scalpel.

She neared the heptagonal cell containing Cortindo, then stopped to look up and down the steel corridor, sensing nothing save the clammy sweat coating her narrow body. Another tremor passed through the floor. This time she was certain.

Whatever was happening, there was danger, and she was its target.

'Fuck you.'

All the decades of medical training, of playing politics with the high and mighty – and immersing herself in the most painful Bone Listener disciplines – fell away now, leaving only her native toughness.

'Just ... Fuck you.'

Mina hammered her fist into the crystalline ward set at the edge of the cell, and watched as the hex-shield flared, then began to fade. Inside that dying glare, the unmoving form resolved itself into a dead body, no different from any of the thousands that had passed through here before.

Except this time, someone wanted the body back.

Someone who was capable of breaking into this place ... but this was *her* place. Mina savagely sliced into the inanimate head of Malfax Cortindo, the scalpel coming away sticky with viscous semi-liquid blood.

There was no time to retrieve the other instruments but that was all right, as Mina hooked her fingers into the flap of scalp and ripped back. She threw herself inside the cell as far as her shoulders, desperate as an explosion banged through the corridor outside. Metal ripped open amid showering dust and noise.

I hear you.

The corpse's exposed skull tasted raw and salty as Mina placed her tongue against it.

Cortindo, I hear you now.

Then Mina pulled her head back. Splaying her fingertips against the bone, she began her quest for one particular song amid the inchoate patterns laid down inside his—

Hands clasped around Mina's ankles.

'*NO!*'

Strong hands, hauling her away from Cortindo ...

'No ...'

... and she shivered as the contact was broken ...

'Please, don't—'

... as they pulled her into the cold dusty air, the two small figures who stared at her, ordinary thick-boned men, less than four feet tall but strong. Mina knew in the instant she saw their stone gazes that the rules she had broken and the rules she had lived by were of no moment, not any longer. This was the day her own life ended.

One of the dwarf-men raised an axe that shimmered with coherent hex-waves, its edge capable of slicing through hardest stone or metal. Biological matter was no kind of challenge. The dwarf drew back his lips; you couldn't call the expression a smile.

Concentrate. Replay.

Mina squeezed her eyes shut, remembering the disciplines.

Remembering the pain.

Concen—

The universe blacked out.

Was finished.

The Robbery-Haunting team were professional. By the time Donal and Alexa arrived, the R-H guys were well settled in place.

They had formed two concentric circles of observation posts around the Illurian umbassy. Harald, his gentle eyes beginning to show the exhaustion, took Donal and Alexa on the tour, walking the quiet streets.

'And the limo,' Harald said, as they crossed one of the narrow avenues that led into the heptagon. 'R-H impounded it from a counterfeit ring.'

Alexa grinned. Donal checked the vehicle from the edge of his vision, not turning his head, just in case their suspect or someone working with him was mounting a surveillance of his own.

In an area like this, where the grand old houses were owned by diplomats and embassies and occasionally an old rich Tristopolitan family, the normal kind of surveillance vehicle would have stood out: a baker's van, for instance. But the dark-windowed limousine was perfect.

'Who's inside?' Donal asked.

'Guy I vaguely know,' said Harald, 'called Ralfinko, and an older guy, a sergeant, looks like he knows what's what.'

'All right.'

Alexa touched Harald on the arm. 'You need to get some rest.'

'No.'

165

'Er ... I know you and I have only just met,' said Donal, 'but I think she's right, old chum.'

'Balls.' Harald spoke softly as always. 'All right. My old sergeant used to say, it's only your comrades who can tell you when you're screwing up.'

They were standing under a streetlamp. Harald dug inside his pocket, and pulled out a small food box. He flipped back the lid, and held out the open box. 'Hungry?'

'Um ... No thanks,' muttered Donal. Inside the box were layered flower petals, orange and darkest purple predominating. 'I don't know how you eat that stuff.'

'It's all he ever eats,' said Alexa. 'Mr Gentle, we like to call him.'

'Right.' Donal looked at Harald, who nibbled at one of the petals. 'And which sergeant was this, that you mentioned?'

'Oh, Bastard Balrooney, we used to call him.'

'And this was in—?'

Harald looked at Alexa, then at Donal, and smiled a peaceful smile. 'The Fighting Sevens.'

Donal had rarely come across the men of the 777th during his own military career, but those few had always lived up to the reputation of their brigade, known widely as the Cursed Commandos. He had once seen a one-eyed old sergeant of the 777th take down six military policemen, before walking back to barracks and handing himself in for punishment.

'Mr Gentle,' Donal said.

Harald smiled again.

'So what do we do next?' asked Alexa.

'The usual.' Harald closed his food box and tucked it away once more. 'We pick the most comfortable surveillance spot and wait.'

That was the way of things. Surveillance consists mostly of watching and busting for a pee. The biggest challenge is boredom, and the tendency to doze off.

From somewhere behind them, an engine started up, then revved with power.

'Did you say we were going to wait?' muttered Donal.

'I am occasionally wrong,' said Harald.

A dark car turned into the avenue, its headlights a liquid malevolent green. Then the driver accelerated hard and the car sped past them. Startled, a reptilian gekkobat launched itself from a stone tree and flapped away into the dark, featureless sky.

'Shit,' said Alexa.

The limousine parked at the kerb started up, as the passenger door swung open. 'You guys want to catch a ride?' The speaker was square-jawed and grey-haired: the sergeant that Harald had mentioned. 'Better hurry.'

The driver had the limo pointing the wrong way, but he swung away from the kerb in a tight U-turn and jerked to a stop next to Donal and Alexa. Donal pulled the door open and pushed Alexa inside, then followed.

'Go ahead,' said Harald. 'I'll catch up.'

'OK.'

Donal pulled his door shut, the sergeant having already done the same up front, and acceleration slammed him back into the seat.

'Don't let him see you,' he muttered to the driver. What was his name again? 'Uh, you're Ralfinko, right?'

'Yeah, and you gotta be kidding. The bastard's already out of sight.'

Tyres screeched as Ralfinko hauled them through a left turn and piled on the acceleration.

At the corner of Silvan Avenue and Five-hundred-and-fourth, a blood-red craggy tower rose from the sidewalk, famed locally for its twisted architecture, for the black oval windows that looked like rows of eyes, and the odd visitors that passed through its doors.

On a window sill on the thirteenth floor, near the junction of a necrotonic cable where it disappeared into the wall, a grey cat hunched. Its crimson gaze followed the embassy car speeding past below, followed by a dark limousine, then another, small car, and finally a bone-coloured motorcycle taking up the rear but accelerating hard.

The cat blinked.

After a moment, it leaped lightly on to the hanging cable, ignoring the potential drop which would be fatal, and walked onwards towards the next roof, dismissing the chase it had seen developing below. Two other cats had relayed the message since the hardbitten tomcat, Dilven, got it from the young Spike; but it was the goings-on at the docks that would concern Laura Steele.

The place where she awaited news, Darksan Tower, stood tall against the purple sky.

Viktor pressed down with his thumbs, and the sniper gave a strangled scream, all that his paralysed vocal cords would allow. At this stage, the sniper didn't even know what information Viktor was after. This was only to establish that Viktor was willing to cause suffering.

Willing, and adept.

'A short woman.' Viktor's voice was low and throaty, designed to reinforce fear. 'With green eyes. Have you seen her?'

'No ...' The sniper could only croak a whisper. 'Haven't—'

Viktor pressed again, hard, and the sniper's back arched off the floor, though his limbs remained helpless. Viktor had worked on the shoulders and hips first, and those joints must be burning in agony by now.

'Is there a prisoner? A woman?'

'I— Yes!' A finger twitched: all that the sniper could manage by way of a warding-off gesture. 'There ... Sal. Got some ... one.'

Viktor glanced at the window. 'In the compound? Sally the Claw's in there?'

The sniper nodded, eyes wide.

'With a prisoner?' Viktor's jaw muscles flexed. 'Tell me.'

'Brought her ... in. Tonight.'

'Her name. What's her—?'

But the sniper was already shaking his head. If he knew the name, he'd say it: Viktor was sure of that.

'Which building?'

'Block ... Three.'

Viktor didn't know which building that was, but he wasn't going to ask: to maintain dominance, he had to appear to already know almost everything.

'What else can you tell me?'

The sniper shook his head.

Viktor stared down at him. The fear and bewilderment, as he regained consciousness, had cracked the sniper's conscious defences; and closed questions had elicited answers ... but now Viktor had run out of specifics to ask about.

'Next time,' said Viktor, 'choose your employer more carefully.'

'No, you—'

Viktor's fist hammered down.

Afterwards, just in case he had missed something on the first search, Viktor went through the beaten man's pockets with care, finally extracting a small brass ID strip. It was stamped with the dragon-wing logo of CalTransPort, the main holding company of Sally the Claw's near-legitimate import-export group.

There was no personal identification to go with it. For a moment Viktor considered stripping the sniper of his armoured hexlar vest, and impersonating him, rifle in hand. But there was no way of knowing whether the guards down below knew the sniper by sight or even by name.

Or perhaps Viktor was too attached to his own leather jacket to want to leave it in this infested joint.

Shaking his head, he picked up the unconscious sniper's rifle, checked the balance, and ejected the magazine. It held a clip of five long, slender bullets. If the sniper had a spare clip, he must have hidden it somewhere; and he was in no position to divulge that information now.

Viktor put the cartridge clip in his jacket pocket. Then, with a last inspection of the sniper – the man would live, provided someone found him within the next few hours – Viktor left the bare room. The landing and the rest of the dilapidated building looked clear, and he went down the old treads quickly but almost silently.

At ground level, he stepped over broken shards on the floor, ducked under the stairs, and groped around until he found a suitable hiding place. He slid the rifle into the gap between a tread and a broken shelf – this had once been a cupboard, but the door had long since been ripped off, probably used for firewood.

There. Good. The rifle was too conspicuous to take inside the complex, but if Viktor had to retreat, this would be a good place to grab a long-range weapon. Five shots would drop one or two pursuers, maybe more.

Viktor hefted the brass ID strip in his left hand, and walked out of the house, pulling the door shut behind him. If someone was expecting the door to be hexed but had no detector, then everything would look as before. If they *did* have a detector, they'd know the defences had been breached. There was nothing Viktor could do to help that.

In the broken alleyway beside the house, Viktor paused, scanning the street, the blackened pits that were paneless windows in other buildings. Then he took a deep breath, held it, and let it out.

Viktor walked out into the open street, and headed for the main gate, his walk loose-limbed and confident, projecting ease. Inside, his nerves crawled. Adrenaline speckled his skin as the fine hairs rose across the back of his shoulders.

Someone, behind the wire fence, swung a flashlight beam in Viktor's direction.

Sixteen

They hurtled through the streets, not yet in open pursuit. If anything, the man they were tracking should be suspicious at the lack of cops. Twice, he'd gone through stop lights at speed.

On the other hand, this was the early hours of the morning, and they were into the less-than-salubrious district known as Vulkan's Vale, otherwise Blood Alley. Here squad cars travelled in convoy or not at all.

'I don't like this,' muttered Alexa, sitting on Donal's left.

'Ralfinko knows what he's doing,' said the sergeant from the front.

'Yeah.' Donal gave a grin that lasted half a second. 'We can see that. But why's the target going so fast?'

'Because he can,' said Ralfinko. 'Looks like he's got diplomatic flags flying.'

'Or—'

Donal stopped as the radio squawked beneath the dashboard. The sergeant pulled the mike from its clip.

'Car oh-seven-niner. What's up?'

'Is Lieutenant Riordan with you?'

'Yeah, affirmative.'

'Could you put him on, please?'

'Er, sure.'

Donal leaned forward, while the sergeant passed the mike back. The coiled cable just reached over the back of the passenger seat. Donal clicked the mike to transmit.

'Riordan.'

'Sir, Bone Listener Carryn said we needed to tell you this. There's been a break-in in the OCML.'

'What?' said the sergeant, while Ralfinko muttered: 'Impossible.'

'There are four fatalities reported so far, sir, including Dr d'Alkarny.'

'Say again?' Donal glanced at Alexa. 'Did you say Wilhelmina d'Alkarny?'

'That's correct. We have possible sightings of a green van leaving the vicinity, possibly with stolen goods aboard.'

'Stolen goods? From the morgue?'

'Sir, Bone Listener Carryn says to tell you, the missing body belonged to Director Cortindo.'

'Damn it,' muttered Donal, with the mike still set to receive. He clicked to transmit. 'Can you contact Commander Steele?'

'Sorry, sir, but no. We've been trying.'

Outside the window the buildings were streaming past. Then Blood Alley was dropping away as the car climbed the steep on-ramp to the ten-lane skyway. Donal realized that Ralfinko had floored the acceleration all the way until the engine howled.

'What is it?'

'Your man from the embassy is up ahead.'

'Yeah, but—'

'And he's driving parallel to a green van.'

Donal stared at Ralfinko for a moment, then clicked the mike. 'Control, do you have any more description on the green van? From the OCML incident?'

'Negative, sir.'

'Shit.'

Alexa said: 'We need to coordinate with our other cars. Can we get a roadblock across the skyway?'

The traffic was sparse, moving fast. There was one more exit ramp before they reached the huge thousand-foot-high skull intersection, passing into the mouth.

'Control,' said Donal. 'Standby by for all points. Listen, have you got any cars down on the flat, that can block exit North forty-seven? We need a barrier.'

'Sir.' There was a loud crackle, then: *'Done it. Two cars moving to block off.'*

The freeway curved and banked, and just for a second Donal glimpsed the white-and-purple flashing beacons, ahead and down below, as the cars closed off the exit at ground level.

'Nice work, Control. We have a possible match for the green van, linking up with our own suspect.'

'I'll relay that information.'

Up ahead, white-and-purple flashes showed from inside the empty right orb of the great skull. More squad cars in position. But on the route that Ralfinko was following, no obstacles were visible. The green van and the Illurian embassy limo increased their speed, drawing away from the pursuit.

Then a long, low bone-coloured motorcycle swept past on the fast lane, as if the cars were standing still. Ralfinko flinched.

'What the Thanatos—?'

'That'll be Harald,' said Alexa.

At the edge of the dock complex, a dark-finned low-slung car drew close to the wire fence. It was a Vixen, top of the range, and more: the vehicle seemed to shrug as it drew close to the wire.

Silvery waves passed across the fence, then faded from sight as the Vixen's door swung open. Laura stepped out on to the cracked tarmac.

'It's hexed, sis,' Laura muttered. 'Can you do something about it?'

A glimmer grew in the headlights. The car rolled forward, edging closer to the fence, until its passenger side was touching the wire. More silver pulses passed along the wire, arcing downwards as if tugged by gravity. Soon there was a dark area of fence directly above the Vixen: the car was diverting the hex flow along her chassis.

'The bonnet's safe?' Despite her skirt suit, with her high heels morphing into combat soles, Laura climbed up on to the bonnet. 'Nice one, sis.'

Laura checked the pistol holstered at the small of her back, slung her handbag diagonally over one shoulder, and leaped lightly from the bonnet towards the fence. She landed like a cat about to scramble up, hands and feet fastening into the wire mesh.

At the top of the fence, razor wire writhed and swirled. But as Laura neared the uppermost portion of the mesh, she was deep in concentration, preparing herself. When she reached the wire, she grabbed with both hands simultaneously. The wire bucked and thrashed, and then the section between her hands grew limp.

After a moment, Laura scrambled over the top and descended to the other side.

That's one thing I couldn't have done when I was alive.

By the time she reached ground level, the razor wire was stirring again, though feebly.

'If I don't come back—'

The Vixen flashed her headlights.

172

'Yes, I will be.' Laura opened her handbag and checked the larger gun inside: a Grauser .35. It was a smaller calibre than Viktor carried, but still a man-stopper. 'Don't worry so much.'

Inside the Vixen, a small furry shape moved, then curled up into a ball. Spike closed his eyes, whiskers spreading as he slipped into sleep.

He had done all he could, passing on the message to the network, and keeping watch on the man, Viktor, as he entered the compound. He had told Laura which building Viktor had entered. Everything else was up to her.

The air in the car's cabin was warm, soothing. In seconds, Spike was breathing softly, paws twitching as he dreamed of the chase, before growing relaxed once more. But the car herself maintained a watch, tracking Laura's progress for as long as she was able, until Laura slipped among piles of shipment pallets and was lost from sight.

They'd blocked the off-ramp, so the green van and the limo were constrained to remain on the skyway. No one had thought to block the next on-ramp, even if there had been cars available, but as soon as Donal caught sight of the second big truck he knew there was a problem.

There were six of them, hauling their way up to the skyway at improbable speed, though they were hauling huge trailers. The trailers must be empty.

'Speed up,' Donal told Ralfinko. 'Get past those bastard trucks.'

'I see 'em, but I can't get there,' muttered Ralfinko. 'Not before— Shit.'

Already the first three trucks had pulled alongside each other in the fast lanes and were beginning to slow. Harald on his bike was just behind them; and then he was level with their tailgates.

Just as Harald started to accelerate into the gap between two trucks, they drove closer together, dangerously close, blocking Harald's bike. Harald fell back.

Two more trucks moved into position, blocking the road. The sixth was back-up, and it pulled in behind one of the others as the whole formation slowed.

'Damn it.'

The sergeant was using the mike, describing the situation to Control. Alexa watched Donal pull out his Magnus and check it before re-holstering. She bit her lip.

'What is it?' said Donal.

'They're well organized.' Alexa was staring forward. 'So far. What have they got in mind for up ahead?'

The sergeant put down the mike. 'We got barricades across every lane beyond the skull. Once they're in, they ain't leaving.'

At that moment, Donal saw something: a shadow high in the sky.

'I don't think,' he said, 'they're planning to leave by road at all.'

'You've gotta be—'

'There goes Harald,' said Alexa.

The motorbike shot forward through the narrow gap, and then Harald was clear of the trucks, accelerating in front of them. Behind the trucks, civilian cars were braking, pulling over; in front, one car was driving too slowly, while the other three drivers that Donal could see were making use of their mirrors and speeding up, drawing farther ahead of the steadily slowing trucks blocking the skyway.

A truck nudged the slow car in the rear, jolting it. The driver panicked, swerving across two lanes before regaining control and flooring the acceleration. Far ahead of him were a green van, a dark limo, and the bone-coloured Phantasm motorcycle fast catching them up.

Then a sequence of white flashes brightened the night.

'What the hell is Harald firing?' Donal leaned forward, trying to make out what was happening.

'Don't ask,' said Alexa. 'I'm sure it's regulation issue.'

Ralfinko snorted.

'Sure,' he said. 'So you got any ideas on how to get past these guys?'

The trucks were slowing right down. Civilian cars had already stopped. The sergeant looked back at Donal; both men nodded, and turned to wind down their windows. Ralfinko's face grew mask-like with concentration, as he drove close up to the trucks' tailgates and kept the car steady.

It took a magazine full of shots from Donal and the sergeant firing in parallel to blow out the rear tyre; but when it happened, it was spectacular. Ralfinko swung the car left, hard, just as the truck swerved and bounced from the neighbouring truck on one side then the other, the skid setting up an oscillation.

Then Ralfinko ripped up the handbrake and slammed his heel into the brake pedal, turning the car sideways-on into a skidding deceleration as the colliding trucks bounced off each other. The crash became catastrophic as four of the six trucks entangled, the fifth lurched and toppled, and only the sixth was braking as the remainder collided, smashed, swerving across the lanes, one going through the central barrier and on to the opposite carriageway.

Flame belched from a truck that was lying on its side.

The car stood still.

'Can you get through?' Donal pointed to a path through the wreckage. 'That way.'

'Got ya.' Ralfinko gunned the engine. 'Sure you don't want to stop?'

'Keep an eye out.' Donal had already slammed a replacement clip into his Magnus.

Alexa said nothing, but her mouth tightened: she knew that Ralfinko had been thinking of helping trapped truck drivers; but Donal and the sergeant were focused on the chase.

More white weapons-fire flashed from Harald's motorcycle up ahead, and the dark limo swerved but corrected its course. They were less than a minute from the orange-lit mouth opening of the great skull, and the chase was getting serious.

Donal leaned out of the open window, eyes squinted against the slipstream, staring up into the sky. Nothing. He must have imagined the—

There.

'Shit.' He pulled himself back inside the car. 'It's big, maybe a pterabat.'

'What the Death have they got going on?' said the sergeant.

'I don't know,' said Donal. 'But let's make sure they don't get away with it.'

The sergeant had the mike again, and was telling Control to get air support organized any way they could, but things were moving fast: everyone knew there was no time left.

White fire flashed up ahead once more, and this time the dark limo screeched across the fast lane and ricocheted from the central barrier. It swerved back and for a moment Donal thought the driver had regained control; but then the limo wobbled and Harald fired twice more and the rear tyres went.

The limo swung wide and span as it headed for the hard shoulder and hit the balustrade.

Concrete exploded and the limo went straight through, sailing out into the air. Donal shut his eyes, trying to listen for the impact, hearing nothing amid the ongoing roar of motor and slipstream and the shocked voices of Alexa and Ralfinko.

'Impossible!'

'What kind of—?'

'It was molyscarab armour,' the sergeant told them. 'The limo's body. I've seen the stuff before. Goes through anything.'

Up ahead, the green van – looking black as it slid into the orange sodium-vapour light – was entering the tunnel, into the great skull's mouth.

'You're not saying the limo's survived that drop?' Alexa was staring back at the gap in the balustrade.

'The bodywork might,' said the sergeant. 'But the wheels'n'axles are a different story, and the driver's probably a mite squished by—'

'This is it.' Ralfinko was pouring on the acceleration. 'Crunch point coming soon.'

'Apt term,' muttered Donal, flicking the safety catch on his Magnus. Even with his finger outside the trigger guard, a sudden jolt could cause an accidental discharge.

'Here goes.'

Ralfinko brought the car swerving through a tyre-burning arc across the tarmac, blue-grey smoke rising from the wheel-arches and then the car was still, diagonally placed across one lane. The green van was stationary, all its doors thrown open. Up on the safety path for pedestrians, a metal emergency exit door was banging shut.

Donal was first out of the car, drawing his Magnus as he ran. A hundred yards further along the tunnel, a bulky man who had left his own car to see what was going on stopped, jerked so fast his jowls wobbled, and then ducked back behind the steering-wheel and pulled his door shut.

There were stone steps a few yards away but seconds mattered so Donal used the bonnet of the parked van as a springboard, caught the iron safety rail one-handed and vaulted over, landing crouched on the concrete walkway. The walkway was for evacuating the tunnel in case of emergencies, which meant the stairwell beyond the metal door led downwards for safety, and also up to reach the higher tunnels.

To the skyways that fed through the empty orbs of the great skull hundreds of feet above.

Behind Donal, Ralfinko shouted: 'The van's empty. Except for a yellow tandem.'

'A what?'

'A bicycle made for two. You know?'

'Shit.'

If the suspects were carrying Cortindo's body it would slow them up. Donal kicked open the metal door, then ducked back. The light inside the stairwell was dim amber pushing back dark shadows: the usual auxiliary lighting.

There was a red alarm button on the wall. Donal slammed the butt of his Magnus against it.

'Hey!'

A shower of artificial rain poured down inside the road tunnel as the sprinklers – in fact they were high-powered nozzles – came on. Purple lights strobed. More importantly, the inside of the stairwell shone with magnesium-white light.

Donal ducked into the doorway, and back out.

'Which way?' called Alexa softly. 'Up or down?'

Donal shook his head. They might be lying in wait with guns at the ready, but he'd caught no glimpse of gun barrels and no one had fired. And he was ninety per cent sure that he'd seen a pterabat earlier, from the car. That would make one hell of an expensive diversion.

Donal pointed up.

The sergeant pointed towards the ground, and Donal nodded. Just in case, it was best if one man went that way.

Ready . . .

Donal ducked into the stairwell.

No shots fired.

Ah, Thanatos.

Gun at the ready, Donal stepped on to the first tread and began to run up.

Viktor crouched on the seventh floor of the office block he'd entered, listening to low voices coming from behind closed double doors. A brass label read Boardroom, but the soft moan from inside the room indicated this was not the usual kind of meeting.

At three o'clock in the morning, that was a given.

To get into the building had been both more and less trouble than expected. From outside, the doors had appeared completely unguarded, with no locks and no watchers. But once he'd pulled open the outer door things had changed.

Viktor had first spotted the small floating orb floating near the ceiling at the first corner. Then he realized that floateyes were hovering at every choke point.

But they were one of the things that Viktor was prepared for. He pulled out his big handkerchief, inspected it – grimaced – then tied it around the lower half of his face. From inside his leather coat, he pulled out two small grey bulbs with atomizer sprays, and took a few deep breaths

He had sprayed a little of the eyesleep mist into the corridor first, letting it drift along to cause inattention in the floating eyeballs. Then he stepped inside properly and sprayed straight into the first floateye.

Its nictitating membrane slipped across the glossy orb, and the eye was asleep and dreaming.

Viktor had continued to spray as he penetrated the building further. At a glass half-wall he had peered into an open-plan office space where a few tired-looking workers were bent over stacks of invoices and bills of lading, processing the legitimate transactions of Sally the Claw's business.

Reaching an inner stairwell, Viktor had climbed past a series of unlit floors, finally reaching the seventh storey. Now, Viktor crouched outside the door.

Another moan sounded from the boardroom.

Sushana!

He was sure of it.

Viktor checked the door. It had a long brass handle, not a knob. Good. Crossing his arms, Viktor cross-drew both Grausers from his shoulder holsters. Then, crouching, he brought his left elbow slowly down on the door handle.

It turned.

And what happened next went very fast.

Through the door, rolling diagonally over his right shoulder, Viktor came up with weapons ready.

Seven, no, eight men were already reaching for their guns. A bulkier figure stood at the far end of the room clad in a pearl-grey suit; and the bloodied form of Sushana sat tied in a chair, her clothing torn, two of her fingers bent and twisted back to sickening angles.

Viktor began to fire: both guns, swivelling his stance, blasting continuously, an overlapping series of loud bangs in the room, deafening. But the corpses dropping around the conference table would never hear anything again.

Maybe one shot in three hit what he was aiming at, but Viktor had seventeen rounds in each clip and that was more than enough. Cordite-smoke hung in the air as Viktor moved quickly around the room, checking the fallen bodies, firing once as a dying man twitched, hand reaching for a dropped, bloodstained weapon. All down.

A stray round had blown apart Sushana's left shoulder and her eyes were wide with shock, face whitened by blood loss. But there was no time for Viktor to help her, because the bulky man in the rich suit at the end of the room was Sally the Claw, and this was the moment he lived up to his name.

Sal's right hand was normal but his left was a great shining pincer. His left arm came up fast and Viktor fired at the movement, rounds ricocheting from the carapace protecting the limb, and then the claw had swept both weapons from Viktor's grasp.

Viktor tried to duck and spin away but Sal was faster, and the claw opened, moved and struck in a tenth of a second, and then it was fastened around Viktor's neck and he knew that he was too late.

'Who are you?' said Sally the Claw.

Donal pounded his way up the echoing stairwell. Twice he stopped, breath sawing, thighs pumped and beginning to burn. A layer of slick sweat coated his skin beneath his clothes, and so far he'd only run up three hundred steps – a part of him insisted on keeping count.

There were scrapes up ahead, but no shots came firing down the stairwell at him. The suspects were headed for the roof of the great skull – they had to be.

'Thanatos. Come on.'

Donal pushed himself back into motion, breathing hard. Then, involuntarily, a sort-of grin pulled his lips back as he ran upwards, a primordial reaction to the hard physical work and the sense of mortal danger: he was in the moment where he belonged, all doubts gone.

He pushed harder.

Laura was hunkered down beside a drain when the gunfire banged out and a series of flashes showed between blinds on the seventh floor of the nearest building. She moved into cover, next to a stack of pallets.

She checked her handbag, which hung at her hip, the strap still slung diagonally across her shoulders. Her firearm was inside.

Then something ripped through the air, parting the handbag strap as other hands tugged the bag away from Laura's grasp. She launched herself forward but two big figures leaped from behind the pallet, grabbing her arms.

179

Yet another bulky man stepped out in front of her and raised a shotgun to her face.

'What shall we do?' said one of the men.

'I suggest,' muttered Laura, 'that you damn well—'

'Tell me what,' came a sepulchral voice, 'is in the bag.'

The man, or kind of man, was seven feet tall and grey-skinned, and a scar ran diagonally across his squarish face. His gaze, when he looked at Laura, was devoid of feeling.

'Automatic,' said one of the men, pulling open the handbag. 'Pretty small ... And ID. She's police.'

Another team of guards was moving towards the building. If Viktor or Sushana were still alive, then the chances of their remaining so were diminishing fast.

'A *commander*.' The grey-skinned man checked Laura's badge, then put it in his pocket. 'We're honoured.'

'You won't—'

'Kill her.' The grey-skinned man turned away. 'Now.'

Laura squeezed her eyes shut.

Donal ...

Then Laura felt a jerk and heard a gasp. Her eyes snapped open to reveal a misty form rising up through the cracked tarmac.

The being reached insubstantial hands inside the rifleman's head and chest ...

'Xalia!'

... and then Xalia manifested her extremities into corporeal existence and squeezed.

Squeezed hard.

Even as the man dropped his weapon and gasped with mortal shock, Laura was spinning aside, flicking back her jacket and ripping her second gun from her back holster, firing three times before the guards had even processed her movement.

Then they broke formation, scattering to every side, only two of them returning fire as they ran. But Laura was already ducking and continuing her tactical movement, while Xalia was insubstantial: the bullets passed through her wraith form.

Then Xalia was upon the two men who were still firing. Blood bubbled from their mouths as she crushed their hearts and they, too, dropped dead on to the tarmac.

The grey-skinned man simply ran, but his gait was controlled rather than fearful and Laura had to decide her responsibility. His back was towards her but he was running for help not escape, she was sure of it, and there were officers' lives at stake and therefore no choice for her to make: no choice at all.

She squeezed the trigger and the small .23 jerked back and the back of the man's neck blossomed dark fluid and he fell and did not move.

There was still a great deal of danger and Laura rolled sideways across the ground and fetched up next to another dead man, and picked up her bigger handgun. But the remaining guards had fled ... apart from one who'd chosen to face Xalia, and then regretted it as Xalia's fingers became talons like steel, slashing downwards.

The man fell whimpering, tendons severed so that all four limbs were useless. He could only shiver as blood spurted out of torn arteries and death closed in.

Laura scanned the environment as Xalia drew closer. There was no immediate danger, and for a split second Laura grinned at her own continued survival. Then, 'Where did you come from?' she said. 'How did you know I'd be here?'

Xalia's wraith-form drifted as though on a breeze, yet the air was still.

Same way as you.

'What's that supposed to mean?' Laura went down on one knee, reloading her automatic. 'The same way as me?'

Why, Laura.

Xalia rose a few feet up into the air, appeared to sniff the air, then descended.

You think you're the only one who talks to cats?

Then another shot fired from inside the building. Laura and Xalia headed towards the doorway, alert for more armed men, moving fast.

Seventeen

Donal was two flights below when he heard the roof door bang open. There was a glimpse of two short, powerful figures carrying something grey-wrapped and bulky – Cortindo's body – and then the dwarves were out onto the roof and Donal was cursing.

Even as he redoubled his pace, sprinting up the last thirty or so steps, he could hear not just the wind from up above but also a deeper grumble, a near-subsonic vibration of total power. It was the pterabat, coming in to hover above the top of the great skull.

Come on.

Donal's breathing was harsh and wheezing now.

Push it.

There was no possibility of silent pursuit as he clattered up the final steps and half-stumbled to the landing, stopping inside the doorway. Outside, the flat expanse of the skull's top reached for two hundred yards before curving down and beginning the sheer descent. The suspects were nowhere in sight.

Donal ran as hard as he could – his legs felt made of molten rubber – out on to the wet slippery surface that was the top of the great skull. Rain was heavy in the gusting wind, and Donal had to squint to see the two squat powerful figures who dropped their burden and scattered to either side as Donal raised his Magnus.

'Desist or I will fire!' The legal words were tugged away by the wind. At least Donal was observing the correct form. 'Stop!'

Overhead, the pterabat filled half the sky as it dropped lower. An abdominal incision puckered and pulled open, and narrow black ropes rippled downwards. In seconds, dark-clad hooded figures were rappelling down.

Donal fired a single warning shot, but the descending figures did not hesitate.

Thanatos . . .

Squatting low, he took aim at the figure closest to the roof surface – *no, watch out* – then span away as one of the dwarves leaped through the air feet first, just grazing Donal's forearm. The Magnus banged out once more, another shot wasted, and Donal swung the weapon down butt-first but the dwarf was already cartwheeling away.

A heavy impact took Donal in the small of the back and he pitched forward.

He threw himself into a twisting fall, firing again at the second dwarf who'd kicked him, the fabric of the dwarf's heavy pullover ripping apart. But it was a surface wound, and a small but heavy foot was swinging for Donal's eye – the other dwarf – and he rolled away just in time.

Hardness thumped Donal's brow, fluorescent yellow spots rippling across his vision as he came up on one knee and cupped his left hand beneath his right, aimed and exhaled – *calm* – and squeezed the trigger.

No shot occurred.

Misfeed . . .

The dwarves were upon him, teeth sinking into his forearm and a small hard fist taking him in the groin, an uppercut that would have downed most men but Donal knew he could take the sickening pain and carry on fighting.

He punched the one that was biting, turned his hip against the second, then pumped three more hooking punches into the side of the biter's neck and the dwarf fell. The other dwarf advanced again, head forward as he came in to tackle Donal at the knees – *not a coward* – but Donal snap-kicked once, catching the dwarf just under the chin.

Then Donal struck with his knee to the same target, followed with an uppercut punch to the same spot again, and the little figure was down.

The first dwarf was already stirring – *what do they feed you guys on?* – but Donal took a running step to kick him in the face, knocking the dwarf back and rolling him over. For the time being Donal was clear.

But the dwarves hadn't needed to beat him, only distract him long enough for the hooded figures to wrap their ropes around the bundled form of Cortindo's corpse.

Donal raised his gun, then remembered the misfeed – *clear, rack and hammer*: that was the dictum Rangemaster Ryan had drummed into Donal – and he clawed back the slide, banging the Magnus with his left fist to fling the unfired cartridge out.

183

Ready.

It took less than a second, but that was too long as the pterabat rose slightly and the corpse of Cortindo came off the roof surface.

'No, damn it.'

A dwarf reached for Donal's ankle but Donal kicked the fingers aside and moved away, swinging the gun up. But the hooded figures clinging from the black ropes carried no weapons.

Donal could shoot them, but he could not reach them with his hands.

He took aim.

For a moment the sight blurred as his focus shifted to the target. The hooded man's eyes were trained on Donal. The man knew he was about to die.

Steady ...

Donal exhaled, tightening the abdomen and the trigger finger together.

'Fuck.'

Then he pulled his finger out of the trigger guard and lowered the gun. He sucked cold wet air into his lungs.

Do you hear—?

No. There was no point in killing the man, that's all.

The pterabat continued to rise.

Perhaps Donal might have fired into Cortindo's already dead body, but what was the point? There wasn't much you could do to a corpse, and it was already tied to the ropes, borne aloft by the pterabat. Killing one of the hooded figures when they were unarmed was not Donal's idea of legitimate force.

He checked the dwarves again – one of them was on hands and knees, shaking his head, dripping scarlet blood mixed with rain – and looked back up. The ropes were withdrawing into the body of the pterabat as it ascended and began to wheel away.

'Oh, sweet Death.' Alexa's voice carried through the pterabat's subsonics with a disconcerting clarity. 'Those steps have killed me.'

She bent over, left hand on her thigh to keep her steady, lungs wheezing. But none of that prevented her from taking out her gun with her right hand and taking a steady aim on the nearer of the two dwarves.

'Don't you bloody ...' She sucked in a breath. 'Ah ... Don't ... Move.'

Then Ralfinko staggered out of the doorway, clutching his coat around himself against a sudden squall of rain, and took aim at the second dwarf. Donal checked them both, then reholstered his Magnus. He looked back up into the dark sky.

Cortindo's body had been drawn into the hold, and the hooded figures were already out of sight. The opening sealed shut as the pterabat banked, diving into the turn and then pulling up, ascending into the cloud layer where its outline grew indistinct and then it was out of sight.

Gone.

One of the dwarves began to laugh.

The claw tightened around Viktor's throat.

'I said' – Sal's voice clenched as though he was the one being strangled – 'who the Thanatos are you? And what is the woman to you?'

'My ...' Viktor forced out the lie. '... Sister.'

The claw which grew from Sal's left arm could snip shut and part Viktor's head from his body in an instant. If he did that, the headless corpse of Viktor would soon reveal the police ID hanging on a cord inside his chest.

Even drenched in blood, Sally the Claw would see the badge straight away for what it was. But every second that Sushana remained alive was a kind of victory, and perhaps that was the best Viktor could—

Sally the Claw screamed.

A wraith's arm was reaching inside his groin, and Sal reacted as a normal man would, bending over, chin coming up and his grip weakening. That was enough for Viktor. The claw's sharpness had pierced the skin of Viktor's neck and it was his own slick blood that allowed him to slip out of that grip now.

Then a pale figure in a skirt suit stepped in through the doorway and raised her gun and fired. Sal's right eye exploded.

Xalia grew insubstantial as Sally the Claw's corpse toppled through her and dropped to the floor with the cold thud of dead meat. Then she drifted to one side and partially manifested, her outline growing steadier.

Are you all right?

Viktor's answer was a croak, scarcely audible: 'Never ... better.'

'Damn it.' Laura quickly checked the corpses scattered around the floor – checked that they *were* corpses, and not wounded men about to revive and reach for their weapons. Then she tried to free Sushana from the ropes that bound her to the chair.

Viktor dragged himself over to where his Grausers had fallen.

'Allow me.'

He picked up the guns, walked over to Sally the Claw's body, then opened fire, aiming at the wrist and blowing it apart in a hail of chitin-piercing rounds. Finally Viktor holstered his weapons, took hold of the near-severed claw, and tugged.

'Almost ...'

Viktor pulled again, and the claw came free with a liquid sucking sound. Then he dragged the thing over to Sushana, and swiped down at the ropes, cutting them apart.

'Well done,' said Laura.

Sushana fainted at last, toppling from the chair. Laura and Viktor caught her before she hit the floor.

I guess ...

Xalia drifted over them.

* ...we should call this a success.*

Laura looked at the bloody bodies strewn across the floor.

'Yes,' she said. 'We damn well should.'

Three hours later, every member of the team apart from Harald was gathered around a table in an interrogation room on the hundredth floor of HQ. Lying on its side atop the table was a stained canary-yellow tandem bicycle.

'What?' said Viktor. 'We should threaten the bicycle until it talks?'

Xalia wrapped a near-invisible hand around the frame, the rest of her body drifting like smoke.

There's no wraith in here.

'That was a joke,' Viktor growled.

Oh.

Alexa smirked. Xalia always could wind up Viktor.

'You said you saw a tandem like this' – Laura was at the back of the room, leaning against the wall with her eyes closed, thinking – 'at Sally the Claw's place. Before Xalia and I turned up.'

And rescued you.

'I was doing all right.'

You were what?

Viktor grinned. 'What, are you feeling under-appreciated, Xalia?'

'Peace,' said Donal. 'And we all know the chances of two yellow tandems making an appearance in two different locations tonight. This was in the back of the van that the Ugly Twins used to carry

186

Cortindo's body. Sally the Claw is part of the network we're tracking down.'

'The Ugly Twins with steel-trap jaws,' muttered Alexa.

That was partly a reference to Donal's bandaged forearm, partly to the way the dwarves had clamped their jaws shut and said not a single word between them since their formal arrest. Nor had they struggled once the cuffs were on: merely went limp and forced the uniformed backup officers to carry them down the many flights of stairs inside the great skull, down to the waiting police van.

'No surprise.' Laura opened her eyes. 'Sal had his fingers – well, claw – in a couple of dozen different pies.'

'Nice if we could backtrack.'

'Yeah. Nice,' said Alexa, 'if the OCML get something out of Sal's corpse.'

Donal blew out a breath, and Viktor muttered: 'Shit.'

'Right.'

The whole team now knew that Wilhelmina d'Alkarny, the chief forensic Bone Listener, was lying on one of her own steel autopsy tables in the depths of the OCML. Viktor and Harald had known her – well enough to call her Mina – and that was why Harald was at the OCML right now, instead of here.

'None of this makes sense,' said Donal. 'Why use the dwarves to blow open the place just to get Cortindo's corpse?'

'How else would they do it?' Alexa reached for the tandem as though to push it off the table, then stepped back. 'Who'd have thought any-one could mount an attack like that?'

'No.' Laura looked at them. 'Donal's right. If the opposition could mount that kind of strike, why do it now? Why reveal themselves because of one dead man?'

'Because Cortindo knew something.' Viktor's voice was like gravel spilling in an iron bucket. 'Because if Mina performed an autopsy, she would learn something about the Black Circle.'

'The name of Cortindo's contact? Maybe,' said Alexa, 'his direct superior. Or someone higher still.'

Everyone was silent for a few moments. Then Donal put his hands in his pockets and looked up at the ceiling.

'You know,' he said, 'it might be interesting to find out why Cortindo hadn't been autopsied yet. I mean, there's a waiting list, but it can't be that long, right?'

Laura said: 'You're thinking someone ordered him put in stasis?'

'Someone important.' Viktor looked from Laura to Donal. 'Someone who could override Mina's authority.'

'Right.'

'Someone,' said Viktor, 'that we should have a little word with.'

Harald was in an outer chamber of the OCML. A young Bone Listener called Brixhan had brought Harald a cup of rose-and-blackthorn tea, then scowled when Harald asked him to stay for a moment.

'You know – knew – Mina, right?'

'I worked for Dr d'Alkarny, yes.'

'What the Thanatos happened, do you know?'

'I believe that Dr d'Alkarny must have decided on an unauthorized—'

Another Bone Listener was entering the room. 'It was her prerogative to check The Honeycomb,' said the newcomer. 'In fact, it was her duty, Brixhan, don't you agree?'

'Um ... Technically, yes.'

'Well *technically* is good enough, wouldn't you say, Officer?'

'What's your name?' Harald's voice went very gentle. 'I didn't catch it, Bone Listener.'

'Lexar Pinderwin. I hope you catch the bastards who did this.'

'I think we already have. At least the ones carrying out the physical act.'

Brixhan frowned.

'You mean,' said Lexar, 'you've got the footsoldiers, but not the principals who hired them.'

'Yeah,' said Harald. 'That's what I mean.'

'Well that's a start.'

'It is.' Harald blinked his gentle eyes. 'Any hints you could give me, might help us to track down those principals.'

'Dr d'Alkarny did nothing wrong.' Lexar was staring at Brixhan.

'Well, that's good.' Harald touched Brixhan on the shoulder. 'She had a day-diary, right? A list of appointments and such?'

'Um ... Yes, I think ... Well, yes, she did. It should be in her—'

'Go and fetch it for me, will you?'

'I don't—'

'Right now, there's a good chap.'

Brixhan swallowed.

'Um, sure, Officer.'

'In your own time.'

With a last glance towards Lexar, Brixhan left. Harald counted to twenty, then walked over to the door and checked the metal-lined corridor outside. It was clear.

'All right.' Harald came back in, sat down, and waved at an empty seat. 'Sit with me, Lexar.'

Lexar sat.

'And talk.'

'I won't tell tales,' said Lexar. 'Dr d'Alkarny was the best examiner who ever—'

'And Mina was a friend of mine.' Harald leaned forward, and suddenly his gentle eyes went as hard as steel. 'A close friend. I want to know *everything*.'

Lexar swallowed, then blinked several times, his eyes growing damp.

'I shouldn't have looked,' he said. 'But she ... There was a body in stasis, under orders. Dr d'Alkarny wondered why.'

'Whose orders?'

'Um ... I'm not sure. Is it important?' Lexar started to rise. 'I can get the—'

'In a moment,' said Harald. 'What is it you didn't want Brixhan to say?'

'He knows nothing. He only half suspects, and that's because of something I said. He doesn't have the sensitivity to have felt it for himself.'

'What are you talking about?' Harald's tone took the sting out of the words. 'Sensitivity to what?'

'To the traces left on her fingers, in her bones ...'

Harald drew back. 'Excuse me?'

'Dr d'Alkarny did the autopsy,' said Lexar, 'even though she was forbidden to, by executive order.'

'You're sure of that?'

'Um.' Lexar hesitated, then: 'Yes, I'm sure of it.'

Harald stared around the room. If Brixhan came back, Harald was going to cuff him to a table and take Lexar outside, because this was important.

'She had focus, did Mina,' said Harald. 'Wouldn't you say?'

'Yes. Better than anyone I've met. Any Bone Listener.'

'Enough focus to hold a dying thought?'

'Oh, Thanatos ...'

'To burn a dying image into her bones?'

'Yes.' Tears began to trickle down Lexar's cheeks, but he allowed the weeping to happen, hiding nothing. 'Oh, yes. She was the best.'

Harald stood up.

'I want you to perform the autopsy.'

'No.' Lexar swallowed. 'I'm only a junior—'

'I want you to carry out the autopsy right now.'

The rest of the team arrived an hour later, while the autopsy was in progress. They'd stopped first in the lowest subterranean level of cells, where the dwarves were fastened against the cold stone walls with silver bands.

Neither of them looked about to talk, not even when Xalia had drifted close and run her fingertips across their brains, reaching through their bony skulls. If only she could read minds ... but as things were, it was all Xalia could do to restrain herself from manifesting her long-nailed fingers and squeezing, hard.

It just wouldn't have done anyone any good.

Donal made a phone call first, direct to the Archives, and spoke briefly to the Bone Listener he'd consulted with, Feoragh Carryn. There was a sadness in her voice overlaid with something more, but it took a minute for Donal to work out what it was. Feoragh was guilty with the knowledge that she'd caused Mina's death; or at least that was the way she saw it.

'No,' said Donal. 'You talked to Dr d'Alkarny because of me, for a start. Let's not have any survivor's guilt here.'

'Please ...'

'I'm sorry, but realize this. At one end of the causal chain are the people who carried out the attack, and at another are my actions, and you're somewhere in the middle. There is no blame.'

'Yes.' Feoragh's voice sighed down the line like a breeze. 'But while I know the theory behind your words, right now I believe none of it.'

'Then what will help?'

'Finding out who killed Mina, and why. And ... dealing with them.'

'Good,' said Donal. 'Then that's what we'll do.'

He put the phone down, seeing Feoragh in his mind's eye, imagining her going down into the Lattice and immersing herself in the bones' Archived memories, digging deeper and deeper. Whatever other result Mina d'Alkarny's death might have, it meant that one Bone Listener at least was probing the Archives with a resolution no one could match.

And whatever the Black Circle, or whatever the opposition called themselves, had intended ... they were going to find a task force on their tail that would not stop.

Donal went down to the ground level, past the glowering deathwolves on the main steps. FenSeven turned to Donal with a smouldering anger in his amber eyes: he'd heard of Mina's death at the Archives. Donal nodded.

The Vixen was waiting at the curb. She swung her passenger door up and Donal climbed inside. Laura was already at the wheel, and as the door came down and clicked shut, she got the car into motion.

'Have the others left?' Donal looked back as HQ slid away behind them. 'Viktor looked surprisingly edgy, after all he's been through.'

'What do you mean?'

'I'd have expected an adrenaline crash, you know? In reaction to everything. Especially since ... I'd say he's quite fond of Sushana.'

The medics had taken Sushana away, and made it plain that no visitors would be welcome for some time, probably days.

'Yeah,' said Laura. 'But he was fond of Mina, too.'

'Oh.'

'Him and Harald both. Some say—' Laura pressed her lips together.

'Say what?'

'That the three of them, Harald and Mina and Sushana, were, er, more than just good friends.'

'Oh,' said Donal again. 'I ... Um. I see.'

Laura reached across for Donal's wrist, then placed his hand against her left breast.

'More normal,' she said, 'than taking up with someone who has no heartbeat, wouldn't you say?'

'I love you.'

'Damn it.' Blinking, Laura shook her head. 'That's not supposed to happen.'

Do—?

Shh.

Donal withdrew his hand.

'And?'

'And, for Thanatos' sake, I damn well love you, too. Good enough?'

'Yeah,' breathed Donal. 'More than.'

The Vixen came to a halt, and opened her doors.

'This is the place,' said Laura.

Above ground, the Office of the Chief Medical Listener was a hunched blue stone building that looked like a frozen animal, with a smaller head-like extension – even the window-strips looked like huge eyes – attached to the main body of the place. Only the twenty police cruisers parked at odd angles around the perimeter gave any clue to the events that had taken place in the subterranean levels of The Honeycomb.

Deeper down than the autopsy level where even now Mina's body was cut asunder, while the young Bone Listener who had admired her so much laid his hands upon her still-warm blood-slick bones, trying to read the message inscribed by agony within.

Eighteen

'I can't do it.' Lexar lay aside the marrow-saw. 'There's nothing I—'

'You can.' Harald's voice was muffled by the surgical mask he wore. 'Try again.'

'No . . .' But, shuddering, Lexar forced his hands inside Mina's splayed and opened corpse once more. 'Ah . . .'

Lexar's eyelids fluttered.

'Shit.' Harald caught Lexar as he toppled over. 'For Thanatos' sake.'

But Lexar stirred immediately and pushed himself away from Harald, and stood on his own feet, swaying.

'Two squat men,' he said. 'Dwarves.'

Harald let out a breath. It confirmed what Laura had said on the phone, about the two prisoners that Donal and Alexa had captured. Whether it could be used as evidence in a trial would depend on whether he could retrospectively get this autopsy declared official.

'Axe,' Lexar added. 'They had an axe.'

Harald shook his head.

Wonderful. Now we can interrogate every hardware supplier in Tristopolis.

This was less than useful.

Can't be more than a couple of thousand of 'em.

But Lexar's eyes cleared and he focused on Harald.

'No ordinary axe,' Lexar said. 'This was a coherent hex-wave resonator. They don't exactly grow on trees.'

'OK.' Harald stared down at Mina's corpse. 'Good. That's something.'

'Looked Illurian to me,' said Lexar. 'Well, to Mina . . .'

There was an odd pain in Lexar's voice, and Harald suspected that there were agonies involved here that only a Bone Listener could appreciate or understand. Then fingernails tapped against the clear glass window inset in the autopsy room door. It was Laura, standing outside.

A misty form drifted through the closed doorway.

'What?' Lexar's hand reached reflexively for one of his surgical cutting-tools.

'She's a colleague.' Harald nodded. 'Xalia, this is Lexar. He's a good man.'

Xalia drifted six feet away, and rose a little towards the ceiling.

Well met, Lexar.

'I'm ... pleased to meet you, Xalia. Pardon my reaction.'

But Xalia was already floating over Mina's corpse, and the shadow and hollows of her near-invisible face were as expressive of grief as Lexar's own.

She was a good person.

'Yes.'

Xalia rotated to face Harald.

Viktor won't come in.

'Can you blame him?'

No ...

After a moment, Harald said: 'I'll go out to him. Lexar?'

'I'm all right here. There's nothing more to do, except to ... tidy her up, you know?'

'Make her look presentable.'

'Yes.' Lexar reached out to touch Mina's dead intact face. 'Presentable.'

A single tear grew in the corner of Harald's left eye.

Are you—?

'Hardly.'

Xalia said nothing more, but drifted almost to the ceiling as she watched Harald leave the autopsy room, trying to keep his feelings under control. She did not know the truth about the rumours of a threesome, though she could float through walls and watch unobserved.

That was because you did not spy on friends, not ever.

We'll track them down. She spoke to Lexar, who was hunched over the corpse, hesitating before closing up the great incision that split Mina's torso open. *Eventually, we'll get them, including the ones who gave the orders.*

'Probably.'

Lexar's tone was empty, and Xalia understood what that signified: revenge meant nothing, justice in the courtroom sense meant nothing, because the only true justice would involve bringing Mina back to life. And that was something no Bone Listener or thaumaturge could ever do.

Perhaps they'll end up here. On your table.

At this, Lexar looked up at Xalia.

'Yes. And if they're not quite dead, I can live with that.'

Xalia wondered what a Bone Listener could do with the feelings and nervous system of a person – an enemy – who was still alive.

I'll see what I can do.

Then she bowed her head, drifted upward through the ceiling, and was gone.

Laura was using the office that had been Mina's to make some phone calls. The first was to the hospital, where it took three transfers and several minutes of holding on the line – one matron in particular was unimpressed by Laura's rank – before learning that Sushana was 'satisfactory'. Laura tried to think of a reply that expressed what she thought of that categorization, failed, and hung up.

Then Alexa came through the door and pushed it shut behind her.

'What's up?' said Laura, looking up from her chair.

'Um ... I may be speaking out of line here.' Alexa paused.

'Or not.'

'Excuse me?'

'You're not speaking, Alexa. So what *is* up?'

'You and Donal.' Alexa swallowed, then continued quickly: 'Was recruiting him your idea?'

'What are you getting at?'

'I know you're close. We – everyone – we think that's great, see ...'

'Thanatos, Alexa. Will you spit it out?'

'It's just ... I'm wondering about the timing. We get deeper into the Black Circle than ever before, and trip something that causes a massive reaction. Breaking into this place.' Alexa gestured at the steel-covered walls. 'That's bringing things out into the open, don't you think?'

Laura crossed her arms.

'What's Donal got to do with this? Other than the way he's cracked the case.'

'I'm not jealous of his success, if that's what you're thinking.' Alexa rubbed her eyes, and Laura reminded herself that living people require sleep.

'So what? I think you've got cause and effect mixed up.' Laura's voice sounded tenser than she'd intended. 'Donal joined us first, and *then* we started unravelling threads.'

'Following lines of enquiry we'd already started.' Alexa shuffled her feet. 'Sorry, but that's why I had to ask about Donal. Cause and effect ...'

Laura held herself still, then: 'Xalia and I virtually dragged Donal from a hospital bed. We had to work on him. Persuade him.'

'Well ... Thank you,' said Alexa. 'You could've just told me to piss off and mind my own business.'

'I nearly did.' Laura smiled, and waited until Alexa smiled back. 'But you're really asking if Donal could have played me, manipulated me. And the answer is no.'

'OK.'

Laura waited again. Then she pointed at an empty chair. 'Sit down, why don't you.'

Alexa sat.

Laura stopped breathing. For the undead, respiration is unimportant.

'Shit,' said Alexa finally, and fumbled inside her jacket pocket. 'Here. You take this.'

She pulled out a bent pink file card, and handed it over to Laura. The writing on the card was in purple ink, a gothic style embellished with heavy curlicues. It read: *Placed in stasis by order of the office of Commr. A. Vilnar, Quintober 3rd 6607.*

Underneath, a different hand had added a note in burgundy. *Duration: indefinite.*

Laura placed the card down on the desktop beside her.

'No need to ask whose body this referred to.'

Alexa bit her lip. 'You trust Donal.'

'You were with him, chasing the body.' Laura frowned, strange highlights shifting through her eyes. 'You're not saying Donal held back? That he could have caught them?'

'I ...' Alexa blew out a breath. 'None of the rest of us were even close. I think he did better than anyone could expect.'

'Well. Good.'

'And there's something else ...'

'What's that?' said Laura.

'I did watch him run up those steps, in the great skull, while I tried to follow.'

'So?'

'So he's got a skinny ass, and he's fit as hell.' Alexa grinned. 'I'd say you're a lucky woman, boss.'

'Thanatos,' said Laura, but she was laughing despite herself. 'Will you piss off out of here?'

Just as Alexa was rising, there was a knock on the door. It swung open, and Donal looked inside.

'Hi,' he said. 'Am I interrupting something?'

Laura and Alexa looked at each other.

'*No,*' they said in perfect unison, then lapsed into sputtering laughter.

'Sorry,' added Laura.

Donal looked at them for a moment, shook his head, and disappeared back into the corridor, and closed the door. But he was smiling as he did it.

The smile faded as Donal continued down the corridor. He was glad that Laura and Alexa were friends; and Alexa seemed like a good person, or at least a good cop. Whether those two concepts were the same was a discussion for a lazy day.

But there had been something in the atmosphere in the room, something that indicated the laughter he had caused had partly been in reaction to earlier tension. And the cause of the tension had been visible: the pink filing card, face up on the desk beside Laura.

Though the handwriting had been upside down, that presented no problem to Donal: he remembered Sister Mary-Ann Styx back at the orphanage, and her sharp questioning of the three-year-old Donal who had claimed to have read the newspaper lying at the far end of the room, and how he had backed up his claims by reciting the headlines back at her.

So Commissioner Vilnar had ordered Cortindo's body to be held in stasis.

'*Follow the paper trail,*' Laura had said.

The thing was, Vilnar *had* asked Donal to spy on the task force. And Laura suspected Vilnar. But none of this was proof.

A prickling crossed Donal's spine, and he turned round. A pale figure – a male Bone Listener – was watching from an open doorway.

'Can I help you?' said Donal.

'Um … It's about Dr d'Alkarny.'

'And you are?'

'Brixhan Dektrolis. I'm not sure, but I think that one of my colleagues might be carrying out a postmortem on Dr d'Alkarny.'

Donal said: 'This is the OCML, isn't it? Where autopsies take place?'

'Of course it's—' Brixhan coloured. 'The person involved is not qualified, and I believe he might have had an emotional attachment to Dr d'Alkarny.'

'Goodness.'

'Well, quite. It's a clear breach of professional—'

'I'll say. Listen, did you assist my colleague, Detective Ceerling? Alexa Ceerling?'

Brixhan blinked. 'Yes, I unlocked the records room for—'

'And cross-checked with the' – Donal was going to say the correspondence files, then quickly changed his words – 'tags in The Honeycomb? Just to make sure we've got the right body.'

'There's no mistake.' Brixhan frowned, probably trying to look authoritative. 'The records are accurate.'

'Of course they are. You people do good work.' Donal let his gaze go unfocused. 'Don't fancy it myself.'

'A lot of people react that way.' Brixhan sounded smug. 'We have the training, though.'

'We certainly need forensic geniuses.' Donal raised an eyebrow. 'And people who know how to be professional. I think you're destined to go far.'

'Ah. Thank you, Lieutenant Riordan.'

So Brixhan had already learned Donal's name, though Donal hadn't introduced himself.

'Perhaps,' Donal said, letting his gaze drift towards the steel wall beyond which lay the autopsy rooms, 'you'll go as far as Dr d'Alkarny herself.'

Brixhan's mouth worked, with no reply sounding.

'Take it easy,' Donal added.

He hitched his jacket, being careful to let the butt of his Magnus show just for a second – it made Brixhan take an involuntary half step back – then turned and walked away, letting Brixhan make of his remarks whatever he wanted.

Unpleasant asshole.

But being a creep wasn't a major crime, more like a congenital disease. It had been a long time since Donal let people like Brixhan worry him.

Conversley Donal knew that making an enemy of Commissioner

Vilnar would not be worrying: it would be terrifying. He had respect for the man. But if Vilnar was involved with the Black Circle, then someone had to take him down.

On the edge of the lab area was a kind of antechamber that acted as a waiting-room for civilians who needed to identify a body or otherwise assist. Donal had been there several times with relatives of victims ... or in one case, in the company of a fat old lady who examined the soapy-looking body of the man thought to be her son, poked it with one gnarled finger and said: 'Looks like a piece a shit, don't he? Too good lookin' to be *my* boy, though. Nice try, Loot.'

He made his way there now, remembering the small acoustically shielded phone booth set against one wall. The room was empty, so he dug in his pocket for the seven-sided coins he needed, picked up the receiver and fed the coins into the slot.

It was a woman's voice that answered.

'Hello? Commissioner Vilnar's office.'

'Hi,' said Donal, unable to use her name, knowing her only as Eyes. 'Um ... Is he in? This is Riordan.'

'One moment.' Eyes was too self-confident to lie and say that she would have to check. She was quite capable of telling anyone that her boss was too busy to talk. *'Putting you through, Lieutenant.'*

There was a click and a scrape, and Donal imagined Eyes flicking a toggle switch on her console. Could she listen in on these conversations?

No matter. If Vilnar trusted her, then she could; otherwise he would have taken countermeasures.

'Riordan.'

'Sir. I'm at the OCML, where Cortindo's body was stolen.'

'You think that's news to me?'

'The theft? No, sir. And I assume you know that Dr d'Alkarny was killed during the break-in.'

There was a long pause, longer than Donal would have expected.

'Is there any progress on that? On her death?'

'Almost certainly the two suspects we have in custody killed her. I'm expecting confirmation on that shortly.'

'Confirmation?'

'Sir, Dr d'Alkarny was a Bone Listener. She might have been able to visualize her dying moments in sharp focus, so that the vision could be ... retrieved. Later.'

'You mean they're carrying out an autopsy.'

'There hasn't been time,' said Donal, 'to get the magistrate's authorization for a PM.'

'*And?*' Vilnar's tone was dry. He might not be a street cop any more, but he understood bureaucratic systems and how to bypass them.

'Someone's doing the autopsy right now. Unofficially.'

There was a sound on the line that might have been static, might have been Vilnar exhaling.

'*Good. Let me know how that turns out. Good work, Riordan.*'

'Er ... One thing more, sir. Cortindo's body was in stasis.'

'*It was? But his death was weeks ago, when you ...*'

'When I killed him. Yes.'

There was more that Donal could say, but this seemed the wrong time to say it. Instead he added: 'But that was just a bureaucratic hitch, I think. It's the dwarves who are the main lead.'

'*Dwarves?*'

'The two suspects we have in the cells. They're four feet tall, if that, but powerful.'

'*Ah.*' Papers rustled at the other end of the line: Vilnar checking documents on his desk. '*Yes. I see.*'

So Vilnar already had copies of the arrest-and-detention reports.

'*And the task force? Are they making any other progress I should know about?*'

Donal hesitated.

'Commander Steele is very capable, sir,' he said finally. 'But one of their other officers was kidnapped and rescued, and none of it looks like leading anywhere. I'd say the task force is ... distracted.'

Let Vilnar think that the trail had stopped, instead of leading direct to his office.

'*All right.*' Vilnar coughed. '*Keep me informed.*'

'Yes—'

But the line was already dead. Donal listened to the oceanic wash of static hiss, learning nothing. He put the receiver down, and left the waiting-room, failing to notice the faint misty movement, nearly invisible, against the wall where the phone was attached. Long wraith fingers curled back, the insubstantial hand palm-up.

Then the wraith raised her middle finger, and gestured towards the doorway where Donal had disappeared.

Screw you, lover boy.

Xalia disappeared back inside the wall.

*

Harald addressed the rest of the team (Sushana excluded – it would be a long time before she left hospital) with his gentle eyes flatter than usual, his voice toneless. The results of the autopsy conducted by the young Bone Listener, Lexar, were conclusive as far as the task force were concerned.

Presenting the findings before a court of law would be a different proposition.

Donal leaned against the wall, his arms crossed, unsure why Xalia had moved away from him when he entered the room.

'Surely we can put the Ugly Twins' – Alexa meant the captive dwarves – 'at the scene. I saw them on the roof, for Thanatos' sake, while an unregistered pterabat took off into the sky.'

'A pterabat,' said Laura, 'that not only failed to file a flight plan, but escaped detection by any surveillance system. None of our launched copters managed to spot it.'

'Damn it.'

'Well, yes. The dwarves' green van wasn't identified for sure, either. The only link' – Laura nodded toward Harald – 'is Dr d'Alkarny's dying memory of the dwarves attacking her. If we can retrospectively get the magistrate's authorization for Lexar to perform the PM, then we'll be able to submit that much evidence.'

Alexa held out both hands.

'Well, then. That *is* enough, isn't it?'

'To get the footsoldiers,' growled Viktor. 'Not the ones who ordered them to kill Mina.'

Harald slowly nodded.

'Shit,' said Alexa.

For a few moments, nobody spoke. Then Donal shifted against the wall. 'You said something about a weapon, Harald? An axe?'

Harald shrugged.

'Lexar says it was Illurian.'

'Another connection to Illurium,' muttered Laura. 'And you've got contacts of your own there, haven't you?'

Donal raised his eyebrows. Harald said: 'I was there for two years, nearly. In the Military Police, seconded from the Marines.'

'Yeah, like one axe,' muttered Viktor, 'is going to lead you to the shop that sold it. One shop from an entire country. Assuming it *was* Illurian ... This Lexar can't be certain, can he?'

'It was ensorcelled in some way,' said Harald. 'Coherent flux thingy ... I can't remember what he said.'

'You weren't taking notes?' Alexa's tone was half-joke, half-accusation.

'No, there was a scribewraith writing an official record.'

'Without a timestamp, I hope,' said Laura.

If the wraith had timestamped the record, then it would flag the autopsy as having taken place before legal permission had been granted. That would be enough to make the findings inadmissible as evidence.

Liquid waves rippling through a melting human body ...

The sudden image passed through Donal's mind, and he shook it away, remembering his fellow hospital patient called Andy: the man with an inability to prevent his body from morphing into random shapes. The man who had nearly ruptured his flowing body and died when the healing-field generator on his bed had failed.

'I might have accidentally discharged a sparkler,' murmured Harald, looking at Xalia. He shrugged. 'Sorry.'

That's not funny.

'I know.'

No you don't. You're not a wraith.

'Sparklers hurt. I know that much.'

Xalia drifted above the floor, making no reply. She obviously disapproved of Harald's using the sparkler to drive the scribewraith out of the autopsy room.

Laura sighed. 'This isn't helping, gang.'

'Sorry.'

'Maybe it is,' said Donal, ignoring the strange look that Xalia seemed to be giving him. 'Are you saying, Harald, that this axe was unusually ensorcelled? And strongly?'

'Um ... Yeah. That's what Lexar implied.'

'So it would leave a strong trace in the Ugly Twins' auras, right?'

Harald nodded. 'You're right. We should get Lexar to—'

'No.' Laura slapped the table. 'We don't use Bone Listeners to torture living people.'

'Maybe we won't have to.' Donal pushed himself away from the wall. 'Maybe there's someone else that can follow the trail. Dig down inside the prisoners' auras.'

His subconscious mind had delivered up the memory of the unfortunate Andy melting on the hospital bed. When the healing field failed, Sister Felice had called in the experts.

What was the young genius called? Kyushol? Kyushen? Something like that.

202

Xalia drifted closer.

I want to be there, when this interrogation happens.

Donal tried to focus on her wraith-form, but it seemed to be slipping in and out of reality.

'All right,' he said eventually. 'If you want to.'

I do.

'Then I'll make a phone call.'

For a moment, Donal thought Xalia was going to say something. Instead, she shook her near-invisible head, and then her whole insubstantial form sank down inside the floor and was gone.

'I hate it,' muttered Alexa, 'when she does that.'

Laura was staring at Donal.

Now what? Donal wondered.

'I'll see you all in a minute,' he said, and went off to call the hospital.

Nineteen

Sister Felice sounded softly charming on the phone, and for a second Donal wondered why he had not tried to see her after leaving the hospital. But there was Laura, and the suddenness of what he felt for her was still startling.

Sister Felice sounded glad that Donal was well, and only a little puzzled by his asking for the young thaumaturge's name. It was Kyushen Jyu, he learned, and technically he was Dr Jyu, but holder of a ThD and not an MD. He never used his title in case someone thought he was a medic.

When Donal got through to Kyushen, it took a while to persuade him that a trip to the city would be interesting enough to drag him away from his normal work. It was only when Donal mentioned an Illurian artefact – an axe – ensorcelled with hex coherence, that Kyushen became interested.

'*Coherent hex-waves? A resonator blade?*'

'Um, yeah,' said Donal. 'I think that's what they said.'

'*Oh, man.*'

'But you can follow the traces inside the prisoners' auras?'

'*Auras? Are you on something? There's no such thing as auras, apart from some people's visual metaphors. They're not, like, real.*'

'Oh,' said Donal.

'*Look, modern thaumaturgical engineering is based on IIC, which makes procedural hex as antiquated as ... as an antiquity. You know?*'

'Do I need to know what IIC stands for?'

'*You haven't heard of Imagine-Inclined Conjuring.*' It was not quite a question. '*Everything in the world has qualia and propensities, and in IIC that's how we model it in hex. We combine the two concepts, see, instead of separating out the teleological functions from the entities they act on. That's the old-fashioned way.*'

'Right,' said Donal. 'Well, obviously.'

'That makes all the … Look, I'll explain it all clearly when I get there.'

'I'll look forward to that.'

'All right,' said Kyushen. *'I'll be there at six am.'*

'Six? That's a little—'

There was a click, and then the line buzzed. Donal stared at the receiver for a moment.

'—early,' he said.

And put the receiver down.

Laura poked her head around the doorway. 'You got through to your contact?'

'Yeah. We're going to try some Image-Inclined Hexing,' said Donal. 'I think.'

'Well. That's nice.'

'It's more fun than sex. Or so my contact implied.'

'And does he have a girlfriend? Has he ever had a girlfriend?'

'I doubt it,' said Donal. 'And how did you know my contact's a he?'

'A lucky guess.' A smile dimpled Laura's pale face.

'Well … You up for some hex later?'

'If you play your cards right, Lieutenant.'

'I'll do my best, Commander.'

Xalia backed out of her concealed position inside the solid wall, coming into the corridor where Harald was standing, a sparkler in either hand. Xalia shivered, which was the wraith equivalent of a living human jumping with fright.

What are you doing here?

'Watching you drift out of the stonework.'

Xalia drifted back a little, wary of the unlit sparklers that Harald held.

I don't like those things.

'And how about Donal Riordan?' asked Harald. 'Do you like him?'

Xalia shook her head, stopped, then nodded.

Like, yes. Trust, no.

'Alexa said he did a good job.'

Like a slow tornado, Xalia corkscrewed around in the air. Then she slowed, untwisted herself, and descended closer to Harald.

He's spying on us. For Vilnar.

Harald blinked, and looked at Xalia with his soft placid eyes.

'That's not good,' he said.

Back in HQ, Donal noticed that Viktor had disappeared. He mentioned it to Alexa, who stared at him for a moment, then said: 'He went to the hospital.'

'Oh, Thanatos,' muttered Donal. 'I'm sorry. Sushana.'

'I know.' Alexa relented. 'You've never even met her, but some of us have known her for a long time.'

'Undercover work is dangerous, in lots of ways.'

'You're saying she was crooked?'

'No.' Donal leaned against a desk. 'Brave and determined and under a lot of stress. It takes guts to do that kind of work. I'm not surprised that Viktor's with her.'

'He's not *with* her, not in the sense you mean.'

'Actually, I kind of worked out that she and Dr d'Alkarny and ...' Donal let his voice trail off.

'And Harald,' said Alexa. 'Did Laura tell you, or did you really work it out?'

'Both, I guess.'

'Everyone needs someone.'

'Um, yeah.' Donal hoped Alexa wasn't propositioning him. It had happened before with other women on occasion; and he hadn't always noticed it coming. 'The thing is, with Laura—'

'If you hurt her,' said Alexa, 'one of us will kill you.'

'Ah.' Donal smiled. 'I'm glad we've got that clear.'

'Well?'

'I won't hurt her,' Donal said. 'And if anyone else does, I'll kill them myself.'

'That's good enough.' Alexa held out her hand.

Donal looked at her, then reached over. They shook.

'What are you two up to?' It was Laura, coming into the main office.

'Team building,' said Donal.

'He'll do,' said Alexa. 'Just about.'

'I'm sorry I asked. Donal, are you sure you want to do this?' Laura held up a long slim envelope on which a stylized silver aeroplane had been embossed. 'Incognito and without official powers, you'll be in a lot of danger.'

Alexa frowned. 'You're not talking about undercover work for Donal, are you?'

Donal said, 'We were talking about Sushana. But this is different. I'm just visiting Illurium as—'

'The department will never pay for that,' said Alexa.

'Er ... What do you mean?' Donal pointed at the flight ticket in Laura's hand.

'Ask Laura who made the booking,' said Alexa. 'Ask her who paid for it.'

Laura put the ticket down on the desk. 'Does it matter? Really matter?'

'Come on,' said Donal. 'Laura ... You didn't pay for that yourself, did you? It'll cost a—'

'I live in Darksan Tower.' Laura looked amused. 'You still haven't worked it out, have you?'

'At least,' said Alexa, 'he's not after you for your money.'

'What are you two on about?'

Alexa pointed at Laura. 'Your girlfriend, Lieutenant Riordan, isn't just your superior officer. She's one of the richest women in Tristopolis.'

Laura shrugged.

'Stinking rich,' she said.

Alexa pointed at Donal. 'But you better still remember what we said.'

Donal nodded.

'I won't forget.'

But Alexa was frowning, and Donal thought that he understood: after talking about the dangers of undercover work, he was volunteering to do the same kind of thing across the border in a foreign country, where the justice system was swifter and harder than the one at home. And while he would not hurt Laura deliberately, if he got himself killed, that would be the worst thing that could happen to her. All this, Donal read from Alexa's expression.

'If we don't get a more specific lead,' he said, 'then I'm not sure it'll be worthwhile going to Illurium at all. Can you cancel that ticket without losing your money?'

Laura shook her head. 'Doesn't matter. But you know that Harald has a lot of contacts in Illurium. You'll have resources to call on.'

'Snitches,' said Donal.

'Maybe. I think some are more highly placed than that.'

Alexa said: 'How can we get more leads? There's nothing to go on.'

'The Ugly Twins,' said Donal.

'They're not talking, are they?'

'Not yet.'

Next morning, at five o'clock, the smell of coffee woke Donal. Laura, already dressed in an olive-green skirt suit, was holding a silver tray with a poured cup of coffee.

'Uh,' said Donal.

'Morning, lover.'

'Mm.' Donal took the coffee and sipped. It was hot. 'Ah ... Thanks.'

'You sure you don't want me to meet the charming egghead for you?'

'Yeah. No.' Donal rubbed his face. 'You'd frighten him off, dear.'

'Is that a compliment?' Laura leaned down and kissed him. Her cold lips felt extra-chilled this morning. 'Or an insult?'

'Not fair. I'm defenceless.'

Laura ran her hand down his cheek. 'Easy prey.'

'I—' Donal picked up his wristwatch from the crystalline bedside table. 'Look at the time.'

'You don't want me to join you in the shower?'

'Well, Dr Jyu will wait for us, I'm sure.'

'You're not sure at all.'

'Um, no ...'

Laura was already walking out of the bedroom. 'Don't delay, lover. I'll wait by the front door.'

The Vixen pulled up just behind the purple taxi that was dropping off Kyushen Jyu before the steps of Police HQ. Donal and Laura alighted, and turned to watch Kyushen, who hadn't noticed them.

As Kyushen passed the deathwolves, the wolves' eyes glowed amber – that was more or less normal – but then the entire pack, FenSeven among them, lay down on their bellies, front legs outstretched, and opened their mouths in lupine grins, tongues lolling and teeth bared.

'That's quite a display,' said Laura.

Donal caught up with Kyushen in the main lobby. Kyushen had already caused a wave of diagnostic hex to pass over Eduardo's counter block, where his lower body was melded into the desk itself.

Eduardo was grinning. 'Why thanks, Dr Jyu. I never really thought of myself as special in that way.'

'Are you kidding?' Kyushen gestured a silvery mist into being, that formed itself into floating runes. 'Best hemimorph I've ever seen, and the integration gradient is spectacular. You mind if I write you up for one of the journals?'

'Uh, sure. I mean no, I don't mind. Will my picture be in it?'

'Yeah,' said Kyushen. 'Definitely some TRS, maybe some—'

'What's TRS?' asked Donal.

'Oh, hi, Lieutenant. Thaumatic Resonance Scanning. Don't your forensic folks use it for analysis?'

'I don't know.' Donal thought back to the shattered corridor in the OCML, where Dr d'Alkarny's body had been found. 'The prisoners I wanted to, er, introduce you to ...'

'Oh, the test subjects. Sure.'

Eduardo frowned, but whether it was the reference to prisoners as test subjects, or whether he resented Donal's taking Kyushen's attention, Donal could not tell.

'They killed the Chief Medical Listener.'

'Surely she didn't try to Listen while they were still alive. Why would she be amused by them, anyway?'

'Huh?' It took Donal a second to recognise Kyushen's misunderstanding. 'No, I mean, they really killed her. Literally.'

'They murdered Dr d'Alkarny?'

'That's what I'm telling you.'

'Awesome. I mean, really bad.' Kyushen put his hands in his pockets. 'Like, how far do you want me to go?'

Donal said: 'What?'

'Look, human thought is kind of transient, but it's formed from neural patterns that build up over time. Pattern persistence is ... Look, say you have an image you form habitually in your mind.'

Donal's eyes shifted up to the left as he thought of Laura.

'That's what I mean,' said Kyushen. 'You've just instantiated a pattern that you've used before, though each instant – that's a technical term – is uniquely different from the previous instants.'

'Um ... If you say so.'

'But you also learn, for example, strategies of learning. That produces metapatterns that are used to create patterns, that are then instantiated. Got it?'

Donal decided it was time to show that cops aren't stupid. 'And there are metametapatterns, I take it, that produce metapatterns.'

Kyushen smiled.

'You've got it.'

'And when you asked about taking it all the way?'

'When you look at the room around you,' said Kyushen, 'most of it's hazy background, but you build a mental model of what the room looks like.'

'All right ...'

'But hidden parts of your mind might find details that the foreground patterns ignore. There are tricks to pulling new patterns out of background haze. You're filtering through a debugging frame because the whole point is you're stochastically analysing apparent noise that the foreground didn't ... Sorry, am I losing you?'

'No.' Donal stared into Kyushen's eyes. 'You were trying to tell me how difficult your job is.'

'Um ... Partly that, maybe ... But the tracing tools dig deep into neural structures. Pain is entirely a neural construct.'

'You mean, the deeper you dig, the more it hurts.'

'Well, oversimplifying ... Yes.'

'And you want to know how much pain the suspects should undergo.'

'Er ... Yes.'

'If you take it all the way, extract everything you can, will it kill them?'

'Unlikely. It's just ...'

'What?'

'Well, they'll probably wish they *had* died. The process may last minutes or an hour, perhaps two hours at the most. But time flow is a matter of internal mental states.'

'You mean it'll last longer for them.'

'For years, or at least that's how it'll feel.' Kyushen gave a soft smile. 'Maybe even centuries. Longer than a normal lifetime.'

'So you'll be doing them a favour. Making it feel like they live longer.'

'In agony.'

Donal shrugged. 'Actions bring consequences.'

Kyushen nodded.

'Yes,' he said. 'They do.'

Harald walked into the task force office and sat down at his desk. There, he stared into space with his gentle eyes, not speaking.

'Hey,' called Alexa. 'Are you all right?'

Harald looked at her. 'I don't think so.'

'So what can I—?

But Harald had already opened his desk drawer and pulled out yellow report folders. He placed them on his desk blotter and began to leaf through loose typed pages. It was movement for movement's sake: Alexa could see that Harald wasn't really reading the reports in front of him.

Laura came out of her office, pulled a visitor's chair into the gap between Harald's desk and Alexa's, and sat down.

'Any news on the pterabat?' Laura asked Alexa.

'Sorry.' Alexa checked the list of official addresses and telephone numbers she'd written down on her notepad. There was now a line drawn through every number.

'I tried every official agency I could think of,' she added, 'starting with the Federal Air Force and the Civilian Flying Authority. I even tried the weather service, in case one of their observation balloons had spotted anything.'

The wraith-enabled sentient balloons were often referred to as Behemoths, an emotionally charged term that Alexa avoided, in case Xalia was offended. Not that anyone had seen Xalia for a while.

'What about the FAF? A pterabat can't have crossed into federal airspace without anyone noticing.'

'Come on, Laura.' Alexa tapped her notepad. 'The border's thousands of miles long, in largely unoccupied territory. The chances of seeing an intruder are minimal if they keep low to the ground, beneath the scan-seers' hexcasts.'

'Is that expert opinion?' Laura gave a half smile. 'You sound pretty definite.'

Alexa coloured a little.

'I got one of the CFA officials talking. He's a nice guy.'

'Oh, yeah?' managed Harald, though his voice sounded empty: ribbing Alexa, but unable to put his heart into it. Not with Sushana still critical.

'What did he tell you?' asked Laura.

'Just what I said. The broadcast masts send out their waves at a thousand feet. In bad weather at night, even a pterabat can fly below hexar altitude, and avoid the banshee patrols.'

Harald rubbed his face. 'Did it definitely come from Illurium? The pterabat, I mean. Couldn't it have taken off and landed inside our own borders?'

'Well David said—' Alexa stopped, and looked at Laura, then Harald. 'Leave me alone. He *is* nice. He works for the CFA's safety board, and he said that a pterabat is too large for a normal small airfield, certainly not the kind of thing you can care for on an isolated farm or whatever.'

'He's not married, is he?' said Laura. 'This David?'

'I don't ... Look, he might not even ring me again.' Alexa blew out a breath. 'Thanatos. Anyway, David doesn't think you could arrange the flight from anywhere but an airport, unless you were *very* well organized. And there were no flight plans of pterabats that could have matched our suspects. None at all.'

'But it's not impossible,' said Harald.

'No. A pterabat could have taken off and landed inside federal airspace. It's just not likely.'

'Why do you ask?' said Laura. 'You got any other information, Harald? A reason for discounting Illurian involvement?'

Harald shook his head.

'Just being logical, is all. Making sure we don't focus all our attentions following one trail, when it's not a definite one.'

Laura said: 'You were the one staking out the embassy.'

'I followed the driver to—' Harald stopped. 'I've got nothing against Donal.'

Alexa looked surprised.

'What's wrong with Donal?'

'I just said—'

'What you said in words and how you tensed up your voice are two different things,' said Laura. 'I heard it, and so did Alexa.'

Alexa looked unhappy. Then she nodded.

Harald closed his eyes, exhaling, then opened them again. 'Vilnar assigned him here, remember? Whether you recruited Donal or not, it was still Vilnar that he reported to before, and who agreed to second him to you.'

'What are you saying?' Laura's voice was like ice.

'Nothing. Absolutely nothing. *You* asked *me*.' Harald stood up, report folders in hand. 'I'm going to the hospital. Give Viktor a break.'

Laura looked at him for an endless moment, then said: 'All right. Send Viktor home to rest.'

'I'll try.'

Laura watched Harald go, expecting the door to slam behind him. When it gently clicked shut, she gave a tiny jump nonetheless. Then she realized that Alexa was watching her with care.

'Do you think I'm losing the plot?' Laura asked Alexa.

'I hope not,' said Alexa. 'Because if you are, so am I.'

Unsure what to make of that, Laura nodded, and returned to her own office where she could sit at the big wallmap of the city that she'd pinned up, and wonder what to do next.

Twenty

It resembled dissection.

When Donal entered the interrogation room, the sights that hung before him were not what he'd expected. Instead of a screaming, twisting body streaked with wet, glistening blood, he saw a still pale dwarfish body almost obscured beneath the multitude of bright, multicoloured images suspended in the air throughout the room's space. The suspect looked in a coma, his face rigid.

Meanwhile Kyushen sat against the far wall before a small table, manipulating a rack of delicate equipment such as Donal had never seen.

Still, it looked like vivisection: but of the mind, or perhaps the soul, rather than the body. Frames of golden light hung in the air, bearing legends such as:

```
[[image schoolJourneyDaily [
    qlist: [duration: variSec dftval=30min,
            painLink: Beating* dtfval = new Beating(severity:=3.2),
            adrenalDump: seq<glandExcrete> = new seq[dftlen = 5],
            tempList: seq<Strategem> = getDump(dumpType.strategem.levelOne).
            ]
    plist: [flee (inp SurroundPic: minGestalt, inp Howling: audioChord)
            [ initRun(speed:=currentState.physioMax()),
             attempt [ executeStrategem(nearFit(tempList))]
            success [ wait(22), watch(maxPoss), continue]
            otherwise [ initRun(speed:=recalc())]
            self.propensityElasticity:=sub1.
            ]
    ]
    ] end_image]]
```

None of which made sense to Donal. The frames were stacked into patterns linked by rune-labelled arcs, like *containment-materialization*, *precursor* and *conjuration*.

'Oh for fuck's sake.'

Donal deciphered what the shining frames meant, by remembering his own childhood.

That bloody orphanage.

Because these were the prisoner's memories of being beaten up travelling to and from school. These were the behaviours that had turned him into what he was.

Kyushen leaned back in his chair and wiped sweat from his face.

'Sorry, Lieutenant. Tough work. He's been neatly ensorcelled with protected hex.'

'Er ... You mean you can't get into his mind?' Donal gestured at the images. 'But aren't these—?'

'Part of Dilvox's soul, yes.'

'Dilvox?'

Kyushen pointed at the strapped-down dwarf. 'That's his name.'

There was a glowing light in Kyushen's eyes that had nothing to do with the flame-script reflected and dancing across his corneas. He was a knowledge-seeker. This was his drug of choice.

'So ...' Donal looked around the glowing frames. 'Are you getting near the core of his thoughts yet?'

'Oh, no.' Kyushen looked surprised. 'That'll take hours at least. These are mesolayer templates for recurrent behaviour. I need to send him into deep trance.'

Kyushen's fingers moved across the dials and tiny switches. New, complicated geometrical patterns of dark-blue and dark-green shifted into being among the flame-script frames.

'We can perform instant-traces, and step through the actions of his potentiated thoughts.'

'Potentiated,' said Donal.

'Yeah, stored.'

More displays opened up, and then Kyushen's fingers moved across the equipment once more, and this time the captive dwarf moved beneath his bonds. Then he screamed, a howl of awful agony that Donal had never imagined a human throat could utter.

Donal opened his mouth to tell Kyushen to stop, then saw the sardonic expression on the man's face: the expression that said all laypersons react this way. Donal clamped down his feelings.

'Is that all you can manage?' he said. 'A bit of pain? I can do that with my bare hands.'

'Wait till you see this.' Kyushen twisted three dials. 'Now I have him reliving his memories of three nights back.'

This time the howling was loud enough to make Donal curl up with his hands over his ears, and it continued until he could take no more. He stumbled towards the interrogation room door, and it swung open at his approach. He stepped through and the big door swung back

Ensorcelled bolts clicked shut of their own accord. In the corridor outside, there was silence.

'Thanatos,' said Donal, to no one there.

But perhaps a ripple of movement passed across the wall, just beyond the edge of his peripheral vision. Donal squeezed his eyes shut, then opened them.

'Shit,' he muttered, knowing he would have to go back in.

My prisoner.

For no good reason, Donal reached inside his jacket to his shoulder and drew out his Magnus. He clicked open the catch, slipped out the magazine to check the heavy load, then pushed the mag into the butt.

Donal grabbed the door handle and went back inside the interrogation room.

Xalia was in darkness, rising through cold stonework, aware of the vertical rivers of not-quite-sound, defined by a nameless sense that was akin to remote touching: a tactile sensation of icy metal pipes that were yards away.

Xalia's density in the material dimensions was close to zero, maintaining the minimum containment necessary to stop dissipation. She was on a knife-edge no human could appreciate: rotate any more of her self out of the mortal universe, and she might never find her way back.

She had been in Darksan Tower, and with Laura's permission had roamed up and down the shafts and communicated with some of the wraiths imprisoned there. The tower was a vast, labyrinthine, ancient place; but it paled beside the dark history and complexity of Police HQ.

Ward-fields repelled Xalia.

If it hadn't been for Sushana in the hospital, for the dead Mina, there was no way Xalia would have tried to penetrate this place.

The ward-fields stretched horizontally across the whole of Police HQ at this level. Layers of standing hex-waves filled resonance cavities in the stone floors for only one purpose: to prevent quasi-material forms like Xalia from passing through to the upper levels of the building.

To the levels where senior officers like Commissioner Vilnar had their offices and secret vaults.

Far below, other ward-fields, beginning at the minus-fiftieth floor, prevented wraiths (and sprites and ectomists) from reaching the dark secrets of the torture chambers. Not to mention the entombed bones of earlier commissioners.

Xalia had never tried to climb so high. Now she floated with tortuous care between webs of high tension hex, among intricate three-dimensional mazes of deadly energy. One lapse of concentration and she would be fried out of existence, in all universes.

Vilnar had sent Donal to spy on Laura ... and worse, to seduce her. Once Xalia had proof that she could show Laura, there was no doubt in Xalia's mind about what would happen next.

Donal would suffer, perhaps die in some lonely alley, waiting for backup that would never arrive.

Xalia was slipping through the third layer of defences when a fiery sentence sprang up in her awareness.

+Who are you?+

Xalia stopped her ascent. For a split second she began a sideways drift, but there were HT hex lines close by. She brought herself to a halt.

Who's asking?

The reply came cold and loud.

+Have you ever considered the nature of eternity?+

What?

+The length of time that persists beyond your existence.+

It took a moment for Xalia to decide that was a threat.

Piss off.

And for a few more moments, silence filled the solid stone. Then a cold rippling passed through everything, including Xalia, and she began to understand the nature of the being that guarded the upper layers. It was a tesselan, an aggregation fashioned from families of wraiths that were torn apart and twisted into new forms and reprogrammed with a single quasi-soul by master practitioners from the darkest schools of mind-control mages.

+I will eat you.+

I don't fuckin' think so.

+And tear you apart, and take you into myself.+

Xalia was already moving.

You and what horde?

+I need no other—+

But they were at the nova-bright webs deep inside the stone now, where lethal energies burned and a vast powerful form like the tesselan guardian dared not move. Sensing the huge capacity for resonance from the tesselan, the dumb, mindless energies of the fire-webs were already closing in.

Xalia elongated her form and slipped *inside* the fire-webs.

And now she was really in danger.

Ah, shit.

From behind, the guardian's words were bright.

+That was fatally stupid, little one.+

Xalia tried to move forward, but the ravening lines of energy beat her back, and a deep realization flooded through her: that she was about to die.

Donal stepped back into the interrogation room. The original frames and glowing patterns were now obscured by arrays of flowing light, webs in which glyphs and icons moved.

Beyond the blaze, Kyushen was scarcely visible at his workbench. Equipment hummed and crackled. The dwarfish prisoner whose soul was being flayed was completely out of sight, hidden by the vast display of light and movement filling the stone-walled room.

'Thanatos ... What are you doing to him, Kyushen?'

'This is the running soul.' Kyushen's voice was made indistinct by discordant clicks and moans from his instruments. 'The actual thoughts generated by the schemata and images. See: there's a propensity being invoked in order to return the qualia associated with ...'

'You're mad.'

'On the contrary. See.' Kyushen's sleeve was painted in kaleidoscopic hues as he pointed into the midst of the visual maelstrom. 'There. *That* structure is completely inconsistent with rational thought, at least of the human variety.'

'Are you saying the prisoner's not human?'

'No, I'm telling you he's clinically insane. It would take some powerful mage-therapists to work any kind of rechannelling to solve the guy's problems.'

Donal stared at the shifting light for a few moments.

'We're not here to solve his problems.'

'No. We're not.'

'But I can't let you—'

'Hush. There. Bloody Death, I've got it.'

'What have you found?'

'Wait. This is the trace I've got to follow, just stepping through these invocations ...'

Donal started to ask a further question, then closed his mouth.

'There's a phone number,' muttered Kyushen.

'You're kidding.'

'It's a resonance impression.' Kyushen looked up at Donal. 'He didn't perceive it directly. I'm going to have to trace the impressions and build a shadow.'

Donal shook his head.

'You mean it's guesswork, not memory.'

'If we get a complete image, it will be accurate.'

Donal wanted to ask how Kyushen knew that, but decided not to. Kyushen's fingers flicked across switches and toggles.

'I'm getting it ...'

Fingers moving faster across the console.

'No. Damn ...'

There was nothing Donal could say or do to help.

'Ah ... Hades.'

'You've lost it,' said Donal.

'Oh, no.' Kyushen looked up. 'I can tell you exactly where the call came from: seven-seven-seven, two-nine, three-five-one, seven-two-zero.'

Donal stared at him, then nodded.

'Keep a log,' he said. 'Of everything you find.'

'Of course.' Kyushen shook his head. 'What did you expect me to do?'

Donal said nothing, but his mind was whirling. This was the second piece of evidence.

I expect you would bury it, if you knew you'd just fingered Vilnar.

Because if there was a more dangerous enemy than a police commissioner, Donal could not imagine it.

Xalia tried but the fire beat her back, the pseudo-fire which could destroy her wraith-form, in pain that would last a subjective century:

a time-dilating immolation. The fire-web was squeezing and burning her out of existence.

Fucking bastard place.

Then a cool wave passed through the web, clearing a passage.

Who—?

They call me Gertie.

Xalia recognized the wraith now. When Laura rode the elevator tubes upwards – elevators which were irrelevant to Xalia – Xalia sometimes flew up alongside, and so she'd got to know some of the captive wraiths.

Gertie? Aren't you trapped in elevator 7? Bound to it?

Well ... there are binds, and binds, aren't there?

Uncertain what to make of that, Xalia matched her own vector's rotational frequency with Gertie's: it was like two corporeal humans holding hands. Together, they slipped through solid matter, heading up towards the place that might unveil the truth.

Commissioner Vilnar's office.

Harald brought his bone-shielded motorcycle to an idling halt. The bike extruded two curved stands, steadying itself as Harald swung his leg over and dismounted.

'Stay ready,' he murmured. 'And keep watch.'

A sense of alertness seemed to radiate from the bike as Harald left it behind him. He strode quickly down an alleyway across which a row of low spiked bollards was set: there to discourage bikes and cars from joyriding between the graffiti-decorated walls.

Tonight was too cold for the neighbourhood youths to be out in force. Even so, a sudden burst of red-and-gold light washed across closed windows and a series of loud cracks split the air: firecrackers and gunpowder candles thrown by young idiots who ought to know better.

As a rookie cop, Harald had nearly shot a fourteen-year-old boy for throwing a firecracker, when his galvanized nerves had reacted as if to gunfire. Now he knew the difference automatically – not just from his years on the street, but from the intervening years as a Marine before returning to life as a cop.

And as a sergeant in the Fighting Sevens, he had once led his troop into a safe haven in the Kongal Rock Forest, in the disputed Fuerile Valley beyond the Zurinese border. Harald had used a native guide, one who'd lived in the military base with them and even cooked their food. The guide's name was Gam Sintil, or at least that's what they knew him as.

Fucking bastard snitches and traitors.

But no one realized that Gam Sintil's true sympathies lay with the separatists. No one knew, until a crescendo of hexlar-piercing rounds crashed from among the fractal forest pillars and half of Harald's troop were dead before they even recognized the ambush.

Kill the fuckers.

Harald had fought his way out with three wounded comrades. His only satisfaction had been when Billy, aka Corporal Bilken Flewelor, had placed a round in Gam Sintil's spine. The bastard had been running and nearly got clear.

Billy's skull had exploded into scarlet mist a second later, from a sniper that Harald had never seen. Harald just managed to get away.

Kill them all.

Just as Harald would do to Donal Riordan, if it turned out the bastard was responsible for what happened to Sushana.

Harald used snitches. He was gentle and friendly with them, when appropriate. But he distrusted and hated them all.

This was an immigrant area, where refugees from Illurium made their homes. Harald already knew where to check first: a café called Stelto's where Birtril Kondalis hung out eight evenings a week (with Hachiday reserved for worship at the Temple of Xithros).

The usual haunting music drifted out of Stelto's, and Harald pushed aside the metal-beaded curtains and slid open the heavy rune-carved wooden door. Its runners were well-greased so the door action was smooth and soundless. Harald stepped into the opium-scented atmosphere.

Three long-faced men were sucking from helical pipes in the far corner. When they turned their eyes towards Harald, the irises were fully contracted, their pinprick gazes focused on a dreamworld that had little to do with Harald himself: it was just a reaction to movement.

On the right hand side, where a family were gathered to eat, a round-faced man with coffee-coloured skin – that was Birtril – closed his eyes and swallowed. Then he opened his eyes and forced a smile.

'Hello, Sergeant,' he said.

'Birtril. What have you got for me?'

'Huh?'

'Information. You know that's what I like.' Harald's gentle-seeming eyes appeared to expand. He dragged a spare chair across the cheap lino floor, and sat down at Birtril's table. He nodded to the thin woman and two young boys who were sitting with Birtril.

'Mrs Kondalis,' Harald added. 'Nice to see you. And the sons.'

Birtril's wife Laxara nodded, but warily. She and Birtril were all too aware of the true legal status of their marriage. Birtril's first – and by law, only – wife remained in Silvex City, back in Illurium.

The money that Birtril sent her every week was the only thing that prevented her raising the matter officially. If Birtril's bosses at the embassy heard about it, his career in catering for diplomats would be ruined for good. And no one would get any money.

'There's, er, nothing going on . . .' Birtril looked up as the cafés owner, Zegrol (the original owner Stelto having passed away during a dispute with a nearby nightclub whose bouncers bore scimitars that they knew how to use) poked his head through the curtains at the rear.

Zegrol spotted Harald, observed his mood, and withdrew immediately. The curtains swung gently after he had disappeared. Birtril gave a long liquid blink of unsurprised disappointment. 'Honestly, Sergeant. No one in the embassy's up to anything.'

'Not even the driver of XSA899-omega-beth-del?'

'Huh?'

'Limo driver. Lean, pale skinned, black hair. Get a grip, Birtril.' Harald leaned towards him. 'And concentrate, will you?'

'Um . . . Sure, Sergeant.'

Harald checked the two sons for signs of anger, but they were not yet old enough to appreciate the bind that Harald held them in, and to realize just how deeply their parents must resent him. Laxara's feelings remained deeply hidden.

'So what's his name? The driver?'

Birtril's gaze shifted to his left. 'Ixil Deltrassol. He's an ex-army driver. Keeps himself to himself.'

'And?'

Birtril glanced at Laxara.

'Um, can we take a walk, Sergeant?'

'Well.' Harald smiled. 'Of course. Let's get going.'

He stood quickly, and helped Birtril get up as though he needed help. It was a matter of maintaining dominance. Harald ignored the opium smokers and Birtril's family – his second family – as he left with Birtril beside him. But he kept watch with his peripheral vision.

Nothing happened as they passed through the hangings and out on

222

to the cold street. Two youths on the corner, one carrying an unlit gunpowder candle, caught sight of Harald and faded into Raxman Alley and were gone. Harald was known here.

That was the way he liked it.

'Talk to me, Birtril.'

'I've no idea what he's done,' Birtril said quickly. 'Deltrassol doesn't make friends. Not enemies, but not friends either, you know what I mean?'

'Only if you use simple words.'

'Huh?'

'Never mind. What are you hiding?'

'I'm not— Shit.' Birtril stopped by one of the metal bollards. 'I don't know about any crime he might have committed, OK?'

'Right, and who are his acquaintances, if he doesn't have friends?'

'I don't know ... He spends time in Sir Alvan's offices, but then he works for the man. That's all.'

'And?'

Harald stared hard, maintaining psychological pressure.

'There were rumours, and ... I've seen Deltrassol's car parked where they said it would be.'

'Uh-huh. Carry on, Birtril. Continue to the end.'

'The See-Through Look'n'Feel,' said Birtril. 'I happened to see him coming out of there.'

'You're sure?'

'Yeah, and the doorman said goodnight to him by name, like he was a regular or something, y'know?'

'Good.'

Birtril let out a sigh of relief.

'That's it, boss. Sergeant. That's everything I know about him.'

'I believe you.' Harald pulled out his wallet, and slipped out three thirteen-florin notes. 'Here, buy Laxara a new coat.'

Birtril slipped the money quickly into his pocket.

'Much appreciated, Sergeant.'

He waited, as if for permission to rejoin his family.

'Go on.' Harald nodded back towards Stelto's. 'Laxara's waiting for you.'

'Thanks.'

Harald waited until Birtril was almost at the café door before calling out: 'And I won't mention anything to Laxara.'

Birtril stopped, stiffening.

'About you being in Quarter Moon Alley,' added Harald. 'I wouldn't want to speculate on what you were doing there. Know what I mean?'

Birtril's head hung forward, and he stood there in front of the door to Stelto's. His face was in shadow against the light, and perhaps he was crying: it was impossible to tell. Then he straightened by a small amount, pushed open the door and went inside.

It banged shut behind him.

Harald stood looking at the closed door for a while. Then he remembered Sushana's battered face, and his own expression turned to stone.

A rocket burst high overhead, throwing out silver and black stars, emitting a screeching howl.

Reaching his bike, Harald swung his leg over the saddle and settled into position.

'If this Deltrassol's a principal,' he told the bike, 'I'm going to rip his nuts off. But if he's just a stooge ...'

The bike rumbled and growled, engine revving as Harald took hold of the handlebars. The bike rolled forward, pulling its twin stands back inside itself.

'... then I'm going to make sure it's Donal bloody Riordan who loses his testicles, and more. For Laura's sake as well as Sushana's.'

The bike accelerated into the street.

Twenty-one

Xalia fought her way through further barriers that Gertie found easy to slip past. For over a hundred and twenty years, Gertie had glided along elevator shafts and the lesser known aspects of Police HQ architecture. She knew where solid stone offered clear passage and where security concerns had resulted in devious defences.

Now, Gertie hung back before the final labyrinth, directing Xalia.

That way. See?

Yes. Thanks.

There were risks in helping a fellow wraith, but Gertie had a perverse streak and in any case she had been bored for days. And Xalia worked with Donal, was part of his new team, and Gertie's fondness for Donal had been growing with the years.

Xalia, meanwhile, slipped and squirmed and attenuated her form to a dangerous extent, fighting to breach the barriers. She wanted proof of Donal's complicity to take before Laura. But this fire-labyrinth was of expert design.

How are you doing, Xalia?

Gertie's message came through blazing curtains of hot hex like a distant echo. Xalia directed a narrow beam of communication back through the labyrinth, more to see if she could than because she wanted to answer. She needed to concentrate.

Fine. What did you think?

Whether it was the tiny distraction of making that reply, Xalia could not tell ... but in the next few moments, the bars of hex floating among the thinner shields grew fatter and hotter, strengthening their manifestation. Xalia pulled herself inwards and held still, floating in place.

Then the bars brightened further and began extruding crescent-shaped horns of crackling energy, and Xalia knew she was done for.

Going further into the labyrinth was out of the question. Secondary and tertiary labyrinths began to swing and rotate through from the orthogonal pocket universes in which they were stored. They inserted themselves into the mortal continuum, filling the labyrinth's gaps.

Vilnar, you mother—

Xalia's curse – directed against the commissioner – was cut off as the first two horns of energy pierced her half-ethereal form and pain flared along the length of her paranerves: a twisting agony such as normal human beings could never experience.

Xalia?

It's got me.

A long thin thread worked its way among the sprouting new bars of the overlaying labyrinths. It was Gertie, extending herself to reach Xalia ... or trying to.

In a moment of clarity, Xalia understood what Gertie was doing, and why. She remembered the way Gertie joked with Donal, and remembering also how Donal had not shown any hesitation in accepting that a task officer member was a freewraith.

Damn it, Xalia liked Donal, but if he was in league with the enemy ...

Gertie, I'm here to gather evidence against Donal Riordan.

For a second, the extruded portion of Gertie's form withdrew, like a blind snake slithering backwards from an electric shock.

Then she extended back into the ever-tightening labyrinth, questing; and after a moment Xalia understood that there was no sense in telling Gertie to get the Thanatos out of here. It would be quicker to show her how bad things were.

Xalia extended herself until her form impinged on Gertie's extrusion, wraith coexisting in the same space as wraith, just as two more crescent horns slipped inside her body and she howled, broadcasting agony along frequencies and energy fields unknown to humankind.

Gertie's form, such parts of her as Xalia could sense, throbbed and flared with shared pain as the cutting hex blasted along her own paranervous system. In the distance, a scream sounded.

Now will you for fuck's sake get out of here, Gertie?

After a hundredth of a second, Gertie's reply rang inside Xalia's paranervous system:

This is my damn building and no one does this to me!

Then Gertie's form began to glow with a concentration of energy such as Xalia had never experienced before.

*

Donal meanwhile had the telephone number that he needed, the second link to Commissioner Vilnar's office, but with no hope that it could be offered in evidence in court. His technical expert, Kyushen, sat in shocked silence, unmoving, while stretcher bearers carried out the unmoving dwarf.

The dwarf's condition, if nothing else, made the evidence invalid.

It was not true death but a Basilisk Trance, unbreakable according to every diagnostic Kyushen had run. Legally, such deep catatonia *was* death. No one, in Tristopolitan legal history, had ever awakened from a Basilisk Trance.

Kyushen stared into nothingness.

'You feel bad.' Donal watched the stretcher bearers leave, and the iron door swinging shut behind them. The displays that had flared so brightly earlier had faded to a few small, minimized and dimmed-out ghosts.

'And you could probably use your own instruments to change how you feel about that ...'

Kyushen looked up.

'... but you shouldn't,' continued Donal. 'Because you *have* killed a man, and you don't get over it, you don't accept it ... you just live with it.'

'But I didn't mean to ... You know.'

'Yes,' said Donal. 'But it was always a risk, and we both knew it.'

After a moment, Kyushen began to shake. His skin was pale and this was the aftermath of shock. Donal watched the fit of shivering take hold of him.

'Relax,' said Donal. 'Don't fight it. Let it pass through you ...'

Kyushen closed his eyes and moaned.

'... because this is natural. Afterwards, you will be OK.'

Some of these words came from Donal's subconscious, from the mesmeric trance the police mage had taken him into after the first fatal street shoot-out that Donal had been caught up in. Donal had killed three men, not just one, after Fredrix's throat exploded in gouts of scarlet arterial blood.

Donal had watched Sergeant Fredrix Paulsen – the nearest to a father Donal had ever known – gasp and shrink as his eyes grew opaque and that was it: nothing left of the man save fuel for the reactor piles.

And after two minutes (though it might have seemed much longer than that to Kyushen) the shaking fit began to fade to a tremble, and finally was gone. Kyushen slumped.

After a moment, Donal left.

Xalia screamed, rotating like washing in a dryer, twisting in and out of reality as Gertie dragged her through tiny closing apertures of pain. Scalding agony defined the tightening labyrinths as Xalia's wraith-form was ripped and torn.

Yet she remained essentially intact as Gertie's cunning use of power and topology took both of them through the fatal hex defences, back to the perimeter. And then they were outside, basking in cool solid stone. Above them, the outer defences roiled and burned.

Gertie's words rolled through Xalia's awareness.

So what point did you prove here today?

Suffering delineated every movement of Xalia's discorporate being.

What ... do you ... mean?

You were trying to accuse Donal Riordan. Implicate him.

Xalia billowed, her wraith-form still ripped, insubstantial inside the solid stonework of the building. Her ability to concentrate was gone; her communication was weak.

Yes ...

Did you get any resonance of a personality in there? In the energies of the labyrinth?

Xalia twisted, trying to focus.

Resonance?

Yeah ... What kind of wraith are you, anyway?

After a moment, Xalia drew enough energy into herself to be able to reply.

Piss off.

Gertie chuckled.

That's better. Now as soon as you can work out whose flavour that was – she meant flavour of resonance – *the sooner you can leave young Donal alone.*

You like ... him.

Again Gertie was amused at Xalia.

I like puppies too. Have you been in the deathwolves' den?

If Xalia had had eyes, she would have closed them. Banter was too much. Everything still hurt.

Don't ... understand.

Young Donal's like a pet to me. You're like a neighbour's kid. And it's time you straightened out your own feelings about Laura Steele.

Fuck ...

Well, you're a wraith, so maybe you shouldn't. Not with humans.

This was too much. But the words that came next from Gertie were softer in tone, soothing, leading Xalia further away from the burning labyrinth. The two wraiths began to sink downwards, remaining inside the cool, solid, protecting stone.

Come on, Xalia. There are groves and grottoes no one knows about anymore. Some have healing energies.

I don't … know.

Gertie drew closer.

Trust me. I can heal you.

After a moment, Xalia replied.

Yes …

Then come.

Their descent through stone became faster.

Donal was in Laura's office. Laura had commanded the internal glass walls to darken, so that she and Donal were alone together. They hugged and kissed, and she groaned when Donal ran his palms and fingertips along her thin blouse, across the silkiness of her bra, but they drew back from going any further.

There were too many officers and other beings in the building capable of sensing powerful resonances; lovemaking would have to wait until they were back in Laura's apartment. Donal blew out a long breath.

'Oh, Thanatos.'

'Yeah …'

Then Donal swallowed and looked at the now-opaque wall, as though there were something to see. He said: 'I don't *want* to go. You understand.'

'You don't want to visit a foreign country?'

Donal shook his head.

'I *am* scared shitless of flying, you want the truth. But I can always get stone drunk, you know? Foreign trips weren't exactly a feature of the orphanage, so I would like to go abroad … That's not it.'

'I know.' Laura's voice grew small and quiet. 'It's scary, isn't it? How fast things happen, like you and me.'

'Exactly.'

'You don't want to be apart from me, and that's good.' Laura gave a half-sad smile. 'I feel the same way, lover. But we both know you're going to Illurium because it's the only way to do the job.'

After a moment, Donal nodded.

'I guess. Listen, I don't want you in danger ... But you could come with me and—'

'No, I don't think so.'

Donal rubbed his face. 'Couldn't we make it a vacation for you, while I do the investigation work? I don't want you undercover – sorry, I know you're the boss – but the thing is, we could set you up in a separate location. I'm good at shifting through alleyways without being tailed ...'

'Oh, my beautiful man.'

Laura stepped close, laid the palm of one cold hand against his face – it felt deliciously soothing to Donal – and kissed him gently.

'What?'

'You treat me just like any other woman.'

'Well ...' Donal smiled. 'Not *exactly* like everyone else.'

'Ha. But that's the point.'

'Uh, what is?'

'What's in here.' Laura gestured towards her left breast. 'I'm *not* like other women. People like me are carefully tracked, wherever we go. I'm not even sure I'd have legal rights in Illurium.'

'Ah, fuck ...'

Laura smiled, beautifully.

'Whatever you say, my love. Just as soon as we get home.'

Donal shook his head, squeezing his eyes shut. Laura laughed.

'All right,' she added. 'We'll get some initial planning done for your trip. Harald's contacts over there will be invaluable ... Where is he, anyway?'

'Haven't seen him for ages,' said Donal. 'Maybe at the hospital with Sushana?'

'No, I just rang there a while back. Viktor's with her. I think he and Harald are taking turns to watch over her.'

'Good.'

Harald was leaning over his bike, accelerating hard as he retraced his route along the Orb-Dexter Freeway, knowing he was within minutes of potentially destroying Commander Steele's happiness. Laura Steele was the best superior he'd ever served under, his Marine service included. When she realized that Donal was a creature of the Black Circle, she would be devastated.

But then Harald remembered Sushana's face, the evidence of things done to her by Sally the Claw and his men. Viktor had been closeted away with one of the hospital doctors for what seemed like an age, before coming out with a dead look in his eyes and brackets of anger in the muscles beside his mouth.

Harald would make someone pay ... make everyone pay, beginning with Lieutenant Riordan, not stopping until he'd taken down Commissioner Vilnar. He just needed one more bit of evidence. But he had always felt there was something wrong in Commissioner Vilnar's domain. Odd energies had flickered and resonated in the Commissioner's office, just beyond the edges of Harald's Marine-trained senses.

The Phantasm bike leaned into a corner, took the bend while startling a finely dressed old woman about to cross the road, then straightened up and increased speed once more.

'Ixil Deltrassol,' Harald's unwilling informant Birtril had said. *'He's an ex-army driver. Keeps himself to himself.'*

Working in the embassy, unaware of the true nature of the Black Circle he ultimately worked for, this Deltrassol was probably a low-life. He was a driver who scarcely ranked as a footsoldier in the extended army of morons and deviants (though their mid-rank officers could be real pieces of work: witness Sally the Claw) manipulated from above by unseen individuals.

But no one would dare to investigate their own police commissioner. If Harald had been half-way sensible, he wouldn't have considered it either.

They're going to pay.

It was Sushana that made the difference, Sushana who had always made the difference in Harald's sometimes bleak world.

Away from the ornate old town houses with polished brass railings, Harald slowed the Phantasm. They entered a Pentangle fronted by former mansions long transformed into decaying hotels. There was a five-sided garden that it was no longer safe to enter at night, not unarmed or alone.

Then he took the bike down a series of narrowing and darkening streets until the lights brightened once more, this time with garish blues and reds predominating. He was into an area that the old rich lady they'd nearly run over would be shocked to realize existed, only half a mile from where she lived out her grand existence.

A tiny chained demonic form fluttered its leathery wings over Sid's Scar Parlour, the curlicued rune-and-knot patterns across its body a testimony to One-Eyed Sid's considerable skill with a straight razor.

Here in Quarter Moon Street, Sid's artistry was well known; but Harald remembered the days of his and Sid's youth, when they had run the streets in the same gang and Sid's use of the razor had been for more immediate purposes than fiscal gain or artistic recognition.

Or perhaps there *had* been a kind of artistry involved in the way Sid had wielded the ultra-sharp blade.

Slowing right down, the bike mumbled with its engine close to idling as they slipped past the black multi-faceted windowless building known as Nameless, past a betting shop and a nightclub whose failing business was driving it inexorably towards the status of knocking-shop, strictly illegal in Tristopolis and always present.

Has there ever been a large city without prostitution? Harald had often wondered at the nearness between this and the Courts of Mercy, less than two miles away yet worlds apart. At least, any Supreme Judge caring to walk down Quarter Moon Street to sample its facilities left his robes of office back at the Courts.

Past the glowing signs of three more establishments on the right, Harald could see the ephemeral beckoning hand that came through the wall and hung above the sidewalk, inviting passers-by inside. The See-Through Look'n'Feel appeared classier than many of the surrounding nightclubs; but there was only type of person who frequented the place. Some of them turned even Harald's hardened stomach.

There was a purple taxi parked just ahead, and Harald pulled the bike in behind it. The three young Zurinese sailors who tumbled from the taxi were laughing and half-drunk, and Harald hoped that whatever adventures awaited them this evening, there would be at least the illusion of happiness involved (whatever sordid transactions might take place) and no traumas to follow them through the rest of their lives.

But in this place, it could as easily be the flash of a blade or the glint of light from a spinning bullet case that would be the last impression to catch their confused awarenesses before darkness slammed in. They might never sense the fingers fumbling for their wallets and ID cards.

It happened here, and it had happened in the foreign ports that Harald had visited as a young Marine, and it seemed to be the way of the world. For a second Harald considered flashing his own ID, his detective's shield, and warning them away ... but they would only get in trouble somewhere else.

And then he remembered the state that Sushana was in, and the sailors faded from Harald's awareness. The bike extruded one stand

– tentatively – and that allowed Harald to lean sideways, to check out the doorway of See-Through Look'n'Feel.

There were four men standing there in deep-purple cloaks – the club's colours – and the largest of them was Stone. Harald had known Stone for a long time (and knew him only by that name). The street moniker was accurate enough.

'All right,' Harald murmured to the bike. 'I'll be going in the front way. Let's just get you tucked out of sight.'

The bike rumbled in agreement and rolled on, withdrawing its stand.

In a darkened alleyway strewn with broken crates and shards of blue and brown glass, Harald brought the bike to a halt. As it extruded both stands, and Harald dismounted, he saw a pale child with reptilian scales across his forehead.

The child looked five years old, but might be as old as eight if his diet was poor.

'Hey,' said Harald. 'Could you do me a favour?'

After a second, the scaly boy nodded. Harald dug inside his pocket and flung over a handful of nine-sided coins. The boy caught them.

'Keep people away from the bike,' Harald added. 'And I'll pay you more when I get back.'

A shimmer passed across the bike's bony carapace. The boy's eyes widened.

'Yeah,' said Harald. 'It's kinda for their own good, not the bike's.'

The boy grinned.

After a moment, Harald grinned back. Then, gun held straight down at his side, he retraced his steps along the alleyway, heading back towards the club's front entrance.

Stone saw Harald coming a hundred yards away, and stepped out into the middle of the sidewalk. He stood like some massive rock half-filling a strait. Passers-by drifted past on either side, avoiding him unconsciously.

'Hey, Sergeant,' Stone rumbled as Harald drew close.

'Hey, Stone.'

'You gonna need that?' Raising one stone-encrusted hand, Stone pointed. 'We expecting trouble?'

'I hope not.' Harald kept the gun pointed down. 'But I like to be prepared.'

'You're not saying one of our clientele has been a naughty boy?' When Stone frowned, the flanges of interlocking granite that shielded his brow scraped together. 'We got a classy establishment here, Sergeant.'

'That's right,' said Harald. 'And I'm sure you want to keep it that way.'

'So who's the miscreant?'

'Miscreant?'

'Why?' The stones shifted around Stone's grin. 'Ya think I can't use big words, like?'

'You won't hear me say that, big guy. The miscreant is called Deltrassol, though who knows what name he uses round here.'

'Oh, that one.' Stone's grin widened. 'He likes the ladies ... insubstantial, like. Doesn't wrinkle his chauffeur suit, at least not from the outside, know what I mean?'

Harald knew pretty well what Stone was getting at.

'You ever thought about getting an honest job, Stone?'

'What, you mean like a police officer? Nice uniform, stroll the streets, nab perpetrators ...'

'We don't actually call them perp—'

'Not since I taught you how to say miscreant, obviously.'

'Right.' Harald smiled at the thought of Stone in police uniform, studying interpersonal skills and criminology at the Academy. 'So where's our Deltrassol?'

'Top floor,' said Stone. 'Right at the back.'

'Nothing but the best for our miscreants.'

'There you go, Sergeant,' said Stone. 'You don't do so bad—'

'—for a dumb copper,' Harald finished for him. 'Thank you so much.'

Inside, Harald stepped through the ectoplasmic curtain that filled the hallway – it slid wetly across his skin – and then he was inside a corridor furnished in red and black. Flame-sprites danced in niches along the walls.

To Harald's right, an archway opened on to the dark interior of the club. Blue-lit booths were sparsely occupied by middle-aged men and their paid companions, some of whom were ordinary humans: the See-Through Look'n'Feel catered to a range of clientele.

There were three wraiths dancing on the bar, their lower extremities just inside the top of the counter, swaying to the too-loud music. One of them looked over towards Harald, the darkness where her eyes should have been now focusing on him. She gave a slow wink as she danced.

She nodded slightly towards the rear of the building, as if she knew what Harald was here for: to take down Deltrassol. It confirmed what Stone had already said, and Harald tipped his forehead to give a finger-tip salute, before continuing along the red-lit hallway.

Twenty-two

Reversed words crawled across the wall, with Harald's shadow blotting out the centre. The light came from the shining sign that floated behind him. Moving to one side so his silhouette would not show, Harald advanced with crosswise steps along the hallway.

At the entrance to the rear lounge, Harald checked inside, in case his target was not where Stone thought, or there was other trouble. The Tiplog brothers were here, their backs to Harald, and he made a mental note to find out later what they were up to. No one else of interest.

So he drew back into the hallway, and crossed to the staircase where two burning wraiths drew aside. One of them opened her mouth to reveal teeth of yellow flames.

Harald ignored them as he began his ascent. The carpet on the treads was sticky and blackened with dirt. Having got this far, the club's patrons no longer needed the illusory glamour that decorated the bar and lounges: a haze of lust obscured the tacky reality, the faded scents of despair and old semen.

The top corridor was floored with bare boards. Paint peeled from flimsy doors; rhythmic groans came from behind two of them. Harald drew his gun. He would kick in each door in turn, regardless of who might be inside.

But one of the wraiths rose up through the floor, anticipating the damage Harald was likely to cause, and pointed at the end door. She hung in the air until Harald nodded. Then she floated downwards and out of sight.

Harald moved fast.

Floorboards creaked beneath his weight but not in time to warn Deltrassol as Harald's heel slammed into the door beside the lock. There was plenty of hip thrust and splinters flew as the door sprang back and Harald swivelled, aiming from the hip – the Fighting Sevens used Instinctual Shooting because traditional targetting takes time – and stopped.

'Hey, Ixil.' Harald used Deltrassol's first name because that was basic intimidation. 'Is everything coming along nicely?'

On the bed, a pale-faced man in a dark suit lay still, eyes widened. The half-manifest wraith sitting astride him pumped her hips several more times before stopping.

Then the wraith turned to regard Harald, then opened her mouth – it looked like darkness pricked with stars – in what might have been a grin.

Then she grew insubstantial, and Harald tried not to look at the tumescence revealed inside Ixil Deltrassol's trousers. The wraith faded almost to invisibility.

Harald laughed.

'Ain't that always the way, Ixil? Here one second, fading away the next.' And, to the wraith: 'Right, darling?'

The wraith was already sinking downwards through the floor. She nodded to Harald and gave a tiny wave in the direction of the bed. In a second, she was gone.

Deltrassol's mouth opened and closed. Then he swallowed and said: 'What—?'

'I'm arresting you for murder,' said Harald.

'No ...'

'Yes. Unless you can convince me there's a reason I should let you go. Then you'd fly straight back to Illurium, wouldn't you?'

'I ... No, I'd stay here. Honest, Officer. I'd—'

'Wrong answer.' Harald's hand seemed to flicker into motion. 'Try again.'

Drops of blood sprang out across Deltrassol's forehead. The Fighting Sevens didn't use traditional aiming, but the sight atop a gun barrel had other uses.

Harald raised the weapon again, ready to inflict deeper damage.

'Uh ... Officer. What— What do you want me to do?'

But Harald's gun was now pointed at Deltrassol's crotch.

'I like tiny targets. It's the challenge, y'know?'

'Look, Officer. I didn't know the dwarves were going to ... do what they did. I swear, I only heard on the radio afterwards what happened. Thanatos ... I'd never get involved in ... stuff like that.'

Harald lowered his aim slightly, to appear less threatening. He could still shoot Deltrassol's thigh and destroy the femoral artery with minimal movement.

'I'd like to believe you.' Harald leaned forward, then closed the fingers of his left hand around Deltrassol's throat. 'But I'm afraid I can't.'

If Deltrassol had had an active hand in what happened to Sushana, then Harald's thumb and finger were going to close, collapsing the laryngeal cartilage. It would take a while for Deltrassol to choke to death.

'No, man ... Please. Don't.'

'One chance.' Harald tapped Deltrassol on the forehead. 'Relax.'

'I don't—'

'... Know whether you know this yet as it's easy to ... lose control and ... just let go of the body and drift ... just drift ...' The tone of Harald's voice deepened and slowed as he looked into Deltrassol's eyes. '... and you can close your eyes ... that's right ... as the threat fades ...'

Deltrassol's eyelids drooped, then closed.

The Marines had taught Harald to kill with guns and blades, with hands and feet; and they had drilled him in the use of subtler weapons.

Ixil Deltrassol slid deeper into trance. Disconcerted by fear, he was totally vulnerable to the unexpected mesmeric tone of Harald's trained voice.

Deeper still.

'... so much pain to sit on ... the fence as ... defence is unnecessary so ... you let it go ...'

As an embassy driver Deltrassol had received trance training, but it was superficial. After Harald penetrated the initial defence, Deltrassol's training made him *more* vulnerable: he had been in trance so often it was easy to return.

'Policeman,' Deltrassol murmured.

Harald modulated his voice to match Deltrassol's neurophysiology. '... because I'm the one who can ... save you from pain ... like a window pane into memory of ... things you have to ... tell me ... as your unconscious knows what it needs ... to help you as it ... always has to ... tell me ...'

'Police. Our contact. He— Set up.'

Harald leaned closer.

'... tell me everything ...'

Laura walked out into the main office area. Donal had been ages getting the coffee – he'd offered to bring back a cup for her – and she wondered what was keeping him. The caffeine meant nothing to her black zombie blood; but it was unusual for Donal to take so long.

On the few occasions Donal had drunk alcohol since coming here, he'd drunk raw cheap whisky that Laura wouldn't dream of putting in her car – the Vixen was more fussy than that. To a zombie, alcohol tastes like sour vinegar laced with something worse: rats' piss, or the lymph fluid of crushed beetles.

Drunk as a zombie was an oxymoron that had somehow passed into the language as a simile. Laura used to consider it one of life's ironies, back when she'd been alive.

'Hey, Laura.' Alexa was on the phone, cupping her hand around the mouthpiece. 'I've got Harald on the—'

Her expression changed to a frown, then she looked up at Laura and shrugged. 'Sorry. He just put the phone down on me.'

'Is everything all right?'

'He told me to cancel an EPB. The one on the Illurian driver. Er' – Alexa glanced down at her notebook – 'Ixil Deltrassol.'

Laura glanced at the door, where Donal was backing in with three cups of coffee clutched between his hands. No wonder he was taking so long.

'What's happened? Don't tell me he's ...' Laura let her voice trail off. 'Never mind.'

Alexa stared at her for a moment.

'I don't think Harald's offed the guy, if that's what you mean.'

'No,' said Laura. 'I don't think one of my officers would do such a thing.'

'Me neither.' Donal approached with the coffees, wincing as he tried to put all three down on Alexa's desktop without spilling anything, and failed. 'Sorry. What bad thing wouldn't we dream of doing?'

'Taking the law into your hands,' said Alexa.

'Well, Thanatos forbid.'

'In a lethal manner,' said Laura. 'Causing a suspect to disappear.'

'Oh.' Donal looked at Alexa. 'Who are we talking about, exactly?'

'Deltrassol, Ixil. Wanted for—'

'The embassy driver, right?'

'That's the man.' Laura perched herself on the edge of the desk. 'And did Harald give any indication why we should kill an Extended

239

Points Bulletin? Doesn't he know how hard I have to work to get one published in the first place?'

'Yeah,' said Alexa.

'But he doesn't care.' Donal half-smiled.

'I think' – Alexa checked her notepad once more – 'he's got the guy and turned him as a witness.'

Laura bit her lip. 'All right.'

Donal saw her expression, and decided that Harald was in trouble, but would probably talk his way out of it. Donal himself had had such arguments with various bosses. You interrogated a witness, an opportunity to lever something out of them came up, and you took it: offering them a lighter sentence or whatever.

The thing was, however spur-of-the-moment the offer might be, the officer had to follow through on it. On the streets, someone who fails to keep their promises isn't *stand-up*, and that is the worst crime of all.

'All right,' said Laura again. 'That's fine. If I'm not around when Harald turns up, get him to hang around until I do.'

'Um ... I'll try.' Alexa sipped her coffee, and nodded towards Donal. 'Thanks.'

Laura took a sip of hers, then put the cup back down on Alexa's desk and forgot about it. She could drink the stuff, but it meant nothing.

'Donal, have you got the remaining travel details worked out?'

'Yeah, hang on a sec.' Carrying his coffee, Donal went to his desk and retrieved a pale-green pad. 'Here you are. Are you sure we can afford this?'

'I can.'

'Well ... all right.'

He was an orphan from the wrong side of the tracks, travelling abroad.

Shit. I'm flying to Illurium.

Sister Mary-Anne Styx would have been proud of him.

Harald leaned closer to Deltrassol.

'... deeper,' he said, 'and then tell me ... whether ... any commands lurk in there.'

He was talking about Deltrassol's subconscious, and there was a reason: if the Black Circle had laid hex-traps or guards in place, even ordinary mesmeric digging should expose their existence.

A buried wipeout trap would cause Deltrassol to scream as inlaid hex scoured his memories all the way back to childhood. Harald was willing to risk that. Part of him wanted it to happen.

'... cashing in on memory where the ... bosses cached their commands ...'

'No.' Eyelids fluttering, Deltrassol shook his head.

His personality was still intact. No mages had buried hex traps in his mind.

'... and you want to tell me ... what shipment the dwarves were stealing ...'

'Yes. Champagne. The expensive stuff. Crates of it, worth thousands. We had the plans, police response plans. How they knew to land the pterabat on top of the skull.'

Champagne?

All this for fuckin' champagne?

'... and when you saw that the dwarves had a body aboard, when you saw the van ...'

'I pulled out, man. Aborted. Don't want that kind of trouble.'

'... is what we want to avoid as you decide you'll do everything to help me ...'

'Yes.'

'... and I need to know, your boss, Sir Alvan ...'

'That's right.'

'... is he your friend?'

'No.'

'... while you spend time in his office ...'

'The club.'

'... because of this place? The See-Through? Tell me ...'

'Sir Alvan comes here. By chance, I saw him. Recognized him.'

'... though he was in disguise ...'

'Yes, a mask. Ensorcelled. But the way he walked. I knew.'

'... that this was Sir Alvan and you blackmailed him ...'

'For small amounts, for a man like him.'

'... who would do you a special favour if you asked ...'

'His secret. Would destroy him. If I told.'

'... and he could arrange to fly you back to Illurium ...'

'Yes.'

So Deltrassol was a blackmailer within his own embassy. He was a low-life, and Harald wanted badly to take him down. But if there were resources available in Illurium, in Silvex City where Donal Riordan was headed ...

Got you, zombiefucker.

The bastards who'd got away with Cortindo's body and the – for Death's sake – expensive champagne had a police contact, someone who'd given them the response plans. By itself the evidence meant little, but it closed the chain of cause and effect that stretched all the way back to Commissioner Vilnar's office.

But first things first.

Riordan. You're dead.

Harald told Deltrassol to sleep for a minute. It allowed Harald time to think.

Then link by link, he put his plan together.

'... and when you return to the embassy, you'll ask him ...' Harald drew the sentence out, hearing a raucous shout from the hallway outside. It was a drunkard's roar, somewhere on this floor: one of the club's clients had teetered out of control.

This could be a problem if it pulled Deltrassol out of trance.

Then a liquid crunch sounded from outside, along with a sudden cessation in the drunkard's torrent of curses, followed by Stone's voice: 'That'll cool him nicely, lads. Be gentle with him.'

The sounds of heels scraping along bare floor followed.

Harald shifted into deep command mode, instructing Deltrassol.

'There is a house ... in Upper Kiltrin North ...'

This was a district containing some of the richer sections of Silvex City, where Harald had spent time in Illurium. The military camp had been twenty miles outside the city. During his secondment to the military police, Harald had spent time in the city proper, liaising with local civilians.

He helped investigate cases, and assisted on the Octemday bar runs where trios of MPs would have to extract carousing Marines from the detritus of smashed tables and unconscious civilians. And do it without inflicting lethal damage on drunken men who were trained to kill.

'Kiltrin,' murmured Deltrassol. 'Pulkwill's Hill.'

'... That's right, and from Pulkwill's Hill you descend ... where it zigs and zags ...' Harald waited for the tiny nod from Deltrassol before continuing. 'To the silver-and-white mansion with the three steel ... gargoyles ... outside, the ones with spread-out wings ...'

'Move.'

'... that move, that's right. The gargoyles move ...' Harald's voice lowered further. '... and in that house ... that mansion ... lives a man called Don Falvin Mentrassore ...'

'Don Mentrassore.'

'... that's right, and the Don has a daughter ... called Rasha ... and servants, and the chief butler might be called ... Adamnol ...'

It had been over two years since Harald's last visit. Adamnol was probably still there, but life was uncertain.

'... You will say the codeword ... that you will remember to forget until ... you remember in that moment ... that Darksong Lightning is the code ... and you won't mind it vanishing from ... your mind ... inside Don Mentrassore's house.'

The Don was a thin elegant man with a silver-grey goatee, usually with a pearl attached at each earlobe, who conducted his affairs with the same kind of diligent yet easy grace that he bore in social situations.

That was why he had been so disappointed in his daughter Rasha when she had fallen in love with a young student of dubious character and family. It had been that student, part of the local underworld with links into crooked quartermasters among the military bases, who had been one of Harald's targets. Harald and four other MPs, all in plain clothes, broke into a camp arsenal just in time to apprehend the men who were making off with firearms and other materiel.

Two of the criminals had reached for their own weapons, and in seconds a firefight blasted the air apart – inside an arsenal filled with explosives: it was good luck that the arsenal had remained intact instead of disappearing in a fireball. It would have taken out the entire camp, including two thousand men and women.

Rasha Mentrassore's fiancé had been too stupid to surrender.

He'd also been too stupid to leave Rasha at home. In trying to show off to her, boasting of his importance among important businessmen, he'd smuggled Rasha into the place in the back of his stolen army jeeplet. She'd crawled out of the vehicle when the gunfire started.

It might have been a stray round of Harald's that took Rasha in the right shoulder; it might have been someone else's. Regardless, Rasha had pitched over with her mouth working but her throat paralysed. Her shoulder was smashed meat, splintered with bones.

After Harald and his team had killed the men who refused to stop, they had got to work on Rasha and two associates of the gang, who had been caught in the crossfire. Using straps from the ammunition cases – nice ironic serendipity – they tied off the major arteries of the wounded trio.

By rights they should have handed Rasha over to the civilian police.

But Harald had judged her to be largely innocent, manipulated by the boyfriend whose body now came in three parts.

And Rasha's father, the Don, had a sense of honour. He always repaid debts.

'... You will explain ... to Don Mentrassore ... that a man called ... Donal Riordan ... will visit him soon ... and will say he is a friend ... of Harald Hammersen ... and the Don should act as if this were true ... tell him that ... *as if it were true* ... but it will be ... a lie ...'

Harald led Deltrassol even deeper into trance, inscribing post-mesmeric commands: Deltrassol would never consciously remember these words.

'... because Riordan is not to be trusted ... *not* to be trusted ... and the Don must lead Riordan ... into a trap ... and spring it shut ... to the death ...'

Deltrassol began to frown, then relaxed, too deep into trance to argue.

'... and this is how ...' Harald slowed his voice, checking the details within himself. '... the Don ... will kill ... Riordan ...'

It was an hour later, when Donal was returning to the task force office with two more mugs of coffee, plus a dark-blue folder tucked under his arm, that he saw Harald walking towards him along the corridor, swigging from a silver hip-flask.

Harald saw Donal at the same time. He screwed the top back on the flask, and tucked it inside his jacket.

'Hey, Donal. How's it going?'

'Good. I think people were worried about y—'

'Can I give you a hand? Here.' Harald took a coffee mug. 'What's in the folder?'

Donal waved the folder at Harald.

'The rest of my travel documents. I really am going to Illurium.'

They continued walking towards the office. Harald went first, opening the door and holding it for Donal.

'Good news,' Harald said. 'I thought it was going to happen.'

'Yeah ... Is there any news on Sushana? We thought you might have gone back to the hospital.'

'Nah. Viktor's there, isn't he?'

They went inside the office, with Donal frowning, unable to read the change in Harald's mood.

'Hey, Donal,' called Alexa. 'You went out for more coffee, and came back with the Marines.'

'Good to see you too,' said Harald.

'Yeah, well.'

Harald just nodded. Then he gave a too-wide smile as Laura came out of her private office. 'Hey, boss.'

'Hey yourself. You OK?'

'Sure.' Serious now, Harald said, 'I hear Donal-boy's going to Illurium.'

'That's right,' said Laura. 'So tell me about Deltrassol.'

'Deltrassol.'

'Uh-huh.'

'I've just dropped him off in Pallas Heptagon. Had to get him past the R-H boys. Robbery-Haunting must owe you a big favour, keeping their team in place this long.'

'Not any more.'

'Well ...' Harald glanced at Alexa. 'Seems our boy Deltrassol's been blackmailing Sir Alvan in the embassy.'

'How?' said Donal. 'What's the ambassador been up to?'

'Oh, let's say, he likes to step out every now and then for a night on the town. Nothing majorly criminal.'

'So why,' said Laura, 'did you let him go?'

'Because he was scared shitless, too scared to lie, and he knew nothing about Sushana being set up.' Harald looked at her. 'You don't think I'd have let him go otherwise.'

Laura thought about that.

'No. Of course not.'

'And now,' said Donal, 'we've got a source inside the Illurian Embassy. Neat work, Harald.'

Harald nodded, mouth tightening, saying nothing.

Twenty-three

The airport was busy. Travellers were dazed by the façade, by the glamour or by weariness. Security wraiths hovered inside walls, occasionally revealing themselves. Away from the check-in desks, hex-protected entrances led to cargo areas and out on to the runways.

Donal had not seen the place since the day the Diva flew in.

Do you feel the song?

For Death's sake you know I do.

Outside, seen through a full-length window, the opaque skies were near-indigo. The wind that blew steadily cut through heavy overcoats, chilling passengers walking to aircraft. The baggage handlers worked fast.

Some of the security men recognized Donal as he stood at check-in. Two plain-clothes officers came over.

'Flying to Illurium?' one of them said, as Donal held his ticket ready. 'Not bad, Lieutenant.'

'Can't discuss it,' said Donal. 'What you might call family business.'

Two of the officers looked at each other. Maybe they knew that Donal had no family, unless you counted the Department.

'You want to look around?'

'Sure,' said Donal. 'Not much changed from before, I hope.'

'Maybe a bit more secure.' Again the two officers looked at each other. 'Wish they'd tried for the Diva here, sir, if you don't mind me saying so.'

'What do you mean?'

'We got trance shielding up the wazoo, is what he means, Lieutenant. And we're not supposed to say so, but there's undercover mages onboard at all times, in among the passengers.'

'I didn't know that,' said Donal.

'Well, not many people do.'

But maybe some senior officers and politicians know. Interesting to find out exactly who.

Because they would have known that the best place to try for the Diva was in the city.

'You want me to check the bags through for you, sir?'

'Um ... All right.'

'Aisle or window?'

'Huh?'

'D'you prefer sitting next to the window, or in the aisle?'

Donal blinked.

'Beats me. I'm a poor boy from the orphanage. This is all new to me.'

'I think the choice is between having a good view or not having to trample on someone's feet to get to the bathroom.'

'Huh.' Donal thought about it. 'Gimme the window, then.'

They checked through Donal's two bags. The older bag was a battered rat-leather suitcase that Sister Mary-Anne Styx had given Donal on the day he left the orphanage. He normally used it to store books, the ones too precious to trade in.

The other case was new and shiny, a present from Laura. Donal tried not to feel uncomfortable about using a piece of luggage whose price could have fed the entire orphanage.

'You want to see the animals, Lieutenant? My name's Piersen, by the way.'

'Animals?'

'The ones that're flying. They have to go in the hold, along with the bags.'

'Isn't that dangerous?'

'The holds are pressurized, some of them. Come on, I'll show you.'

Donal followed Piersen through a door marked *Airport Staff Only*, and felt the cold touch of wispy fingers trail across his skin. Donal subvocalized a thank-you, not because he enjoyed the sensation but because he made no assumption that the security wraith enjoyed searching him.

'Did everyone hear about what happened?' Donal asked Piersen as they walked along a bleak corridor. 'About the Diva?'

'Some of us knew people who were on duty that night, Lieutenant. At the theatre, I mean. One of the uniforms told us the place went crazy. He's been seeing a police mage for trancework, trying to get over it.'

Piersen stopped at a set of doors made from some heavy, oily-looking material.

'Looks like the audience got ensorcelled, and a couple of dozen or more dropped into complete parazombie mode. Am I right?'

'That's about it,' said Donal. 'What's through here?'

'Cargo.' Piersen pushed open the doors. 'Waiting to be shipped.'

'Thanatos. So many?'

There were trolleys with baggage piled high, and stone-faced handlers manoeuvring trolleys into position near the big outer doors. And there were grey hexagonal cases with animals inside, scarcely visible through the small barred openings.

Donal caught a glimpse of sliding metallic-blue scales inside one case, pale pink membranous wings in another. He heard pitiful mewls and psychotic growls of despair.

'Can't they be tranquillized or something?'

'Yeah,' said Piersen, 'but it doesn't work too well. Some of them probably *have* been drugged by their owners, but the stress wakes them right up.'

It had taken Donal an hour in trance last night, to replace his fear of flying with excitement at visiting a foreign city for the first time. This was a reminder that he didn't need.

'Those cages look pretty tough.' Donal heard the doubt in his own voice. 'The airlines wouldn't place their own aircraft at risk.'

Piersen laid a hand against one grey case, ignoring the hiss that sounded inside. 'They'll be asleep soon enough.'

'I thought you said—'

'Right.' Piersen grinned, baring his teeth. 'Every flight's got a mage or witch on board, didn't you know? You sure won't get attacked by parazombies on the plane.'

Donal blinked.

'And is it right you had to waste a bunch of 'em,' Piersen continued, 'at the Energy Authority?'

'Uh ... Kind of.'

'Damn.' Piersen looked at the crates, then hammered one with the side of his fist. 'I wish I'd been there. Zombies of any kind give me the creeps, you know?'

Donal let out an extended breath. 'Really?'

'What, you never wanted to draw a bead on one and—?'

'Go fuck yourself, Piersen.'

248

Donal turned away and walked out, back to the check-in area and the regular passengers.

At the portal for boarding – meaning, exiting on to the tarmac and walking several hundred yards through the cold, biting wind – a uniformed woman was checking tickets and replacing them with boarding passes. Donal queued up along with everyone else. Finally it was his turn.

'Travelling alone, sir?'

'Yes. First time, too.'

Donal stopped. The clerk's skin was very white, and the faint tracery of grey veins implied that her blood ran black and cold.

Do you feel the bones?

Yeah.

The clerk's nostrils widened. She stared at Donal for a long silent moment.

Then she looked down, scrawled something in purple ink on a silver ledger, then annotated a white card that she handed over to Donal.

'The flight's a little under-booked, sir ...'

'Um, what does—?'

'... and I've upgraded you to first class.'

Donal looked at her, not knowing what to say.

'Have a nice flight, sir.'

'Er, and you. I mean, have a good day.'

The clerk smiled her icy zombie smile.

'I will now. *Thank you.*'

It was Harald's turn to watch over Sushana at the hospital, so Viktor – after two hours' sleep – had forced himself back to work. When the front desk called to say that a Bone Listener wanted to talk to Lieutenant Riordan – to talk in person – it was Viktor who picked up the call. He went down to meet the Bone Listener.

There he found her staring in silent communication with two deathwolves, their eyes glowing darkly amber. Unnerved, Viktor allowed his hands to move unconsciously to a crossed-wrists position, ready to draw his twin Grausers, before realizing what he was doing.

He cleared his throat and said: 'I'm Viktor Harman. I work with Donal Riordan.'

'Is the Lieutenant unavailable?' The Bone Listener, Feoragh, looked up at Viktor with odd, gentle eyes, dark against her pale skin. 'What is the matter?'

'He's flying out.' Viktor checked his watch. 'Probably just getting on the plane.'

'That's a pity.' Feoragh stood up. 'I'd like to share some information with him.'

'What about?' Viktor realized how his tone sounded. 'I mean, can't I help? Or one of the others?'

'Who else works with him?'

'We both report to Commander Steele. She's—'

'Laura Steele?' A glistening look slid across Feoragh's big eyes.

'Er ... Yes.'

Feoragh held a hand out to each of the deathwolves, and murmured something in an archaic tongue that Viktor could not have named, much less understood. The deathwolves opened their mouths wide, large tongues lolling as they revealed their fangs in a shared lupine grin. They nodded once as they rose and wheeled away in one motion, and padded towards the outer doors.

From the solid desk that he was part of, Sergeant Eduardo Kolemann watched with widened eyes as the deathwolves left. Meanwhile Feoragh was already striding towards the nearest bank of cylindrical brass lift-tubes.

Viktor blinked three times before regaining his composure and following her.

'You know Commander Steele?' he asked, catching up.

'We know who she is.' Feoragh gave a smile that shared no warmth with Viktor. 'And we have an interest in your case. Your ongoing operation.'

They rode in the lift-tube together. When the wraith enclosed Feoragh, it shone with a soft blue glow that Viktor had never seen before. Its grasp on him was the usual cold ethereal grip; but when the wraith ascended, it was smoother and faster than normal.

Feoragh turned to Viktor as they rose. When she spoke, her words echoed with disconcerting overlays in the airflow.

'The people you're hunting,' she said, 'killed more than a colleague. Mina d'Alkarny was headed towards becoming one of the greatest Bone Listeners in history. Don't think you can understand what I mean by that.'

'Um ... We're trying to—'

'I know what you're trying to do.' Feoragh looked upwards as their ascent-rate slowed, then back at Viktor. 'And we're on your side, otherwise I wouldn't be here.'

'All right.'

But a strange softening passed across Feoragh's face then, and she waved her fingertips in front of Viktor's forehead as the wraith came to a halt and held them in place, suspended in the shaft. Viktor felt waves of alternating warm and cool pulses passing through him.

Feoragh nodded, and the wraith pushed her and Viktor through the opening, into the grey-carpeted corridor.

'You have a hurt of your own to deal with, Viktor Harman,' she said. 'And I hope that you heal properly and soon.'

'Partner,' muttered Viktor. 'Only one of them's hurt.'

'Physically at least,' said Feoragh. 'But we have to watch out for more than that in these matters, don't you think?'

Viktor started to open his mouth, before realizing he had no idea what to say to her.

'Come,' Feoragh added. 'Introduce me to your commander. I'm looking forward to meeting the famous Laura Steele.'

Viktor led the way, yet it felt as though he were following her. It was an unusual feeling, and he blinked his gritty eyes, checking for ensorcelment as he did so – a tendency to blink rapidly and yawn was a symptom of having been recently mesmerized.

There was nothing, and he went through the internal visualizations that he'd been provided with in trance-training. Again, nothing.

Laura came out of her office to greet the Bone Listener.

'Hello, I'm Laura Steele.' She held out her hand. 'I'm sorry about Dr d'Alkarny.'

'Yes.' Feoragh bowed, then touched the back of Laura's hand. 'It seems that you are.'

'Um ... How can I help you?'

'Are you able to contact Lieutenant Riordan,' asked Feoragh, 'before he departs for Illurium?'

'I'm not sure ...' Laura turned to Alexa. 'Get the Commissioner's office, and ask Eyes to ring the—'

Laura broke off as Harald shook his head.

'Scrub that,' Laura continued. 'Do it yourself, via the ordinary switchboard. Ring the control tower or security, whoever you can get hold of. Keep them on hold.'

'I'm on it.' Alexa tugged the receiver from the hook and span the wheels to all zeroes. 'Switchboard? I need to—'

But Laura was already leading Feoragh through the doorway to her office and pulling it shut behind them.

Alone with Feoragh, Laura asked: 'You have information from the Archives?'

'From deep in the Lattice,' answered Feoragh, 'having searched far. Lieutenant Riordan was working on a conspiracy case, or the possibility of one. That was what brought him to your attention, I'm guessing.'

'That's right. And you know about the Diva.'

'Yes, and of the precedents. The famous performers who died prematurely so that others might enjoy their bones.'

There was a silky tone in those words that made even Laura shudder.

'Am I missing something?' Laura said. 'Those performers weren't even in Tristopolis, they were ... Oh, shit.'

'The Illurian connection is strong, otherwise Lieutenant Riordan would not be going there. But there is more. Have you heard of the Tringulian Triplets?'

'No.' Laura thought back to visits to the theatre with her parents, back when she was young and the world was warm and bright and simple. Her mother had followed the newspaper columns about theatrical stars. 'Wait ... They're opera singers also, is that right?'

'Yes ... And the thaumaturgical geniuses of Svaltirno recently operated on the triplets, not to separate them, but to ensure their continued health. The triplets' condition had been worsening, but after the operation' – Feoragh sounded as though she were reciting a newspaper article verbatim – 'a hospital spokesman said the prognosis was more than excellent, and the chief thaumaturgical registrar declared the operation a resounding advance in modern operating techniques.'

From the outer office, visible through the glass walls of Laura's office, Alexa waved and pointed at the handset, indicating that she had the airport on the line. Laura raised a hand, signifying: *Wait a moment.*

'Look, Bone Listener, if you want to tell me something of importance to Lieutenant Riordan, you need to—'

'I can tell that you and he are intimate,' said Feoragh. 'Perhaps the airport control tower can send a message to the flight deck, before they are out of range. Even if the aircraft has taken off, I mean.'

'We don't do this kind of thing every day,' answered Laura. 'What do you need to tell Donal?'

'I'm ninety-seven per cent certain that the conspiracy which I suspect you codename the Black Circle are going to target the Tringulian

Triplets. The Triplets match the profile of famous performers whose bones make a tempting target for those ... people.'

This time there was manifest hatred in Feoragh's voice.

'And the announcement,' she continued, 'that the Triplets are going to live for several decades longer than anyone anticipated is going to annoy the conspirators intensely. The fact that the Triplets are performing shortly in Silvex City is going to present an opportunity they won't be able to—'

'There's going to be another hit? In Silvex City?'

'Yes, and that's the message you need to get to Donal Riordan. That, and that I've narrowed down the list of possible contacts. With the layers of indirection they've put in place, I cannot tell with an accuracy of more than fifty-three per cent, but my intuition says I'm right.'

Laura looked at Feoragh steadily. A Bone Listener's intuition was worth more than facts, or at least that was what Laura's mentor, Captain Felthorn (who died a month before Laura herself did, but in his case permanently) had often told her.

'You think you know who the Black Circle member is? The one who organized the hit on the Diva?'

'I'm not sure if that operation was his ... But Councillor Gelbthorne has banking and energy interests that have to coincide with the Black Circle's long term strategy. He's the person that Donal Riordan has to apprehend. I take it he has Cross-Border Warrants?'

'Yes, three blanks hex-entangled to Judge Prior's office.' If the judge filled in a name and signed any of the local copies, the corresponding warrant in Donal's possession would display the same information. 'If you're really sure about this, we can go over there right now.'

'And the airport?'

Laura looked out at Alexa. 'You still got them on the line? The airport cops?'

'Just hung up,' Alexa called back. 'Some guy called Piersen, said Donal's already gone through. I'll have to see if we can call the aircraft, but Piersen said it's impossible.'

At his desk, Harald gave a tiny smile, his face hidden at an angle where no one should notice.

Purple gloom enveloped the city, and Alexa had switched on her bright desk lamp. Earlier, wraiths had cleaned the windows inside and out, so that the lamp now shone to produce a reflected interior; and in that reflection, Alexa had seen Harald smile.

Seen him smile when she said Donal was unreachable.

Alexa picked up the phone again, and tried a different tack, asking the operator to put her through to the airline's reservation desk. If that didn't work, she would think of something else.

Harald stood up quickly, and muttered something about going down to the range. He looked like a man who needed to let off steam, but a gun range wasn't always the best place for that. The range master would soon spot an officer whose emotional state meant they were not best suited to be firing right now.

Alexa watched him go.

Twenty-four

Laura slid open a desk drawer, and stared at the Magnus lying inside. It was Donal's gun, the one he had not been able to take because no airline allowed anyone besides on-duty sky marshals to fly armed.

She wished he'd been able to carry it with him.

'I can wait,' said Feoragh. 'The judge can wait. It will be three hours at least before the plane lands in Silvex City, maybe a lot longer ... you know what the storms are like at the Illurian border. And the warrants amend themselves instantaneously.'

'I know.' Laura looked back through the glass wall, seeing Alexa on the phone, gesturing as she argued. 'But we're not getting anywhere here. Let's go.'

Feoragh blinked her liquid eyes.

'I intuit the movement of powerful enemies against you, Commander Steele.'

'Uh ... Right,' said Laura. 'Who in particular?'

'Unknown so far, or I would tell you. But the thing is ... they have made a mistake. Because they never should have killed Mina d'Alkarny.'

'How—? What do you mean?'

'There are ripples of causation spreading through the Lattice, patterns that will reveal themselves among the information vectors. And ...'

'What?'

'... and we are only human, or' – with a humourless smile – 'at least as human as you, Commander. Bone Listeners are supposed to be impartial, and we are, but there is the matter of motivation.'

Outside, Alexa slammed the handset down again, and swore.

'You want to get her killers too, huh?' said Laura.

Feoragh gave the minutest of nods.

'Then you two get moving.' Laura watched Alexa check the revolver inside her handbag. 'Judge Prior takes a while to get motivated, but I think he'll be impressed by you. At least he'd better be.'

'Yes.'

Alexa snapped her handbag shut. 'I'm ready.'

Donal thanked the scanwraith as he passed through the final gate to the outside. A cold wind held steady across the tarmac, and in front of Donal a thin woman clutched at her wide white hat with one hand, her dress and coat with the other. She walked with tight paces, trying to keep balance on her stiletto heels.

They headed for the steps that attendants had already wheeled up to the plane. The aircraft's propeller blades were still, pregnant with the possibility of whirling motion, waiting to drag the metal craft aloft.

The thin woman's husband, portly and dressed in a double-breasted suit, kept his head down as he walked, making no attempt to help his wife. Donal shook his head, and checked out the other passengers walking with him. All of them looked more richly dressed than him, though they couldn't all be flying first class.

And he wondered, as he continued across the tarmac, whether the scanwraith would have allowed him to carry his most precious accessory aboard after all. But that was spilled milk: the Magnus was safely locked in Laura's desk drawer back at HQ.

The first of the passengers was already climbing the steps, while at the top two stewardesses in black capes smiled their welcoming smiles.

Travelling first class still meant having to climb the steps by yourself, though Donal could imagine some future service whereby wraiths lifted the passengers up into the aircraft. The wind tugged at Donal as he ascended. When he gripped the rail he felt how cold it was: almost enough to make the skin stick.

He waited a moment for the woman ahead to reach the top, then moved up two steps at a time to reach the hatchway and enter the plane.

'Welcome aboard, sir.'

'Thanks.'

'You'll be seated over here.'

In first class, the portly man with the thin wife was already making himself comfortable, having sipped the brandy that a steward-ess had poured for him. Drawing a fat cigar from a silver case, the

256

man placed it between his lips and sucked hard, igniting it. A near-invisible curtain surrounded his chair, sealing him off from the rest of the cabin.

Donal had always hated cigars. The thought of the essence-of-flame-wraith that was used to soak self-igniting tobacco ... that was a new wrinkle that made him despise the man further.

'May one fetch you a drink, sir?' The steward who spoke was thin and effeminate. 'Perhaps a sherry?'

'Whisky,' said Donal. 'Single malt, raw as you like.'

'Ah, very good. Thank you, sir.'

As the steward went aft, Donal checked the other cabin crew, seeing the limp-wristed men gossiping with the stewardesses, and noting the two stewards who looked different: lean rather than thin, with enlarged knuckles and some scarring around the eyes.

If any of the other passengers noticed, they would probably feel worried, but for Donal the Federal Sky Branch officers represented added security. Still, he regretted now having asked for a window seat: if there was to be some kind of action, the best place for Donal to be sitting would be next to the aisle.

Yet it had been twelve years since the Goladol Separatist Alliance had hijacked a series of aircraft, seven in all, and forced them to fly to Zurinam. Since the last two loads of passengers had been executed by the Zurinese authorities – deliberately the hijackers had landed the plane during the eighth day of Weeping Week, when non-believers were not allowed out of their homes, and the gladiatorial bishops had wept even as they carried out the sentence on the innocent foreigners who'd been forced into Zurinam – people had fought back and security had been tightened.

The last two attempts had been only partially successful, and the rebels had not even tried for the past nine years.

Still, Goladol Province remained part of Illurium. If the few news reports that made it past the border censors were credible, then trouble persisted in the region. No wonder that the Tristopolitan and federal authorities collaborated to keep security tight.

'There you are, sir. One fine whisky.'

Donal hoped it was not too fine, but when he sipped it the liquor seemed to become mist, an intoxicating mist. He closed his eyes to appreciate the overlaid tastes.

Despite himself, Donal laughed.

'Make sure your seat belt is secured, sir.'

'Yes, thank you.'

There was a central bulkhead up front, some ten feet back from the entrance to the flight deck. Black curtains screened off the small area, and at first Donal assumed it was a secondary galley, perhaps a wet bar for first class passengers only.

But then he saw the steward returning the whisky bottle to the galley that was set aft, and noticed the watchfulness of one of the hard-looking stewards as he passed the black drape. This was some kind of secure facility.

Maybe an armoury?

It was another eight minutes before the last of the passengers was aboard, still filing down the aisles towards the economy seats in back. The propellers jerked and began to rotate even while eight insubstantial wraiths were hauling the steps out of the way.

The cabin vibrated, and the plane slowly turned on its nose wheels until it was pointing along the runway for take-off. Overhead the blank purple sky seemed darker.

The engines rumbled.

Donal took another sip of whisky.

'Welcome aboard, ladies and gentlemen. I'm Captain Yershwin, and we are ready to take off. Please settle back and enjoy.'

Sister Mary-Anne Styx, back at the orphanage, had been big on explaining the basic laws of physics, those that she knew, to her audience of mostly disbelieving young charges.

But Donal had always paid attention, and now he knew it was inertia that pressed him back into the upholstery as acceleration dragged the aircraft along the runway. The lights outside became a blur as the engines dropped in pitch. Then the lights were dropping away and the aircraft was rising, a pale green glow emanating from the engine housings, as hex-protected turbines drew power from the necroscopic cells embedded in wings and fuselage.

Going to Illurium.

Donal shook his head again, then tossed back the remainder of the whisky in one long beautiful gulp.

Alexa was alone in the task force office. She had another mug of coffee on her desk, but she wasn't going to drink this one: she'd spend the rest of evening having to go pee. How Donal drank the amount he did, she didn't know.

Perhaps men's bladders were bigger, or something. Maybe when

Sushana was well enough to chat again, Alexa could ask her. She might know.

Having failed to get a message through to the airport before Donal left, Alexa wasn't sure what to do next. A sensible person would go home.

A sensible person would never have volunteered to be on Laura's task force.

If they scored a spectacular success, then perhaps the task force members would be slated for recognition and promotion ... but no one likes a snitch, let alone a police officer who rats on fellow officers. So long as they investigated corruption *outside* the Department, it was manageable.

Even then, the City politicians could damage anyone's career prospects with a whisper or innuendo, or even a discreet (yet unsubtle) spot of blackmail.

But Alexa was determined to make Commander herself some day. When she pulled open the left hand drawer of her old desk, it revealed a stack of books from the collection she mostly kept at home: the dry tomes she needed to memorize and understand in order to pass her sergeant's exam next month.

Some of the books were slim volumes with cheap covers, and the one on top was one she'd hardly looked at: *Surveillance II – Reading Lips*. Alexa had all seven volumes of the Surveillance series, plus the 'unofficial' eighth volume that no officer could afford to be seen reading: the one subtitled *Running Away*.

The author was a retired street cop, and in *Surveillance VIII* she described the geometry of hiding, the vectors of light and shadow, and angles of escape. (Suddenly changing direction to one side is a common tactic, but often it allows the pursuer to run along the hypotenuse of a right-angled triangle, while the pursuee runs further, along the other two sides. A fatal error.)

Everyone knew that the books were intensely practical; but to be seen reading a book on running away was to invite weeks or even months of ongoing taunts and insults. It wasn't just this department: surely every police force in every city of the world was the same.

Alexa pulled out the volume on lip-reading and opened it atop her desk. She skimmed through the chapters, looking for interesting passages to re-read. (The author was good at telling personal anecdotes, humorous and possibly exaggerated, in order to highlight the points she was making.) Then Alexa put the book down and closed it.

There were other esoteric skills of use to plain-clothes officers, and one of them consisted of deep trancework. Harald had given her some pointers, taking her through basic mesmeric inductions and suggestions, showing her how to manipulate other people's minds, and her own.

Since beginning the work, Alexa had not yet put a suspect into trance; but she had used visualization to improve her scores on the gun range, and she had Harald to thank for it.

Harald. I don't like the way you smiled tonight.

Beneath his gentle ways, there was a dangerous side to Harald: the product of his years in the Marines, where he had learned skills that were unknown and unthinkable to the civilian populace ... and to most police officers.

Something's wrong.

Part of trancework, deriving from its original uses in medicine, entailed developing the ability to revisit memories, to relive past events in such detail as to allow the person to explore stimali they had not consciously perceived when the events happened.

In therapy, such work allowed the patient to make happy memories more vivid, more intense, and to anchor them in a world of confident thinking. The reverse procedure allowed them to make a traumatic memory lose its painful hooks.

For police officers, for surveillance officers in particular, such skills had additional uses.

Alexa's eyelids fluttered as she thought back to the sight of Donal and Laura, visible through the glass sides of Laura's office, after Donal returned from the Archives. It was the day he met the Bone Listener, Feoragh, who came here today ...

No. Wrong time. Alexa shifted her memory to when Donal came from the interrogation that he kept silent about, working with Dr Kyushen Jyu. After that, black-suited medics took one of the dwarf twins away to a secure ward.

Yes ...

Alexa sank a little deeper.

This memory.

There was something here, something going on. She thought that Harald might know what it was, because of the way he'd looked at Donal.

Alexa had the time pinned. Now she had to slip back in memory and revisit that time. She closed her eyes and began to count backwards from seven hundred, her eyelids fluttering as she leaned back in her chair and smiled.

Her awareness slid deep inside.

In the past, she saw Laura's lips move, saw Donal turn so his back was to Alexa, but the tension in his shoulders was a kind of eloquence ... Then he turned, and in her memory this time (unlike her first experience of these events) Alexa could lip-read every word that Donal said.

'Seven-seven-seven.' Donal paused, then: 'Two-nine-seven-two, six-six-nine-six.'

'That was in the dwarf's—?' Laura stepped to one side, so that Donal's shoulder obscured Alexa's view of her face.

But it was enough.

I don't believe it ...

Shuddering, Alexa began taking deeper breaths, feeling like a diver beginning to ascend. Donal had been saying that the Commissioner was implicated. That Commissioner Vilnar's involvement was confirmed, from a second source of evidence. Alexa was sure of it.

Donal had *told* Laura that Vilnar was a suspect.

Yet Harald's attitude towards Donal had changed for the worse.

Not him.

It was hard to believe. Especially with Sushana in the hospital.

Harald, a spy for Vilnar? Impossible.

Eyelids fluttering, Alexa slipped back into her memories.

Five minutes later, her eyes snapped open.

'Harald, you fuckin' cretin.'

An hour into the flight, there was a soft moan from beneath the deck. Startled, Donal looked outside in case part of the wing had dropped off. There was nothing save the strong green glow of turbines against the indigo night.

Another moan sounded, followed by a drawn-out growling. The hard-faced stewards were already moving towards the rear of the aircraft. Donal realized they were heading for whatever part of the plane connected with the cargo holds.

Was one of the animals down there emitting the sounds? Donal remembered his glimpses of the caged creatures. Some of them could be dangerous if they got out.

Outside, in the far distance, a sheet of white lightning flared. This was a sign of the Transition Tempest, of the turbulence and concentrated hex that for ever roiled in the skies above the Illurian border.

Yet the flight time, according to Captain Yershwin's announcement shortly after take-off, included two more hours before they reached the perpetual storms. This was too soon for hex-induced phenomena to manifest themselves.

But down in the hold, an awful screech was followed by a chorus of yowling. Whatever the disturbance was, it was affecting more than one of the beasts. In fact, it sounded like all of them, as they gave howling vent to fear and rage.

One of the stewardesses hurried forward, complexion pale, then stopped as she reached the black drapes beyond the forward bulkhead. Donal had wondered what was hidden there.

'Excuse me.' He raised himself up, and stepped over the feet of the white-haired woman in the next seat. 'I beg your pardon.'

'You be careful, young man.'

'I'm really sorry, ma'am.'

'No, I mean, if you're going to help with those dangerous animals, you be very careful.'

'I'll try.'

But without a weapon, Donal wasn't sure what he would do if the beasts got free.

'Please don't worry.' It wasn't Captain Yershwin's voice over the tannoy, but a younger man. 'This is First Officer Smeltil. Please be assured that we have everything under control. Remain in your seats with your seat belts fastened.'

Another stewardess, not the woman who'd hurried forward, reached out and touched Donal's arm. 'Sir, please return to your—'

Donal leaned close to her ear. 'I'm a police officer. Let me help.'

'Oh, Lieutenant, yes ...'

So Donal's rank as well as name had been noted on the passenger list.

'Excuse me.'

It was the first stewardess, followed by a dark-complexioned woman Donal had not seen before. This woman was dressed in black and purple robes, and the eleven-sided amulet between her small breasts shone silver and jet.

Moving heptagrams rolled across the exposed areas of her skin: her taut lined face and her bony hands. Her age was impossible to determine. She looked like some sand-weathered sculpture left out in the desert for decades.

Donal was about to hold up his hand and suggest that the woman remain where she was; but her eyes held a strange glint, like oily pools in whose strange depths creatures swam.

A witch?

That's right.

The thought seemed to be Donal's own.

After a few moments, Donal blinked back to full awareness. The two stewardesses yawned, eyelids fluttering, then came awake.

'What—?'

The witch had already reached the rear of the aircraft.

'I'm glad she's on our side,' muttered Donal. 'Er, she *is* on—?'

'Oh, yes.'

'Thank Hades.'

At that moment the plane lurched sideways. A dozen people yelled or screamed.

'Shit.' Donal caught hold of the nearest seat as a tray crashed on the deck.

'Hurry.' A stewardess was pushing him.

'All right.'

Donal moved towards the rear galley, where the witch had disappeared from sight. A grim-faced steward was holding open an internal hatch. Metal steps led down into a shadowy space. Donal leaned inside, catching a glimpse of the witch's robe.

'Thanatos. Here goes.' Donal grabbed hold of the steel rails and jumped. He slid down the rails on his palms, just like the stairwell in the orphanage. Then his feet hit the lower deck.

'Hush.'

The witch was sitting cross-legged before the row of cages, her arms outstretched, her eyes closed as she bent her head forward and sent waves of energy – whatever that might mean: Donal could almost hear Sister Mary-Anne Styx's sceptical voice debunking mysticism whenever it was mentioned – towards the fearful animals. Silver scales and purple skin and grey talons flashed inside the cages.

A thump sounded behind Donal, then a curse. Donal turned to see one of the hard-faced stewards – an undercover marshal, had to be – lying on his side. One knee was pulled up against his chest.

The plane had bumped again just as he was descending the steps. Donal could see straight away that the man's leg was broken.

'I'm Riordan,' said Donal. 'Have you got a weapon?'

263

'Yeah ...' Through clenched teeth, the injured man forced out: 'Ankle ... holster. Other leg.'

'I've got it.'

Donal moved fast, whipping the black short-barrelled revolver from the holster. The injured leg needed to be immobilised, but if the animals got free – or the turbulence got worse – first aid would be irrelevant.

Crouching, Donal took aim at the nearest cage, then swivelled the weapon from one cage to the next. A translucent streamer of pale light washed through the cargo hold.

It was only in that moment that Donal finally acknowledged the obvious. This was no ordinary storm, and these were not ordinary animals. And it would take more than bullets to resolve the situation.

A dark glow surrounded the witch.

The plane pitched. Screams and tinkling glass sounded overhead, attenuated by the deck in between and by something more: a thickening quality to the air, a new vibration just below the limit of human hearing.

Around the witch, the air darkened further. Inside the cages, animals quietened as their eyes brightened. Then they too began to hum and warble, reptilian throats joining the witch's near-subliminal chant. Donal lowered his weapon.

Go forward.

For a moment, Donal could not work out who had spoken. The witch continued to hum and chant, but somehow it was her words that he was thinking.

Touch the animals, came the thought. *One by one.*

'I don't—'

Now.

Donal looked back at the officer with the broken leg. The man's eyes were shining and damp with suffering; but he was determined to remain conscious. Donal handed him back his weapon.

'I won't be needing it,' Donal said.

'What are you ... doing?'

'I wish I bloody knew.'

The plane tipped sideways again. Donal rolled along the smooth deck, coming up on one knee. Somehow the witch remained fastened in place, seated cross-legged on the tilted deck, her attention focused inwards.

Donal could never appreciate what battle she was fighting, nor how much energy it required. He could only do as she had asked. He crawled to the first cage.

'Don't.' It was the wounded sky marshal. 'Don't do it.'

'Have to,' muttered Donal, grabbing hold of the bars and hauling himself half-upright. 'I know it makes no—'

A cold black tongue rasped across Donal's hand, and was gone.

Do you feel the bones?

'Thanatos,' he whispered. 'That was a Basili—'

Hurry. It was the witch again, inside his mind. *There's little time.*

Another thought, of a different flavour, followed.

And do you taste the song?

Twenty-five

The plane was straightening up. There was a series of bumps, and once more a scream sounded from the passenger deck overhead. Loud, it pierced the sound of ongoing panic. Donal pulled himself forward to the next cage, and thrust his hand inside.

'Ah ...'

Teeth fastened on his wrist. Sharp teeth. An acid burning pierced his skin. Donal forced himself to hold still and not jerk back: those sharp curved fangs could rip his tendons apart.

Do you feel—?

Hush. Let me work.

It took all of Donal's trance-trained willpower to override his reflexes and hold in position until the pressure released. Burning still swept through him as he crawled forward. There were four more cages.

There was more danger here than the hex-laden storm outside. Somehow Donal's presence was part of it.

Do you hear the music?

It's here because of me.

One of the beasts was ethereal, akin to a wraith yet not remotely human. The bars of its cage acted as conductors for the necromagnetic field that held it in place.

When Donal put his hand inside the field, the burning across his skin was followed by an icy blast as the strange form melded with him, just for a moment. The geometries of space rotated through impossible angles and directions. Donal saw the world like some cuboid painting, from perspectives no normal person could maintain.

Then a massive migraine seemed to cleave his head asunder like an axe. Falling backwards, he cried out ... and felt fine.

'What the Thanatos?'

The witch juddered. There were no words in Donal's head, but he got the message: the witch couldn't hang on for much longer. He had to make peace and create some kind of rapport with the remaining animals fast or the aircraft was going to fall out of the sky.

It's my fault. They need to understand I'm no threat.

There were three cages left. Donal grabbed the next with both hands, steadying himself as the aircraft tilted again. He forced his face between the bars.

Foolish risk ...

This time he got what should have been a clear view of the beast, but purple scales swirled in helices too fast for his eyes to follow. It spat something acidic into his face and he jerked back, releasing the bars and rolling across the hard metal.

He bumped up against a cage.

Not ... The witch, bent over, looked close to collapse. *Not an attack.*

'It forgives me,' Donal said. 'I understand.'

No ...

For a moment Donal thought the witch was disagreeing with him. Then the plane bucked and she fell and Donal realized that it was over: the plane was going down with everyone aboard and it was his fault.

The fuselage screamed as metal twisted. Donal slammed his fist into the nearest cage and something slid across his skin. It corkscrewed and twisted inside, some quicksilver insertion sliding into Donal's bones, delivering pain.

Donal yelled as a percussive wave of air hammered across the hold, slamming him against a bulkhead.

Collapsed on the deck, the witch looked unconscious. The wounded man was curled up, shivering.

One cage left.

The plane was dying but there was a chance. Donal leaped from the deck towards the final cage as the cargo hold span upside down and everything went ...

NO!

... away.

When Donal came to, several people were taking care of the wounded man. One of the stewards plus a well-dressed passenger were tying emergency splints in place with linen napkins. There was no sign of the witch.

Someone had left a water bottle next to Donal. He picked up it, unscrewed the top, and drank. After draining it, he checked the label: mountain water from Goladol, in northern Illurium.

The plane was flying steadily.

'Ugh.' Donal dragged himself upright. 'There's a medical chest ... upstairs. I saw it earlier.'

'Yeah, we know.' The steward looked up at him. 'Problem is, there's a dozen injured people upstairs. One of them's had a heart attack.'

'He'll be all right,' murmured the well-dressed man, continuing to work on the splint.

'There'll be an ambulance waiting when we land,' said the steward.

'Assuming we don't hit more storms. Wouldn't it have been better to turn around?'

The steward said nothing for a moment, then: 'Um ... Keep this to yourselves, but the weather's worse behind us than it is up front. Nothing like this was predicted by the Met Bureau.'

The medical man chuckled. 'Never trust a seer, is what I say.'

'What happened' – Donal gestured toward the deck – 'to the ... lady?'

'You mean the witch?' asked the steward. 'She's fine. Why?'

'Nothing.' Donal had last seen her collapsed; but there was nothing normal about witches. 'What about the animals?'

The cages were silent.

'They're quiet. Don't know what spooked them earlier. Well ... the storm, right? I mean I don't know how they knew it was going to happen.'

'Me neither,' said Donal.

But he had a bad feeling that somehow he did know, that the witch had been right and his presence here triggered everything. He remembered being back in the theatre when the front rows of the audience, ensorcelled, had risen in parazombie trance and stepped forward in exact unison, advancing upon the Diva ... and upon Donal.

Do you hear the bones?

No.

'Where is she now?' Donal added. 'The witch.'

'Working on one of the passengers' – bitterness surfaced in the medic's voice – 'that I couldn't do anything for. I'm making myself useful down here.'

Can you feel the music?

It was not *my fault.*

The injured steward moaned with pain, then slipped out of consciousness once more.

Donal grinned, and glanced back at the cages.

'What's funny?'

'Nothing,' Donal answered. 'Sorry. I had a bang on the head. I'm having a strange reaction to it.'

I feel wonderful.

The medic looked concerned. 'Just sit down and I'll look at you in a—'

'No, no. I'm not concussed. See?' Donal raised his right hand, using the thumb to keep the little finger bent. 'Three fingers, right? No, the weird thing is ... how wonderful I feel.'

Really wonderful.

'Euphoria,' said the medic. 'Perhaps the oxygen in here is ... Never mind. If you're able to move OK, perhaps you should get back upstairs to the passenger deck. See if there's anything you can do to help. You look capable enough.'

'All right.' Donal climbed, chuckling to himself. 'All right.'

Knowing this was a strange reaction to have.

When Donal reached the top of the steel ladder, a thin hand took hold of his wrist then grasped with steel strength and hauled him up. It was the old witch, clothed in black and purple. When she released her grip, Donal's wrist throbbed.

'Er ... Thank you,' he said.

No one had taught him how to address a witch. Nuns, yes: the steel ruler across his leg taught him to respectfully say Sister (or Mother in the case of the Reverend Mother who ruled the orphanage, cold bitch that she was). But the witch was different, and Donal knew that a lack of ceremony would not bother her.

'The touch of black blood,' she said, 'is upon you. The tempest field is unusually widespread tonight, to have picked up the resonance this far from the ... Could there be intelligent direction behind it?'

'I may have enemies in Silvex City, though I've never been there.' Donal shrugged. 'Part of the job.'

'That does not make it a good thing, young man.'

'No, ma'am.'

A smile cracked the witch's old skin. 'But you will face the dangers anyway? Good for you, Donal Riordan.'

'How did you know my name?'

The witch nodded towards the rear bulkhead of the galley, where a small typed list stood in a transparent glass pocket. 'They call it a passenger manifest.'

'Oh ...'

'Be observant of the world. That's the way to thrive, don't you think?'

Donal inclined his head in a kind of bow.

'Here.' The witch reached inside her robes, tugged, and brought out the silver and jet amulet that Donal had seen earlier. 'This is for you.'

'I can't—'

'Take it. *Now.*'

'Er ...' The amulet was already in Donal's hand. 'Thanatos. How did you do that?'

'I didn't do anything. Are you saying I can control your hands?'

'Well, I don't suppose it's possible to—'

'Put the amulet around your neck right this moment.'

'—command me to ...' Donal finished fastening the cord at the back of his neck, and left the amulet drop against his sternum. '... um, do anything I didn't want to do already ...'

'Exactly.' The witch smiled again, and this time Donal could see the warmth of her spirit: young and dancing, despite the age of her physical body. 'Aren't you so glad you wanted to do the right thing?'

'Right ...'

'You'll excuse me.' The witch touched Donal's arm. 'There are still a few people who need my help.'

'Yes. I'll just—'

'Go back to your seat.'

Donal let the witch slip past him in the galley, then he headed back towards first class. People were snoring softly, despite the earlier panic.

Back in his seat, Donal allowed his eyelids to droop, enjoying the soft orange glow of light seen through closed eyes. Somehow the witch had given him permission to enjoy this. He slipped slowly down into warmth.

Do you ...

Smiling, Donal fell asleep.

The Transition Tempest's core was formed of huge billowing sheets of silver and purple fluorescence, the aurora heart of a centuries-old (maybe millennia-old) storm that raged in place above the Illurian border. Silver lightning could strike at any time.

Suddenly, it did. Strike.

White light flared inside the cockpit and ripped back along the aisles and concave walls, and then was gone. The plane's systems continued to function, and nobody panicked.

Only the witch was capable of panicking at that moment, but she was too busy to worry about anything as she poured her strength into maintaining the calming spell that enveloped all the passengers, particularly Donal Riordan as he smiled, deep inside some happy dream, and murmured one word: *Laura*.

Hearing it – or sensing it somehow – the witch also smiled. She had been in love, and had remained married to the mage of her dreams for thirty-five years, until his confrontation with a group of parazombies controlled by some unknown power. That had been in a 'secure' hospital wing.

The medics had tried to retain control of the ensorcelled parazombies, refusing to let police officers inside the ward to help them, while her husband Valkton attempted the group exorcism single-handed, unwilling to wait for help to arrive. The concentration of hex increased by the minute: the parazombies' controller was travelling physically towards the place, increasing the strength of his broadcast (by the straightforward geometry of an inverse-square law) the nearer he drew.

The witch had tasted the resonance of the Black Circle upon the emanations remaining around her husband's corpse. She had not known the conspiracy's name at that time; but she read the same traces upon Donal Riordan.

And you realize, don't you?

All of this she obtained from Donal's subconscious, during the twenty-minute interrogation that she had conducted in the galley when he ascended from the plane's cargo hold. In Donal's memory, the conversation had lasted only seconds.

You begin to realize what they did to you, Donal Riordan.

When Donal came awake the plane was commencing descent. He pulled back the small white curtains inside the window – or were you supposed to call it a porthole? – and noticed two things at once: the near-black sky above, and the glistening reflections on the perfectly flat ground beyond Silvex City.

He'd missed the beginning of the Glass Planes, the hundred-mile-square glass sheets that were supported like some god's three-

271

dimensional chessboard, stacked one plain (or plane) above the other, separated by fifty or a hundred feet of air (for the spacing alternated). The supporting pillars were of marble; each was as wide as an ordinary city.

There were legends, plenty of them, about the aeons-past origins of the Planes. Each legend had thousands or hundreds of thousands of believers. Yet so many of the legends contradicted the others. No one knew the truth; many people claimed to.

Donal had slept through the aircraft's passing inside the Transition Tempest and emerging on this side, over Illurian territory. What was strange, was that in his mind's eye Donal could see every detail of that vast, long-lived storm guarding the border.

The engines' pitch changed. Their emerald luminescence shifted hue, glowing a deeper green as the plane banked left and downwards, beginning its miles-long arcing trajectory to the waiting runway.

Silvex City shone scarlet and emerald, gold and cobalt-blue, with glass spires picked out in violet light. In them, yellow patterns like nebulae swam.

Another country.

A huge grin stretched Donal's face as he watched the cityscape grow larger and more amazingly detailed as the plane came in to land. Soon there was touchdown. Donal's head rocked back as the tyres span across the roughened opaque glass that formed the runway. Then the brakes were on and the aircraft was braking, a controlled deceleration down to taxiing speed.

Only the final ground manoeuvres remained before Donal could walk inside Silvex City itself.

Finally the plane rolled to a halt parallel to a terminal building, one of seven that spread out in a star-shaped configuration across the glass plain. An oval detached itself from the wall and moved towards the aircraft, dragging behind it an elongating tunnel formed of overlapping metal leaves.

'We would like to thank you all for choosing Air Illurium for your journey, and we look forward to—'

While the first officer's pronouncement sounded over the tannoy, even the most jaded first class passengers were murmuring their appreciation. One heavyset woman pulling on a fur stole said to her husband: 'Wonderful time, dear. Shall we do it again soon?'

'—seeing you next time. Thanks again, everyone.'

'I think we absolutely should.'

None of the stewardesses blinked at this, not even the young lady with the bandaged hand. How would she explain the wound to herself? Handling a broken glass?

The injured steward with the broken leg was out of sight. And the black drapes were pulled across the witch's cubicle, though Donal was sure she was inside.

Everyone's happy.

Donal waited until the last, pretending to take time over getting his belongings from the under-seat locker, though it consisted only of his overcoat and the battered paperback of *Human: the Heretics*, the next volume he'd intended to read.

The black drapes concealing the witch did not even twitch.

Donal waited. He was the last passenger on board.

'It was a great flight,' he told the effeminate steward. 'Apart from the interesting bits.'

'I know just what you mean, sir.'

Donal stopped by the drapes, considering whether to pull them back. If the witch were in some kind of trance, an interruption might be dangerous.

The amulet, now inside his shirt, felt cold and hard.

Do you ...?

Shhh.

Three black-robed men were coming aboard the aircraft. The tallest of the trio stared at Donal with eyes that seemed to expand as they focused.

'Who are you?'

'I'm Donal Riordan.'

One of the other mages pointed at Donal's chest, straight towards the amulet concealed beneath Donal's shirt and tie. 'It was passed on, not stolen.'

'Truth,' said the third mage.

And all three mages bowed at once.

'You are blessed,' their leader said. 'Go with our blessings added to hers.'

'Er.. Right,' said Donal. 'Thanks. Especially ...'

Donal glanced back at the drapes.

'I'd better let you get on with it.'

None of the mages moved until Donal had left the aircraft.

*

There was a five-sided bronze clock powered by water-wraiths. It was ornate, hanging from the ceiling via a braided cluster of bronze chains encrusted with faceted glass drops, like jewels. The floor was tiled in some lustrous dark-green mineral through which dark spirals swirled.

And this was merely the baggage hall.

Donal's fellow passengers were waiting for their cases to come down the glass chute set high in the wall. As Donal reached the chute, it was his case that came sliding down. Some of the other passengers stared at Donal as if he had arranged it.

Obviously that was nonsense, but Donal smiled as if it was his due anyway, picked the bag up, and looked around. He could not see a sign, but from the way some of the people were standing around the hall, he intuitively deduced which archway to use.

He walked through, saw the floating flame-wraith pointing the way to Customs, and followed that corridor.

It was decorated in something like the gothic-deco style that Donal was used to, but heavier in its use of glass and bronze. The air smelled clean, almost antiseptic. At the final gates leading to the open concourse, Customs officials were checking documents and people were standing in nervous queues, waiting to be called.

But a white-gloved officer beckoned Donal forward, and nodded as Donal began to raise his passport, waving him through.

'Welcome to Illurium, Lieutenant.'

'Um ... Thanks.'

Everything was easy.

In an office off to one side, almost hidden, a figure in a dark robe that might have been black or deep-purple made a tiny hand gesture. A good feeling swept down Donal's body at the sight of that benediction. Whether it was a mage or a witch that had cast the hex, he could not tell.

Do you—?

Soon. Soon enough.

Donal walked through the barrier and into the vast domed edifice of the concourse. He found a bureau de change, not having had time to buy Illurian currency back in Tristopolis, and winced at the smallness of the pile he received for his florins.

There was a bank of red payphones, and he used the nearest, pushing two fourteen-sided coins into the slot before dialling. The line hummed and hissed, then a switchboard wraith answered, and Donal told it the extention he needed.

Five seconds later, Laura came on the line.

'Guess what, lover? You're off to the opera again—'

Twenty-six

Overhead, crystal shone amid steel spars, among which amber shapes encapsulating flame-wraiths floated. Shops and eateries, glistening and clean, were arranged across a bewildering array of stacked tiers, the floors mostly of glass. The sound of two thousand chattering voices washed over Donal, echoing back and forth in the great space.

A coffee bar caught his attention. According to the hand-painted sign, they offered twenty-three varieties of coffee and seventeen of tea. Donal smiled at the sight and the dark aroma.

He carried his bag across and sat down at a table against the wall. A small translucent sprite rose up from the table and hovered there, beating her almost-invisible wings to stay in place. Donal pointed at the Choco Zurinese and said: 'I'll have a medium ... No, make it large.'

The sprite smiled, or gave what passed for a smile on those tiny, delicate near-human features; then she slipped back inside the tabletop for a second. She reappeared and glided towards the counter where three ordinary humans worked.

It was the prettiest of the waitresses who brought Donal's coffee, and he gave a brilliant smile and said: 'That looks fantastic.'

Responding to his cheerfulness, she beamed back.

'You'll enjoy it.'

Everything was peaceful.

When the waitress returned to the counter, she smiled at one of her colleagues, who was cutting a piece of cake from a dish.

The colleague was serving a portly middle-aged man, who responded to the little joke she made – Donal couldn't quite catch the words – with a gentle remark of his own, and sat down at a corner with his cake and tea. Cutting a piece of cake with the side of his fork, the man then raised it to his mouth and closed his eyes in pleasure.

Somehow it seemed to Donal that his simple pleasure in receiving the coffee had communicated itself and spread among three more people in the space of seconds. Wouldn't it be wonderful if life could always be like this?

And why can't it be?

The only thing Donal knew about the future was that it hadn't happened yet.

And the one thing about the recent past he was sure of was that he hadn't felt this good when he got on the plane in Tristopolis, but he'd been feeling fantastic since he woke up high above Silvex City. Could be something to do with the altitude? Or even the make-up of the atmosphere here?

After he'd finished the coffee, he took the cup and saucer to the counter himself, and thanked both the waitresses who were there (the third having disappeared around the back). Their eyes crinkled up as they smiled in genuine happiness, and they voiced cheerful farewells as he left.

This was not seduction. They were far too young for Donal.

And if there was one thing about the present he was sure of, one melancholic fact marring the perfection of this moment, it was that he would have loved to share this adventure with Laura. Provided it could be safe.

Craning his head back, Donal looked up at the glass dome, and the perpetual blackness pressing against it. Unused to sky that was anything but purple of varying hues, he wanted to see what things were like here. Was the near-black sky featureless, or was there some kind of visible topology? Visible to the naked eye?

He looked around the exit signs. *Ground Transportation* one of them read, which Donal assumed meant taxis and buses. A separate sign for trains pointed down a flight of stairs.

What Donal wanted was a place where he could— There. A sign for *Observation Lounge* directed him to a moving strip that began horizontally and then rose to form an escalator. It carried him up, past two levels of restaurants and clothing stores.

At the top he got off and walked past the glass bar, ignoring the inviting drinks, and walked to the exit that led outside. Most of the people were content to sit beside the glass walls and look out; but there was a door to the exterior patio, so Donal opened it and stepped out into cold darkness.

There were tiny points of yellow in the black sky. Here and there, pale-blue orbs were scattered.

277

It's true night.

This was what you could not see from Tristopolis or any part of Federal airspace. This was humanity's glimpse of the greater universe, of starlight that had crossed the void over epochs.

As Donal watched, a crimson meteor streaked across the sky, followed by another, and then a third.

He spent a long time drinking in the vastness.

When Donal returned to the concourse, his two bags in hand, it was gone twenty-five o'clock. He'd been outside longer than intended.

Alexa had arranged a hotel room by phone for him, not relying on the Department's travel office: it had been painful enough getting them to authorize the foreign travel, even though Laura had paid for the air ticket. Whether the Nova DeLuxe would let Donal check in during the early hours of the morning, he had no idea.

Descending a helical escalator, Donal passed through seven storeys of concourse until he came to the Ground Transportation level. There, among families waiting for relatives or cheap unofficially booked taxis to arrive, stood a disconsolate group of drivers. Some wore dark uniforms, and held up placards on which visitors' names had been written.

E. Aalsighsen; *Councillor Livko* read one; a scrawled legend that might have been *The Family Labrusvhjo*, however that was pronounced, was another; and *D. Riordan*; then a sign that just read *LexCo Inc Reprezentativ*, which was either a foreign language or bad spelling, and—

Donal went up to the man with the peaked cap and the *D. Riordan* sign.

'Who sent you?'

No one is expecting me.

'Ah ... Mr Riordan. Can I take your bag?'

Concentrating on his breathing, allowing his vision to become very sensitive to motion on the periphery of his awareness, Donal said: 'But who is your employer?'

'Sorry. I was supposed to say ... Don Falvin Mentrassore, sir, is a friend of Harald Hammersen.'

'Ah. Right. Lead on.' So this was one of Harald's contacts. 'And I'll carry my own bag, thanks.'

'Yes, sir. We're headed that way.'

'Were you here when the flight landed?' Donal checked his watch. 'That was nearly an hour ago.'

'Um, yes, sir.'

'Sorry I kept you waiting. D'you need to take a break or anything before we travel?'

Donal knew what it was like when you were on stake-out, which was why every car or nondescript room needed at least one large empty bottle, if not several, in case it became an observation point.

The driver hesitated, then said: 'I'll just be a minute.'

Donal grinned at him. The driver headed off towards the restrooms. Donal put his bags down on the polished tiles and looked around the concourse.

There were shops selling trinkets and ordinary foodstuffs and even pharmaceuticals. Perhaps, if this place was easily reached from the city's lower levels, it served as a shopping centre for local people. And for airport staff.

A shabbily dressed young man with a lute hanging from one shoulder by a leather strap was heading towards Donal.

'Excuse me, sir.' The man's complexion was ivory, his eyes bore epicanthic folds, and his accent was Shorinese. 'D'you know how to get to Dalishville Range?'

Donal's knowledge of Illurian geography was shaky, but he knew the place was hundreds of miles away at least. 'Not really. The train station's that way.' He pointed back towards a ramp. 'That's the cheapest way to travel, I think.'

'Yes, no buses here.'

He meant long distance buses.

'Good luck,' Donal told him.

'Thank you, sir.'

The youth headed in the direction of the ramp.

'Who was that, sir?' It was the car driver, returning. 'Someone bothering you?'

Everyone was calling Donal sir.

'Not really. He was just looking for directions.'

'Oh. And he came to you first.'

Donal shrugged. If you looked calm and watchful, people assumed you were at home. But this was a city like any other, however polished and gleaming it—

Do you feel the bones?

No, but there's something nearby.

Donal stared at the sign for the train station.

'Sir? We really—'

'What's your name?' Donal asked. 'And you can call me Donal.'

'I'm Rix.'

'Well, Rix, how about if you take my luggage, after all?' Donal picked the bags up and offered them. 'And take them to Don Mentrassore's house.'

'Er ...'

'Right, just the bags. I'll be along later. What's the address?'

'Of Don Mentrassore's home?' asked Rix, as if unable to believe someone could not know where the Don lived.

'Uh-huh.'

'It's in Upper Kiltrin North,' said Rix. 'The road spirals down from Pulkwill's Hill, and the Don's mansion is—'

'What's the name of the road?'

'Pulkwill's Hill *is* the main public road. The house is on a private street with no name.'

Donal wondered how the mail was delivered; but for now all he had to know was how to get there. 'A taxi will know the way, I presume. What do I ask for, Mentrassore Mansion?'

'Sure, and it's easy to find,' said Rix. 'Drive slowly down the road until you see the place with the three steel gargoyles out front, usually with their wings spread out like this.' Rix gestured wide with both hands. 'Or maybe you'll see two gargoyles and an empty whatcher-maycallit. Plinth.'

'The Don's renovating?'

'No, it's just ... Things move around, you know? Just never while you're looking.'

Rix held Donal's bags with no more effort than Donal had.

'Sir? Er, Donal ... What do you need to do? The Don's got every facility.'

Donal glanced back at the storefronts. 'Just a few supplies I forgot to bring. Might poke around for a little bit, and see some sights.'

Do you—?

Get a move on.

Rix looked at his watch. He wore it inside his wrist, like Donal. Ex-military.

'Don't worry about me,' Donal added. 'I won't be sleeping on the streets.'

'Right then.' Rix tipped his cap. 'Good luck, sir.'

Donal watched Rix go, then headed towards the storefronts. When he reached them, he glanced at his watch as though remembering something, then turned back and followed the path that Rix had taken. Looking down to a paved area where limousines and dark-green taxis waited, he saw Rix climbing into a low black limo.

The limo pulled out smoothly and followed the roadway, disappearing from sight beneath a ceiling of opaque glass.

Do—?

Yeah.

Donal headed for the ramp that took him down to the rail station. In Tristopolis, it was the bus depot that attracted low-life predators. Here, subtle indications of geometry and cleanliness told him to make a different choice.

Down in the subterranean station were seventeen long dark platforms. The air was cold; everything was bathed in the silvery strangeness of fluorescent lights. Three of the platforms, at the far ends, had ramps that led up to the roadway level.

A taxi was ascending one of those ramps as Donal watched, leaving behind a platform on which only bales of sacking-wrapped goods were left standing. A couple of railway workers walked past the train whose carriage lights winked out one by one.

Few passengers waited at this hour. As Donal descended to the nearest platform, he noticed a squad car pulled up behind a large pillar close to the nearest ramp. Two uniformed officers came from behind him and walked slowly past. The larger man, his shoulders huge and his neck thick with muscle, slowed further as he looked at Donal.

Pretending he had not noticed the officer's regard, Donal slid his ticket wallet out of his inside pocket and opened it, then glanced up at the platform sign – a moving wraith hand was repainting the next train's destination in a cursive purple script – and nodded to himself, as though confirming his travel arrangements. The officers walked on.

Examining the small knots of passengers and the lone individuals standing hunched with hands in pockets, or huddled alone on cold benches, Donal began to think he had this wrong.

Still, he noted the young woman – girl – on one of the benches. Had the officers questioned her on their patrol? She looked fourteen years old and alone, therefore vulnerable.

The officers were getting into their squad car and pulling the doors shut. Donal watched as they reversed, made a screeching U-turn, then accelerated too fast up the ramp, heading for the roadways above.

Seconds after they were out of sight, a lean unshaven man came out from behind a pillar and began to walk along the platform, his too-big eyes staring at everyone in turn. Donal hunched his own shoulders and subtly bent over as he looked away, feigning the body language of uneasy fear.

Most ordinary citizens *would* feel fear at this hour, in this place.

The man uttered a low growl as he passed Donal; and Donal shivered and hunched up tighter inside his overcoat. Then the man was past, heading for the lone girl sitting on the bench.

I thought so.

A swagger entered the man's walk as he reached the girl's bench, produced a smile and said: 'Hi, can I sit here?'

The girl, shivering slightly, gave a shrug. She glanced up at him, then away.

'Don't worry about me, girl,' the man added. 'I'm a preacher. Nothing to worry about.'

Preacher. Perhaps Donal had got it wrong.

Do you feel the bones?

Well, now you come to mention it ...

Head down, Donal drifted closer. Analysing the man's stance, he thought there might be an iron rod or truncheon in the right coat pocket. The gun was on the man's left hip, presumably butt-forward; he'd left his long coat open despite the cold.

That was a shame. A stupid or overconfident man might have buttoned the coat up, hindering access to the weapon.

Closer now.

'Looks to me like you need a friend.' The man's tone was sympathetic. 'And a hot meal. I know a house where—'

That was when he noticed Donal.

'You.' His lips pulled back from his teeth, and the chill that entered his deepening voice told Donal everything he needed to know. 'Back off. Now.'

'Huh?' Donal blinked.

The man was rising from the bench, uncoiling, hand reaching inside his coat, spitting as he said: 'You. Fucking. Want ... *This?*'

Lapsing into single-word sentences meant he was about to attack and the time had collapsed to zero.

Now.

As the man's hand tightened and began to pull the gun out, Donal's mental state flipped. He was pure reptile as his left hand smacked palm-first into the man's face, then grabbed for the gun hand as he hook-punched his right first to the side of the man's neck, using every ounce of torque from the hips. The man dropped, already out.

But Donal followed him down knees-first. There was a sickening crunch.

Finally, Donal stripped the gun from the man's hand. You don't take the weapon away until they're no longer capable of using it.

Then he searched the unconscious man's clothes, finding an extending steel truncheon – that might prove handy – and a handful of loose shells. Unprofessional.

But the man's real profession was befriending young girls, before introducing them to the wonderful world of turning tricks. Then he could take the larger cut of everything they earned, while they sank deeper and deeper into that life.

Not this time.

The man had a wallet, and Donal pulled out all the notes and eight-sided Illurian coins. He handed them over to the girl.

'Here,' he said. 'I believe he wanted you to have this.'

'Mister ... I'm sorry.'

'For what?' said Donal. 'He was going to turn you into a victim, but you're not that, you're a person and you *will* ... *stand up* ... for yourself, all right?'

The prone man groaned.

'All right?' Donal continued. 'And you'll buy yourself food and make a phone call. Do they have the Sisters of Death in this city?'

Memories of Sister Mary-Anne Styx emerged, amid the scowling coldness of the other nuns. But the order was used to dealing with runaways. And they did not do brainwashing: it was literally against their religion.

'I guess ...'

'Then go back up to the main shops,' said Donal, 'and do that now. Get something to eat. Make that call.'

'Yes, sir.' The girl got off the seat. 'OK.'

She began to move towards the pedestrian ramp. Then she looked back at the prone man. 'What will you—?'

'Just get going.'

Ducking her head, she turned and left, climbing towards the concourse levels which at least were bright and safe for the immediate moment. Donal had a feeling she would follow his suggestions. He could do no more.

There was a twitch from the man's hand.

Donal hauled the man up to a sitting position, legs outstretched still on the cold platform. He glanced along the platform: no one was watching; every waiting passenger had blanked out their perceptions of what was happening here.

Working the pressure points at the back of the neck, Donal brought the man back to painful half-awareness.

'If I'd left you here unconscious,' Donal whispered into the guy's ear as his eyelids fluttered, 'you would have died. You think anyone would worry about trash?'

'Uh ...'

'If you come back here, you die.'

The man groaned, swallowed, opened his mouth, and gave a kind of shortened gasp. Donal's hands squeezed tighter.

'If you go back to running the girls, you die.'

Only a croak sounded now. Donal released his grip a little.

'Did you run them from a house? The girls?'

'Yes ...'

'Which road?'

'Gruytliwik Avenue.'

'Number?'

'Huh ...'

'House number. What was it?'

'Seven ... teen.'

'Go back there,' said Donal, 'and you die. Do you understand?'

The man gave a painful nod.

'Then get up.' Donal hauled him to his feet. 'And go.'

'Where—?'

'Out of here. Out of your life.'

'Yes ...'

Instead of heading towards the ramp, the man stumbled to a yellow-painted metal door and – with difficulty – hauled it open and half-fell through. His footsteps dully clanged down metal steps. Donal followed.

It was an emergency exit down to a grubby road tunnel where stinking rubbish was piled at the sides, next to the dank walls. This was the rottenness that Donal had known must live even at the core of Silvex City.

He watched as the injured man tottered then moved out of sight. Perhaps another shadow moved within the darkness, some predator hunting another of his own kind, sensing injury and weakness. Donal looked at the gun in his hand, back down into the darkness, then shrugged.

He pushed the heavy door shut.

Then he walked back on to the platform just as a cheerful rumble sounded along the silvery tracks. A train slid into the station. Passengers began disembarking, some with cases because they had flights to catch.

Donal walked up into the concourse as part of a large extended family who were chatting among themselves about their forthcoming holiday, lively despite the late hour, accepting Donal's presence as sheer chance. They ascended from the station.

Then Donal was back among the glittering façades that promised a civilized world where two-legged rats did not survive; or so people innocently hoped.

Twenty-seven

Alexa caught up with Laura in the steamy, overheated canteen. New notices proclaimed that this was VOLKOWAN'S RESTAURANT, but it was the same old canteen with the same old food, now cooked by an outside company instead of civilian employees of the Department.

Laura had no need to eat, but she did have to keep her contacts happy, to befriend and manipulate those who were useful to the task force ... and to her ongoing career. When you got to the level of Commander, there was no other way to play the game.

Understanding that much, Alexa did not care. Her goal was to reach the level of Commander herself, and to be younger when it happened than Laura was now. Oh, and ... she wanted to be alive when the promotion occurred.

Snitching on a fellow officer who was guilty of poor judgement ... now that was rarely the best way to advance one's career. Harald had endangered Donal – Alexa was sure of it. What she ought to do was confront Harald first, without telling anybody else, however dangerous a course of action that might be.

But there was another worry. Xalia.

Laura was saying goodbye to a precinct captain whom Alexa didn't recognize. Alexa waited until the captain was leaving before walking up to Laura.

'Hi there.'

'Oh, Alexa. Is everything all right?'

'Kind of ... I haven't heard from Xalia at all. No one's seen her and she hasn't checked in.'

'Don't worry,' said Laura. 'I know what she's ... No. Wait.'

'What is it?'

Laura was looking at her watch. 'She hasn't reappeared?'

'No.' Alexa, remembering her trance and the lipreading, made an

286

intuitive leap. 'Is it something to do with the Commissioner? What you've got her doing?'

'Why do you say that?'

Both of them were glancing around, checking that no one could overhear their conversation. But they were far enough away from any wall or pillar that a wraith might be lurking inside. The floor in this portion of the restaurant was covered in a kind of hemp matting that played hell with stiletto heels but was good insulation.

'I guessed.'

'All right.' Laura looked around, spotted a black internal phone affixed to a blue-tiled wall. 'I need to ring and check on Xalia. Come with me.'

'Thanks.' Alexa walked alongside Laura. 'Does Donal feel the same about Vilnar as you do?'

There was a crinkling of Laura's eyebrow and the beginnings of a smile before she caught herself. 'What do you mean?'

Alexa let out a breath.

'I mean, either Donal's a spy for Vilnar, or Donal's your spy in Vilnar's camp. Am I right?'

Laura shook her head. Reaching the phone, she picked up the handset and asked the switchboard operator to put her through to Wraith Resonance. She waited, then said: 'Commander Steele here. Can you locate Xalia for—?'

Her voice trailed off.

'What do you mean?' she said then. 'How long? What happened to her?'

Laura listened a moment longer, then thanked the operator and replaced the handset.

'Shit.'

'What's happened?' asked Alexa.

'Xalia's hurt. Can't speak, and won't be able to until she's spent time in a healing field of some kind. Could be days, or longer.'

Alexa and Laura looked at each other, both thinking of Sushana lying in her hospital bed. The team wasn't doing well.

'I'm going to try and see her now,' added Laura. 'You'll get back on duty?'

'Yes, of course. And Donal's on our side, right?'

'Bank on it.' There was no hesitation in Laura's voice. 'If at some time in the future I'm not around and Donal is, treat him the same way as me, right?'

'Um ... Right.'

'I'll see you later.' Laura strode quickly out of the restaurant, her pace quickening until she was out of Alexa's sight.

Alexa remained staring in the direction that Laura had gone. Then she picked up the internal phone that Laura had used, and asked for Viktor's extension. There was a single ring, then Viktor's voice said: *'Hello?'*

'Hey, it's me. Alexa. Are you going to be on duty for another hour or so?'

'I'm right here, me,' answered Viktor. *'Why do you ask?'*

'I'm going out for late supper.' Alexa didn't want to lie to Viktor. Perhaps she would grab something while she was out. 'Can I bring you back anything?'

'No. Wait ... Maybe a bagel. Anything.'

'Sure thing. You all right?'

'Kind of ....'

Alexa could hear the pain in Viktor's voice. She dared not say anything about Xalia's being hurt. The poor guy was suffering enough already, and Viktor had always liked Xalia, however provocative she got.

'Take it easy, big guy.'

'Yeah.'

A click sounded and the line was dead. Alexa rehooked the handset. Then she followed the route that Laura had taken.

There was a group of people waiting near the first elevator shaft. Alexa hurried on along the corridor to elevator 7. Alexa stepped inside the lift field.

Where ya going?

'Ground floor, Gertie. Thanks.'

Alexa closed her eyes as she fell through the shaft. Gertie was a sensitive wraith who had read the stress in Alexa's voice and knew she was in a hurry.

There you are.

Gertie pushed Alexa out into the foyer.

'Thanks again.'

Then Alexa went out past the desk sergeant, through the huge doors and past the deathwolves. She descended the big steps to the street where two people were climbing out of a purple taxi. Alexa leaned inside and called to the driver: 'You OK to pick up another fare?'

'Sure thing, doll. Where ya headed?'

'The hospital, please.'

The two plain-clothes officers waited while the driver wrote out their receipt, and paid the exact money, no tip. The driver scowled but said nothing until the two men were climbing the steps up to HQ, and Alexa was sliding into the back seat.

'Skinflints,' he muttered.

Internal Security, Alexa nearly answered, but kept her tongue. The problem with being a cop who investigated other cops was that you could never step out of line yourself. You had too many enemies who would love to get their own back.

'Visiting somebody?' the driver asked, pulling the taxi out into the traffic.

'Kind of,' answered Alexa.

Perhaps she should try to buy flowers from the hospital shop on the way up. But Harald was the one she needed to talk to, not Sushana; and what Alexa had to say would not be softened by a cheap gift.

Harald, I think you're in deep, deep shit.

But what mattered to Alexa was the danger threatening Donal.

Donal's cab halted before the wide gateway. The last two hundred yards had been a slow zig-zag down a sloping ice-smooth road, with the driver growing nervous. There were few streetlights: a discouragement for idle pedestrians.

'They call it Billionaire's Row,' the driver said. 'Ain't too comfortable around here myself.'

'Not your biggest customers, huh?'

'Nah. They got their own limos and such, right?'

'Gotcha,' said Donal. 'Look, you can let me out here. No need to drive inside.'

The driver's shoulders slumped in relief, and Donal wondered what kind of reputation these mansions had. He counted out coins while the driver wrote the receipt.

'Keep the change.'

'Hey, thanks. You want I should bump up the amount on the receipt?'

'Nah, that's all right.' Donal slid out of the seat.

'Take it easy,' said the driver. 'Have a good night.'

'And you.' Donal stepped out on to the smooth road, and closed the taxi door. He looked up.

A strange glimmering hung suspended across the night sky, that startling black curtain of sky pricked with yellow and pale-blue stars. When another scarlet meteor slipped across night's vault accompanied by a paler counterpart of identical velocity, Donal realized there was a vast layer of glass overhead, insulating the street and the city from the true sky above.

The taxi's engine changed note, as the driver manoeuvred through a five-point turn so that he was facing back up the snaking hillside street. Then he stopped, watching Donal: checking that Donal was all right.

Donal raised a hand, then walked into the open gateway, between the big pillars. Immediately the hairs rose on his head and across his entire body as he passed through some powerful hex scan.

He stopped, then walked on, his shoes scrunching on gravel.

Pale shapes slipped across the gravel in silence, then sat down, panting. Their eyes glowed crimson rather than the amber of their Tristopolitan counterparts.

Deathwolves, privately owned.

After a few moments, Donal decided they weren't going to attack. He took one pace towards the house, then another. The wolves rose and walked alongside him.

The bronze front doors swung open as Donal reached the silver-chased marble steps. A tall uniformed man stood smiling.

'I'm Hix, sir. Welcome, and please come inside.'

'Hix.'

'That's right, sir.'

Donal walked into the vast hallway, which was as richly appointed as he had imagined.

'Any relation to Rix, the driver?'

'My cousin, sir, I'm afraid to say.'

'But he spoke highly of you.'

'Ahem ... Very good.'

There were statues and paintings, nice to look at; but it was after one o'clock in the morning and Donal was tired. Hix led the way to spiralling stairs, and gestured for Donal to go first.

The stairs came to life as Donal stepped on the first tread. They flowed upwards, carrying him to the upstairs landing. There, he waited for Hix.

'Just along here, sir.'

'Shouldn't we keep our voices down?'

'Sir? Oh, no ... There's no else here. Not in this wing of the house.'

'Ah. Of course.'

Hix stepped inside a room and held the door open. Donal followed.

The bed was huge, with soft pillows and a gold frame, over which a pale-blue canopy gently stirred, though there was no draught in here.

'The bathroom is through there.' Hix gestured towards an inner door. 'And have you eaten? Would you care for a drink?'

Donal nodded towards a cabinet. 'Is that a wet bar?'

'Absolutely, sir. And if you check at the bottom of that wardrobe, you'll find your garments have already been hung up for you.'

'Well, Thanatos. I could get used to this.'

'Very good, sir.'

'What does that mean?'

'Excuse me, sir?'

'What does "very good, sir" mean? Does it mean I've made a witty remark? Does it mean you're having a nice night?'

'Um ... I couldn't say, sir.'

'Don't worry, Hix. I apologize.'

'Sir ... There's no need to do that.'

'Nevertheless, I'm sorry. And I'm grateful that you're putting me up for the night.' Donal checked his watch. 'What's left of it. Don't let me keep you from your own bed.'

'Sir.'

Hix gave a practised bow, then backed out of the room, closing the doors shut behind him. They clicked into place, then clicked again: additional locks sliding into place.

Trapped.

But Donal was in the place he was supposed to be, and he was very tired. He looked around for light switches, seeing nothing appropriate.

Shit. How did he operate the bloody lights?

Is it always like this in a foreign country?

Tiny flames flickered in the bedside lamp; but there were no knobs, switches or buttons. After a moment, Donal took a guess and snapped his fingers, feeling foolish.

Every light in the room switched off.

Donal stripped and got into bed. He lay down, and slid into ...

Do you feel the—?

Yes, they're everywhere.

... sleep.

291

Soft beeping and moans and twittering sounded from watch-sprites hovering above the patients. Harald held Sushana's hand while she slept. The IV tube into her arm delivered the narcotic coma she needed to kill the pain and allow her body to heal ... of external wounds at least.

A pool of light surrounded the bed; beyond it, curtained-off beds remained in darkness while their occupants slept and, for the most part, crept their way towards death. Harald was in no doubt about how gravely injured Sushana was.

Then Alexa came walking down the aisle between the beds, re-pocketing her golden detective shield that she'd had to flash to be allowed inside. Visiting hours were long over, and Sushana was a colleague rather than a relative.

But it was Harald that Alexa had come to see.

'What is it?' Harald looked surprised, then stone-faced as he clamped down on his expression. 'Has something happened?'

'Is that what you're expecting?' Alexa remained standing, having few other psychological advantages over an ex-Marine with so many years experience. 'That something bad might have happened?'

'What do you mean?'

'Maybe something bad in Illurium? To Donal Riordan?'

Harald looked at her, then spread his hands. 'Hush ... I don't know what you're talking about, but this is a Serious Cases Ward where—'

'Donal Riordan is spying on Commissioner Vilnar for us. For *Laura*. I wonder if you're aware of that.'

'No.'

'And Xalia's hurt, too. Someone's doing the Black Circle's work for them. Perhaps there's something you're not telling us, Harald. Something you've never told Sushana as *you* betrayed us all.'

Even deep in narcotic coma, Sushana groaned and moved her head from side to side before lapsing into stillness. There was a frown on her battered, swollen features. Her eyes remained closed.

'You can't think' – Harald was on his feet now, as though there had been no act of standing up but an instantaneous change in position – 'that I'm a traitor. Look at what they've done to ...' He gestured towards Sushana in her bed.

'Just as I can't think Donal's a traitor,' said Alexa, her voice low but fierce, 'when he's risked so much and suffered so much from us. Who the fuck d'you think got us Vilnar's phone number in the first place?'

'What?'

'If Donal hadn't brought in Kyushen Jya, the person that Donal met when he was in hospital thanks to the Black Circle … and he was the one that talked to Feoragh Carryn, remember? Both evidence trails come from Donal's work. '

'I don't—' Harald was frowning now. He turned to stare at Sushana's battered face. 'No. I can't have made that mistake.'

'Perhaps you need to think more deeply.'

Harald's jaw muscles clenched. 'Thanatos.'

'I saw a chapel to the Sacred Thanatos downstairs. You want to go and pray for a minute, Harald? And think about what you're doing?'

Alexa knew she was taking a risk. This was an accusation of criminal activity, and if she made it official and Harald was convicted … interesting things happened to cops who went to jail.

And it had to be obvious from the way Alexa was speaking that she'd told no one else what she suspected. 'Harald?'

Perhaps she should have been more open with Laura.

'Yes,' Harald said, surprising Alexa. 'I think I'll do that.'

'You'll—?'

'Go into the chapel to pray.'

Then he slipped past Alexa with silent footsteps and padded out of the ward like a ghost. She stood there confused, not knowing what to do.

Barefoot on the deep soft carpet, Donal used the luxurious bathroom first, then made his way to the nearest window and peeked out. The sky was still black, with scarlet meteors streaking past.

So beautiful.

Gardeners were working down on the lawn. A handyman was raking the gravel of the huge drive.

According to an ornate clock sitting on a baroque table, the time was after eleven o'clock. Late morning, and Donal had felt no need to rise earlier.

He wondered if Don Mentrassore worked from home, or whether he would be elsewhere by now, doing whatever it was he did for a living. Or perhaps all he needed to do was count his money and spend it.

Donal realized that he had little idea how really wealthy folk lived their lives.

He went back to the bathroom and filled a glass from the tap and drank it. Then he limbered up, and worked his calisthenics and shadow-boxing, feeling the exercise come easier and with a new sense of fiery joy.

Everything was falling into place. He'd felt that way since the ...

Can you feel the bones?

It doesn't matter.

... witch on the plane had given him the amulet, the one he wore even now.

Donal stopped halfway through a five-punch combination. An amulet for luck? A charm that let him move through life taking serendipity for granted?

At the orphanage he'd learned to make his own luck. Yet Sister Mary-Anne Styx used to say that a boy with the right frame of mind would create luckiness purely by being aware of opportunities, by having the fearlessness to follow them.

So ... He was in a mansion owned by a rich ally, all set to help. He had a name to hunt down: Councillor Gelbthorne. That was the name Feoragh had retrieved from the Lattice.

Perhaps it was time Donal Riordan allowed good luck to enter his life.

Laura. I wish you were here.

Twenty-eight

Dressed in a clean shirt and the same suit, Donal went looking for breakfast. He'd tried wearing the amulet outside his shirt but it made him look like a Lower Southside pimp, so he'd tucked the thing out of sight.

'Mr Riordan.' It was a familiar snooty voice.

'Hix. Good morning.'

'If you'd care to dine, perhaps the kitchen could help. They're preparing the Don's luncheon.'

'Which way is the kitchen?'

'Along that corridor.' Hix pointed downstairs. 'Then turn left and it's the second door on the right.'

'Got it. Hang loose, Hix.'

Donal gave a sunny smile because he felt good and because, whether you were stone-faced or smiling, you never let other people break your composure.

Hix sniffed, and turned to polish an antique shield that hung on the wall. A short sword was slung diagonally across it. Donal had seen cheap imitations; but this one probably would have been at home in a museum.

Whistling an old dance tune, Donal followed Hix's directions and poked his head inside the kitchen. It was red-tiled and copper-faced and looked like a chef's dream.

'Hey, guys,' Donal said to the four cooks. 'Any chance of some breakfast?'

'No problem. Sit down.' One of the men pointed to a wooden table off to one side. 'What d'you want? Sausage, omelette? What?'

'An omelette sounds brilliant,' said Donal. 'Any kind you like yourself.'

It felt good to let someone else do the cooking, like being in a

Rix frowned as the lift platform resumed its descent. Then he looked at Donal and shrugged. 'Sorry. I've a hard time memorizing names.'

'Oh. No problem.'

After a minute, the platform settled, and doors opened. Rix went through first, and Donal followed. There were no other staff here as they passed along a stone walled corridor with a plain carpeted floor, then another utilitarian corridor.

They came out on to a square-edged stone balcony overlooking a rectangular hall in which hundreds of seated statues were arranged in rows.

Not moving.

They were static, but the figures were not statues.

Instead, row upon row of shaven-headed children, dressed in pale-blue tunics, sat cross-legged. Their eyes were directed straight in front, focused on infinity.

'What ...?' Donal could not understand what he was seeing.

From the centre of each child's chest, a flexible glass conduit led down into the floor. Part of Donal sensed waves of – something – passing along those conduits, glowing bright in a colour that had no name. The amulet burned against his chest.

Every one of the two thousand children blinked, at exactly the same time.

Dread squeezed Donal's heart. He saw how the children's pale chests rose and fell in synchrony. He knew that if he could hear their heartbeats they, too, would beat in time. The atmosphere was heavy with cold energies.

Rix's gun hand came up very fast.

Now.

Donal swept his left forearm across as he pivoted away from the line of fire, trapping the sleeve.

The weapon banged, loud in the great echoing space.

There might have been a collective gasp from the imprisoned children but Donal was deep into the movement, flowing with the necessity of the situation as he fired a knee shot into Rix's spleen, drove the top of his head against Rix's face, and stripped the gun from Rix's weakened grasp.

He clubbed Rix above the eye with the butt of his own gun.

The gun he'd acquired last night was more familiar so he drew that now, transferring Rix's gun to his left hand. There was dark movement at the edge of Donal's vision and he dropped to one knee as he span

302

and fired once, twice, then twice more as armed guards scattered for cover.

Do you—?

Not now, for fuck's sake.

Rix moved behind Donal, so he kicked him in the throat.

Then Donal was rolling to one side as a fusillade sounded from the guards. The corridor was a temporary shield and a long-term trap, but he needed the immediate advantage so he leaped across the balcony and out of sight from the guards.

Now what?

He checked the weapon he'd taken from Rix: a Magnus. Donal smiled. One gun in each hand, he aimed out at the hall and back along the corridor simultaneously, while his mind whirled as he tried to plan his next action.

A low moan sounded from Rix, failing to disguise the faint running footsteps of rubberized combat boots. Guards ran to new tactical positions.

How many of the bastards are there?

They would use a leap frog system, one group providing cover as another ran forward. Soon they would be at the balcony and then the corridor entrance. Meanwhile, reinforcements would be coming from deeper in the—

'ALL ARMED PERSONNEL, STAND DOWN! DO NOT FIRE UNLESS IMMEDIATELY THREATENED. STAND DOWN NOW!'

The voice blared from tannoy speakers and echoed around the hall where the imprisoned children sat.

'WE RECEIVED A FALSE REPORT, REPEAT FALSE REPORT. LIEUTENANT RIORDAN IS NOT REPEAT *NOT* A THREAT TO THIS FACILITY. LIEUTENANT RIORDAN, YOU NEED NOT LOWER YOUR WEAPONS, BUT KNOW THAT YOU ARE SAFE NOW.'

It was a persuasive voice. That was exactly the reason why Donal dared not trust it.

After a time, a cough sounded inside the corridor. Donal took aim around a pillar, but the man who advanced was dressed only in dark-green boxer shorts. He looked thin but soft, no kind of fighter. He bore a pale-blue sheet of paper in one hand.

'Um ... Sir? Can I give you this?'

Donal kept his gaze flicking back and forth, both ways along the corridor. 'Put it on the floor, then go.'

'Sir!' The man placed the paper at his feet then backed away, skin trembling. Then he was around the corner and running on his bare feet, panting as though expecting a bullet in the spine.

Donal placed one gun on the carpet, unbuttoned his shirt, and drew the amulet from over his head, and wrapped the chain around his left hand before picking up the gun once more. Then he duck-walked over to the paper note and dangled the amulet above it, waiting for the slightest tingle of reaction, watching for the smallest spark or glimmer from the amulet.

There was nothing from the amulet. These were ordinary words on everyday paper.

Message received from Don F. Mentrassore:
Visitor called Lieutenant D. Riordan is an ally on police business.
Earlier information that he was engaged in criminal activity was
untrue. Cooperate with this man in every endeavour.

Donal backed away from the paper without touching it, and pulled the amulet back over his head. It dangled against his shirt.

'You expect me to believe this?' he shouted to no one there.

He settled back down, weapons at the ready.

Twenty-nine

Laura sat back on her heels on a padded blue mat. The stone cell around her was dry. It was also too cold for a human to kneel while wearing only a skirt suit: too cold for a *living* human.

Beside Laura, the ethereal form of Gertie drifted. She had abandoned her lift shaft duties again. She floated above the silver bars concealed in the floor, bars that extended through the walls and ceiling.

This was designed as a holding cell for temporarily psychotic mages who might damage others by intention or by accident as their hex forces underwent hysteresis and slipped beyond control. But the silver caging had other uses, and with Gertie's help Laura would be able to see sights most humans, including the no-longer-living, could not dream of experiencing.

Gertie's insubstantial fingertips touched Laura's zombie-cold skin, hesitated, then slipped inside. She reached into Laura's brain, inside the visual cortex. Neurochemical pathways swirled with spillover energies from Gertie's wraith parametabolism.

In a few moments blue shapes swam across Laura's vision and she gasped.

'What is it?'

Can you make out images?

'No ...'

Wait. Things will settle.

'Oh. There.'

An ovoid shimmering field of blueness became sharper in Laura's vision, or perhaps in her mind's eye. There was no longer much distinction to be made between the two. And inside the blue—

Can you see her?

'Xalia, yes. I see Xalia.'

There.

305

'Who the fuck,' said Donal, standing at the open study door, 'do you think you are?'

Beside him, Hix swallowed, looking as wide-eyed as his master. Then the Don gestured for Hix to leave.

'I deserve that,' said Don Mentrassore. 'And please come in ... Except that I acted on false information, as you might have gathered by now. And I *did* manage to stop Rix in time.'

'Not exactly.' Donal entered the study. '*I* managed to stop your fuckin' stooge. If he dies that'll be good riddance.'

Don Mentrassore winced, though whether at Donal's tone or the images he conjured up was impossible to tell.

'I apologize. And I've already arranged for what you said, the seats at the theatre.'

'What?'

'The performance of the premiere. It's tonight. And I've spent a great deal to ... Well, never mind. But you'll be able to attend the performance every night for the next three weeks, if that's what you want.'

Donal's teeth remained clenched.

'I don't care what arrangements you've got with Hammersen. Cross me again and I'll take you down, Mentrassore. All the way.'

The Don swallowed.

'I believe you,' he said.

It was three hours later that Donal took his seat in the plush box in the theatre, high above the stalls. He adjusted the winged collar of his shirt, and ran his fingers down the lapel. It was the first tuxedo he'd ever worn.

Looking like a waiter had never been an ambition in his life.

Beside him, dressed in a plum velvet version of Donal's tuxedo that would have looked ridiculous on most people, the Don sat down and adjusted the lace cuffs of his shirt.

This is stupid.

Donal had no weapons, because he'd known in advance there would be scanwraiths at the theatre entrance. Although they were invisible, having been chosen for their ability to be that discreet (since the theatre's patrons were rich), the wraiths had triggered a warning tingle in Donal's amulet.

Finally the lights dimmed, the orchestra in the pit began the overture, and Donal settled back. With his opera glasses, he scanned the rest of the theatre once more in the gathering darkness. He caught a

momen
answer
brass pl
'Can
'It's ...
here.' L
'Well
'I'm '
'Oh, ;
Laura
the hall
interior
voice ar
Mrs 1
hallway
Judge
gown, a
and pus
'Well,
His sn
'Since
The ju
moved t
'Than
His ha
down.
'You'r
This v
'Your
vellum 1
arrest w
'My d
night du
'Or wo
'So wl
to arrest
Laura
'Comr
'The C
'Impossil

glimpse of two late entrants in another box, on the opposite side of the theatre.

One of them he didn't recognize, a man dressed in a dark velvet suit similar to Don Mentrassore's ... but the other's features were vaguely familiar, and in a second Donal had it.

This was Alderman Kinley Finross from Tristopolis.

Scarcely anyone had mentioned him during the entire investigation and yet ... Donal remembered the letter which had set up the meeting with Malfax Cortindo.

Xoram Borough Council
99 Phosphorus Way
Xoram Precinct
Tristopolis TS 66A-298-omega-2

Tristopolis Police Headquarters
1 Avenue of the Basilisks
Tristopolis TS 777-000

42nd Quatrember 6607

Re: Meeting with Malfax Cortindo, Director, City Energy Authority

Dear Commissioner Vilnar

It has been absolutely my pleasure to arrange a meeting between one of your officers and Director Cortindo of the City Energy Authority. The latter body are of course a credit to our city, and the Director evinced no hesitation in ensuring me that any technical assistance which is germane, he will be overjoyed to provide.

I have communicated with Director Cortindo that Lieutenant Donal Riordan will be meeting with him, as per your indicated request of 40th ult., on the evening of 37th of Quintember at nineteen o'clock, at the Downtown Core Station. All facilities will be placed at the Lieutenant's disposal.

Kindest regards

K Finross

Alderman Kinley Finross

'No,' said Laura. 'Anything can be done, if you're willing to sacrifice enough.'

She reached inside her purse.

Thirty

Halfway through the second act, several entire rows of the audience began to breathe in unison, and the amulet began to burn against Donal's chest.

'Thanatos.'

Someone turned round to shush him.

Shit shit shit.

Donal ripped the amulet away from him, and after that events accelerated. Down on stage, the triplets were singing so impressively that memories of the Diva had been threatening to overwhelm Donal.

Do you feel the bones?

Oh Death yes.

The amulet lay on the carpet, its light slowly fading. Its protective hex was dying now that it no longer nestled against Donal. It could no longer shield against dark tidal forces.

Stage spotlights brightened to gold (for in the opera's story a village festival in the enchanted land of Brismangidor was about to begin). Donal noticed white flickering like indoor lightning. Overhead spotlights were flashing runes into the audience's eyes, a subliminal induction that for some reason Donal was able to detect.

And now that he was exposed, the Black Circle could use him again.

Thanatos, I've played into their hands.

Because the amulet wasn't to guard Donal from external forces ... It was to hide his internal darkness from the world. But now that shield was gone.

Do you feel the bones?

'NO!'

Some of the audience looked up at Donal, startled; but most were spellbound by the flashing runes. The mass parazombie spell would already have fallen, except that the Black Circle had not realized that Donal Riordan would be in the audience. Not here, not tonight.

But if they had, the audience would already have been ensorcelled exactly as they had been in the Théâtre du Loup Mort. Because it was not the Diva who had been the focus of that mass binding spell. She had been the target, but someone else had focused the thaumaturgical waves transmitted to the theatre, acting as a kind of lens for the Black Circle mages.

Do you taste the music?

'Yes! Yes, I do.'

For Donal was the focus.

Donal was the lens.

He was the weapon that had caused the Diva's death.

Donal stood rigid, every muscle tensing into catatonia. All the rehab, all the memory reburning, all the suffering. He had tried so hard to become the old Donal, the man he had been before the bones' influence took him.

Strange harmonics swirled all around: moans and wails that had nothing to do with the orchestra below.

Can you hear the bones?

Always.

Do ...

Every damn moment.

Across the theatre, in a guest box as plush as the one Donal shared with Don Mentrassore, two men were intent on the audience. No ... Alderman Finross was dividing his attention between the increasingly entranced audience and the triplets on stage.

It was Councillor Gelbthorne whose eyes glittered as he channelled thaumaturgical energies down into the theatre.

Gelbthorne.

Some part of Donal's mind perceived wave upon wave of blackness beating downwards, though this was an illusion, a kind of metaphor: the energies involved had nothing to do with light. The human retina could not perceive necrons.

Laura.

Do it for Laura.

His old boxing coach, Mal O'Brien, had picked Donal up off the ring floor once. It was supposed to be a sparring match, but his heavier opponent was filled with hate for his own reasons and Donal had gone down with his forearm snapping from the impact on the floor, his ribs already fractured from an angled punch he'd not seen coming.

Mal had said: *'It will heal, boy. And your spirit? That's still whole.'*

And Donal had called out to his opponent leaving the ring: *'Hey. You running away?'*

What had happened after that was a moment of dark joy as Donal ran forward with his one good arm ascending, powering from the hips, and the uppercut he delivered was the best of his life. The heavy bastard fell backwards and did not move.

But it was what Mal said later, as they tied the splints on with wormskin bindings, that came back to Donal now.

'Never worry,' he told Donal. *'Broken bones heal* stronger *than before, didn't you know?'*

Here in the theatre, waves of shadow ebbed and flowed around Donal. Then the secret mage, the real enemy, Councillor Gelbthorne, looked at Donal from across the auditorium. He recognized the kind of person, the kind of *device*, that Donal was, that a mage could make use of.

Gelbthorne focused.

Can you hear the bones?

Deep inside, Donal fought, holding on to his thoughts, because being human was all it took: to reinforce his real thoughts, not repattern his neural pathways to become a filter for Gelbthorne's transmission.

Broken bones heal stronger than before.

Do you feel the music?

It was an illusion, but from across the auditorium Gelbthorne's eyes became bright, became huge, like widening spotlights focused, now, only upon one thing. Upon the vessel that could focus his energies.

Upon Donal.

Broken bones ...

Do you—

Heal ...

—feel—

Stronger ...

—the—

Than ... Before.

—music?

And every moment of hate from his orphanage days, and every

second of love he felt in Laura's presence, strengthened Donal now as he fought back and deep inside him a kind of laughter rose.

No.

I am the music.

The ensorcelment ripped apart.

Donal was free.

The audience remained partly mesmerized because of the earlier influence. Stage spotlights still beamed their subliminal gestalt-runes directly into their eyes. Not everyone would be susceptible enough to obey whatever commands Gelbthorne managed to channel, but there would still be plenty.

Donal was on his own against hundreds. Gazes from across the theatre turned towards him.

A group of men in medics' uniforms stood in the shadows near one of the ground-level fire exits. Their attention was fixed on the triplets. When the moment was right, they would seize the dying (or already dead) triplets and take them away, fleeing through the emergency exits.

Would they flense the bones? Or was that a pleasure reserved for Gelbthorne himself, with Finross perhaps assisting?

I am the music.

Exits ... Donal remembered a fire alarm button in the corridor outside: the memory offered itself up to him now.

So flow.

He vaulted backwards over his seat, brushing aside Don Mentrassore's grasp – the Don was now under Gelbthorne's influence – and took three long steps out into the corridor and hammered the red triangular button with the bottom of his fist.

A klaxon howled.

Overhead nozzles sprayed water down from the ceiling. Further down the corridor was a hose cabinet, with a sand bucket, and a fire axe. Donal grabbed the axe, and went back into the box.

Water was spraying downwards in the auditorium, the performers suddenly coming to a halt and the orchestra sound falling apart in discord. Those audience members who'd been mesmerized were jolted out of trance.

A woman screamed, starting the panic.

'Fire!'

Across the gap, just for a second, Councillor Gelbthorne's gaze locked on Donal's. Gelbthorne concentrated, willing Donal to drop into trance.

'Fuck off,' said Donal.

The Don reached for him from behind, but Donal slammed his elbow back into the Don's face, blood spattering as the nose broke, and then Donal was spinning out of the box, axe in hand as he ran out into the corridor.

He sprinted, pouring on the speed. Gelbthorne was not going to get away.

I am *the music*.

But people, panicking, were filling the halls and corridors.

Donal reached the door that led to the stage. It was opening slowly from the other side. Donal grabbed the knob and ripped it open fast, then slid past the stumbling man he'd surprised.

Keeping hold of the axe, Donal ran backstage. With pandemonium among the audience, this was the quickest way to Gelbthorne's box.

And Finross. He shouldn't forget Alderman Finross.

Threading his way among performers and stagehands, Donal reached the far side and looked out. A blocky figure in police uniform was there, directing three other officers to keep the frightened audience streaming out through the fire exit. One of the uniformed men looked familiar: it was Reilly, the officer who'd driven the car.

No sign of Gelbthorne.

But there was Temesin in his dark-blue coat, improbably smoking a cigarette, standing calm while water showered down and hundreds of civilians fled past him.

Donal decided to trust him.

He made his way through the pouring water to Temesin, and said: 'He was up there. In that box. The mage who kicked off the spell ... Must have backfired.'

'Yeah, right.' Temesin stared at the axe in Donal's hand for a second, then looked up. 'That would be Councillor Gelbthorne. Had a visitor with him.'

'From Tristopolis. Alderman Kinley Finross.'

'Wonderful. Another politician. And what spell was that, by the way?'

The paramedics who'd been waiting were now in handcuffs. Five uniformed officers surrounded them.

'I suggest you—'

'Gelbthorne's disappeared, before you go on.'

'Does that mean you've had men outside trying to spot him?'

'Maybe.' Temesin took the cigarette out of his mouth. Finally, it was sodden. He flicked it on to the wet carpet. 'I'm not sure we've enough for a warrant.'

'An arrest warrant?' asked Donal. 'Or a search warrant?'

'Either one.' Temesin squinted at Donal through the artificial torrent, which was not letting up. 'Too bad.'

'Yeah ...'

Donal looked back up at the box he'd been in. There was no sign of the Don.

'You ever notice how things happen in twos or threes?'

Temesin jammed his hands in his pockets.

'What are you thinking of?'

'Just that if there was an emergency, like a fire or some such, in Councillor Gelbthorne's house, you'd have no hesitation in breaking in with your officers to bravely rescue the good man ... Wouldn't you say?'

'Maybe.' Temesin looked at Reilly, who was still ushering people out through the fire exit. 'I take that back. Definitely.'

Something like this should take planning ... but Donal knew that Alderman Finross was a coward who would be on the first flight back to Tristopolis, now that the attempted murder and bone-stealing had blown up in front of his eyes. Donal had to take him down tonight.

Two thousand children, breathing in time ...

Perhaps it was the synchronized respiration of the audience, as they had begun to fall under Gelbthorne's spell, that reminded Donal of the captive children in the Power Centre.

Or were they specially grown inside the Power Centres from newborn? Donal wasn't sure he'd seen true awareness in their eyes. He wondered if using living beings was truly worse than using the bones of the dead.

He remembered his conversation in the Energy Authority complex, and Cortindo saying: *'The conglomeration does not truly think or feel anything.'*

'Not even pain?' Donal had asked.

'No. At least, that's what I'll tell anyone who asks me officially.'

Now, he let out a breath.

'How is power delivered to the houses? Big houses.'

'Like Gelbthorne's? He's even got his own ... generators, if you can call them that.'

322

'I've seen what your Power Centres are like.'

'Yeah ... At least we bury them in peace when they die.'

'Shit.'

'Right. But subgenerators have long shafts linking them to the main Centres, in case of power shortage and in case of accidents. Probably, if you knew someone with influence in the Corporation, you could even get schematics of the system.'

The nozzles' spray was lessening to a light drizzle.

'If only I knew someone like that,' said Donal.

'Mm.'

In his study, Judge Prior leaned back in his chair.

'Young lady,' he said to Laura. 'I knew your father for many years, and I remember your every birthday party, you and the other toddlers—'

'Other rich folks' kids.'

'If you like. But I can't let you ask me to do this.'

'Please, Your Honour. This is important.'

'As is the order of justice. And propriety.' The judge removed his reading glasses and put the warrant aside. He rubbed his nose. 'I'm sorry, Laura.'

Alexa took a step, thinking Laura was about to leave, then stopped.

'Excuse us a moment.' Laura hefted a small object from her purse. 'Can we talk in private?'

'Is that a privacy cone?' Judge Prior glanced at Alexa. 'Well, my dear. If you like. But I'm not changing my—'

Laura activated the talisman's spell, and an inverted cone of silence rippled through the air as it slid into place, enclosing Judge Prior and Laura in a volume from which no sound could escape.

A *transparent* volume.

Watching carefully, Alexa held herself very still, hoping that both Laura and the judge would forget about her presence. She watched for perhaps two minutes.

Finally, the privacy field shrivelled out of existence and Laura put the talismanic device back into her purse. She twisted the clasp shut. Then she waited as, hand shaking, Judge Prior undid the cap of his expensive fountain pen, and slowly signed his name at the foot of the warrant.

'There,' he said. 'You're satisfied now.'

'I am. Thank you, sir.' Laura picked up the warrant. 'We'll see ourselves out.'

The judge watched Laura and Alexa until they reached the study door. Then: 'You've changed, Laura Steele. You didn't used to be like this.'

'Yeah,' said Laura. 'Death has a way of doing that.'

Outside, the Vixen's headlights sprang into full brightness as Laura and Alexa came down the steps. Neither woman said anything until they had climbed into the car and it was rolling down the driveway.

When they were on the public road, Alexa sighed.

'I don't believe that.'

'We got the document,' said Laura. 'What else matters? I hope your lipreading is as good as ever.'

'Just about. Did your father really tell you that he'd bribed a judge? And Old Incorruptible Prior, at that?'

'Not exactly. Dad said it all right, just not to me. I was listening at the keyhole.'

'Oh.'

As the car drove on past the park – it looked dark and dangerous – Alexa added: 'What did you mean earlier, about being willing to sacrifice? The Judge?'

'No ... I'm the one who's made an enemy tonight.'

'Shit.'

'Do I look like someone who cares?'

Don Mentrassore, his nose covered in a green wormsilk dressing and his manner furious – though not at Donal – did more than furnish the information. With Hix (not Rix) driving, the Don accompanied Donal to the Power Centre, where they bypassed the generation halls with their enslaved children.

Donal wondered whether he was right to be pursuing one man in the midst of this, before remembering the Diva and what had happened to himself.

Uniformed technicians handed over a rolled-up purpleprint and a large flashlamp.

'There's bogeys,' said one of the men, 'that can take you most of the way.'

Still dressed in his theatre finery, the Don nodded to Donal and said: 'That's a little too adventurous for a man of my age. But I wish you luck, sir.'

'Yes, thanks.' Donal nodded, unable to warm to the man any more than that. He waved the purpleprint. 'Appreciated.'

It was now around five hours since the Don's driver had tried to kill Donal in this place. Perhaps later he would be able to blame Harald for that attempt, not the Don.

'This way.'

Two technicians led him through a hatchway and down a metal ladder to a narrow maintenance tunnel along which a single rail ran. There was a bogey as promised, a small flat bed atop two wheels side by side. Donal could not see how it stayed upright, nor how it was powered.

'Necromagnetic induction,' one of the techs said. 'And look, see up there?'

Donal looked. There was a glowing number in orange, 327, high up beside the hatchway.

'You carry on going,' the tech continued, 'until you reach 201, then get off and ascend the ladder, where the domicile tunnels – that's the tunnels to private homes, right? – radiate outwards. Ya gotta take number five, and it's the second house.'

'All right,' said Donal. '201, 5, second house.'

'And you'll want these.' The technician handed over heavy goggles. 'It goes pretty fast.'

Donal pulled the goggles over his head, clambered on to the bogey, then sat cross-legged on the flat bed, thinking again of the cross-legged mindless children sitting in rows not so far from here.

'What do I—?'

A rectangular portion of the bed, next to Donal's right hand, began glowing a soft orange.

'Press that, keep pressing it . . .'

Donal pressed down and the bogey rolled into motion.

'. . . and keep pressing until you want to stop, then just let go.'

No one had to tell Donal that this was called a deadman switch.

Acceleration was building up, but something prevented him from falling off.

Good ride for kids.

If only the orphanage could see him now, ignoring the plight of hundreds, no, thousands of children. If Sister Mary-Anne Styx were here—

But already the tunnel had arced to the left and downwards, and if Donal looked back there was no sign of the Power Centre, only the plain walls and rows of safety lights streaming past.

I am the music.

With his left hand, he checked the gun at the small of his back once more.

In Tristopolis, Viktor was leading a group of R-H detectives up the short path to Commissioner Vilnar's blackstone residence. It was unfair of Laura, by Viktor's reckoning, to expect Robbery-Haunting to help out in the slightest way – forcing your way into a Police Commissioner's house didn't seem like the best method of enhancing anyone's career prospects.

At least, Viktor decided, he himself would do all the talking. Warrant in hand, he banged on the door. In maybe five seconds, it swung open. A scowling woman with a lined face stared at Viktor.

'What the bleeding Thanatos do you want at this hour?'

Viktor held up the warrant.

'Is the Commissioner in, ma'am?'

'No, he's not. He went to the Death-damned office for something. You married, Detective?'

'Uh, no, ma'am. Not exactly.'

'Well do some poor woman a favour and think about whether she wants to be married to the entire damned Department. And was that a search warrant I just read?'

'Yes, that's—'

'I don't know what's going on, but Arrhennius is going to be pretty pissed at you guys. You want some coffee?'

'Arrhennius?'

'You're busting into a man's home and you don't even know his first name?'

Viktor rubbed his face.

'Sorry, ma'am.'

'No, you're not. But I suspect you will be.'

At exactly the same moment, Laura and Alexa were leading another team of R-H officers, six of them, towards the lift shafts. Gertie's wraith hand beckoned briefly before slipping back inside the entrance to her own.

The eight women and men looked at each other before stepping into the shafts in tandem. No information indicators showed on any of the lift shafts.

They rose in silence, and came out on the 187th floor, into a corridor ringed with alternating bands of icy cold and searing heat. Laura said nothing as they passed through the outer office.

Eyes was at her desk as always, her long black hair glistening with reflected highlights from the silver cables that linked her eye sockets, via the console, to the rooftop mirrors ... to what was in effect the Commissioner's private communication and surveillance network above the city streets.

Perhaps Eyes somehow knew about the warrant that Laura carried, because Alexa noticed her reach beneath her desk to press a button. The door to the inner offices slid open.

Then Alexa was following Laura into the Commissioner's office, with the R-H officers behind them.

'What's gone wrong?' This was the Commissioner himself, gesturing back the metal visitor's chair that was transforming itself into a hooked, talon-bristling monstrosity, ready to attack. 'What is this?'

There were other defences in here, many of them subtle and unexpected, down to the ashtray that could double as a percussion grenade.

'It's the Black Circle,' said Laura, holding out the warrant so that the Commissioner would be unable to see his own name written there. 'They've penetrated higher in the city apparatus than anyone suspected.'

'And you've got proof?' said the Commissioner.

'Enough, we think.'

'Are you sure about that?' The Commissioner's fists clenched. 'Really sure?'

'Certain enough,' said Laura, 'to get a judge's signature on this.'

The Commissioner's squarish face split in a predatory smile.

'Then let's go and get her,' he said. 'I've waited a long time for this.'

Laura froze, still holding out the warrant.

'What did you say?'

'I said— Well what the Thanatos did you think I said? Are you deaf?'

'No, but—'

A crash reverberated through the office, a vibration that rippled the air or perhaps just the eyeballs of everyone inside. They toppled to the floor and lay there. The warrant spilled across the floor, right next to the Commissioner's blunt-fingered hand. He levered himself up to a seated position on the floor, staring at the paper.

Then he looked up at Laura.

'You bloody fool,' he said.

After a long moment, Laura regained her voice.

'Sir?' Her certainty had slipped. 'We have evidence from corroborated sources. We know the phone number you used to contact the ...'

Laura's voice trailed off.

'What number?'

Alexa answered: 'It was seven-seven-seven, two-nine, three-five-one, seven-two-zero. There's no doubt.'

The Commissioner huffed as he struggled to his feet.

'Which'll be the phone on Marnie's desk.'

There was no doorway. The R-H officers had already crawled to the wall where the door had been. Two of them slipped deep into trance, trying to determine what hex enchantment had been wrought. One of their colleagues hammered his fist in frustration on the solid stonework.

'Who?' said Laura.

'Marnie, my secretary.'

'Oh, you mean Eyes,' said Alexa.

The Commissioner's lips twitched.

'Yes, I mean Marnie Finross, the Alderman's niece whom I thought I was keeping under adequate surveillance, until you blew the whole thing wide open.'

Laura tried to focus on what was happening. Commissioner Vilnar was tough but slippery when it came to confrontations: everyone knew that.

'Nice try, Commissioner. But hasty lies won't cover up the evidence.'

'No, but impetuous actions will certainly mean Marnie gets away, don't you think?'

Laura opened her mouth to reply, but one of the female R-H officers said: 'He's telling the truth, ma'am.'

'And you are—?'

'Petra Halsted. They said I should help out.'

'Laura, I've heard of her.' Alexa's tone was quiet. 'She's a truthsayer. Certified before federal spellbinders.'

'Shit.'

The Commissioner cleared his throat.

'Recrimination is for bloody idiots,' he said. 'Why don't we see if we can get ourselves out of this Death-damned mess?'

Donal had his gun out now, walking crouched along the narrow access tunnel. Back in the main tunnel, the wraith-enabled bogey had moved away from Donal as soon as he'd stepped off. There was no means of fast escape.

As far as he could tell, all the narrow branching tunnels led to the subterranean levels of the great houses; none led directly to the open ground. That would have been a security risk.

He came to the next door, and stopped. Its necromagnetic lock looked huge, and Donal realized that he had not thought the problem through adequately.

Then power coils hummed and heavy bolts slammed back.

The door swung open.

'Shit.'

Two huge men with zombie-pale faces raised their submachine guns – Grauser Howlers with the disc-shaped magazines – straight at the centre of Donal's body. One twitch of a finger, and a stuttering burst of fire would rip Donal in two, and the bloody halves would fall with a wet thump to the floor and that would be that.

Thirty-one

Disaster whirled in upon Donal, tumbling in on all sides as he admitted the depths of his stupidity. Without the chaos he'd intended to cause there would be no reason for Temesin's officers, even assuming they were outside Gelbthorne's mansion, to break inside under the pretext of rescuing the Councillor.

Laura. I'm sorry.

Sorry that he'd let her down. That he would never see her again.

Thanatos.

And then the strangest thing happened, the like of which Donal had never heard of during a police operation.

Both zombie guards lowered their weapons, stared at each other, and shook their heads. Then they turned to Donal and one of them said: 'You have the touch of dark blood. It is upon you.'

'Er ...'

'This house,' said the other, 'is a place of turbulence and mischief.'

'Say what?' Donal felt he should not be arguing, but what exactly was going on?

The first zombie handed his weapon to his colleague, then pulled open his own shirt, and pressed his fingertips against his white chest in an exact sequence. There was a wet, soft ripping sound, and Donal could not turn his gaze away as the man's chest split open.

Inside, black and glistening, was the zombie's rhythmically pumping heart. The zombie placed his fingertips against its pulsing surface and said: 'I will not harm you, brother.'

And the zombie's colleague placed his Grauser Howler on the floor, then straightened up and likewise touched the other's beating black heart.

'I too swear, that this human shall be my brother.'

The zombies looked at Donal.

'Um, thanks. I mean ... Thank you.'

'That is good enough.'

The zombie pulled his chest together, and the wound – or access orifice, whatever – sealed up straightaway. The zombie did his shirt back up.

'We've just resigned from Councillor Gelbthorne's employ,' the other zombie guard told Donal. 'By our actions, we've resigned. We have never liked this place.'

'Gelbthorne,' said the other, 'disturbs the darkness.'

Donal still could not process what was happening.

'My name is Brial,' said the first zombie, 'and this is Sinvex.'

'I'm ... pleased to meet you,' said Donal.

Then both zombies turned away and walked off along a featureless passageway. Donal stared after them, bemused, wondering what the Thanatos had happened here.

A submachine gun still lay at his feet.

'Hey ... You forgot something.'

But the zombies were already gone.

'Waste not, want not.'

Donal picked up the submachine gun, checked its magazine and action – full and perfect – and grinned, remembering the time he'd come second in the Battalion shooting competition in the machine gun category. He'd always thought it was an accident: he was hopeless with this kind of weapon.

Perhaps this time he could come first.

It was Gertie who rescued them, her wraith form slipping through the walls to check their condition, then accessing the trip-switch contained beneath Eyes' desk. Beneath Marnie Finross's desk: Laura was still angry with herself for having missed the obvious.

The big door reappeared.

Wraith-enabled furniture scampered out of the office. The living metal chair exited first, followed by a cloud of assorted items surrounding the big lumbering desk on its stubby legs. Finally the humans, when they were sure it was clear, hurried out after the furniture.

Behind them, the portal to the Commissioner's office sealed up once more.

Sorry, Arrhennius.

'What for?' said Commissioner Vilnar.

I think your office is lost for ever.

The Commissioner smiled.

'I can always get another one.'

Laura blinked. The Commissioner was on first name terms with a lift wraith? Perhaps she had misjudged the man.

'Commander Steele,' the Commissioner said. 'What are you waiting for?'

'Um ... Sir?'

'I want you to arrest Marnie right now.' He gestured at her empty desk. 'Find her and bring in.'

'Yes, sir.'

Laura left the room fast, followed by Alexa. The R-H officers exchanged glances, then nodded to the Commissioner and exited.

The Commissioner reached inside his jacket and pulled out a big blue-steel handgun, checked the safety, and reholstered. Then he went to the coatstand and got down his heavy overcoat, and pulled it on. As he did so, he noticed a discarded tissue in Marnie's wastepaper bin, stained with lipstick. He picked up the tissue and pushed it into his overcoat pocket.

'Gertie?'

Yes, Arrhennius?

'Can you drop me down to street level the quick way? Just like the old days?'

My pleasure.

'Then let's do it.'

A strange presence was prowling the lower corridors of Councillor Gelbthorne's mansion. Strange waves of coldness passed through the air.

Maids and other personnel were scurrying along the corridors, hurrying into offices or boltholes and locking the doors, as Donal passed amid the chaos. Donal saw two hulking grey-skinned men, with mosaic armour woven into their skin, who were squeezing their bulk into a linen cupboard, glancing down the corridor.

Whatever had been set loose in here, Donal didn't want to see it.

Donal took a short flight of steps up to an open redbrick landing. It was a vast atrium of white walls and red tiles and fifteen or more balconies arranged at odd angles. Donal caught a glimpse of dark scales and then he was moving again, racing up steps as silently as he could manage.

More staff bolted out of his way as he hurtled towards double glass doors. Then he saw a tiny red button that reminded him of the fire alarm in the theatre so he did the natural thing: he hammered the thing with his fist.

Nothing happened.

'Shit shit shit.'

It had to be a fire alarm. What he hadn't figured was that it would be silent, broadcasting by some means to the house staff but not wailing sirens that might bring outsiders to investigate. But that had been the whole point of—

A metal barrier was rising up out of the floor, cutting off access to the suite of rooms ahead.

Move.

Donal reacted by instinct, trusting his intuition – *I am the music* – and sprinted forward – *fast* – feeling a wash of stinking coldness rise up in the atrium behind him – *faster!* – and then he was hurdling the rising steel, foot touching the carpet beyond, catching it, and he stumbled.

Ceiling and walls rotated past him and he continued the roll to one side, catching one hallucinatory sight of a vast dark reptilian eye focused on him as the steel barriers slammed shut, cutting off the outside world.

Donal was safe.

It sings . . .

He felt a cold, eerie singing deep in his bones, and knew what it meant. A mage was very close.

Commissioner Vilnar came down the outside of the building like a descending bat, his overcoat billowing cape-like as he dropped on to all fours. Startled deathwolves could see the glowing bluish form that enveloped him: Gertie, the wraith whose servitude in Police HQ had always been associated with a certain . . . latitude.

Gertie billowed and fluttered back into the safety of the vast dark tower. Around the Commissioner, the deathwolves growled, their amber eyes glowing.

'FenSeven,' said the Commissioner. 'And FenNineBeth. Are you ready for the hunt?'

'*Grrr . . .*'

'Come on.' The Commissioner led the way, moving fast for his bulk. 'Let's check . . . Damn it.'

The Avenue of the Basilisks was filled with people spilling out of theatres, heading for the restaurants. Marnie could be anywhere among thousands of people along the vast long canyon-like thoroughfare, or in any of the two-hundred-storey-high towers that walled it.

'She's got dark hair,' muttered Commissioner Vilnar, 'and this is her scent.'

From his overcoat pocket he drew out the tissue that he'd retrieved from Marnie's wastebin.

'Unless she's hexed this with some kind of trick,' he added to the deathwolves. 'So you be careful, boys.'

The deathwolves flitted off into the crowds, lean and dangerous and scarcely visible to rich folk who were unaccustomed to seeing true predators. They would not have cared to realize that there were dangers deadlier and more immediate than wheeling and dealing in boardrooms and clubs.

Laura and Alexa ran out on to the street. Alexa stopped dead, seeing the Commissioner, her mouth opening though she was unable to speak.

Then the Vixen, Laura's car, came hurtling towards them and span sideways-on in a squealing handbrake turn, its doors popping open as it slewed to a halt. The car was empty inside.

Laura looked at the Commissioner.

'Go on.' He made a pushing gesture. 'Get after her!'

Blinking, Laura jumped inside the car and got moving before Alexa could even react.

'All right,' said Commissioner Vilnar to Alexa as the Vixen moved off into the traffic. 'You're with me.'

Alexa turned to follow the Vixen, then stopped.

'No,' said the Commissioner. 'We're going back inside.'

Donal entered a gallery of bones. Unmoving, they dragged at him.

Petrified skeleton hands, some gold-framed displays (lit by quiet spotlights) that were only a single knucklebone, then some isolated ribs and, in a special triptych arrangement, three entire skulls that grinned at Donal as he stumbled past.

They sang.

Unfocused visions swirled around Donal, and he dropped the sub-machine gun without even noticing as the pains and cramps shifted through him, a warning against fighting the beautiful dreams.

They sang to him.

No. Help . . .

All around, the bones were calling, promising their wild, seductive, artistically sublime dreams.

Diva, help me.

Or was she the last person who would want to help, even if she were alive to come to Donal's aid? Perhaps he deserved to fail, to die immersed in wondrous trance.

There were inner doors with ornate handles, and Donal had already grasped them in his bare hands before he realized his mistake ... for the handles were of carved bone: the bones of long-dead artists.

No ...

A maelstrom of visions pulled him down.

There were ruby seas where the song of small-breasted mermaids lured him to—

No.

—the living forest where flowers breathed scents such as he had never—

I will not ...

—their myriad hands trailing softly down his skin, cupping his—

...allow this to ...

—pulling him into—

...happen.

—swirling pastels and the feel of—

NO!

He broke the visions apart.

Because ...

And stood there, chest panting, soaked with sweat, having thrown the doors open to reveal the final chamber within.

I am the song.

By his own will Donal had thrown off the bones' ensorcelment, but it was far too late as he saw what lay inside the chamber.

He fought back the urge to vomit.

Three men stood around a flat altar: Councillor Gelbthorne and Alderman Finross and another whose shock of white hair and photogenic features were familiar, as of someone famous seen only in newspapers, and Donal thought he might be a politician. But the corpse that was stretched out on the altar was more than familiar, since it was at Donal's hand that the man had died.

It was the corpse of Malfax Cortindo.

While all around ...

Sweet Thanatos, no.

... lay the pale discarded detritus of the components they had used up in their work, the power source that had fuelled whatever strange hex they had cast and shaped. It was almost an anticlimax when the corpse's eyelids twitched, because it had to be worth it, even for the perverted mages of the Black Circle: worth it to have used up the resources they had.

The floor was littered with dozens of dead children, their blank eyes open, never to see anything again.

Gelbthorne raised a hand, and pointed at Donal. Orange lightning spat across the room.

And burst apart as it struck Donal's chest. He took a half step back, knowing he had no time to run back into the gallery of bones and retrieve the submachine gun he had dropped, while the visions had clutched him.

Last chance ...

But that was the moment when Malfax Cortindo's corpse jerked into movement, span on the altar and sat up, then stepped down on to the floor, his bare feet squashing the dead children on which he stood.

There would be no complaints from those soft corpses.

'Fuck you,' said Donal, and ran.

Laughter followed him as he threw himself out through the doorway, into the room where the bones' attraction pulled like riptides through his soul. But it was a second's work to snatch up the submachine gun, turn, and squeeze the trigger.

The deafening, stuttering crash of automatic fire banged and reverberated in the enclosed space. Donal's teeth were clenched as round after round poured back through the doorway, clustered on the targets: the sitting corpse and the three standing men who ...

There was a click as the magazine emptied.

... were still on their feet.

A mist of black powder hung before the trio: the remains of the bullets dissipating as they struck whatever shield the mage, Gelbthorne, had gestured into place.

Now the gesture that pulled back the lips of Cortindo's dead face was anything but human. The decayed tongue inside the blackened teeth moved. There might have been a glimpse of maggots within, before the corpse closed its mouth once more.

At least this thing could not yet speak. By the time it had regenerated that far, Donal would be dead.

Oh, Laura. I'm ...

All four mages, Cortindo included, raised their hands to destroy him.

... sorry.

An explosion behind Donal blew the steel doors open. The percussive pressure hammered Donal through the opening, back into the chamber where the mages stood.

He fell atop dead children.

In the doorway, a tall figure stood with a heavy hexzooka over one shoulder. Beyond, revealed in the great atrium, a riderless bone motorcycle was harrying prey, darting at a great scaled reptile that was spitting in fear.

'The Marines have descended.' Donal smiled.

'We always do,' said Harald.

Orange lightning gathered around the four dark mages as they prepared to counterstrike ... but in that moment, more motorcycles growled and screeched into the atrium, dark-green with flashing lights.

Officers on foot in dark-green uniforms with white helmets, automatic weapons held at port-arms, flooded in after them. And bringing up the rear, looking calm and relaxed, came the narrow figure of Temesin, smoking a cigarette, holding his detective's shield out in front of him.

Donal looked at the four mages.

'Game over,' he said.

'Aaah ...' The sound that came from Cortindo's dead mouth was inhuman.

But then Councillor Gelbthorne and the white-haired man took hold of the reanimated Cortindo, wrapping their arms around him in a kind of bizarre group hug.

The white-haired man spared time for one malevolent glance at Donal before they lowered their heads and concentrated. The air shifted and wavered and began to rotate. Strange geometries were manifesting themselves.

'No. Don't leave—' This was Alderman Finross, terrified.

But the trio of mages had formed a conglomerate whole that was revolving, faster and faster until it twisted, turned through an angle that was entirely impossible, orthogonal to every axis of Donal's experience ... and was gone.

All that was left was the broken, weeping Alderman, leaning against the abandoned altar, surrounded by two score dead children, maybe more.

Donal got to his feet.

'No! It was Blanz. He ... He *ensorcelled* me!' Alderman Finross was almost babbling. 'Please, please don't kill ... I'll tell you everything. They left me no choice but to—'

He stopped as he realized how much he was incriminating himself.

'Senator Blanz,' said Donal. 'That prick.'

Alderman Finross toppled to the floor and lay outstretched.

'I think he fainted.' Temesin had walked inside unnoticed by Donal. 'Too bad. I was enjoying the sound of his voice.'

Donal's nostrils flared, and he gestured around the room. 'Doesn't this bother you?'

Temesin considered the small corpses. 'I've seen worse.'

'Shit ...'

Then Temesin turned to Harald.

'Impressive entrance,' he said.

'Yeah.' Harald spat to one side, then grinned. 'Want me to bust up any other buildings while I'm here?'

Laura, inside the Vixen, cruised along the Avenue of the Basilisks, scanning the crowds, looking for the dark-haired figures of Eyes ... Marnie Finross.

The problem was that Laura could only envision the woman with those silver cables depending from her eyes, attaching her to the refractive apparatus that led to the rooftop mirror system. Actually recognizing the woman's features would be impossible.

And there were so many hundreds, thousands of people on the street. If she'd fled inside a building—

'I give up,' Laura told the Vixen. 'I don't see any chance of spotting the bitch.'

But then she saw two low shapes flitting among the people's legs, then a sudden scuffling, and the deathwolves had pulled a woman's coat off with their fangs. The woman's long white hair swung as she sprinted away from the deathwolves ...

'Damn it, that's her. Even her hair colour's changed.'

...and the woman kicked off her high heels as she sprang towards the sheer wall of the nearest tower and began to slither upwards. Marnie Finross's palms and soles adhered to the surface as she quickly ascended, while all the two deathwolves could do was sit down on their haunches and howl.

The Vixen screeched to a halt, then trembled.

'Come on,' said Laura. 'I know you can do it.'

Then Laura touched the gear stick – just a touch – and the Vixen turned and rolled forward, heading straight for the building as Marnie Finross had done. Then the Vixen morphed her rear wheels fast like springs and bounded ten feet upwards.

The Vixen's wheels quickly span and re-formed into splayed talons arranged like steel flowers, and the car hit the wall with all four spiked wheels and began to climb upwards, rolling straight up the surface slowly, engine growling with the effort, slowing ... then the car stopped and hung there, quivering.

Laura bit her lip.

Then the car backed down to the sidewalk, groaned and rolled back on to the roadway, not bothering to re-morph her wheels back to normal configuration.

'It's all right,' Laura said, patting the steering wheel. 'Really.'

Even as a youngster, the Vixen had been scared of heights.

Then the Vixen's engine sighed, and her headlights swivelled upwards and became impossibly bright, all power diverted into the bulbs, transforming them into spotlights whose brilliant white beams swung high up the tower. They pinpointed the still-climbing figure that was Marnie Finross.

'Oh, that's good,' murmured Laura. 'I think that's all we'll need.'

The Vixen's spotlights followed Marnie Finross all the way to the top, where she climbed on to the roof and was lost from sight. For a second Laura thought that was it, the end of everything. Then a tiny red glow, then several red glows from high above told her that it was fine, it was all right, the case had come to a conclusion.

Laura touched the driver's door and it popped open. She stepped on to the sidewalk.

'I won't be long,' she said.

The building's doorman used his passkey, accompanying Laura inside the penthouse express elevator. It shot very fast up towards the top level and only slowed in the last few seconds. He walked with her along the hallway, and opened the armoured glass doors that led outside, and then he stopped and gasped.

'Don't worry,' said Laura. 'They won't hurt you.'

But the same could not be said of Marnie Finross.

'They're, they're ...'

'My friends,' said Laura. 'Just my friends.'

Ranged all around the rooftop were cats.

Hundreds of cats.

And every cat's eyes glowed crimson in the night, entrancing the one who had dared to look upon them, to match the masters of the entrancing game.

Marnie Finross had tried to outstare cats.

Her catatonic body lay curled and paralysed like some hardened fossil of bygone aeons, her mind disintegrated into madness, shattered into shards that could never be repaired.

Laura smiled.

'Thank you.'

Meanwhile, deep in the hidden basements of Police HQ, it took all of Alexa's strength to haul Commissioner Vilnar's senseless body out of the chamber where he had sought answers. He had known the quest would knock him unconscious, had trusted Alexa to remove him from the place that would kill him if he stayed inside for too long.

She strained – he was heavy! – and pulled and eventually dragged him into the stone corridor, clearing the doorway. She glanced back inside the chamber at the roiling, nova-white light ... and then the door slammed shut of its own accord, hiding the chamber's interior.

On the floor, Commissioner Vilnar moaned.

'Here.' Alexa unstoppered the water bottle he'd told her to bring, raised his head, and poured a few drops between his lips. 'Good.'

In a minute, he had come round again. Whatever was in the bottle, it was more than water. He took a deep breath, then held out his hand so that Alexa could help him heave his bulk upwards and regain his feet.

'You'll go far in this department,' he told Alexa. 'Not every network of allies is as corrupt as the Black Circle.'

'Um ... No.' Alexa could not help glancing at the closed door.

'But you won't ever tell anyone what you saw in there.' Commissioner Vilnar's eyes seemed very large and round. 'Will you?'

Alexa swallowed.

'N-Never.'

'That's what I thought. Now you and I are going to brief the others. All right?'

'Yes, sir.'

The smile that crossed Commissioner Vilnar's face looked inhuman. After what he'd just been through, Alexa was surprised he could smile at all.

'That Senator Blanz,' he said, 'thinks he's such a tricky bastard.'

'Sir?'

'Hiding right out in the open. But we'll fix him ... No.'

Alexa stayed silent, not daring to ask questions. Things were moving fast.

'That honour belongs to the team. Laura Steele will lead the arrest. Somewhat appropriate, don't you think?'

Alexa smiled at last.

'Yes,' she said. 'I think that would be brilliant.'

Thirty-two

The State Capitol was a great nine-sided, distorted polygon over which permanent dark clouds floated, like streamers of black ink through the indigo sky. Despite the quicksilver rain, journalists were arranged on the steps to photograph the arriving senators. Today was an important day.

It did not matter that the man who had proposed the bill was not here. Voting on the Vital Renewal Bill did not require Senator Blanz's presence. Part of the interest among the journalists, of course, was to enquire about the conflicting rumours surrounding the senator's disappearance. No one among the state legislature was willing to comment ... at least not on open record.

Flashbulbs popped as paramedic-mages carried a light palanquin from a newly arrived ambulance. Today's vote was likely to be a close-run thing, so that even councillors who were on their sick-beds – possibly their death-beds – had answered the summons to the Capitol.

This wizened figure belong to Councillor Will Sharping, a grand old liberal who was an icon for the younger generation. Sharping was respected even among his opponents as a gentleman of the old school, one who would never stoop to the sharp tactics seen so often nowadays.

There was speculation as to how the Councillor might vote, because he could influence others decisively, and not just members of his own party.

Inside the Capitol, from the viewing gallery, Laura and Donal stood beside a stone pillar. They watched the councillors take their seats, observed as the mages bore the palanquin inside and somehow collapsed it, causing it to fold up so that Councillor Sharping appeared to be sitting like an ordinary councillor, on an ordinary chair.

'Let's do it,' whispered Laura.

'Yes.'

It was three days since Donal had returned from Illurium, and every nerve was taut with tension as he and Laura descended among the politicians. Could it really be over soon?

The Speaker of the House was enunciating the terms of the Bill, prior to the voting.

'—that the rights to counsel, to marriage, and to employment be immediately revoked from all non-human, in-human and ex-human beings—'

The man's voice faltered as he caught sight of Laura and Donal coming down the steps. Perhaps the Speaker was more of a mage than he looked, being able to detect that Laura was a zombie just by glimpsing her.

'—to, er, take under state ownership all liens and properties currently held in title by such—'

Laura halted first. Behind her, Donal pushed his jacket open, revealing his favourite Magnus in its new shoulder holster, which was a present from Laura.

Then Laura reached inside her bag, pulled out her detective's shield, and cast her voice: 'I'm Commander Steele, Tristopolis PD. And' – replacing the shield inside her bag, she withdrew a vellum document inscribed with purple ink – 'this is a warrant for the arrest of Senator Blanz—'

Murmurs grew all around the chamber. Didn't this woman know that Senator Blanz was missing?

'—in other words, I'm arresting *you*.' In her other hand she already held handcuffs, and now she headed towards the wizened figure with the wispy white hair.

Above her, the Speaker of the House coughed.

'Young lady, you're making a risible mistake. That is most manifestly Councillor Sharping, whose—'

But Donal stepped forward then, taking solid hold of the wizened man's wrist. As Donal had expected, the strengthening of his sense of his self – which was the witch's and the bones' true gift – held fast now.

He saw through illusion.

I am ...

And he dispelled illusion in the eyes of others.

...the song.

To the assembled state government, it appeared that the air shook and broke apart, until the man in Donal's grasp looked strong and vital, and the hair atop his head, though white, was thick and bushy.

'We've got you, Blanz.'

Orange lightning cracked through the Capitol chamber.

The impact flung Donal back. Protected as he was by a hexlar vest, reinforced by federal spellbinders flown in for the job, Donal was unharmed by the blast itself. For a second he thought that everything remained fine, that the operation was going down as planned.

Then he saw that Senator Blanz had pulled off a trick that was more sleight of hand than true sorcery.

He held Donal's Magnus in his hand, aimed directly at Donal.

No ...

Then Blanz swivelled his aim and squeezed. Donal lunged forward, knowing already what had happened.

Laura's head blew apart in a spray of bone splinters and liquid brains.

NO!

And Donal's fingers clawed for Blanz's eyes as the impact took him in the heart and the bang that followed seemed far away and everything went black as Donal died ...

Thirty-three

... and woke, while the medic mages were still working on him. He was lying on the stone floor of the Capitol chamber, and some of the councillors were staring in horror at the scene taking place below them.

Donal tried to work his mouth.

'Don't talk,' murmured one of the mages. 'It'll be all right.'

No, it won't.

He raised his chin, and stared down at his open chest cavity. Two mages were working inside him, their hands and forearms slick with black fluid. And inside his chest ...

Oh, Thanatos.

...was a beating, slick black heart ...

Oh, Death.

...taken from the one who would need it no more.

NO NO NO NO NO!

For not even a zombie can survive without a brain. With a skull blown apart into splinters and wet fragments.

No ...

Three days later, against all medical advice, Donal stood at the grave-side, on a dark heath in the Dispersed Vale, at the edge of Black Iron Forest. The diggers shoved wet soil into the grave and quicksilver rain fell and fell, unceasing.

The priestess and the task force team stood watching. Behind them – against his political advisers' advice – was Commissioner Vilnar. Whatever Laura had been in her original life, this was a zombie being buried now ... and Blanz might be discredited, but his movement was not.

Her heart beat steadily.

Laura.

Steadily, inside Donal's chest.

I love you.

But at least Laura was spared the reactor piles. As Donal would be, when his turn came.

Oh, Thanatos ...

For undead bones are strong and their song is wild.

Too wild to tame.